Also by Karen Swan

*Players*
*Prima Donna*
*Christmas at Tiffany's*

# The Perfect Present

Karen Swan began her career in fashion journalism before giving it all up to raise her three children and to pursue her ambition of becoming a writer. She lives in the forest in Sussex, writing her books in a treehouse overlooking the Downs. Her first novel, *Players*, was published in 2010, followed by *Prima Donna*. In 2011 Karen's third novel, *Christmas at Tiffany's*, was a *Sunday Times* Top Ten Bestseller.

Visit Karen's website at www.karenswan.com, follow her on Twitter @KarenSwan1 or find her on Facebook.

# The Perfect
# PRESENT

## KAREN SWAN

MACMILLAN

First published 2012 by Macmillan
an imprint of Pan Macmillan, a division of Macmillan Publishers Limited
Pan Macmillan, 20 New Wharf Road, London N1 9RR
Basingstoke and Oxford
Associated companies throughout the world
www.panmacmillan.com

ISBN 978-1-4472-2560-7

Typeset by Ellipsis Digital Limited, Glasgow
Printed and bound by CPI Group (UK) Ltd, Croydon, CR0 4YY

*To my father, Malcolm*

*Best dad and inspirational man*

*My role model*

# *Prologue*

My darlings,

There is no easy way to say goodbye – not after our hello. What a day that was, your matching pink faces blinking up at me like two old souls come to guide me through our adventures together, for I was so young when I had you. And thank goodness for that! We snatched six precious years that ought not to have been ours, and we made them dance, didn't we?

It was all so clear to me in that very first instant: you are why my heart beats and my eyes open, why my skin breathes and my spirit soars. You are my heart, my soul, my love, my life. I have rejoiced in every moment with you – not just the wondrous look on your faces on Christmas morning, but the little miracles too: how the freckles on your noses flower like daisies on summer days and how your bodies turn gasps into laughter as I give you cowbites on your ribs – never forget those, by the way, even when you're all grown-up. They make everybody smile.

What else will I miss? The smell of your heads – I would bottle it and wear it like perfume if I could. Heaven scent, I always called you, and I was right. I'll miss the feeling of your 'loving hands' in mine; I'll miss the three of us sleeping in our bed together, all messy and noisy like hibernating bears and no one there to tell us off when we sleep late. Please make sure you sleep enough. It's so important. And brush your teeth twice every day. And eat fruit.

There are also, I suppose, lots of things that aren't important, even though grown-ups say they are – things like not wearing your shoes on the carpet, or eating all your broccoli. It doesn't matter if you never grow to like courgette. I didn't start eating quiche till last year and it didn't do me any harm – at least I don't think it's the reason I'm writing this letter. (Oh dear, bad joke.)

Just try to be open to new things; I think that's the message to get across. Life is big and noisy and exciting and colourful, but sometimes it also feels scary and you have to be brave. Even when people let you down and break your heart – and sadly, they will – just keep going, and never give up. You will recover. I made you strong.

It had been my Big Plan that we would all go round the world together when you were bigger, maybe ten? I would take you out of school (I know, cool mummy!) and teach you myself. I wanted us to travel through Asia and South America, but I don't think Aunty Lisa's going to be able to do that with Uncle Martin's job. So just travel as soon as you're big enough and explore the world.

By the way, your grey eyes are rare – did you know that? You get them from your daddy. When Queen Elizabeth I ruled England, grey eyes were considered the very height of beauty. It's why I gave you your name, Lillibet. As the oldest, it went to you. As for my Laura, you were supposed to be Flora, for I saw all the colour and life of the gardens in your face, but it was a letter too far from your sister and I wanted you both to be as close as shadows, so Lillibet and Laura you are, my Elizabethan beauties.

2

## The Perfect Present

I know you will be sad for a while, maybe for a long time, but try to laugh at least once every day. And sing – you'll be amazed how much better it makes you feel. Being happy won't mean that you've forgotten me, or that you love me any less. It's what I want for you, more than anything.

I know you'll get through this, because you have each other. Ever since the doctors told me the news, I've been so grateful that I made two of you; I thought it was so that you'd always have a playmate, but now I think it must have been God's way of making sure you wouldn't ever be alone. As long as you have each other, you will be all right. Be kind to one another; share, and try not to fight. Aunty Lisa will try her best to make it better for you, so let her.

When I was your age, I wanted so badly to be a twin or a princess or a fairy. They're not what I'm going to get to be, but even though you won't be able to hear me or see me, I'll do everything I can for you to feel me. I'll be the butterfly in your tummy when you get nervous before Sports Day. I'll be the shiver running up your skin when you climb out of the swimming pool; I'll be the giggle in your throat when you want to laugh at Mr Benton's moustache in Sunday school. And one day, when you are really old ladies – much, much older than I am now – we will be together again in heaven. I will be right by the gates waiting for you, my darlings, just like I do at school. Until then, I will be an angel on your shoulders, loving you.

Mummy xxxxx

# Chapter One

Laura looked at the shoes in her hand and knew before the assistant had come back with her size that she would buy them, even if they didn't fit. They were red, and that's all they needed to be. She was almost famous for them around here, and Jack always teased her about it – 'You know what they say – red shoes, no knickers.' Of course, he knew full well she'd be the last person to go knickerless. Maybe that was why he found it so funny. Anyway, she preferred him saying that to his other response, which was to roll his eyes. 'You've got almost fifty pairs!' he'd cried last time before he'd caught sight of her expression and quickly crossed the kitchen to apologize, saying he secretly quite liked that she had a 'signature'.

The shop assistant came back, shaking her head apologetically.

'All I've got left is a thirty-six,' she shrugged. 'We're completely out of thirty-eights, even in the other colourways.'

Laura bit her lip and stalled for a moment as the assistant moved to return the shoe to the display shelf. 'Well . . . I'll take them anyway,' she muttered, looking away as she reached into her bag for her credit card. 'They're such a good price now. There'll be someone I can give them to . . .'

'Okay.' The assistant hesitated, casting a glance at Laura's red patent slip-ons, which she'd polished so hard at the breakfast table that morning that their eyes met in the reflection.

A minute later, she savoured the jangle of the bell on the door as it closed behind her and stood for a moment on the pavement, adjusting to the brightness outside and the change of pace. The day was already limbered up and elastic, the late-November sun pulsing softly in the sky with no real power behind it, local businessmen rushing past with coffees-to-go slopping over the plastic covers and pensioners pushing their shopping carts between the grocer's and the butcher's, tutting over the price of brisket; a few mothers with prams were congregating around the bakery windows, talking each other into jam doughnuts and strong coffee to commiserate over their broken nights.

Laura turned her back on them all – glad their problems weren't hers – and started walking down the street in the opposite direction, swinging the carrier bag in her hand so that it matched the sway of her long, light brown hair across her narrow back. Her studio was in a converted keep, just beyond the old yacht yard, eight minutes away. People tended to have a romantic notion of what it must be like when she told them where she worked, but it wasn't remotely pretty to look at. Tall and ungainly on its stilts, it towered over all the corrugated-panel workshops and dilapidated boat huts on the banks, and her square studio-room atop them looked like it had been bolted on by an architect who'd trained with Lego. The wood was thoroughly rotted, although you wouldn't know to look at it, as it had been freshly painted two summers previously by a student at the sailing club who was after extra cash. She loved it. It felt like home.

She turned off the high street and marched down the shady

grey-cobbled lanes, past the tiny pastel-coloured fishermen's cottages with bushy thatched roofs – which were now mostly second homes for affluent Londoners – and over the concrete slipway to the compacted mud towpath that led down towards her studio. It sat on a hillock in the middle of the estuary. 'St Laura's Mount', Jack called it. The brown water merely slapped at the stilt legs during the high spring tides, but the path over to it was only accessible at low tide, which was why she was enjoying a late start this morning. Strictly speaking, if she really cared about doing a nine-to-five working day, she could have bought a small dinghy to row over in, but she rather liked the idiosyncratic hours it forced upon her. But even more than that – and she could *never* admit this to Jack – she loved the occasional stranding overnight, when her absorption in her work led her to ignore the alarm clock and the path became submerged. After the first 'stranding', she had brought a duvet, pillow and overnight bag to the studio so that she was properly set up for the eventuality, but Jack hated it. He felt it encouraged her – enabled her – to continue working when it was time to stop and come home.

The tide was almost fully out now, and the mudflats looked as glossy as ganache, but Laura didn't stop to watch the avocets and bitterns picking their way weightlessly over them. Their mutual fascination with each other had worn off a while ago and now they existed in apathetic harmony. She walked quickly up the two flights of metal stairs and unlocked the door. Jack was forever telling her they had to up the security on the place. She had thousands of pounds' worth of materials in the studio.

Dumping her handbag on the floor and carefully lifting the too-small shoes out of their box, she placed them on the windowsill. They looked like two blood-spots in the all-white interior. The wide planking floorboards had been painted and overvarnished so that they looked glossy and more expensive than they really were, and it had taken over twenty tester pots and Jack on the edge of a nervous breakdown before she had found the perfect white for the walls. She hadn't wanted it to look cold in the winter, but it did, in spite of her best efforts – there's precious little that can counteract the pervasive grey light that characterizes the Suffolk winter. She had had some blinds run up in sandy-coloured deckchair stripes and that had helped warm things up a bit. It had to – the windows ran round every side of the room so there were lots of them. Jack always used to worry that she was too exposed working up here, with 360-degree views where anyone could see her alone in the creek. But Laura insisted that neither bored teenagers nor avid bird-watchers had any interest in her.

The red flashing light on the answering machine caught her eye and she went over to listen. After several years of working alone with only Radio Four for company, it was still a surprise to realize that people were actively seeking her out and calling her up with commissions. The move from jewellery hobbyist to professional goldsmith had been accidental, when the charm necklace she'd made for Fee's mother had provoked a positive response at the WI. After weeks of ignoring Fee's nagging, well-intentioned demands to set herself up properly, her friend, young as she was, had taken it upon herself to place a formal advert in the *Charrington Echo*. Rather serendipitously, the editor of the *FT* magazine had been holidaying in neighbouring Walberswick at the time and happened to chance upon it whilst waiting for her lunch order in the pub. An hour later she had knocked on

Laura's door and from there it had been but a hop, skip and a jump to the prestigious placement in the *FT* magazine's jewellery pages.

Today there were two messages, both from Fee – now working as her self-appointed PR and manager on the days she wasn't manning reception at the leisure centre. Through squeals and much clapping, she was forwarding appointment dates for three prospective new clients. Yesterday there had been another one, and this was several weeks after the article had come out. Laura scribbled the dates and times in her diary, shaking her head over the fact that the commissions were still coming in. The feature had been about new-generation jewellers, and the box on Laura had been the smallest, squeezed in at the very last minute. She had pretty much dismissed it as soon as she'd seen it because they'd cropped the photo so you couldn't see her shoes, but clearly lots of people hadn't, because the little red light was still happily flashing most mornings when the tide finally let her in.

Laura walked over to the bench and began casting a critical eye over the previous day's work – a necklace that was for a wedding next week. She caught a glimpse of the grey heron beating past the east window, and knew her eleven o'clock appointment had arrived hot on her heels. Good old Grey. He was better than any CCTV system. He stood for hours in the reed bed, only retracting his neck and leaping into flight when one of her customers passed by on the path to the studio. Like the avocets and bitterns, he just ignored her now.

'Hello?' a male voice drifted up questioningly, and she heard his shoes on the patterned metal treads.

'Come up to the top,' Laura called before taking a deep,

calming breath. She slid the unfinished necklace into a drawer and refilled the kettle, somewhat aghast to notice that the limescale had flourished unchecked so that it looked more like a coral reef in there.

'Hello,' the voice said, near now.

She set a smile upon her lips, took a deep breath and turned. 'Hi,' she replied, as a well-dressed man emerged through the doorway.

He stopped where he was, either transfixed or appalled by the sight of her. In keeping with her 'take me as you find me' defiance (and in direct contrast to Fee's 'take me, I'm yours' dress sense), she was sporting a grubby pair of boyfriend jeans that fell so low they exposed the upper curve of her hip bones, and a faded black Armani A/X sweatshirt of Jack's. The only things about her that were shiny were her teeth and the glossy red flats on her feet.

'Ms Cunningham?' he enquired, holding out a hand.

'Laura,' she replied, shaking his hand so lightly that her fingers slipped away just as he squeezed and he was left gripping her fingertips. He looked down at their star-crossed hands and released hers.

He straightened up. 'Robert Blake. You were expecting me?'

In her dreams, maybe.

His movements were assured, extending a sense of total control and purpose, and Laura immediately understood nothing ever happened in his life accidentally or without reason. He was utterly imposing and yet curiously boyish – as though she could still catch a glimpse of his twelve-year-old self in his face.

It was an intriguing clash. His voice was deep and he was tall, five foot eleven or so, mid-thirties with coppery-brown eyes and a wide full-lipped mouth of extraordinarily even teeth. His hair was carefully combed from his face but she could see it would only take one of the easterly zephyrs that zipped round the yard to unleash a riot of light brown curls and an easy smile. His bespoke shirt and mannered formality told her he'd seen the world; the light in his eyes told her he'd seduced women on every continent.

Laura nodded, knowing she was probably blushing. 'Of course. It's a pleasure to meet you.'

His eyes lifted off her to scan the room and she saw them rest on the tiny new shoes, still in their box.

'You found your way here okay, I hope?' she asked quickly, motioning for him to sit on one of the huge white sofas.

'Eventually, although I thought my satnav was playing up at first. It took me a while to believe you'd *really* be down that tiny track. I don't usually have to pack wellingtons for a meeting,' he said, giving her a small, amused smile that made her stomach flip for joy and confirmed all of her instincts.

He sat down and looked back at her, and she caught a flash of the oyster-coloured silk lining of his jacket and the hand-stitching on his shoes. She could see nothing of the twelve-year-old in him here.

'All my clients have problems trying to find me on their first visits out here. I suppose I really ought to move to somewhere more accessible, but . . . I like to be near the water.' She shrugged, all out of small talk. 'Would you like a cup of tea? Or coffee? It's only instant, I'm afr—'

'No,' he interrupted, before softening it with a 'thanks'.

Laura picked up her notebook from the workbench and sat on the sofa opposite. It was set just slightly too far back and she had to perch on the front of the cushion.

She took a deep breath and exhaled quickly. Soonest done, soonest over. She wasn't a great people person at the best of times, much less dealing with people who looked like that. 'So, how can I help you? What is it you're after?'

He took his eyes off her and paused for a moment, bringing a fist to his mouth as though he intended to cough into it. 'Well, it's for my wife,' he said, his voice quieter than before, as though his wife might be hiding out on the stairs. 'Obviously Christmas is coming up, but it's her birthday, too, on the twenty-third. I need to get her something special.'

She nodded, knowingly. Obviously he wanted it in time for Christmas. Obviously he was married.

'Is there enough time? Are you busy?' he asked.

'Rushed off my feet. Everyone wants their pieces for Christmas,' she said, scribbling his name in her notebook.

'Is that because of the article in the *FT*?'

'Yes. Did you see it too?'

'It's how I found you.'

'You and thirty others,' she murmured, resisting the urge to roll her eyes. 'Not that I'm complaining.' She looked up to find him staring at her intently, and knew he was finding her odd. From the cut of his suit, she guessed the women in his life wore jeans in child sizes with crystals on. 'What were you thinking for your wife?' she asked.

'I want a charm necklace for her. With seven charms.'

His certainty was surprising. Most clients didn't have a clue what they wanted. 'That's specific. Why seven?'

'That's just how many I want,' he replied, shrugging.

'I see,' she said, getting up and lying the notebook on the coffee table. 'Well, I've got a selection of some charms I can show you now, just to give you an idea of what kinds of things I can do.' She reached into what looked like a filing cabinet, pulled out a shallow drawer and brought it over, setting it down on the table in front of him. Some miniature charms were lined up in a neat display in military rows upon red velvet. 'And of course, if you've got anything specific in mind that you don't see here, I can make it to order.'

She sat down again, waiting for his response to the little treasures – her collection was small but refined – but he didn't even look at them.

'The entire necklace must be bespoke,' he said.

Laura sat back. 'Ah, well now, that will be significantly more difficult to arrange in time for Christmas, I'm afraid.'

'It's four weeks away,' he countered, sitting up straighter.

'Yes. But as I said, I am incredibly busy at the moment.'

'Can't you delegate?'

'It's just me,' she replied, her politeness stretching to gossamer-thinness.

He looked out through the east window opposite him for a few moments and she could tell by the set of his jaw that he was irritated.

'Okay. Let me explain fully what it is that I'm looking for here,' he said, leaning forward so that his elbows were on his knees, his hands clasped together. He looked like a president come to read to schoolchildren. 'My wife's birthday is on the twenty-third. She *hates* that her birthday is on the twenty-third. Every year we throw a big party for her birthday, and every year we open the door to people saying, "Merry Christmas". It puts a lot of pressure on me to come up with something really special that makes her birthday stand apart from Christmas. Are you with me?'

Laura sat back and frowned at him. She most certainly was not. Gorgeous he may be, but his patronizing tone was pushing all her buttons.

'When I read that article on you, about your charm jewellery, it gave me the idea for the perfect present for her – a charm necklace, but with a difference. I don't just want it to be decorative, or to signify last year's holiday. I want every charm on this necklace to represent her relationship with each of the most significant people in her life. That's why there are seven. And that's why I can't just . . . choose one off a tray. They have to be unique to her.'

Laura nodded, intrigued. 'It's a great idea. It goes a lot further than most of the jewellery I'm asked to create. Most of the time, people want charms for notable life events such as christenings, twenty-firsts, wedding anniversaries and suchlike. I've never been asked to . . . well, tell a life *story* before. It would be an exciting project for me professionally, and I can guarantee your wife would finish up with something incredibly special. But that's a very labour-intensive commission. If you'd be happy to wait till after Christmas . . .'

'No. Categorically not.'

'Well then, let's see – if you'd consider dropping the number to, say, three or four charms, there might be enough ti—'

'No,' he said firmly, interrupting her again.

Laura sat back, irritated and offended. He wasn't even trying not to be rude. 'Well then, I'm afraid we're at an impasse, Mr Blake. There simply isn't enough time for me to interview your wife for that many charms.'

'You can't interview her anyway,' he said briskly. 'It's a surprise. It's absolutely imperative that she knows nothing about it.'

Laura pursed her lips grimly. The project – ambitious though it might be – was fast losing its appeal. He might be easy on the eye, but she did not fancy several hours in his company, listening to stories about his no doubt twenty-two-year-old wife.

A BlackBerry buzzed quietly in his suit pocket and he took it out.

Laura watched him with building anger as he frowned at the message on the screen before pocketing it again. His behaviour since arriving here had been bullish and arrogant. 'There won't be anything for her to find out about,' she said, shutting the notebook to signify that the meeting was over. 'Not from me, anyway. I'm sorry to disappoint you, but I have to be realistic about my delivery times and my commitments to my existing clients.'

'Are you saying . . . ?'

'I'm saying it might be your wife's birthday, but it is also Christmas for everybody else. If you cannot wait or compromise, then I can't help you.'

They stared at each other, horns locked, and Laura felt the red mist descend. She didn't fool herself for one second that she was Miss Congeniality. She knew perfectly well how tricky she was. But even she was more capable of compromise and basic manners than him.

Robert Blake stared at her for a moment, his anger seemingly matching hers, then walked away – but not towards the door. He went to the window, taking in the view. Laura's own eyes were drawn to the horizon beyond him, and she could see, further out in the estuary, the newly exposed mudbanks drying out in the sun. In another four hours it would be slack water, and then the tide would start its silent creep back, rustling the reeds and smothering the mud that always sucked at it so greedily.

He noticed the shoes beside him and picked one of them up. It still had the tissue and toe-shaper in it.

'For your daughter?' he asked.

'I don't have a daughter,' she replied briskly.

'Boy?'

'What? No,' she snapped, flummoxed by these forays into personal chit-chat. She watched him replace the shoe carefully.

He jammed his hands casually in his pockets and wandered back towards her. 'We've got off on the wrong foot,' he said with no apparent trace of irony. 'Perhaps I should have stated earlier that I'm paying double your fee.'

'Double my fee?' she echoed.

'That's right,' he replied, and she saw victory creep into his eyes, the unassailable conviction that this would seal the deal. Christmas would belong to his wife alone after all. He was a businessman used to winning. No doubt the car parked on the quay with the perfectly correct satnav was a Volante or Carrera; no doubt he had a mistress who was already jockeying to be his second wife; and no doubt the fact that he was here for his wife's present and not trawling Bond Street meant he'd already bought her the W1 trophies of the Cartier Tank watch, the Asprey tennis bracelet, the Theo Fennell diamond key and the Tiffany eternity ring.

Laura stretched herself an inch taller. 'It's not a matter of price,' she said with impressive firmness, revelling in her own small victory. He had picked the wrong person to lord it over. As far as she was concerned, this was a matter of wills now, and when push came to shove, *she* chose which commissions she took. She was going to win this. 'I have other clients. I can't let them down.'

'*You* don't need to. I arranged for your assistant to contact them all on your behalf this morning and reschedule.' He checked his watch. 'And naturally I'll compensate you for any commission that you lose on account of this reshuffling.'

'Fee's cleared my diary? On your orders?' Laura croaked. Her head was beginning to spin.

'You'll find the timings much more convenient now.'

She stood up hotly, hoping to God Fee hadn't installed CCTV for training purposes. She felt his eyes on her as she marched towards the door. There was simply nothing more to say. She had been reasonable; she had been polite. And now she was all out of both. 'You need to leave now. I'm sorry not to have been able to help you,' she said coldly, opening the door. She held out an arm and motioned for him to leave. 'I hope you're more successful hijacking Christmas for your wife somewhere else.'

His shock was palpable. 'Now hold on! Did you hear the terms I offered you? I'm paying *double* your fee.'

'There's no need to talk to me as if I'm an idiot. You're the one who's not hearing, Mr Blake.'

'Surely this is an offer too good to refuse.'

'I don't think so. This is *my* business and I work for exactly who I like, and that does not include people who rearrange my diary for their spoilt wives. It will no doubt surprise you to learn that I don't do this for the money.'

There was a flinty silence as he took in her cold anger and her firm hand on the open door. 'Okay, look, I've offended you, I can see that,' he said, backtracking quickly. 'But you are the only person I can come to for this.' It seemed he'd decided flattery was now the best form of attack.

'I find that hard to believe. There are plenty of jewellers out there and most are a lot more experienced than me.'

'But the charms . . . no one else is doing what you're

doing. Look, I've bought Cat everything over the years – watches, diamonds, you name it. But this necklace, it'll be the only piece that actually *means* anything to her. Please.' His voice cracked suddenly. 'This gift has to show her how much I lov— What she means to me.' He paused for a moment, his previously gloating eyes now boyish and appealing. 'Everything rests on it.'

But Laura was unmoved. 'You had the nerve to order my staff to rearrange my commitments to suit your schedule, and that is bang out of order in my book. Now I'll ask you again: Please. Leave. I have a lot of phone calls to make.'

They both knew she had won. Slowly, he walked to the door, then stopped by the steps in front of her. 'You're making a big mistake.'

'That's my loss, then. Goodbye,' she said stonily, slamming the door firmly behind him. 'And good riddance.'

She was pretty sure he heard that.

# Chapter Two

'Hi, Tom,' Laura said tonelessly, leaning on the tall mahogany bar and giving the crowded room a quick once-over. In contrast to her studio, which was all about driftwood and artist's light, Tom's Seafood and Champagne Bar had gone the other way with the nautical theme, lifting materials direct from the shipyard: the highly polished floor was teak, thick rope intended for tethers had been used for the banisters, the blinds were made from brown clinker-sail canvas, and brass cleats had become coat hooks. Sepia shots of Gatsby-esque schooners adorned the walls, and upturned half-cut boats had been fitted with shelves and were used to store the glasses. Half the tables were already taken, and most of the chairs were turned towards the panoramic windows to watch the dusk blooming like a feather-edged peony against the vanilla sky.

The portly barman looked up from polishing two glasses. 'Laura,' he acknowledged.

'Busy tonight.'

'Aye. The new chef's bringing 'em in. His lobster tagliatelle's a treat. Fresh saffron, white crab meat . . .'

Laura nodded approvingly.

'Tempted?'

She shook her head apologetically, her fine hair polishing her shoulders. 'I'd love to, but Jack's already got dinner on. I've got to make this quick. I don't suppose—'

'No. Not seen her,' Tom said quickly, opening a bottle of crème de cassis and pouring it into two glasses.

Laura raised an eyebrow and rested her clasped hands on the counter. 'Where have you not seen her?'

'Well, not behind that pillar, for a start,' he said, uncorking a bottle of the house champagne and pouring it on to the crème de cassis.

Laura took two steps to the right and caught sight of a skinny ankle jigging furiously next to a plastic Hello Kitty bag. 'Send over two fresh glasses when you get a chance, will you?'

'Sure thing. D'you want to try one of these? Kir royale?'

Laura looked at the glass suspiciously. 'Not unless it's on the house – otherwise just our usual.'

She picked her way cautiously through the tables, taking care not to knock anyone's drinks with the bags looped over her arm. The furious ankle seemed to pick up speed as she approached, almost as though its owner was picking up on her presence.

'How did you know I was here?' Laura asked, looking down at the fresh-skinned, heart-shaped face that was cringing up at her.

'Your squelch.'

Laura looked down at her red Hunter wellies. They were still shiny from her wade through the water on the way back from the studio; a tendril of seaweed clung limply to the seam around the ankle.

'You're the only person Tom allows to wear wellies in here. Working late again?'

'Thanks to you,' Laura said pointedly, dropping the shoe bag on the floor and taking the empty seat.

Fee nervously reached for the drink she'd been nursing since she arrived, grateful that there were too many witnesses present for Laura to make an attempt on her life. 'Look, Laur, I know you might be a bit cross . . .'

'A bit?'

'Okay, maybe more than a bit—'

'Try bloody fuming.'

'Okay, okay, I know you might be a bit bloody fuming that I took the order without telling you, but I only had your interests at heart, I promise.'

'Oh really? And that's your job, is it?'

'As your manager, yes.'

'Self-appointed manager. I never asked, and I can't afford to pay you,' Laura reminded her.

'Well, you can now,' Fee winked, hopeful of raising a smile. Nada. 'Anyway, I'm doing this out of love, aren't I?'

Laura looked at her perky, buoyant friend. Petite and whippet-thin with a heart-shaped face, prominent blue eyes and shoulder-length blonde hair as wispy as candyfloss, she was Laura's opposite in every way. Fee was bright, bouncy, bonny, bubbly and all other happy things beginning with B. Laura was brooding, belligerent, bony. She always felt heavier-footed than her feather-light friend, as though she trod through her life with a weighted soul – or at least with wellies on.

'It isn't up to you, or the *client*, to say how I run my business.'

'Well now, I hate to point it out, but you wouldn't have a business if it wasn't for me. You don't always know what's best for you. You'd still be tinkering with dodgy brooches no one ever saw, much less wore, if I hadn't had that ad of Mum's necklace made up.'

'That was different.'

'Yes, it was. And it's why you're doing so well now.' She leaned forward on her skinny arms. 'Come on, Laur, the guy made an offer that you couldn't walk away from.'

'Funny how I did, then.'

'Yes, well, you're just—' Fee's mouth dropped open. 'What?'

'I chucked him out. I'm not doing it. I've spent all afternoon reinstating the appointments.'

'Oh no, you didn't?' Fee moaned, dropping her head in her hands and showing off this week's colour on her gel nails – a strong lilac that seemed better suited to a little girl's bedroom. 'Laur, why didn't you at least speak to me about it?'

'Why didn't *you* speak to *me* about it?' Laura hissed back. 'How could you let me go into that meeting and be totally banjaxed like that? You know how much I hate meeting new people. It's the reason why I didn't want to go professional in the first place. And you just left me to be bullied by some rich guy who walks in and starts telling me he's cleared my diary.'

'I thought you'd be made up,' Fee moaned, raking her hands through her fine blonde hair.

'What, because he offered double?'

'It was more than double, actually.' She dropped her hands flat on to the table. 'As soon as I told him you were booked up till Christmas, he offered double on the spot and I hadn't even given him your rates.' She gave a little shrug. 'So I bumped it up from eight hundred a charm to twelve hundred.'

'Twelve hundred?' Laura's voice was suddenly quieter.

Fee nodded. 'And he was going to pay *double* that. Don't you get it, Laur? That was your biggest commission yet. You'd have netted nearly seventeen grand.'

Seventeen grand?

The two women stared at each other, one with a look of dawning horror, the other with a look of despair.

'But I . . . I mean, I . . . Well, I didn't realize it was so much,' Laura whispered. She picked up Fee's glass and took a hefty slug. 'Shit.'

'Yeah, I'll say,' Fee muttered, wrangling the glass back and draining it herself. 'I could've paid off my credit card with my thirty per cent take.'

'Thirty per cent?' Laura looked at her sharply. 'Who said anything about thirty per cent?'

Fee shrugged. 'That's the going rate.' She patted Laura's hand lightly. 'And you don't need to look so shocked – that does cover PR *and* managerial duties.'

'Oh God, I can't believe I chucked him out.'

Fee looked at her optimistically. 'How badly did you chuck him out? I mean, what are we talking about here – did you chuck his briefcase in the river? Or did you just do your mega-posh Ice Queen voice that you do when you get pissed off?'

'I slammed the door in his face and told him good riddance.'

'Huh. A mix of both, then. Excellent. Well done.' Fee collapsed her head into her nested arms.

Tom came over with a tray and set down two slim flutes and a bottle of the Prosecco that passed as the 'out of season' house champagne. 'What's up with you two? Thought you said you were going to be celebrating, Fee?'

Fee shook her head. 'She kicked him out. It's not happening.'

Tom looked at Laura and she gave a helpless shrug. 'I didn't do the maths.'

'Her temper got the better of her, is what she means. You'd better take the bottle back, Tom. We'll just be on the one glass tonight.'

Tom shook his head. 'Pity,' he muttered, taking the bottle back to the bar.

'Well, I was still right to turn him down,' Laura spluttered finally after they'd both downed their glasses and were sliding their fingers round the rims. 'I mean, it's the principle, isn't it? You can't just let people run your life because they're richer than you are.'

Fee hiked up her eyebrows, completely unconvinced. 'And that's what you're going to say to Jack, is it? That you turned down, on one piece of jewellery, nearly as much as he makes in a year?'

'He makes more than that,' Laura argued tetchily. 'The workshop has never been busier. The reupholstery business is recession-proof.'

'Yeah, but you get my point, though. It doesn't matter how many people want their sofas resprung – he's not ever going to be doing so well that you can afford to turn down that kind of money. You've got to be really raking it in before you can afford to sniff at seventeen grand. And just before Christmas too.'

Laura slid her elbows along the table and dropped her face on her arms. 'I just won't tell him,' she mumbled into the table. 'There's no point in torturing him with what could have been.'

'What was, you mean. It was all signed and sealed when

I put the phone down to him. There were no ifs or buts about it.'

'Yes, yes, all right! Stop going on about it, will you?' Laura snapped, more furious with herself than Fee. Fee had been right. She had allowed her temper to get the better of her. 'There's nothing I can do about it now. What's done is done.'

They sat in miserable silence, which was punctuated by the solitary beep of an incoming text on Laura's phone. She read it and sighed. 'Dinner's nearly ready. I've got to go.' She stood up and looked over at Fee, who appeared genuinely crestfallen. 'I'm sorry. I'll make it up to you next time.'

Fee tried to raise a smile. 'Sure.'

'Hey, look. Slow and steady wins the race,' Laura said, trying to raise her spirits. 'I've always believed that. We'll be okay.'

'You might be. You've got Jack. Meanwhile, I'm fifty short for my rent this month.'

Laura looked down at her friend, who would no doubt be eating a Pop Tart for dinner again. She reached down and rifled in her purse. She handed over a twenty- and two five-pound notes. 'All I've got, I'm afraid.'

Fee cracked a grateful smile that made even Laura respond in kind. 'You're a true friend, you are.'

'Huh, you think?' Laura murmured. 'One who undoes all your good work.'

'Nah, you're just principled, that's all. There's not many people about like you.' Fee's slender tapered fingers reached up and squeezed Laura's knobbly ones. 'You're a contrary fairy all right. You might be an acquired taste, but *I* love you, babes.'

# Chapter Three

Jack was expertly chopping parsley and Arthur was nosing around for the last morsels in his gleaming food bowl when she walked through the front door seven minutes later. 'The terrible two', she called them. They were inseparable: Arthur, an Irish terrier, slept soundly in the workshop as his master stuffed and wove and reupholstered rickety chairs on the point of collapse.

'Hey, boys,' she said, dropping her handbag and the new shoes on the pine bench in the tiny porch as Arthur bounded over to her, hair flying off him like dandelion puffs in the breeze. 'You beat me to it, then.'

'Well, I knew that if I wanted something more than beans on toast for supper . . .' Jack teased, pausing in his chopping and reaching over the worktop with puckered lips.

'Good day?' she asked, kissing him and then watching him as he crushed a clove of garlic beneath the knife. He was so pretty – girlish almost, with his lanky frame, shaggy light brown hair and fine nose; only his bright blue eyes with their distinctive dropped irises that fell into slits like cat's eyes gave him any kind of edge. Fee was always saying he looked like a boy-band singer, although at thirty-four he was probably more like their manager – but she took the point.

## The Perfect Present

'Well, I finished that chesterfield finally. Wept my way through it, of course. I mean – tartan? With all that buttoning? It gives me a headache just looking at it.'

'Yes, but what the client wants . . .'

'Mmm. Well, it's done now; nothing a run home couldn't shake off. Which Arthur loved, of course.'

'Of course.' Laura smiled, bending down to scratch the daft mutt lovingly around the neck.

'The downside is, the car is still at the studio, so I'll have to leave early to walk there in the morning.'

'And yet again, Arthur's a winner!' Laura cheered, waving the dog's forelegs in the air.

She stood up again, investigating the chopped ingredients, all placed in separate bowls, practically colour-coded along the worktop. 'I thought you said dinner was almost ready,' she said.

'Ah, busted!' he grinned. 'Well, I'm afraid Arthur and I were missing you. This is going to be another half-hour. Why don't you take the paper – it's on the table there. I've already run you a bath, and I'll bring a glass of something cold up in a minute.'

'Oooh.' Laura smiled, nicking some red pepper. 'Mr Ambassador, you are spoiling me.'

She meandered lazily upstairs and peered into the bathroom. Fresh, fat bubbles foamed at the rim tantalizingly, and the scented oil burner was already lit on the windowsill. Undressing quickly, she climbed in, listening to the clatter of Jack in the kitchen below as she opened the local paper.

It was Thursday, publication day, and she always liked to start with the classifieds at the back, her keen eyes eager for a bargain. Most of what they owned had been 'pre-loved', as she preferred to call it – the grey linen Habitat sofa adopted

27

after a customer never returned for it, the iron bedstead in their room (which had been a mistake: it creaked like an arthritic knee every time they turned over), the French painted armoire with the mesh front where she kept the towels in the spare room.

Jack came in with a glass of wine a few minutes later, true to his word as ever. 'Here you go,' he said, planting a kiss on the top of her head. 'Seen anything you like?'

'No. Not really,' she sighed. 'Although I see you did.' She indicated an ad at the bottom that had a faint pencil mark around it.

'Oh, that,' he said dismissively. 'It's nothing.'

'It's for a beach hut,' Laura said, reading the ad more closely.

'Yes. A private sale. That was why it caught my eye.'

'I thought you could only get them through the council? Fee once told me there's a crazy waiting list.'

'Everything's crazy in Fee's world,' he grinned. 'But yes, she's right on this occasion.' He sat on the edge of the bath and began gently ladling the water over her shoulders. 'You either have to get your name on the list and wait until you're in your mid-eighties to get one, or you remortgage to get one that comes through a private seller like this.'

'Remortgage? For a glorified shed?'

'Mmm-hmm.'

'I bet that's just hype. It says POA here. Why don't you ring them and ask how much they want? It can't be much. I mean, those things don't even have running water, do they?'

'No power,' he corrected. 'I rang when I got in. They're asking fifteen for it.'

'Hundred?'

'Thousand.'

'Fifteen *thousand*? No! No one would spend that kind of money on a glorified shed.'

Jack smiled at her outrage. 'And that's a bargain, trust me. It must be fairly shabby. The really smart ones go for well over double that. They're investments as well as heirlooms.'

'How do you know that?'

He sighed. 'I've wanted one for years. When I was a kid, my grandma had one in Sandwich. We used to spend all summer messing around in it.'

'I never knew that. What happened to it?' she murmured as he soaped her shoulders.

He shrugged. 'I don't know. It got sold, I suppose. Such a shame, though. I really loved it.'

Laura looked up at him. She could tell by his tone that he really had.

'Well, do you want to go and look at it, maybe?' she asked after a minute. 'I mean, if you really want one that badly, we've got some "rainy day" savings we could dip into. And with my business taking off, it's providing us with a nice little extra income too.'

Jack shook his head. 'I'm sure, but it's not coming in quickly enough for this, sadly. That baby will be gone by dinnertime tomorrow. And we won't see another one for ten years.'

'No!'

'Rarer than hen's teeth.' He reached a hand down and gently squeezed a soapy breast. 'Anyway, I only came up to do that.' He grinned, kissing her on the lips. 'I'd better go back down and check Arthur's not sitting in the wok.'

Laura sighed as he shut the door gently behind him. Her earlier victory was growing evermore hollow by the moment:

the biggest opportunity of her career, Fee's Visa bill and now Jack's boyhood dream – all dashed with one tantrum. She'd messed up properly this time. She'd blown it for them all.

Hadn't she?

# Chapter Four

'You seriously need to get a boat,' Fee panted as she slid the straps of the rubberized waders off her tiny shoulders the next morning.

'Yeah, well, if this comes off, I'll be able to afford one,' Laura replied, hanging hers on a rusty nail banged into one of the stilts and rooting around in her tote for her red Converse.

'I still don't see why we couldn't have waited till low tide. I mean, what's the rush? Why do you have to ring now? It's barely eight o'clock.'

'Because I didn't sleep a wink last night. Time quite literally is money, Fee.'

'Something I never thought I'd hear you say. But I don't understand what's changed your mind. You were adamant yesterday that you wouldn't work with him.'

'That was before I realized that working for him would allow me to make Jack's dream come true.'

Fee pulled a face. 'Come again?'

'There's a beach hut for sale in the *Echo*. They want fifteen thousand for it, and Jack's desperate for one. He tried to play it down, of course.'

'So, what – you've told him about the commission, then, have you?'

'Don't be daft! There's nothing to say Robert Blake will

take me on again, and even if he does, the beach hut might have already gone – that's if Jack's to be believed and these things really do walk off the shelves. But if all the stars do line up, it'll be his Christmas present. A surprise.' She gave an excited grin. 'I thought I'd put a Christmas tree and his stocking in it. You know, insist on taking Arthur for a walk on the beach first and then – ta-da!'

'Not getting ahead of yourself, then,' Fee quipped.

Laura smacked her lovingly on the arm.

'So what about all the very legitimate objections you had to working with him, then, like too many other jobs?'

'For knocking on twenty grand I'll mine the damn gold myself! No, I'll make it work somehow. It's not that bad. I didn't like his attitude more than anything. He got my back up from the start, staring at me like I was some kind of freak. I bet he's never seen a woman without a fake tan before.' She threw a sly smile at Fee. 'He'd bloody love you,' Laura said, double-knotting her laces as Fee pulled on her Uggs. Laura looked over at her orange-streaked, bare-legged, mini-skirted friend who had all the fat – and therefore warmth – of a string bean. 'You know your legs look like threads hanging down from your skirt when you wear those boots, right?'

She could feel Fee stick her tongue out at her back as they started climbing the stairs.

'And God forbid you should put on a pair of tights. It is November, you know,' Laura called from in front.

'Yeah, yeah, yeah,' Fee said, pushing her on the bum.

Laura swiftly unlocked the door and they bundled into the studio, Fee automatically shivering in the cold all-whiteness.

'So have you worked out what you're going to say to him?

I mean, you, Laura Cunningham, apologizing? It's never been done before, has it?'

Laura bit her lip and shook her head. 'Oh God, I feel sick just thinking about it. He might not even take the call. I completely humiliated him, Fee.'

'Well, there's no point in torturing yourself with it. The sooner you get it over and done with, the better,' Fee said, handing her the phone.

'I think I'll just make a cup of tea first.'

'You're delaying.'

'I know. Want one?'

'Go on, then. I'll need an extra sugar this early in the morning.' Fee flopped down on the sofa, her denim mini flashing a pair of pink polka-dot pants and her terrific legs.

Laura, as ever, was in Jack's jeans – he was, depressingly, the same size as her – a Metallica tour T-shirt she'd found in the Heart Foundation shop and a navy M&S cardie. It was as far from Fee's pretty, girly look as you could get, but that was how she liked it, and Fee had long since given up trying to get her into stripes or florals or pastels. She preferred camouflage clothing of the 'don't look at me' kind.

'Have you got his number?' Laura asked as she stirred three sugars into Fee's tea.

'Yup, it's right here,' Fee said, fishing it out of her bag.

Laura set down the teas on the driftwood coffee table and read it. 'That's a London number.'

'You don't think he works in Walberswick high street, do you? Cayman Islands more like.'

Laura took a deep breath. 'If anything should happen to me, tell Jack I love him, all right?'

Fee laughed and tossed a cushion at her as Laura punched in the numbers.

It rang only once before it was picked up and a woman who sounded like Joanna Lumley's daughter breathed down the line. 'Mr Blake's office.'

Laura closed her eyes and prayed for an out-of-body experience. 'Er, hello. I'd like to speak to Mr Blake, please.'

'I'm afraid Mr Blake is in a meeting. Who may I tell him called?'

'Uh, uh, it's . . . I'm, er . . .' she stammered. 'My name's Laura Cunningham.' There was a silence and Laura wondered whether the woman had hung up on her. 'Hello?'

'The jeweller?'

So her reputation preceded her, then. 'Yes, that's right.' She braced herself for the click – the sound of the death knell on Jack's dream.

'Hold, please.'

Laura clamped her hand over the receiver. 'Shit! She's actually putting me through,' she whispered, grimacing anxiously. Fee was kneeling on the sofa, quite literally gnawing on her own fist. Her Visa bill was huge this month.

'Robert Blake.' His voice was brisk.

'Mr Blake,' she almost whispered down the phone as her nerve fled. 'This is Laura Cunningham speaking.'

Slight pause. 'Yes?'

'I'm ringing to . . .' She swallowed hard and thought of Jack. 'I'm ringing to apologize for my dreadful behaviour yesterday.'

'That's decent of you,' he said after a moment.

'And I also wanted to say that if you would, uh . . . still like me to make the necklace for your wife in time for her birthday, then it would, uh . . . be my pleasure.'

'I see,' he said, following up with another long silence.

Laura didn't know what to say. What else was there to

say? She had apologized for the first time *ever* and offered to do the job on his terms. She'd given him all the power. He got to choose now whether to take it or leave it.

'So I'll leave that with you, then, to think over,' she mumbled. 'You've got my number if—'

'What made you change your mind?'

The question stumped her. She didn't think her boyfriend's childhood dreams would be of interest to him. 'I just took another look at my diary. I figured if I can fit in four charms, I can surely squeeze in another three.'

'Fine.'

'You mean you want me to do it?'

'Yes.'

'Oh. That's great, then,' she said, trying to keep the squeal out of her voice, amazed he'd made the decision so quickly. She'd guessed he would string her along at least for a day or two. 'Well then, how do you want me to proceed with this? If I can't meet your wife, I mean?'

'I want you to interview her family and friends.'

Laura's heart sank. For seven charms? That meant seven separate interviews. She'd been hoping he was just going to ask her to interview him, get his stories. That would have meant she had a chance of getting all the material she needed in one day. 'I see.'

He had obviously heard the hesitation in her voice. 'Is that a problem?'

'No, no,' she replied quickly. 'I'm just thinking about the time it's going to take to collect all the material I need from so many different people. Most people aren't used to being interviewed. It takes them a while to relax before they really start to share and confide. And then there's the travelling time as well. Where are they based?'

'London and Surrey mainly. Although one's in Milan and there's another in Frankfurt.'

'Milan! Frankf—'

'I'll do what I can to streamline the process for you. I might be able to get them over here. But if not, I'll cover all your expenses, naturally. My PA can arrange your flights.'

He wanted her to fly around Europe collecting stories for his wife's necklace? 'Or I could interview them over the phone,' she suggested hopefully.

'You won't get anything more than dinner-party anec-dotes out of them if you do that. It'll have to be face-to-face.' His tone brooked no further discussion on the subject.

Laura suppressed a sigh. 'Okay then, if you're sure.' It's your money, she didn't add.

'We'd better start by having the meeting we didn't have yesterday, but you'll have to come to me this time. My diary is non-negotiable at the moment.'

Laura's hackles rose again, even though she knew that his point was fair. 'Fine. Where are you?'

'In the City, off Whitechapel. I'll email directions through to your PA. Then we can go over the list of people for you to meet, and my expectations for the piece.'

Laura swallowed, wondering what on earth that meant – something gold, pretty and sentimental, surely?

'Can you make lunch on Monday? Oh, wait . . . I'm just checking my diary. No, I've got lunch on already – it'll have to be coffee.'

'Yes. Fine.' Laura rolled her eyes.

'Three o'clock?'

'Fine.'

'Okay, I'll see you then.'

'Uh, wait!' Laura called out, sensing his hand hovering over the disconnect button.

'Yes?' Impatience flickered at the edges of his words.

She swallowed hard. This was not going to be easy. 'I'm afraid I'm going to need to ask for the money upfront,' she said quickly, like ripping off a plaster. 'I've got to, uh, order all the materials in advance and gold isn't cheap, obviously.'

'That's fine. We can sort it out when we meet on Monday.'

'No, I'm sorry, but it has to be today,' Laura said firmly, grateful that this was a telephone conversation and he couldn't see her eyes closed in prayer. She needed that money today to secure the beach hut and it had to be ready cash or nothing at all. Even if her savings weren't tied up in accounts that took ten working days to release, there would still be no question of accessing them. She had to live within the bounds of *this* life, not her past.

There was a terse silence. 'I'll have the money wired to your account within the hour. Send my PA the details.'

And the line went dead. Laura stared at the phone in her hand – was that his riposte to her shutting the door in his face?

'Oh my God,' Fee gasped. 'Did he just hang up on you?'

Laura replaced the phone on the handset. 'Yes. He's so damned rude. And self-important, and . . .'

'So it's all off,' Fee breathed, her shoulders sagging.

Laura looked at her in surprise. 'No. Quite the contrary. You need to send over an email with the bank details. He's paying in full within the hour.'

'Seventeen grand? Within the hour?' Fee screeched, doing a jig on the sofa. So Christmas was back on! 'How the hell did you manage that?'

'Well, not by making friends,' Laura grimaced, drifting

over to the east window. The dawn haze was drifting off and the estuarine waters were being leeched out to sea, leaving Old Grey standing monumentally, like the last watch, on the banks.

'It'll be fine once you start.'

'Mmmmm.' Laura chewed on her thumbnail anxiously.

'Stop doing that. You look like you're harming yourself,' Fee tutted, pulling her hand down. 'That'd be all we need. Laura Cunningham with a self-harming disorder.' She rolled her eyes exaggeratedly.

Laura shook her arms out. 'I just haven't been able to swim this week, that's all. And I get twitchy . . .'

'Yep, I know. But you're still coughing from that chest infection last month. That'd be all we need. Laura Cunningham with double pneumonia.' Fee rolled her eyes again.

Laura laughed. 'You drive me insane, do you know that?'

'Oh great. That'd be all we need!' Fee cried, throwing her arms in the air dramatically. 'Laura Cunningham with a mental breakdown . . . ' She giggled, giving a sudden shriek as a cushion flew through the air and hit the window, forcing Old Grey, who was now flying past, to turn a sharp right and find somewhere more peaceful to fish for his dinner.

Two hours later, she found the man waiting by the bus stop at the top of the steps, as promised, wearing a black shiny bomber jacket and a pleased expression.

'Laura?' he asked, his shorn light brown hair immovable in the wind.

'Hi, Roger,' she said, shaking his hand.

'She's just down here,' he said, heading down the steps that led on to the beach.

He waited for her at the bottom and they stomped through the sand together, bodies braced against the wind.

'Have you had much interest in it yet?' she shouted across at him as they walked past the rows of huts that she'd never bothered to inspect or lust after. She always preferred walking in the surf – the water was why she came, not the sand – but up close, she saw they were as different as children. Aside from the obvious differences in decor – pastels or brights, painted interiors or wallpaper – some were double-fronted with verandas, terraces and steps, others were little more than painted garden sheds that had been craned on to a beach. Some were painted in contrasting candy stripes; others were super-minimal in unpainted timber with fully glazed sliding doors. One had a wood-burning stove pipe sticking out through the roof.

Roger threw his head back and chortled as though she was being funny. 'I've had to turn my mobile off,' he hollered back. 'My wife's totally fed up with it. It's insane! You were lucky, I'm telling you. The next person called literally as you rang off.'

Laura felt her pulse quicken. Was this man playing her, trying to justify the price? Or had Jack been right after all?

They slowed down as they approached a row of huts that had been painted in a harmonious palette of ice-cream shades – pistachio, baby pink, vanilla, ice blue and lilac sorbet. They appeared to be middle-ranking in terms of their size and position on the beach, Laura thought – double-fronted with small verandas, a window either side of the door and three steps off the beach.

'And here she is,' Roger said proudly, resting a leg on the steps of the one hut that looked like it was about to blow down. 'This is Urchin.'

Indeed she was one. The hut was third in a row of seven, peach-coloured, paint peeling off in huge flakes like some sort of architectural psoriasis, and the door was – well, it wasn't a door. It was just a slab of plywood bolted to the front.

Laura looked back at Roger with her mouth agape.

'I know. She's a bargain, that's for sure,' he said, looking up at the decrepit structure. 'She's been in the family for three generations now, but my kids want to go to Center Parcs on holiday nowadays and, as you can see, I haven't got the time for the upkeep.' He blew out through his cheeks regretfully, but still Laura couldn't say a word – he wanted fifteen thousand pounds for this pile of *firewood*? 'Come on, I'll show you inside,' he said, bounding up the steps and unlocking the deadbolt.

He took off the plywood and Laura stepped in. It was freezing inside, at least five degrees colder than on the beach, and an overpowering musty smell, born of years of damp towels, assailed her. The floor was so sodden the boards actually bowed, and the flimsy curtains were covered in mildew. What was supposed to pass for a counter appeared to be part of a chemistry experiment with unidentified black fuzzy fungi creeping over the silicone sealant like bees over honey.

'So what d'you think?' Roger asked, checking his watch. 'You can see the potential, I expect?'

'No, not really,' Laura murmured, rooted to the spot. She didn't want to touch anything in case it broke or infected her. Clearly the entire structure would need to be gutted and completely refitted.

'So, there's running water . . . well, more like gentle-walking-pace water,' he said cheerfully, clearly only hearing what he expected to hear. 'No electricity, of course, but that's part of the charm, I guess, isn't it?'

Laura rotated on the spot and looked out of the rotten cracked window. The view was the best thing about it. Was this *really* what Jack dreamed about? Would this really be a dream fulfilled for him? He was handy at DIY, but giving it to him as a 'doing-up' project seemed like more of a burden than a gift. She would have to get a proper carpenter in to restore it if she was going to bother doing this at all, but that would be another couple of thousand on top, eating up all her immediate easy-access savings.

'I hate to rush you on this,' Roger said, checking his watch again, 'but I'm going to need a decision from you, I'm afraid.'

'I'm sorry?' Laura looked at him. He was insane if he wanted her to make a snap decision about throwing fifteen grand at *this*.

'The fella who rang after you is coming any minute. He was dead determined to get it, but I said you rang first, so . . .' Roger shrugged gallantly.

Laura sniffed doubtfully. She knew he was playing her. She couldn't earn and blow that kind of money in one day without at least giving it some thought. Even if it had been a super-fancy hut with underfloor heating, Bose surround-sound, an Aga and a helipad on the roof, she'd have had to think about it.

The sound of heavy treads on the steps outside made them both jump. A stocky man who looked like he bench-pressed old ladies for laughs looked in, his bulging arms resting on the door jambs. 'Well?' he asked, out of breath. 'Did she wannit?'

Roger looked at her and Laura felt her mouth dry up. She didn't see the attraction, couldn't understand the clamour around these things. Jack had told her – when he'd had no inkling that it was even a possibility – that he'd jump at the chance, but would he really jump at this? Would anybody, except for Knucklehead here?

Roger shifted position impatiently. The big man was eyeing her twitchily.

'Fine, I'll take it,' she said sullenly, pulling out her cheque-book. Handing Jack his dream was within her gift now. It was the very least she could do.

# Chapter Five

It was late when Laura stirred the next morning. Saturday. In spite of Jack's best efforts to help her drift off the night before – a glass of wine, a relaxing bath, a massage and some routine but satisfying sex – she had still slept badly, waking with her usual start at two a.m., her heart beating triple-time.

She had lain in the dark for four hours, part of her wanting to get up and go downstairs and work on some ideas for a new bracelet she was starting. But the other part of her wanted to stay in the warm bed where at least there was the prospect of sleep coming back for her. And besides, she hadn't wanted to risk waking Jack – he loved sleepy sex. It had been safer to just lie still and let her head fill up with all the things she needed to do on the beach hut. She had signed the contract and paid the full horrid asking price there and then. It was legally hers and there was so much to get on with in the next few weeks if she wanted to have it ready for Christmas Day it made her head hurt. First on the list was hiring a carpenter, so that it at least had a door and a floor that wouldn't sag beneath a flip-flop, and she needed a plumber to come in and replace the pipes. Once that was done, she could concentrate on the fun things – painting and decorating it, buying some furniture. She'd seen some very nice wooden bunting at the gift shop by the pedestrian crossing that she thought would look good strung up along the gabled roof, and she rather fancied one of those designer-paint sludgy-colour combinations . . .

Sleep had come to her only when the winter songbirds had finally woken, their busy chatter the signal that it was safe to close her eyes again. The darkness had gone for another night.

From her bed, Laura heard the telltale creak on the second step from the top and knew Jack was coming up with her breakfast. She stretched languorously, her eyes on the light that escaped around their blind, as she assessed from its dimness exactly which shade of Pantone grey the sky was going to be today. She felt the cool air on her bare arms – both she and Jack liked a 'fresh' room, leaving the windows open even in the winter – and quickly tucked them under the duvet again, just as Jack bumped the door open with the tray.

'Morning,' he smiled, setting it down on the bed as Laura took in the just-orange-enough tea and thickly buttered toast.

Jack passed her the tea, but it was too hot to sip, so she took a bite of toast instead, self-consciously munching in the quiet room as he watched her.

'What do you want to do today?' she asked him after a minute or two.

Jack shrugged. 'Well, they've started selling Christmas trees at the supermarket, but it seems a bit early yet, don't you think?'

'Yes.'

'We could go for a walk on the beach.'

'We could. Arthur would be happy.'

'But there is a strong north-easterly today.'

'Oh. Cold.'

'Yes.'

'We could always go to the leisure centre and have a swim and a sauna,' Laura suggested, but Jack just wrinkled his nose.

'Saturday morning. Too many kids running around.'

'Mmm.' Laura started on the second triangle of toast.

'Actually, I do need another phone charger for the car. It's barely working at all now,' he said brightly. 'We could go to Carphone Warehouse and get a new one. Plus we need some batteries for the Sky remote.' He smiled. 'How does that sound?'

'Great,' Laura nodded.

'Okey-dokey,' Jack said, getting up, reaching over and kissing her lightly on the tip of her nose. 'I'll start running your shower, then, and we can get this show on the road.'

Laura looked back up at their cosy cottage as Jack locked and double-locked their glossy pillarbox-red front door. His insistence upon vigilant security was a foible that Laura found alternately sweet and irritating. Today it was sweet. Charrington – a tiny fishing village on the Suffolk coast – was hardly a crime hot spot. The most the police ever had to bother about was drunk teenagers dropping chips on the pavement on a Friday night, and parking violations on the promenade.

Laura waited for him as he pushed a hand against the door for good measure, and she looked up at the deep stone windowsills, wondering whether some boxes might look good on them. Lead planters would look particularly fine against the red door and would tie in nicely with the bushy grey thatched roof. It wasn't a big house by any means –

just a two-up, two-down – but it was so pretty; all the houses in Pudding Street were. It was true what they said on the telly – location, location, location. Here, they lived in one of the best-maintained streets in the town and they were only three streets back from the beach and a four-minute walk from the town centre.

Satisfied that their home would be adequately protected during their short absence, Jack took Laura's hand and started leading her down their narrow, pedestrianized lane, ambling past their neighbours' thickly plastered old walls that, still now, looked to Laura like roughly spread royal icing. She loved the names of the cottages – the Old Pilchard Shed; Thistledown; Old Owl; Sunny Corner. Theirs – East Cottage – seemed rather humdrum by comparison, but Jack had put her off changing it when they moved in, as he'd said it was bad luck to change a house's name. A couple of bicycles were chained to black metal downpipes, and there were more and more scooters parked in front of the cottages every month – what Rome had known for generations and London for a decade, it seemed, had finally trickled out to Charrington.

They turned left, inland, at the end of the road, a sharp gust of wind buffeting them as they stepped out of the protection of the lane. Arthur dropped his tail and Jack held her hand more tightly as she shivered. It had been a mild, wet autumn, but the Met Office had predicted arctic conditions for the winter, and if this wind was anything to go by, it looked like they had it right for once.

The lines of small red, blue and metallic silver cars parked along the outer streets alerted them that, for most people, the Christmas countdown had begun, and as they turned right into Main Street, they heard the mechanized music of the Santa's Grotto in the town square. It was nothing more than a mobile home painted dark green, with tinsel around the window frames and garish lights fastened to the sides in the shape of Rudolph pulling a sleigh. At the front, a scowling teenager Laura recognized as Ruth, on an apprenticeship at her hair salon, was dressed as an elf. In truth she would have made a better Santa. She had the shape for him and, in time no doubt, she'd have the beard.

Laura and Jack walked by without making eye contact. Laura didn't want to antagonize her. She used her nails when washing Laura's hair as it was.

'What do you think about the new Rav?' Jack asked her as they queued at Greggs for some apple turnovers – their weekly treat.

Laura looked at him. 'I haven't made my mind up about what I think of the old Rav yet,' she replied drily.

Jack grinned – her sarcasm always amused him. His hands squeezed her waist and she laughed out loud, squirming away from him. 'Because I was thinking it's probably about time we considered trading up. The Volvo's getting pretty tired now. It's up to a hundred and eighty thousand miles; the gearbox is sticking. Plus the MOT's coming up in a few months.' He shrugged nonchalantly. 'I just thought the new shape looked good for us. The boot's just about big enough, good mpg and . . .'

Laura crossed her eyes, and this time he laughed out loud. 'What. Ev. Er.'

'Does that mean you'll come and look at some, then?'

'So long as I get to choose the colour – inside *and* out.' She narrowed her eyes. 'How are we going to pay for it, though? It's not like we'll get much for the Volvo.'

'I've seen some good HP deals around. I think I can

negotiate them down to the numbers I've got in my head,' he nodded assuredly.

'HP?' Laura echoed, taking the paper bag from the assistant as Jack handed over the change. *And I've just spent fifteen thousand on a heap of painted kindling.* 'I don't know, Jack. I'd rather we didn't get into that.'

Jack's face fell. She'd seen the thumbed copies of *Autocar* under the mattress on his side of the bed.

'I just mean, can't we wait a bit till we could pay upfront instead?' she pleaded. 'I've already told you I've got money coming in pretty regularly now.'

'Babe,' Jack said, hugging her around the shoulders and kissing the top of her head, 'I appreciate the gesture, but any money you make is yours to spend as you see fit. It's treat money, and it wouldn't make a tangible difference to the sums we're talking about anyway. It would just get swallowed up and you'd have lost out on something special for no real gain.' He kissed her again. 'But I do appreciate the offer. Really I do.'

Part of Laura wanted to tell him that she'd just made in one month what he made in eight. But she didn't. Being the principal breadwinner mattered to him above all else. It was his proof that he was providing for her, taking care of her.

They wandered through the pedestrianized square, where the giant Christmas tree – an annual gift from Charrington's twin town, Farsund, in Norway – was being erected in its usual spot next to the war memorial opposite WH Smith. Jack squeezed her hand that little bit tighter as they passed Costa Coffee, where a group of six or seven men – twice Jack's size and dressed as pantomime dames – were setting up a pitch, carol singing to raise money for the local rugby club. They eyed up Laura appreciatively, instantly falling into a rendition of 'Uptown Girl' that made her blush and Jack increase their pace.

They wandered through the thickening crowds without aim or deadlines, Arthur lifting his paws like a Lipizzaner horse to prevent anyone treading on them. Carphone Warehouse was heaving with teenagers pointing out to their weary, baffled parents the mobiles and packages with unlimited free texts that they wanted for Christmas. It wasn't the relaxing leisure opportunity Jack had been hoping for, and he found the car charger and paid for it quickly whilst Laura waited outside with Arthur.

He returned the favour a few minutes later when they passed the shoe shop. Laura ducked in on the pretext of finding some snow boots, but really she wanted to check whether they'd got any new stock in – and whether any of that stock came in red.

They struck gold in Accessorize, buying Inuit-style slippers for Jack's eleven-year-old niece, a Fair Isle beret and scarf for his sister, and a fake-fur hat and muffler for his mum. It was half their Christmas shopping list done at a stroke, but they stumbled on the male counterparts: Jack was sure his nephew – fourteen and carrying a licence to sulk – would want the newest PSP FIFA game, but couldn't be sure he hadn't already bought it, and even Jack conceded that he couldn't buy his father another grey cashmere-blend V-neck. Three years running was quite enough.

Laura saw several things to consider for Fee – some sheepskin-lined boots (she had to find a way of keeping her warm somehow), a shaggy black 'rock princess' coat in Dorothy Perkins, a pink pleather handbag – but she wouldn't commit this soon before Christmas. She had to be absolutely sure there wasn't something better for her that she just hadn't seen yet. Apart from Jack's, it was the only other present on her list, so it had to be right.

Finally, driven by waning inspiration and budget, to Arthur's intense delight they made the right turn he'd been waiting for and headed for the beach. The sea breeze lifted their hair up as they walked hand in hand away from the chattering crowds and towards the thickening band of gold ahead.

As they passed the beach huts, Jack stopped. 'Look, that's the one they were selling,' he said, looking up at Urchin.

'It's a wreck,' Laura replied, doing her best appalled face and watching him closely.

'Yeah, but it could be amazing,' he said, carefully climbing the steps. 'It wouldn't take that much to get it back.'

'I hate peach.' She stuck her tongue out to prove the point, beginning to enjoy the charade.

'Imagine how good it'd look in a really dark grey, though, with a pale accent on the trims,' he said, cupping his hands around his face and peering in through the window. He inspected the joists and collapsing door frame, wobbling the veranda for good measure. 'Oh well. Maybe in the next life,' he sighed, jumping over the steps back to her.

Laura squeezed his hand as they turned away and walked down to the water, feeling giddy with joy. Suddenly, she couldn't wait for Christmas.

'Cooeee! It's just me!' Fee trilled, closing the back door on the cold night behind her and rubbing Arthur's broad head as he bounded up to say hello and investigate the glorious smells emanating from the paper bags she was carrying. 'Where is everybody, hey?' she asked him in a deep, silly voice as she massaged his ears. 'Where are they? Come on. Let's go find them. Where are they?'

Arthur led the way and Fee followed him through the pale blue Shaker kitchen, her eyes taking in the bottle opener and unopened bottle of Marlborough on the worktop as she passed. The table was already set for three, with the chicken-printed oilcloth spread protectively over the fancy Farrow & Ball-painted tabletop. Fee knew it was for her benefit only – she had never yet eaten a curry without ruining one of the items of clothing she was wearing at the time, so Jack took no chances with the furniture. In fact, it was a small blessing that he didn't spread newspaper over their seats too and make them all wear bibs for their Saturday-night ritual.

'You'd better not be bonking!' she hollered up the stairs as she walked past them towards the living room. 'I'll put *X Factor* on pause!'

She burst into the sitting room, and for a second was surprised to find the TV already on, muted.

'Oh no,' she whispered, and looked behind the door. Laura was lying on the big grey sofa, Jack sitting next to her, his arms outstretched so that each hand rested upon her shoulders. Slowly, rhythmically, he was squeezing each one, first left, then right.

Arthur gave a small whine as he saw the stiffness in his mistress's muscles and pushed his wet nose against the hand that lay inert on her stomach, but she didn't flinch or respond in any way. Her eyes were like marbles, her breath rapid, and a mist of sweat glossed her skin.

Fee sank to the floor in dismay as Jack looked up at her, despair in his eyes. She watched in silence as on and on he squeezed, neither speeding up nor slowing down, just a constant pulsing beat that echoed through Laura's rigid body, until the repetitions, slowly balancing her horror-frozen brain into an REM-like trance, began to drive into her muscles and they started to droop like warmed wax, heating up and losing tone. He let his fingers keep the slow beat for another two minutes, then laid his hands like hot towels across her shoulders. Her breathing had calmed, she was coming back – and yet her eyes were still glazed, as though part of her remained locked inside.

Jack and Fee watched as Laura began to come to, growing more alert as she tuned into the music that was playing and the scent of the candle that was burning. She seemed puzzled momentarily to find Jack kneeling beside her. And then her face crumpled and she hid her face with her hands. 'I'm sorry.'

'Babes, you've got nothing to be sorry for,' Fee cried, flinging herself forward to the edge of the sofa and taking her friend's hands in her own. 'We're the ones who are sorry. How are you feeling now? Better?'

Laura nodded. She looked pale and her eyes still weren't focused. She turned towards Jack. 'Thank you.'

Jack smiled, thinly and wearily.

'What was the trigger?' she asked, trying to remember.

'The headlines came on. I couldn't turn over the channel in time.'

'It's not your fault,' she said, trying to soothe him.

'I *should* have known. It's the anniversary. They were bound to show it. I should never have turned the telly on.'

'Jack, you were watching the match. You couldn't have known they'd show it then.'

But Jack shook her absolution away. 'I should have thought. They always read the headlines during the ads. How bad was it, on a scale of one to ten?'

'. . . Eight.'

Jack's mouth twitched very subtly. 'It's gone up again. You haven't been there for months.'

Laura shook her head. 'No.'

After a moment, he gave a small shrug. 'Well, it's the four-year anniversary. It's a more powerful trigger. I'm sure it'll drop back next time.'

'If there *is* a next time,' Fee said fiercely. 'That might've been the last one, for all we know. Have a little faith. You're getting stronger every day, aren't you, Laur?'

Laura nodded obediently. She and Jack both knew she had tonight to get through. She swung her legs round so that her feet touched the carpet.

'Please let's not dwell on it. I really just want to forget about it.'

'Well, are you hungry?' Fee asked quickly.

'Starving,' Laura lied.

'Great! I got extra naan.' Fee smiled. 'Let's eat while it's still hot and get back to our Saturday night. Louis' act's going out tonight, I just know it!' Fee looked over at Jack as they filed through the door. 'I don't suppose there's any chance you'll let us eat it on our laps?'

His strangled expression in response made even Laura laugh, and she felt the regression lift off her entirely: Fee's light spirit was every bit as remedial as Jack's carefully learned medical approach.

'Well, it was worth a shot!' Fee guffawed as they trooped into the kitchen and began peeling back the foil-covered tubs, the three of them doing a fine job of pretending it was just another normal Saturday night.

The next morning, as Old Grey sailed past the window, his wings beating with slow stateliness, his neck retracted, Laura looked towards the door. She could already hear the foot-steps on the stairs, and the absence of slapping flip-flops or single-stab stilettos told her it wasn't Fee.

Jack knocked with his customary rat-a-tat-tat and peered round the door. Laura was wearing leggings and one of his T-shirts, sitting at her bench, goggles pushed back on her head. A sheet of gold and her jewellery torch lay in front of her.

'So this is where you're hiding out.' He smiled, walking into the room. It was blazing with light although it was freezing outside. Arthur was lying in the middle of the floor, pools of white sunshine beaming down on him like a heat lamp. He raised a quizzical head and cocked a curious ear at Jack's presence here. Like Laura, he hadn't been expecting him.

Jack leant down and kissed Laura's pursed, closed mouth. She wondered if she still tasted of peanut-butter toast and coffee. 'Back on crunchy?' he asked.

She rolled her eyes, knowing he hated the taste of both. 'If I'd known you were coming, I'd have had honey and tea.'

'Not on my account, please. I'll kiss you regardless,' he said, sliding a hand over her breast and squeezing lightly. She wasn't wearing a bra and he knew she'd got dressed in the dark.

Laura smiled faintly, looking back down at the miniature silver pram she was working on – one of the charms for a christening bracelet that was due in a few weeks' time.

'How come you're in so early?' Jack asked, perching on the arm of the sofa. She was aware of his eyes watching for the occasional press of her nipple against the flimsy fabric.

'Tides.'

'I missed you.'

'I just have to keep up with these orders,' she replied,

lowering her eyes again. 'If I fall behind, I'll never catch up again, and I can't let the clients down. Everyone needs their pieces for Christmas.'

She felt him watch her as she heated the gold again with a green flame, hammering it lightly at just the right moment, her brow furrowed, her mouth set in a line of concentration. Her body language was closed and remote still. It always was after an attack. She'd slept on the far side of the bed the night before, her hair – wet from her inevitable protracted shower – soaking the pillow, a sea of unarticulated despair between them both. Would it ever be over?

Jack walked towards the far window and scanned the tide line. High water was only an hour or two away. He looked back at her.

'Are you going to be working here all day, then?'

'Yes. Why? Have you got to work today as well?'

He shook his head. 'It's Sunday, Laur. I believe in having a day of rest.'

She kept her eyes down. 'These wheels are a nightmare. I want them to spin.'

'Is there any particular reason why they have to?'

She shook her head. 'I just want it to be authentic, that's all.'

'And yet again, Laura Cunningham makes life easy for herself,' he teased.

Laura grunted her reply.

He heaved a sigh of defeat. 'Well, in that case, I'd better go and get us some supplies. We'll be stranded within the hour and that's a prospect I could quite enjoy, as long as it involves the Sunday papers, plenty of food and you joining me at some point on the sofa. Is the milk fresh, or do you need some more?'

'More, please.'

He nodded. 'I'll be back in twenty, then. I'll stretch out on the sofas and you won't even know I'm there.'

But you always are, she thought to herself as the door clicked behind him and his footsteps faded beneath her. You always are.

# Chapter Six

Laura sat on the train frantically texting Fee – she couldn't get enough signal for a call – to contact Robert Blake's office and explain about the signal failure. Her train was running forty minutes behind schedule and there was still a short walk from there. It was going to be an hour, best-case scenario, and it was already 2.20 p.m.

She rested her cheek against the window and closed her eyes again, trying to nap – she was generally better at napping than sleeping and had learnt to rest more deeply in ten minutes than most people could in three hours – but the teenage girl opposite insisted on sharing her iPod playlist, and had turned it up so loudly that her earphones were effectively redundant.

After several minutes, Laura gave up and stared out of the window. A cold white light was slanting across London, bleaching the pavements and forcing pedestrians and drivers to squint against it. Soon she would be out there too, her shoulders hunched, her thighs chilling quickly in the wind, away from this uncomfortable heat that was blowing hard from under the seat against her calves and forcing her to occasionally throw her legs forwards and kick the iPod girl.

She sighed frustratedly, prompting discreet stares from her neighbours. This was the last thing she needed – another bad start on top of the first bad start. And she'd tried so hard, too, putting on the black trouser suit she always wore to funerals, trying to match him in his uniform and show a little respect.

Eventually the train pulled in to Liverpool Street and she allowed herself to be carried along by the sea of travellers swarming towards the gates. It took three attempts to get her ticket through before she realized it was back to front, and she inhaled nervously as the double-height halls opened up before her. She still wasn't good with crowds.

Tucking her chin down, she looked for the exit sign and moved nimbly towards it. Just breathe.

'Laura?'

She looked up in surprise. Robert Blake was coming towards her, his overcoat splaying out behind him, like Heathcliff roaming the moors. He was more gorgeous than she'd remembered. How on earth had she ended up slamming a door on *him*?

'H-hi!' she stammered. 'I thought we were meeting at the Guildhall.'

He nodded. 'I got your message. I've got a meeting in an hour. It just seemed easier to see you here. It's just as quick from here back to my office.'

'I'm so sorry about—'

'It's fine. Hardly surprising that the trains fall apart at the first dip in temperature.' He stared down at her, his hands on his hips. 'I barely recognized you, actually. You look so different to last time.'

'Oh yes. Well I thought I'd better try to blend in.'

'It was the red shoes that gave you away. Not many of those around here.'

Laura looked down at her red pumps, feeling conspicuous.

They stood awkwardly in silence for a second, busy commuters rushing past them with irritated expressions and pursed lips.

'Well, why don't we get a drink over here?' he said, motioning towards a small café.

'Sure,' Laura replied, noticing a striking redhead do a double-take as she passed by. Not that he seemed to notice. He seemed genuinely oblivious to his looks and the effect they had on people.

They walked into a tiny coffee house with four round tables, chocolate-brown walls and plumes of steam decorating the air. Behind the counter, a stocky barista was practically tap-dancing the beans underfoot to grind them as he flamboyantly put together exotic coffee combinations that had precious little to do with cocoa beans, hot water and milk.

Robert ordered for them – espresso for him, cappuccino for her – and they found seats towards the back.

Laura cleared her throat as Robert took off his coat and laid it on the spare chair. 'Look, Mr Blake, before we go any further, I want to apologize again for the way I behaved the other d—'

'No,' Robert replied firmly, his gold-flecked eyes holding hers. 'You were absolutely right. I was out of line. I should never have gone behind your back like that. I don't blame you at all for how you reacted.' He gave a tiny smile. 'In fact, I rather respected it. And please call me Rob.'

Laura's face showed her surprise and she looked down at her hands on the table. The waiter set down their coffees. They each had a tiny chocolate on the saucer, and Rob held his out towards her questioningly. 'If I have any understanding of women at all . . . ?' He raised a speculative eyebrow. 'We could call it a peace offering.'

Laura cracked a smile. 'Fine. Thank you.'

He heaved a sigh of relief as the tension between them slackened, and Laura took a sip of her coffee without breaking up the chocolate-dusted heart sitting on the foam.

'So,' she said quietly, checking with her finger that there wasn't any residue on her top lip. 'Seven charms from seven people. Who are they all?'

'Me, Cat's sister Olive, her best friend Kitty, her ex-boyfriend Alex, her friend from university Sam, her business partner-stroke-personal trainer Orlando and her boss Min – Cat works three afternoons a week at an art gallery in Holland Park.'

Laura nodded. 'And who are the people living abroad?'

Rob reached down into his briefcase and pulled out an envelope. 'Alex and Sam. But as I said, I'm trying to get them over here. Everyone's details are in there.'

Laura peered into the envelope before looking up at him. 'You're going to a lot of trouble for this. Is it a significant birthday for your wife?'

'They all are, aren't they?' he remarked with a smile. 'But she's going to be thirty-two.'

'Oh.' Laura's age. 'Well, look, if you've got a bit of time, we could start with your interview now. It would be helpful for me to get some background on her.'

Rob shifted in his seat. 'Okay. What do you want to know?'

'Let's just start with some basic background stuff – where you live, family, how long you've been together.'

'We live in Virginia Water in Surrey, and we've been together for five years, married for over four of them.' He answered with the slightly frozen look of a game-show contestant.

'Oh, so it was a fast engagement, then.'

'Yes. I suppose you'd say it was a "love at first sight" scenario. I couldn't risk letting her get away.'

Laura nodded. 'And do you have any children?'

It was an innocuous enough question, but she might as well have asked him his favourite sexual position. His face froze, his muscles setting to stone in front of her. '. . . No, not yet.'

The 'yet' was telling and Laura's cheeks flamed. 'Oh, I'm so sorry.' She felt like she'd been prying rather than just doing her job.

He gave an embarrassed smile, raking a hand through his hair. 'No, it's not . . . It's a perfectly reasonable question. I am paying you to reflect her life, after all. It just feels quite early to be talking about my private life with you when we've only known each other for two and a half minutes, that's all.'

Laura nodded and fixed a patient smile on her face. If everyone was going to be as reticent about being interviewed as Rob, she'd never get the necklace made for next Christmas, much less this one. 'If you'd rather wait a bit, I can always interview you later on. Last, even.'

He looked at her for a moment and then nodded. 'Yes, perhaps that would be better.'

Laura took a sip of her coffee, smudging the heart out of recognition, and they watched a woman in a suit order a latte and panini. The woman's eyes slid over Rob and then to Laura as she sat down. Laura straightened up.

He looked over at Laura guiltily as they sat in continued silence. 'I suppose I could have just emailed this over to you rather than making you come all the way here to see me.'

'No, it's fine.'

'It's just that I thought we'd be better off clearing the air properly before you begin. You're going to get to know an awful lot about my wife and her life in the next few weeks. It wouldn't be right if there was . . . an atmosphere between us.'

'I completely agree.'

'It's just that I really need this to be perfect.'

'I understand.'

'My wife is my life.'

'Of course.'

He nodded, looking over at her. 'Are you married?'

Laura shook her head. 'Boyfriend. Four years now.'

'Four years?' The exact opposite to his relationship – a slow burn. 'Is marriage on the cards?'

Laura shook her head again, more vehemently this time. 'Not the marrying kind.'

'Who isn't? Him or you?'

'Both,' she replied. It was only a half-lie, or half-truth, whichever way you wanted to look at it. Jack had only asked her once, three years ago, on New Year's Eve, and he'd been so appalled by her mute tears that he'd never brought it up since. Now she had no idea whether he still wanted to marry her. Their gentle, aimless drifting side by side seemed increasingly to suit them both perfectly.

'Free spirits, huh?' His BlackBerry buzzed in his coat pocket and he reached over for it. 'Damn. The clients are early. I'll need to head back to the office.'

'That's fine. I'll wait here for the next train.'

He stood up and she followed suit.

'We'll speak soon, then?' he asked, shrugging his coat back on.

Laura nodded.

'And call me if there's anything. But there shouldn't be any problems. Everyone's waiting to hear from you.'

'Sure. Great.'

He shook her hand briskly. 'Bye, then.'

'Bye.'

Laura watched him go – his upright, almost military bearing and purposeful march as he disappeared headlong into the crowds that frightened her so much. People moved aside for him, men and women casting sly interested glances as he passed, and then he was gone.

Laura slumped in her seat and untwisted the blue foil wrapper on the chocolate Baci he had given her – his peace offering – unable to get his words out of her head. *Free spirits, huh?*

As if.

# Chapter Seven

Even on the motorway the next morning, Laura's yellow and cream dolly car – a near-extinct Citroën 2CV that needed pushing up hills – stood out. For the last two junctions, Laura had gradually become aware that on every side of her and in front and behind she was hemmed in by sleek saloons and executive coupés in metallic navy, silver and black. Jack needed the Volvo for work, of course – he needed the boot space for ferrying furniture to and from clients' houses. She'd been adamant about not having a van as their main car, and the Volvo had been the compromise, but it had been on its last legs when they'd bought it as it was all they'd been able to afford of the model.

Still, she could only get up to two-thirds of the speed of all the other commuters in Dolly, and had trundled along in the slow lane since joining the M11. Her sole company – the radio didn't work, and CDs, much less MP3s, hadn't been invented when this car was built – was a pale blue Rover, which she'd sat behind ever since they'd both emerged from the Dartford Tunnel. It was driven by a white-haired, tweed-jacketed man accompanied by his wife, who kept handing him sandwiches, and Laura was passing the time trying to guess what was inside them – chicken salad? Cheese and pickle? Egg and cress? Perhaps he was a potted-meats man.

Nine-thirty in the morning was too early, she reasoned, for coronation chicken.

She was settling on ham and mustard when her junction came up and she reluctantly peeled away from them, resisting the urge to wave goodbye. She followed the signs for Riverton, as Fee had instructed her to. The roads became ever narrower, ever leafier, and she slowly became aware of an indigenous predilection for floral-stickered wheelie bins, glossy red Cinquecentos and candle shops.

After a few miles, a sign for 'Ottersbrook' took her off to the left, and she was soon driving past a set of white pick-eted mock-gates that heralded the boundary of the village. There was a newly built housing estate to her right, with boxy red-brick maisonettes set along a series of sweeping cul-de-sacs. The village store seemed to be set in a scarcely adapted house that had simply given over its ground floor to washing powder, fresh bread and bags of jelly sweets, and a couple of young girls – aged twelve, maybe thirteen – were sitting on the railings of the disabled-access ramp, dipping sherbet Dip Dabs.

There was no pavement to speak of, and the lawns of the central village houses ran down to the road. The aban-doned bicycles and Nerf guns casually left out overnight showed that this was a close-knit community-watch neigh-bourhood.

Laura glanced down at the directions Fee had written in her large, looping script – all the Is dotted with hearts – with her gold metallic pen. She was only twenty-three, and sometimes the nine-year gap between them was glaringly obvious.

'*Past the village store on the right . . .*' she murmured. 'Done that. *Follow road to the end, turns into unadopted road . . .*' Oh great, because Dolly couldn't even make it over gravel. '*Last house on left, look out for the . . .*' She squinted. 'What's that say? *Ca . . .* ? *Camel*? *Candle*? Tch, what's she on about?'

Dolly bumped along from wheel to wheel, as if she was doing a commando crawl down the unmade track. 'As if there are any camels in Surrey, Fee. There probably aren't even any mongrels,' she mumbled, just as a long brown face peered over the hawthorn hedge and spat at the window.

'Oh my God!' she shrieked, slamming on the brakes and bringing the car to a skid-stop with the front left and back right wheels in potholes so deep that Dolly's tummy grazed the muddy lane. She sat with her hands on the steering wheel and stared unseeing through the windscreen for a moment. Had that really been a . . . ? She got out, leant one arm over Dolly's roof and one foot on the door frame, and stared at the camel that had gone back to eating sloe berries, masticating quite disgustingly, so that a velouté of black foamy spit collected in the corners of its mouth.

It stared back at her, clearly unrepentant at the mess it had made of her window, and for a moment she wondered how it might be possible to exact revenge on a hostile camel.

'Her name's Sugar,' a voice called out.

Laura looked over, to find a rosy-cheeked woman with deep-set blue eyes and a jumble of black curls piled high walking down a garden path towards her. She had an orange-faced toddler on her hip who looked like he shared the same table manners as the camel, and a white duckling was waddling alongside her feet. 'You know, one hump or two?'

Her face split into a delighted chuckle – as though it was the first time she'd ever heard the joke – and Laura nodded, too shocked to find a laugh.

'She's the best landmark ever. Everyone in the village uses

her as a reference. You know, "second left past the camel" and all that.' Laura stared at her. The woman spoke at the speed of light. 'Plus she's a great security guard. Spits like buggery – I expect you just found that out. I heard your holler all the way back in the kitchen. No one'll even try to walk past her on the lane. I've had to fit our postbox a hundred yards further back. Postman got fed up with it all.' She smacked her forehead with her free hand. 'Damn! I should've thought to mention it to your secretary and you could've picked the mail up for me on your way past. Never mind, you're here now.' She caught sight of Dolly – the automotive equivalent of a beached whale – shrugged at the sight and smiled. 'I'm Kitty, by the way,' she said, throwing open a small gate and thrusting forward a hand. 'And this is Samuel. You must be Laura.'

Laura nodded. 'That's right. Pleased to meet you.'

They shook hands, and Kitty – now that she'd stopped talking – looked at Laura with interest. 'Rob's told me all about you. I'm so fascinated to find out how this will work. Well, come on. Come inside. Everything's a tip, I'm afraid. I haven't even seen the cat for a month. I'm sure she's been sat on or buried under a pile of washing,' she said, leading Laura up the garden path and straight past the fat tabby sleeping in the wintry sun on one of the deep stone windowsills. 'Have you had breakfast?'

'Uh, well, I had a coffee and a Danish when I stopped for petrol,' Laura said, trying not to step on the duckling that was waddling around her ankles.

'That's a "no", then,' Kitty smiled, leading her into a low-ceilinged cottage. It was a limed wattle and daub house with black timbers, tiny leaded windows and a climbing rose around the door. Inside it was predictably dark and beamy, with oak-panelled walls and a short, lethally steep staircase with child-proof gates at the top and bottom.

They stepped into the kitchen, clearly the heart of the house, for at one end of it there was an enormous inglenook chimney. An ancient racing-green solid-fuel Aga stood against the opposite wall, and there was a huge round table in the middle. The terracotta-tiled floor was covered with dozens of kilim rugs, all touching end to end like dominoes so that the overall effect was of a patchwork quilt. A small thread-bare orange velvet sofa – pushed against a wall – was covered with an Ikea throw, and an Irish wolfhound was dozing happily on it. Unlike the camel, it clearly held no security qualifications whatsoever.

'That's Pocket.' She winked. 'You can guess why, can't you?'

Laura nodded, quickly getting the gist. That dog was too big to fit in most cars, much less a pocket.

'Don't mind her. She's the gentlest of giants. I always get her to look after Samuel if I have to help Joe in the yard with something.' She lifted a heavy-looking kettle off a trivet and plonked it down on the Aga. 'Joe's my husband, by the way.'

'Right,' Laura replied, wondering where to place herself. There were towers of crispy, yellowing newspapers everywhere, a huge log basket by her knees, and plastic chew toys – whether for Pocket or Samuel, Laura wasn't entirely sure – on the counters. 'So is Samuel your first?' Laura asked, reaching for some small talk.

'My fifth,' Kitty replied, pulling a tray of slightly over-cooked bacon, sausages, black pudding and mushrooms out of the warming oven. As if on cue, a tousle-haired boy with bold, splodgy freckles wandered in through the back door, holding the duckling – or was it a different one? – under one arm. 'Oh, Tom, there you are. Go and get me five eggs, there's a good boy.'

Tom's shoulders dropped automatically. 'Oh, Muuuuum,' he whined.

'Go! And put that duck down. Your father will be after you in a minute to help with the hedging.' Kitty wagged a stern finger at him and he turned in his muck boots and headed back to the hen house.

'You have five children?' Laura echoed.

'Yes. All under eight, would you believe it? Tom there's my eldest.' She put a cup of blue-rinse tea in front of Laura. 'Earl Grey okay? Help yourself to sugar,' she said, pushing a bowl over, then picking up some of the bacon and sausages with a pair of tongs and dividing them between two plates. One of them had a massive chip on the rim and looked like it had at some point been glued back together again.

Tom came back in with the eggs, and Kitty hurriedly cracked them and scrambled them up.

'Here you go,' she said, setting the plates down on the table. The wafting aroma finally piqued Pocket's interest and she raised a languid head as the two women began to eat.

'This is wonderful, but really, you needn't have gone to so much trouble for me,' Laura said, watching Kitty heartily smack huge dollops of HP sauce on to her plate.

'Nonsense. Rob said you were coming all the way from Suffolk. You must have been driving for what – three hours?'

'Thereabouts,' Laura agreed, munching on some sausage. 'My car isn't really geared up for motorway driving any more. I might have been quicker driving in reverse.'

'She's pretty, though,' Kitty smiled, and Laura liked the way her eyes crinkled into themselves.

'Yes.' Laura took a sip of the tea. 'It's a lovely place you've got here. Have you lived here long?'

'All my life. The farm's been in my father's family for four generations. I grew up in this house.'

'Seriously?' Laura exclaimed through a mouth full of food, suddenly ravenous. She'd been on the road since six this morning, and hadn't appreciated quite how hungry she was.

'Yes,' Kitty said, spooning some beans on to the heel of a cob loaf. 'Sometimes I think it'd be nice to have somewhere new, though, with bigger rooms and straight walls. I even went and had a look at the show home for the new estate on the edge of the village.'

'But a new place wouldn't be a patch on here. This is bursting with character.'

'That's estate agent speak for poky, with rising damp and no right angles or insulation,' Kitty chuckled. 'But no, you're right. I could never leave this place. It's just an idle fantasy for those days when it gets too much – you know, kids fighting, animals wandering in and out like they own the place, Aga's gone out, half the roof tiles have blown off in the night. The thought of magnolia paintwork and wall-to-wall carpet, a thirty-foot garden and a damp-coursed utility room – aaaah, bliss!'

Laura nodded. Put that way, she could see the attraction.

'I suppose you have it much the same yourself, don't you?' Kitty asked, wrapping her hands around her mug, her pretty eyes peering curiously over the steaming mug. 'Husband, kids, animals . . . ?'

'Boyfriend. And no kids. But we have a dog called Arthur. He's gorgeous, an Irish terrier. He's nearly four now. We love him to pieces.'

'Have you been with your boyfriend long?'

'Almost four years, although . . . we were friends before that.'

'Oooh, think he might propose?' Kitty asked excitedly.

'No,' Laura said briskly, wondering how, within five minutes of stepping into this stranger's house, she was tucking into a full English and sharing her private life. She didn't 'do' intimacy. With anyone. Well, possibly Fee, but she always complained it was more like surgical extraction than genuine intimacy. 'I'm not sure marriage is ever going to be my bag.'

Or motherhood, she thought to herself as Samuel staggered back through. His face was still stained orange and he was sucking on a wooden Thomas the Tank Engine, the legs of his babygro sleepsuit tied round his waist to reveal a yellow-tinted and very low slung nappy that hung to his knees.

'Just look at him,' Kitty tutted, a blend of adoration and exasperation in her voice. 'I'd better change his nappy before Joe comes in and insists he lives out with the pigs. You don't mind, do you?'

'Of course not.'

'I'll just be a sec.'

Laura watched as Kitty scooped Samuel into her arms and headed up the creaky staircase. Kitty was not at all what she'd spent most of last night bracing herself for. Given Rob Blake's power-trip dynamics and 'international set' appearance, she'd been expecting his wife's friends to be Russian models with endless legs and coke habits. But Kitty was so . . . well, *normal*.

She noticed Pocket was staring at her through one open eye – doubtless getting ready to lay her claim on the scraps – and she got up, taking the plates over to the worktop by the sink for something to do. Pocket followed at a trot. Laura found a bowl of leftovers on the windowsill and proceeded to scrape the bacon rind and beans into it, tossing a few stray pieces of eggy bread to Pocket, who caught them in clashing teeth.

'What are you doing?' a voice asked abruptly.

Laura wheeled round to find the silhouette of a tall, rangy man in overalls and gumboots standing in the doorway.

'I was just giving her some titbits.'

'And who said you could do that? She's diabetic.'

'Oh! I'm sorry.'

'As you should be.'

Laura shifted her weight nervously from foot to foot as the man stared at her. She felt strange to be the one standing so familiarly in the man's kitchen, at his sink, whilst he hovered at the threshold as if he was the visitor.

'I'm Laura. I've come to interview Kitty for a necklace I'm making for Cat Blake's birthday.'

'I heard.' From the withering tone of his voice, he clearly didn't approve. A nigh-on twenty-thousand-pound piece of jewellery that required people to be *interviewed* was clearly a ridiculous frippery in his book. He stepped out of his boots and into the room, and as he came out of the light, she saw that he was younger than he had at first appeared – mid to late thirties, with pale blue eyes in a long, rectangular face with greying stubble. He walked towards her, his eyes staying on her all the while. 'And I suppose that's your car that's just been abandoned in the middle of the lane.'

'Oh – yes. The camel gave me a fright and I ended up in some potholes.'

'Damn near drove over it in the tractor. Useless car for driving around here,' he muttered rudely as he poured himself a cup of tea.

'Well, to be honest, when I was told I was coming to Surrey, I didn't expect I'd need an off-roader,' Laura replied, her hackles rising at the sustained attack.

'I'll have to pull it out. You've managed to well and truly strand yourself,' he grumbled.

'I'm sure I'll be able to manage,' Laura replied stiffly.

'Oh no, let Joe help you. It'll only take him a second,' Kitty interjected, and Laura looked up to find her standing by the doorway.

'Where's Tom?' Joe asked her brusquely.

'Waiting for you. Probably playing in the barn.'

Joe shot his wife a look and, stuffing his feet back into his boots, stomped out into the yard without another word, taking his tea with him.

'Don't mind him,' Kitty said breezily as she began clearing the table. 'He's better with animals, that's all.'

Laura nodded politely as Kitty slid the dirty plates into a bowl of soapy water. 'Was he a farmer when you met him?'

'Yep, his family owned the neighbouring farm. I always say he asked for my land in marriage,' she chuckled. 'I've known him since I was five. We were at school together.'

'Are your children going to carry on with the farm?'

'Who knows? Tom's saying he wants to. That's why he's home today and not at school. Joe's usual man's having an op, so he's kept him home to help out with the hedges,' Kitty rambled, cleaning the plates vigorously and handing them to Laura to dry. 'But he might change his mind as he gets older. There are no guarantees, are there?'

Within a few minutes, the washing-up was done and Pocket was back on the sofa, sleeping soundly again.

'Well, where would you like me to interview you about Cat Blake?' Laura asked, folding the tea towel over the Aga rail to dry. Kitty was easy company, but after Joe's hostility, Laura was keen to get her work done and get out of there.

'I thought we could do it on the way to Samuel's music group,' Kitty smiled, drying her hands.

Laura's face dropped. 'Sorry?'

'He's got his music group in half an hour – a dozen three-year-olds banging the cymbals. Really it's hell on earth, but it's a lovely walk and I can show you the village. We can talk then. Come on.'

# Chapter Eight

The old part of Ottersbrook was much prettier than the new residential part she had driven through. The church, primary school and village hall were clumped together down a narrow stretch of winding lanes, where thatched cottages stood directly on the road, corners and bay windows jutting out like sharp elbows.

Kitty – in Next jeans and a blue Sherpa fleece – was pushing Samuel on an old Raleigh tricycle that Laura suspected had also been part of Kitty's childhood. It had taken half a packet of baby wipes to get the orange stain off his face – sweet potato mash apparently – and Laura had been horrified when Kitty had casually asked her if she'd strap the wriggling, protesting toddler into the buggy whilst she dashed upstairs to the loo. Sensing her lack of experience in dealing with the mini-limbed, Samuel had proceeded to make himself as rigid as a scaffolding board and started to scream so hard his lips went blue.

'So, Rob told me you're Cat's longest-standing friend?' Laura began, restless and somewhat irritated by this scenic, long-winded way of extracting information.

'You'd better believe it,' Kitty replied, an ever-present smile on her lips. I've known her as long as I've known me. She's my oldest and dearest friend in the world.'

Laura looked across at Kitty as she bent down to pick up the engine Samuel had just lobbed into a neatly clipped privet hedge. Living in the home she'd grown up in, married to her childhood neighbour, best friends with her oldest companion . . . She seemed to belong to another era somehow, one where people corresponded by letter, not Twitter, and to whom community didn't mean the number of friends on your Facebook page.

'Her family came and lived in one of the farm cottages when she was five, and we spent all our time together. She's only four days older than me, so we shared all our parties. When we started at primary, we were supposed to be in separate classes but we refused to release each other's hands until they let us sit together. We used to swap a shoe each at break time and skip around the playground arm in arm, me with her left shoe, her with mine . . .' Kitty shook her head and laughed at the memory.

'It sounds like you were as close as sisters.'

'Closer. Twins. *Siamese* twins even – sometimes I wasn't sure where I stopped and she began. I could always finish her sentences. I always knew every thought that was in her head. People talk about twins having ESP, but we had it too, you know. Other people – teachers, the kids at school, even our mums – found it a bit creepy.' She looked over at Laura. 'You can guess what they called us, can't you?'

Laura shrugged.

'Go on, take a guess.'

Laura looked at her blankly. How the heck would she know?

'KitCat,' Kitty smiled. 'And Kitty Cat. "Here, Kitty Cat," they'd shout, and we used to pretend we were kittens and we'd run over to them, pretending to lick our paws. Talk about role playing.' She shook her head at the memory. 'And Dad used to go mad at us because every time the farm cat had a litter – which was often! – we'd hide the kittens in our rooms and the number of rats in the hay barn would just double. Poor Mum would find them all sleeping together in the sock drawer. The kittens, I mean, not the rats,' she giggled. 'Do you like cats?'

Laura shook her head. 'I'm a dog person. Arthur's my baby. I have to respect his enmities.'

Kitty smiled, appreciating the attempt at humour. 'Of course.'

They had reached a low prefab building that looked like it had been put up in the war, and a melee of buggies had congregated by the front door. Kitty added hers as she unbuckled Samuel one-handed. She opened the door and as Laura followed her in, she walked straight into a wall of screams. Instantly she felt the breath snatched from her lungs, leaving them empty and deflated like week-old balloons. She instinctively squeezed her eyes shut, trying to block out the sound, both hands gripping the half-open door.

'It's just over h— Laura? Are you okay?' Kitty asked, coming closer as she saw that Laura was paralysed on the spot. 'What's wrong?'

Slowly Laura opened her eyes. The first thing she saw was Kitty's concern; the second was a woman dressed as a jester playing a recorder and being followed around the room by skipping children; the third was a row of curious mothers sitting on felt conference chairs, staring at her.

'Laura, what just happened?' Kitty asked in a quiet voice.

'Low blood pressure. I've got low blood pressure,' Laura

murmured, beginning to straighten herself up. This wasn't unusual after a bad episode. It was like aftershocks following an earthquake.

Kitty nodded, but alarm rippled through her eyes like the blips on a heart monitor. 'Let's get a coffee and have a sit-down. Samuel's fine in here,' she said, taking Laura by the arm.

She led Laura through to a smaller room next door, where a few plastic catering tables and stacking chairs had been laid out. Kitty got them each a cup and a saucer full of sugar-sprinkled Nice biscuits as Laura fiddled with the cuff buttons on her jacket.

'Do you want to talk about it?' Kitty asked kindly, sitting down.

'There's nothing to say,' Laura said, replacing her cup so sharply on the saucer it was a wonder it didn't crack. She caught sight of Kitty's hurt expression and a voice in her head instantly berated her. 'I'm sorry. What I mean to say is . . . I'm not a good talker. I don't like talking about myself. I'd honestly much rather hear about you and Cat.'

Kitty nodded, but her voice was quieter when she spoke, and she kept her eyes down. They had taken a step back-wards. 'Okay. What would you like to know?'

'Um . . . well, what was the tone of your friendship? Was it jokey, mischievous; were you always getting into trouble?'

'Yes. All those things and more. One day, we'd sit in a tree for six hours, looking out for red kites coming back to nest; the next, we'd be explorers, trawling up and down Dad's fields with the metal detector, absolutely certain we'd find Roman treasure.'

'Did you?' Laura asked hopefully.

'A few old coins, bones, some pottery. Nothing of any

great age or value. But we liked the hunt more than anything. It was the *idea* of discovering something that excited us.'

'What else?'

'We built a den in the woods at the bottom of the long field. My father put up a platform in a birch tree for us, and we hung webbing underneath it, which we filled with ferns for camouflage. Cat got given a beginner's archery set one Christmas, so we set up the board on a nearby tree and would pretend to be Robin Hood, shooting through the leaves.' She bit her lip and grinned. 'We ought not to have, of course. There was a public footpath down there. Can you imagine?' She held up her hands and widened them. '*Walker harpooned!*' she announced, laughing, as if it was a newspaper headline.

'Ouch.'

'Yes. We were lucky more than anything else. Cat took out a squirrel once, as I recall.'

'Was it just the two of you down there?'

'Oh yes. And no boys allowed, naturally. We'd raid the fridge and just stay out there all day. It had to be pretty cold or wet to drive us back in. Usually we wouldn't leave until we saw my parents coming down the field with their torches, shouting at us to come in for dinner. We were permanently covered in mud and scratches.'

'You sound like real tomboys.'

'I guess so, although we loved being girly too. We'd have discos in our bedroom, jumping around with the lights off and our headlamps on, and Mum gave us a box of her old clothes – including her wedding dress – that we could dress up in. We used to practise getting married to each other, always in the car for some reason,' she puzzled, frowning at the memory. 'Drive-thru weddings in Surrey . . . Huh.'

She shrugged. 'And we took it in turns learning to walk in her mum's heels. When we reached thirteen, we were both allowed to have our ears pierced. We'd pull off the wax strips on each other's legs. We were never apart, basically.'

Encouraged by this easy stream of consciousness, Laura leant forward. 'What's the most vivid memory you have of her?'

'There are so many,' Kitty said, looking up at the polystyrene-blocked ceiling. 'But I suppose . . . I suppose it was at Guide camp when we were about eleven. We were in Devon, and it was the first time we'd both been allowed away from home. It was the second day there – I remember because our tent collapsed on the first and we had to go out in our vests and knickers in the middle of the night and try to fix the guy ropes using our hairbrushes as mallets.

'Anyway, we were cooking dinner. I was dumped with peeling the potatoes and Cat had to get some more water from the stream two fields away. I must have chopped up well over fifty potatoes when I saw her staggering back towards us, carrying something.'

Kitty smiled and shook her head, but her eyes were far away.

'It was a lamb, just a tiny thing. It had got caught in a roll of barbed wire and a fox had separated it from its mother. Cat had seen it and started screaming and waving at it, but the fox must have been starving or something because Cat said nothing she did would make it run off. There she was in the middle of a field, with not so much as a stone to throw at it, so she started beating and kicking at it with her own fists. Can you imagine? This little girl physically fighting a fox? She got a few really nasty bites herself, of course, and ended up having to have stitches and all kinds of shots afterwards, but I'll never forget the sight of her coming up with that lamb in her arms. Her arms and legs were smeared with blood but all I could see was the whites of her eyes. Her delight! She was so happy she'd rescued this lamb. She said it was the best moment of her life.' Kitty sighed. 'I think she loved the fact that for once she was given all this praise for something that wasn't about how she looked.'

Laura threw her a puzzled glance. 'What do you mean?'

'Well, that was always the first thing people talked about when they met her. The only thing, really. They never seemed to notice – or even care – that she was kind or funny or clever.' She gave a pitying shrug. 'I always kind of felt sorry for her about it really.'

'You don't think she's pretty?'

'Of course I do. But I spent so much time with her, hers was the face I spent more time looking at than any other. I knew it better than my own.'

'What happened to the lamb? Did it die?'

'Ordinarily it would have been put down. It was lame and clearly in pain. But the farmer took one look at Cat's big, pretty, hopeful eyes and everything she'd done to save it, and he called the vet out. They had to amputate, but other than that, it recovered well and was hopping about on three legs within a few days. Cassidy, we called it.'

'You *kept* it?'

'Well, the farmer couldn't do anything with it, and there was no way Cat would leave it. You should have seen her mother's face as she got off the coach at the end of the week with a three-legged lamb in her arms!'

Laura paused. 'Why Cassidy?'

Kitty's eyes were shining. 'As in Hopalong?'

Laura groaned. 'You have a thing for naming your animals after bad jokes.'

'It's the glue that binds us,' Kitty replied, collapsing into giggles as Samuel headed up the stampede of children chasing into the room and making a beeline for the biscuits.

It was three o'clock before Laura finally got into Dolly, and even then it was only because Kitty had to do the school run and Laura was keen to leave without bumping into Friendly Joe again. He had, as Kitty had assured her he would, lifted Dolly out of the potholes, but any goodwill this might have engendered was undermined by the fact that he'd deposited her right next to Sugar's hawthorn hedge, and the driver's-side window was now several inches thick with black camel spit.

She sat in the slow lane of the M25, surrounded again by all the sleek executive cars ferrying all those tired, not-so-sleek executives home. Laura wondered whether Robert Blake was somewhere among them, battling the hordes to get home to his beloved wife – a wife she now knew was kind to animals, brave, inordinately pretty and prone to bad jokes.

Her mind wandered back over the stream of anecdotes and stories Kitty had machine-gunned at her over the course of the day. Samuel's music class had led on to lunch – a fish pie Kitty had thrown into the Aga on the way out to music – and Kitty hadn't stopped talking once.

It was clear the two girls had been each other's gate-keepers, and she was toying with the idea of a portcullis icon. It was a strong image and a powerful testament to the strength of the friends' protective support for each other. But how could she ignore the lamb? The self-proclaimed best moment of Cat's life, and Kitty's abiding image of her – the lamb in her arms as she carried it home, bloodied and brave and jubilant.

And what about a cat? Cheesy it might be, but it represented their shared 'kitty cat' identity in childhood. Or what about a play on words: Kit-Kat? Wouldn't that be fun? It would look great in metal, and Laura was sure she could capture the texture of the all-important foil.

Then there were the reminiscences about high school ('the English teacher likened her to the heroine in Shakespeare's Sonnet 18') and how someone ('never identified') had graffitied a marriage proposal to Cat on the railway bridge. But no, she thought, dismissing them; they didn't specifically relate to her relationship with Kitty, merely recounted the acts of passion that pretty girls inspire in men. Wasn't this very necklace an example of just that, with her husband, in this instance, the smitten fool?

What else? Achieving the school's lowest ever grade in a geometry test was a dubious distinction, albeit somewhat satisfying for Laura to hear after all the plaudits. Kitty had kept the side up by coming second last. And being picked as Mary for the school nativity play every year was frankly just predictable. No, their pranks were of considerably more interest to Laura – their week of detentions for growing cress in the staffroom carpets during half-term when they were in the sixth form, or putting a banana in the exhaust pipe of the geography teacher's Nova and watching his car splutter down the road, black smoke bellowing behind him.

Kitty had thrown the stories at her like clothes from a window – the two women's shared escapades intertwined into a single narrative like a plait – and their sound and colour filled Laura's head as she drove along the motorway with all the speed of a pensioner who'd left the handbrake on. By the time she parked the car in the little garage behind the cottage, the sun had long ago sunk below the watery horizon. She locked the car door quickly and jogged down the back garden path, dodging the icy patches and knowing Jack would already be in the kitchen waiting for her, the bath run and their dinner on.

The moon was full and low on the water tonight, casting a bright, lambent glow across the entire bay. But for once Laura wasn't watching the horizon. Her eyes were following the condensation beads dripping slowly down the windowpanes, one after another, in a meditation, like counting rosary beads.

She pulled her cardigan tighter around her, shivering as she watched the first prickles of frost begin to creep up the outer sides of the window glass. She looked back at Jack – his face slackened with sleep but still so handsome – in their bed. He always slept so deeply. He had half kicked the duvet off him so that one leg was free, and he was breathing so lightly she could barely hear him at all. He's even considerate in his sleep, she thought, watching him.

Her eyes scanned the room, falling first – as always – on the polished walnut box on the mantelpiece, then on their clothes folded neatly on the bedroom chair in the corner, on all the drawers pushed fully into their cavities, the water carafes freshly filled each night before bed. Everything was in order and absolutely just so. This was the perfect life Fee envied and wanted for herself; so why didn't Laura want it too? Why couldn't she feel the gratitude she ought to for living this life? As Fee was always at pains to tell her, Jack was Mr Poppins – practically perfect in every way. She couldn't ask for more. She didn't want to want more. And yet every night after he fell asleep, she lay in the dark, straining against the despair that threatened to suffocate her.

She hadn't missed the expression that had swept over him like a breeze just an hour ago – exasperation; weariness. *Again?* it had silently asked as she'd jump-started them both awake. She didn't blame him – precious few men would come home every night to a girlfriend who struggled to find enough appetite to swallow the food he cooked, who found smiling a physical exercise, who cried almost every time they made love, who screamed every time she dreamed.

She turned back to the moon, her old confidante, and rested her head against the wall in contemplation. How many nights had she spent gazing at it from this spot? Night after night, as it fattened and thinned and tugged along the tides that shaped her own days, it showed her that life works in cycles: what had been lost would, in time, be returned to her, it seemed to say. But she had never believed it, no matter how many nights she tracked its progress in the overarching sky. What she had lost she knew she could never get back.

Except that now . . . now she was in a different cycle. One that she had never asked for, and had never wanted. The sudden realization that had woken her so suddenly tonight was still a mystery to her. Twelve days late. How could it have happened? They were always so careful – she insisted on it, and Jack, sweet Jack, knew better than to push the issue.

But he would push her on this if he knew about it. *If.*

# Chapter Nine

Laura hugged her knees in closer and rearranged the blanket, tucking it under her bare toes, the chair rocking slightly on the rickety veranda. They were still pink and throbbing from the stinging cold water, and the easterly morning breeze, scarcely impeded by the confines of the beach hut, kept making her shiver with its unexpected breaths.

She watched the sea take another run-up at the beach, spreading heavily for a few moments before gravity dragged it back like a stern mother. The heavens had opened overnight and now the sky was busier than it had been for weeks, with billowing clouds jostling against one another like sale shoppers as the laughing wind zipped between them.

Arthur was sitting beside her, watching a split purple tennis ball bobbing madly on the surf. He gave a low, desolate whine as it buffeted the sand, but his mistress didn't hear. She was lost in her own thoughts.

Laura couldn't take her eyes off the light dancing over the water's skin, those malted, silty waters that rippled from mink into dazzling caramel with every exuberant dash the sun made from behind the clouds. It was one of those days when the view was more hindrance than help, teasing her in the studio with its capricious moods and whimsical lights, and given that she couldn't focus on work after last night's shock realization, she figured it was better to be in the weather than watching it. She wanted to melt like butter in the heat spots; she wanted to pitch herself against the gale-force gusts and be blown through from the inside out. Cleansed. Cleared of this mistake.

A long silhouette moved over the sand, differentiated from the others somehow, and a low growl rumbled through Arthur's body. The vibrations beneath Laura's hand caught her attention and her eyes flickered down towards him and then followed his gaze. A man was walking in front of the huts, his back to them as he scanned the beach.

'Rob?' she asked, startled, standing up so that the blanket fell to her feet. 'Are you looking for me?'

The man turned, apparently astonished to find her wearing just an oversized man's jumper on this freezing cold November day. 'Hi!'

He looked odd standing on the beach in his suit and overcoat. His shoes were covered in wet sand, but she could tell he wasn't the type to roll up his trousers.

'How did you know I was here?' It was more of an accusation than a question. How on earth had he tracked her down? Only Fee had been here with her so far.

'You left your studio open and—'

'I did *what*?' She shook her head. She was all over the place today. How the hell was she going to keep this a secret from Jack if she couldn't even shut a door behind her?

'The door was open,' he said, watching the disbelief on her face. 'I went in and saw you from the windows, walking down by the water. I dashed down here and knew you couldn't have gone far.' He looked at the forlorn structure barely protecting her from the elements. 'I didn't know you had one of these.'

You didn't know you paid for it either, she thought to herself.

'Have you had it long?' he asked, running an admiring hand along the timbers.

She shook her head. 'No. I've only just bought it. As a Christmas present for my boyfriend,' she mumbled. 'It's a surprise.'

Rob walked around the hut as though inspecting it for his own purchase. Laura waited for him to reappear. 'I read somewhere that these are hard to come by,' he said finally.

'I caught a lucky break. But it needs a lot of work doing on it, obviously,' she said, moving around a bit. 'Most of the shiplap's rotted, so I'm getting that replaced, and the floor's going to be ripped up.' She pushed down with one of her feet as if to show him, catching sight of her bare legs as she did so. 'Oh God,' she said, looking up in horror and pulling the jumper further down her thighs.

'I did wonder if you were, uh . . . cold,' he murmured.

'I forgot,' she said, twisting round to see if her jeans were any drier than when she'd wrung out the hems five minutes earlier. Hmph. Barely. 'Paddling,' she muttered, pulling them on anyway. 'I get done every time.'

'Well, at least now you have somewhere to shelter afterwards,' Rob said, politely turning towards the sea.

'Yes.'

'Does it have power?'

She shook her head. 'No. But it will have running water once some new pipes have been put in at the end of this week. The old ones are completely blocked. I've got a bottled-gas camping stove for boiling the kettle and things.' She pulled up her zip and clattered the kettle to indicate it was safe for him to turn round.

'It's great. I can't wait to see what you do to it. I helped my father renovate an old gypsy caravan in our garden when I was young. You know – one of those "father and son" projects that are so fashionable now? It was great. It's left me with a bit of a fascination for quirky bolt-holes, and a misguided belief in my abilities with power tools.'

Laura chuckled. It was hard to see him as a lumberjack.

'My uncle bought one of those Silver Bullet caravans – you know, those 1950s American ones?' she said.

'I love those!' Rob remarked, enlivened. 'They're so hard to find now.'

'Well, he did it up. We stripped it back to a shell and rebuilt it. All I did was pass him the hammer or his cup of tea, but I felt like I was helping. I sat out with him all day long, while he'd tell me about the places we'd go to in it – Scotland, Cornwall, France . . .'

'And did you?'

'Yup, and every campsite we went to, it was like we were rock stars or something. All the other campers would come and stand around, watching my poor uncle reversing fifty times trying to get it into the pitch.'

'*That's* pressure,' Rob grinned. 'Nobody wants an audience for that.'

'It had these amazing wooden bunk beds, and I used to lie on them, reading a book and looking out of the window as we trundled up the motorways. That was in the days before seat-belt laws, of course.'

'I remember those! My parents had a Volvo estate, and we used to sleep in sleeping bags in the boot on the way to Cornwall.'

'Whereabouts in Cornwall did you go to?'

'Well, not to Rock, although we must have been the only people in Cornwall *not* there. We used to go to a tiny place called Gunwalloe Church Cove on the Lizard. My father went as a child. No one's ever heard of it.'

'I have.' Laura stared at him in astonishment. 'That's where *we* went. '

'You're kidding?'

Laura shook her head. 'Every June half-term.'

'But that's when we went too.'

Laura grinned. 'Who knows? Maybe you nicked my bucket. Or ran through my sandcastle.'

'Hey! Why the bad rap? Maybe I gave you my cornet.'

'Actually, a boy did give me his cornet once,' Laura laughed. 'I was walking back from the little café at the back, and—'

'A seagull swooped down and took it?' Rob finished for her.

They stared at each other in amazement. *Had* their paths crossed before?

Laura looked at him, eyes bright and hair ruffled on the beach, and could so easily imagine what he had looked like that she could almost believe that she was actually remembering. But it could only be a fantasy. Her life didn't work like that.

'No, it couldn't be,' Laura murmured, pulling herself back in, her smile fading. 'A nice idea, but it's the kind of thing that happens all the time down there, isn't it? I mean, the gulls are such a nuisance.'

He took in the change of her tone and nodded. 'Yes. The councils are really struggling with it. It's particularly bad in St Ives, I believe.'

'Yes . . .' They fell silent, back to being awkward again.

'We didn't have a meeting scheduled, did we?' she asked after a moment.

'No. But I have a client nearby and I thought I'd drop in on my way back from seeing him.'

'Oh. Where's your client based?'

He coughed. 'In Norwich.'

'But that's fifty miles away. I'd hardly call that nearby.'

Rob cracked a grin. 'I know. But I was on the M11 when I had an idea. I've thought of a way to make your life easier.'

'You're going to clone me!' she deadpanned.

'Not quite. You can come to Verbier with us.'

'W-what?' she stammered. 'Who's us?'

'Everyone on the list, pretty much. Me, Cat, Kitty, Orlando, Sam and her husband, and Alex and his girlfriend.'

Laura stared at him in disbelief. She didn't even know where to *start* with that statement. 'But how can I possibly go if your wife's going to be there? You said you wanted it to be a surprise.'

'It's fine. We'll tell her you're Orlando's plus one. He's the only person not bringing someone so it'll even out numbers anyway.'

'Look, it's a kind offer, but I really don't think it's going to be necessary. I've arranged to see Orlando tomorrow, and I've just done Kitty. So I'm two down already.'

'But what about Sam and Alex? They're both overseas. You'd have to make separate visits to see them in Milan and Frankfurt instead. This way is far more time-efficient.'

'Couldn't they come over here?'

'I tried, but they can't – or won't. They were miraculously free when I suggested meeting up at our chalet in Verbier, though.' He shrugged lightly. 'Cat and I go there every year, usually for New Year, but I thought we could go for opening weekend this year – they're predicting record snowfalls; plus, as it's Orlando's fortieth, we're going to have a surprise party for him and stay for a long weekend.' He shook his head. 'Although God only knows how *that's* going to pan out. Orlando's been on the brink of a midlife crisis since he turned thirty. But it would give you plenty of time to talk to everybody. There's no reason why Cat should suspect anything.'

'And . . . and . . .' Laura's head was spinning. 'And when were you planning this for? I mean, it's December tomorrow,' she said, planting a bare foot on the floor. 'It's party season. I might have plans. It's highly likely I do,' she lied.

'The weekend after next. The ninth to the twelfth.' He looked at her. 'Can you make it?'

She didn't need to check the diary to know that the pages were still stark white and empty. They always were. It was only ever her, Jack and Fee. 'I'll have to check with my boyfriend. I'll get back to you.'

'Okay,' he said, looking at her evenly, so that she saw the copper clouds reflected in his eyes. His face was kind, and she knew he was just being considerate, doing what he could at his end to ensure she met the deadline. It wasn't unreasonable. In fact, most people would consider a free trip to Verbier as far from unreasonable as it was possible to get. But then she wasn't most people. She was a riddle that only Jack knew how to answer.

He patted the hut again before folding his collar up and turning into the wind. 'Your boyfriend's a lucky man, Laura,' he said, beginning to walk off. 'I hope he appreciates it.'

'Right, so that baby's bracelet is ready to go out, yes?' Fee asked, as she brushed the last sandwich crumbs off the sofa.

Laura looked up through her goggles and grunted her assent.

'It's very cute,' Fee purred, spinning the wheels on the tiny pram.

'Just be careful with it, will you?' Laura said snappily. 'It's very delicate too.' She carried on soldering.

Fee pulled a face at her grumpy friend as she silently retrieved one of the pale pink leather boxes and set the intricately crafted bracelet delicately inside, along with the handwritten note card Laura had written, detailing the story for each charm and giving a key quote. Then she packed it in a snug cardboard box, finally writing out the recipient's address in her very best gold wannabe calligraphy.

'There!' Fee said, pulling back to her admire her handiwork. 'Pretty good, even if I do say so myself.'

'Gee, thanks,' Laura drawled. 'Your best handwriting was just the finishing touch needed for my thirty hours' worth of work!'

'Sarky,' Fee muttered, privately dying to draw a daisy in the corner. 'We can't all be creative geniuses, you know.'

'And remember that needs to be out before the end of the day, or it won't be guaranteed for delivery by tomorrow, and the christening's on Sunday. To be safe we really need it to get there before the weekend.'

'Yeah, yeah,' Fee yawned, watching her friend manipulate a strand of gold into a tiny fret-worked birdcage. 'What's that, then?'

Laura looked up through her lashes. 'It's for the golden-wedding couple.'

'What's it gonna be?'

'I'm putting an enamelled nightingale inside the cage,' Laura murmured, concentrating on the task in hand. 'The motif is "songbird". The husband said he fell in love with his wife when he overheard her singing.'

'What, in the bath?'

'No. He used to have his lunch in the same café every day and he could hear her singing in the back. He started sitting closer and closer to the kitchen door, determined to catch sight of her when she came out. But she never did.'

'So what happened?' Fee gasped, sitting bolt upright, hands clasped above her heart.

Laura took in her friend's melodramatic posture. 'It's all right, Fee. We already know there's a happy ending,' she said drily. 'This *is* for their golden wedding anniversary.'

'Ugh, just tell me already!'

Laura rolled her eyes. 'After several months of waiting and listening, he couldn't bear it any longer and one day he just marched into the kitchens. They were engaged by the end of the day,' she said, watching a dreamy smile creep across her friend's face.

'That is one of the most romantic things I've ever heard,' Fee sighed, rocking back into the sofa, hugging her knees tightly to her chest. 'Although he'd have had to do a quick U-y if she'd been a moose,' she added earnestly.

Laura chuckled in spite of herself. 'Quite.'

'Hey!' Fee exclaimed delightedly. 'That's the first smile you've cracked since you got here all blue-lipped and frosty. Finally the Ice Queen melteth.'

Laura scowled at her. 'Melteth?'

'Yeah. You've been in a foul mood since you got here. Wassup?'

'Nothing is up. I'm simply concentrating on my work.'

'Yeah, right,' Fee said, disentangling her long limbs and

walking over to the kettle. She noisily tapped the instant coffee into the two Emma Bridgewater seconds mugs and slopped milk on to the work surfaces. She set the coffee mug down in front of her friend. 'Want to talk about it?'

'There's nothing to talk about.'

'Did you and Jack have a fight?'

'Me and— What? No!'

'So what is it, then?'

'I am fine,' Laura said defiantly. 'I have just got a shed-load of work to do and I can't spend my days sitting around gossiping like you do. People are waiting for their commissions. I can't miss a single deadline. You know that.'

'All right, all right. I was just asking,' Fee said, raising one hand in surrender.

The phone rang and she walked over to pick it up.

'If that's Jack, tell him I'm with a client,' Laura said hurriedly, shoving her goggles back down over her eyes and going back to the birdcage.

'So you have had a fight . . .' Fee said, peering at her through suspicious eyes as she picked up the handset. 'Hello? . . . Yes, that's right . . . No I'm sorry, she's engaged at the moment. Can I help at all? . . . Right . . . I'm not sure, she'll have to get back to you herself on that.' Fee walked over to the calendar of Suffolk beaches hanging on the wall and ran a finger over the dated squares. 'Uh-huh . . . from the looks of things, she can do that . . . Okay, fine – I'll tell her . . . Thanks. Bye.'

Laura cocked an eyebrow.

'Well, it wasn't Jack, you'll be pleased to hear.'

'Who was it?' Laura asked, defiantly ignoring Fee's leading comments.

'A guy called Orlando asking if you're going to

Verbier. And if so, do you want to postpone your interview tomorrow?'

Laura nodded, still without looking up. 'Fine. I'll ring him back in a minute.'

'Ahem! *Verbier?*'

Laura laid her equipment out patiently on the bench. 'Don't get your knickers in a twist. It's nothing exciting. It's to do with Cat Blake's necklace. A bunch of them are going skiing before Christmas, and Rob thought it would make my life easier to go along too and interview everybody out there.'

'Blimey! Nice work if you can get it.'

'I'll be working, Fee. Not skiing,' Laura muttered.

'What did Jack say?'

'I haven't told him yet. Rob only mentioned it this morning.'

They sat in silence for a few minutes, and Laura knew that Fee was staring at her.

'Stop it, Fee,' Laura warned.

'I know there's something. What's he done? Too many rose petals scattered in the bath and they clogged up the drains? The scented candles leading up to the bedroom dripped on the carpet?'

Laura dropped her head to the side, exasperated.

'You know I'm gonna keep on going until you tell me.'

There was a long pause and Laura's eyes darted around the room as if they were chasing shadows. 'I think I'm pregnant,' she murmured finally.

Fee slapped a hand over her mouth, staring over at Laura through enormous blue eyes. Laura blinked hard.

'But you can't tell him, Fee!' Laura demanded, panicking at the sight of Fee's shock. 'You have to promise me. Not a word.'

'But—'

'Swear it!' Laura cried, standing up agitatedly.

Fee raised a hand in surrender. 'Okay, I swear. I swear.'

'Swear on your life.'

'I swear on my life. Shit.'

Laura sank back on to her stool, her breath coming fast. Saying the words had been like lifting weights, piling flesh and muscle and sinew on to a bony whisper.

'Why is it a bad thing?' Fee asked tentatively.

Laura looked at her in amazement. 'You know perfectly well why. There is no question of me becoming a mother. How could *I* bring a life into the world?'

Lead lined the air between them. 'Laur, you'd be a fantastic mum,' Fee said quietly.

Laura shot her a dark look. 'Just don't.'

'But it's true. Jack would be such an incredible father, you know he would. And you wouldn't be dealing with it alone. Jack and I would support you all the way. Oh please, at least talk to him about it,' she implored, holding her hands together in prayer.

Laura jumped off her stool and advanced towards her in fury. 'You swore, Fee!'

'But this isn't just about you, Laura. Jack has a right to know. You have to make the decision together.'

'At the end of the day it's my body, my decision.'

'But don't you see? This could change everything for the two of you.'

'That's precisely what I'm worried about, Fee. I don't *want* anything to change. I want everything to remain exactly as it is.'

'Do you?' Fee asked, and Laura saw sadness in her eyes.

'What does that mean?'

'Life keeps moving forwards, Laur, even when you stay standing still. Nothing stays the same for ever.'

Laura narrowed her eyes and planted her hands on her hips. 'You two have been talking again, haven't you?'

Fee sighed. 'Jack's worried about you, and I'm worried about you *and* him.'

'Why? What's wrong with him?'

'He's unhappy, Laura. You must be able to see it?'

'I see no such thing,' she said defensively.

'You won't go on holiday. You won't make other friends. You won't move house. You won't get married. You won't get a new car. And now you won't have a baby?'

'Jack likes routine as much as I do. It's why we're so well matched.'

'That is *not* the reason you're together, and sooner or later you're going to have to face it.'

'Says the girl who doesn't keep a boyfriend for more than ten days.'

But Fee didn't react. Laura's eyes filled with tears and Fee stood up and walked over to her, placing a gentle hand on her arm. 'All I'm saying is that I think your life is not healthy the way it is. You have to let some light in. Some fresh air. If something can't grow, then it decays.'

'Well, thanks for the biology lesson, but I don't even know for sure that I am pregnant yet. At the moment, I'm just late.' Her voice was defensive and tremulous all at once. Breaking.

'Then buy a test and at least get some peace of mind. It might be that there's nothing to tell and you're just shouting at me for the fun of it.'

Laura relented a little. Her tiny, wise best friend had a point. 'Well. It is fun,' she muttered, a glint of mischief in her eyes.

'I know,' Fee grinned, hugging her tightly. 'I know.'

# Chapter Ten

'Have you seen my phone?' Laura asked, rummaging through her bag as Jack squeezed past her on the way to the Bran Flakes the next morning.

'Can't say I remember seeing it, no. When did you have it last?'

'Well, if I could remember that . . .' she muttered, giving up with the bag and smacking her hands on her thighs 'Uuuugh!'

'Don't flap. It's not far,' Jack said with frustrating calm as he poured the milk and cereal into a bowl and began eating with speedy efficiency. 'Have you tried ringing it?'

'It's out of juice.'

'Of course it is.' Jack cast his girlfriend a knowing look. Laura was notorious for never charging her phone. 'Well, is it urgent? Do you want mine for today?'

Laura shook her head. 'I just wanted to see whether there were any messages from the sister yet.'

'Whose sister?' His voice was muffled as he dabbed at a milk spot on his shirt.

'For this charm necklace I'm doing. I was supposed to speak to her before all the others, but Fee's left several messages and she hasn't come back to us yet, and I need to get on. I was hoping I could get two lots of interviews done in one go today. Surrey's a long way from here.'

'Reversing up the drive is a long way in that car.' He refused to use the name that Fee and Laura used so affectionately for her. 'Maybe she's away.'

'Who is?' Laura asked, checking under a pile of magazines on the worktop.

'The sister.'

'Oh. Yes. Maybe.'

Jack checked his watch. 'Dash! I'm late. I've got to run. What time will you be back?'

'This meeting's arranged for eleven o'clock so I shouldn't be late. That early start almost killed me on Tuesday, and besides, it isn't a good idea to get there too early. I don't want to get caught doing an all-day interview again.'

'I don't want you to either.' He kissed her on the tip of her nose. 'Your place is here, with us, isn't that right, Arthur?'

Old Faithful looked up at his master adoringly, knowing that in a second he'd hear the jingle of the car keys and they'd head off to Jack's workshop together. 'I thought I'd do a casserole tonight. How does that sound?'

'Mmmm,' Laura replied absently, still wondering in her head where she'd put the damn phone and only vaguely aware of the front door clicking shut.

Ten minutes later, phone still not found, she was jerkily reversing down the drive in Dolly and heading towards the motorway with the rest of East Anglia.

In the event, she shaved thirty-five minutes off the journey this time round, partly because by the time she hit the M25 rush hour had eased and all the school runs had cleared from the local roads. She followed Fee's terribly written directions (keeping a wary eye out for camels this time) before finally pulling up outside a double-height smoke-tinted glass cube with rows of black Discoverys parked in front.

'Well, this is it, all right,' Laura muttered, her chin resting on her hands as she leaned against the steering wheel and saw that 'The Cube' was discreetly etched into the glass panel above the door. She watched as the doors swished open and a sleek brunette came out, iPhone to her ear and wearing white Lycra cropped leggings with a tight white tank beneath a sleek fur-trimmed padded jacket. The patron saint of exercise, perhaps? She was followed moments later by two more women, this time in all-black ensembles high-lighted with fluoro piping and offset by yoga mats, glistening legs and long, sleek ponytails that swung in unison.

Laura reluctantly got out of the car, realizing how low Dolly sat to the ground compared with these monster-sized 4x4s – their wheel arches were almost at her roof-height. The little yellow and cream car looked incongruous amidst the glossy black beasts, like a tortoise in the company of panthers.

Shuffling through the tinted glass doors, she walked up to the reception desk – a long, long expanse of white gloss. Two tanned women were sitting behind it wearing headsets and talking intensely at the screens in front of them as if they were reading the latest indexes from Reuters.

Laura waited for one of them to hit a button and give her their attention, fiddling absently with her top and feeling ridiculously overdressed. If Fee had only left her alone, she'd have just pulled on her usual baggy jeans and a jumper of some description, but her friend was clearly living in terror that the commission might be cancelled at any moment and the spectre of Visas unpaid would come knocking in the night, so she'd insisted she put on one of her best tops – a grey and jade silk tunic from Monsoon that Jack had bought her last Christmas.

'This woman moves in gilded circles,' Fee had told her sternly. 'And you have to be an ambassador for your brand. She's not going to want to wear something with your name attached if you insist on walking around looking like a bag lady, now, is she? Her friends will report back later, you can be sure of that.'

'Can I help you?' The receptionist was looking at her – well, past her, really, as a courier staggered past with an enormous container of bottled water on his shoulder. 'No. No. Excuse me! That's for the Lotus Room. Over *there*,' she added, as though he was an idiot. 'The vanilla room.'

She rolled her eyes at Laura as the poor man made his way back in the opposite direction.

'I'm here to see Orlando Morelli,' Laura said, watching the man try to lock his knees.

'Do you have an appointment?'

'Yes.'

'He'll be a few minutes,' the receptionist said, looking back at her screen. 'He's just finishing with his Zumba ladies. What's your name?'

'Laura Cunningham.'

'Okay.' She pressed 'send' on her keyboard and nodded to a white leather chesterfield. 'Take a seat. He won't be long.'

Laura walked over and sat down. She could hear the muffled *thwump* of conflicting base beats coming from the rainbow-tinted glass studios that flanked the lobby area. The pink-and-yellow tinted rooms appeared to be mellower, with lots of women lying on the floor in contorted stretches listening to whale music, whereas the green-and-blue tinted rooms sounded like they were conducting illegal raves. Neither option appealed. An iPad had been left on the seat next to her with a *Vogue* app open – a woman draped over an elephant appeared to be advertising turquoise eyeshadow.

After a few minutes or so of bewildered browsing, she felt someone's eyes upon her and looked up. A robustly muscled man in navy shorts and a very expensive-looking grey slim-fit T-shirt was standing by the reception desk staring over at her. Laura stared back, not because she'd never seen a T-shirt look that expensive before – although she hadn't – but because even from fifty feet away there was no way she could be *his* plus one. Was Rob Blake blind?

'Laura?'

Laura rose to meet him as he crossed the room in athletic bounds.

'Orlando Morelli. A pleasure.' His accent was as rippled as his muscles, his words tumbling like quavers on a score.

'Pleased to meet you.'

'You are here to discuss Cat.'

'I am,' she replied, disconcerted by his gorgeousness. He had a nose Rome could have been built upon and a jaw so square she'd seen rounder right angles. He was the most chiselled, handsome man she'd ever seen. And that meant he was gay.

'Come, let us talk in my office.'

He led her towards the staircase, past the vibrating glass rooms. In one, Laura spotted a class full of women crouched over bikes, all going nowhere really fast.

'You spin?' Orlando asked, catching her eye as they started climbing a cantilevered glass staircase.

'Usually only when the credit-card bill comes in.'

'Funny,' he laughed, wagging a finger. Ahead of them, spanning the width of the building, she could see a vast gym with running machines, elliptical walkers, weights and vibration plates, all in use. This wall was yellow-tinted.

'What's with the coloured glass?' Laura asked as they climbed.

'It influences mood, and therefore energy levels. We have cooler tones in the rooms where higher-intensity classes are held – like spinning and Zumba. Warm, pink hues are used for the floor- and mat-work classes like yoga and Pilates and ballet, where we work on muscle tone and core strength. And the yellow in the gym is happy; it feels sunny. Releases lots of endorphins and makes the clients feel energized.'

It sounded like hogwash to Laura. Walking Arthur on the beach always made her feel happy – or the closest she got to happy, anyway. 'Wow,' was all she could manage.

He led her down the corridor towards the front of the building and stopped outside a frosted-glass door. He opened it and let her pass through into his office. 'Please. Take a seat.'

Laura reached down into her bag and pulled out a small voice-activated recorder. 'Do you mind? It's useful for later on when I'm back at the studio. I might miss something here that I pick up on later.'

Orlando shrugged. 'Sure. We must get it right, no? Before we begin, would you like some water?'

What she really wanted was a coffee. 'Sure,' she replied, waiting whilst he poured her a glass from an opaque bottle that spelled out in red diamanté letters *Bling*. Even the water here was rich.

'So, Cat's your business partner here?'

'Yes, that is technically correct. But Cat is also one of my best friends. She saved me not once, but twice. I can never thank her enough.'

'Saved you?' A comic image of him being pulled from the water by a petite blonde flashed up and she repressed a smile. 'But how?'

He grinned, his teeth spectacularly white against his tanned skin. 'We first met when I was a trainer at another gym. I had only just come over from Italy and knew no one, was not paid very much. Then Cat came along. She wanted to run the London Marathon – it was her dream, one of her "bucket list" ideas – and she needed a running mate.' He shrugged. 'Most of the trainers there had never done more than run around the supermarket, but I have run the marathons in London, Berlin, New York . . . So I drew up a training schedule for her and we started meeting three, four times a week for sessions.'

'So then you grew pretty close.'

'Absolutely. And I fell madly in love with her, as everyone does.'

'I've heard she's very beautiful,' Laura said dutifully.

'And gentle, and so funny. Who can resist her?'

'I suppose she was running the marathon for charity?' Laura heard the bite in her voice and finished with a half-smile.

'Of course. She ran for a local hospice.'

'Did she raise much money?'

'Quite a lot,' he shrugged. 'Twenty-three thousand pounds.'

Laura's jaw dropped. 'How many times did she run it, for heaven's sake?'

Orlando laughed loudly. 'She and Rob know a lot of very wealthy people.'

'They must do.' Laura thought of the £179 cheque she had

handed over to the RNLI for a sponsored swim the year before. And she was a good swimmer. Lots of lengths.

'Do you run?' Orlando asked her.

'Only when I'm late,' she quipped. 'I don't believe in running, actually. I think it's bad for your knees.'

'Correct running shoes make all the difference.'

Laura shrugged dismissively. To date she'd never found a red pair she liked. 'So you met when Cat started training for the marathon,' she prompted. 'And fell madly in love.'

'Yes. But sadly for me, she is madly in love with her husband,' he said slowly. 'And sadly for her, so am I.' He burst out laughing. 'That is how she saved me, you see. I came to England because I thought my family would not understand. But it was hard to bear. I have always been very close to my mother and sisters, and I was sliding into a bad depression, drinking too much . . .'

'And Cat talked you round?'

'She wouldn't leave it alone. For miles and miles while we ran, until eventually one day she just came in and handed me some tickets to go back to Rome the next day.' He closed his eyes for a moment as he stepped back in time, and when he looked at her again, big, proud Italian tears started falling, unembarrassed. 'My mother said she had always known, from the day I was born. She said I was too handsome to be a straight man.'

The woman was right – Laura had known it the second she'd clapped eyes on him – but she couldn't help but feel it had been a risk. What if his mother hadn't known? What if she *hadn't* been able to accept it?

'You said Cat saved you twice,' Laura said, narrowing her eyes in concentration. 'What was the second thing?'

Orlando gestured all around them. 'This. It was her dream

to set up her own business, so she backed me in this entire venture – put up the deposit, got Rob to go through my proposal, ironing out all the figures and projected growth, came to the bank with me, searched for the plot for me, helped with the concept and design. You name it, she did it. The Cube is as much Cat's vision as it is mine.'

'Really? So all the tinted glass . . . ?'

'Her idea. And the heated floors in the changing rooms. And the lavender piped through the air-con. And the Parma violets frozen in the ice cubes. And the sweet almond oil dispensed for massage during the yoga classes. It does wonders for your skin, you see.' He trailed a hand up his own smooth arm.

'It sounds like she knows her luxury, then,' she said.

'Cat knows her market, and she was after a holistic feeling. We wanted the Cube to be a place you come to for a sense of well-being, not just another gym with banks of treadmills looking over the car park.'

Laura nodded. It was certainly a far cry from Charrington Leisure Centre, where the floors boasted verrucas, not ambient temperatures, and the municipal tiles had scarcely been cleaned, much less replaced, since the war.

'And our pool is ozone treated.'

'What's that?' Laura asked suspiciously, half expecting him to say it had been personally blessed by angels.

'Chlorine-free. Cat said none of the women would get in it if the chlorine was going to damage their highlights, and I think she was right,' he grinned. 'It has proved very popular. Plus we have a hair salon in the changing rooms.'

'You have a *hair salon* in the *changing rooms*?' Laura echoed, remembering those swingy ponytails.

'Yes – nourishing masks, blow-dries, cut and colour. Cat

understands how busy our clients are. They have school runs and shopping and lunch appointments to fit in. Gym and hair need to be one stop.'

Laura sat back, deep in thought for a moment as she took in the level of detail at which this woman operated. It was little wonder Rob had looked so genuinely perturbed by the sight of her in her studio that day when his wife went to the trouble of making sure that the very air she breathed was lavender-scented. It was also a long way from sitting in trees and rescuing lambs. Somehow, she didn't see Kitty fitting into this version of Cat's life.

'She sounds . . .' Laura floundered for the right word. OCD. Neurotic. Irritating.

'Perfect?'

'Is that how you'd describe her?' Laura countered.

Orlando put his elbows on the table and leant forward. 'You hate her,' he said, scrutinizing her face.

Laura was taken aback. 'Absolutely not. I've never even met her,' she lied, thoroughly sick to the back teeth of listening to the idol worship of Cat Blake, having to force a smile while the person sitting opposite her rhapsodized, fantasized, memorized and damn near immortalized a woman who was really nothing more than a pretty Surrey housewife. It was increasingly a wonder to Laura that she had got this far in her life without hearing about the woman. It was a wonder that her movements of the day weren't discussed on the national news. '*And finally, today Cat Blake ordered a loin of venison from Ocado for the white-tie dinner party she's hosting on Saturday in aid of Save the Children. Her hair has already been highlighted in readiness for the event, and hairdressers all over the country are reporting a run on her favoured shade, salty popcorn . . .*'

'But you don't want to meet her either. I can see the disdain on your face,' he said, drawing a circle in the air.

'It's not that.'

'What is it, then?' he grinned.

'Nothing at all, really. That's just how my face is in repose. A little bit . . . scowly.'

He raised a disbelieving eyebrow and waited.

'Fine. She maybe sounds a little *too* perfect, that's all. I can't help wondering whether she's a little too good to be true. You know – reuniting your family, setting up your business, taking care of her clients' scheduling problems, running marathons for charity . . . Can anybody really be that nice?'

Orlando's chocolate-brown eyes twinkled naughtily. 'You want dirt,' he grinned, rolling the word over his tongue like a cork on water.

Laura fidgeted beneath his scrutiny. He had her number, she knew it. 'Well, maybe just a flaw would be good. You know, for balance.'

'It would make you feel better.'

'It would,' she nodded.

Orlando sat back in his orthopaedic chair and considered her words, one finger pressed thoughtfully against his bow-shaped lips.

'That's not helping,' Laura said after they had sat in silence for a while, and Orlando laughed at her deadpan expression.

'Don't worry, I am actually just filtering out all the atrocities I could tell you about her,' he said, one hand fluttering. 'So many. Just terrible.'

This time Laura cracked a smile.

'Well, there is one,' he said finally. 'But you will be horrified.'

'I certainly hope so.'

He took a deep, nervous breath. 'She likes her coffee instant.'

Laura sighed, deflated. 'I'm going to pretend you didn't just say that.'

'Really. It's true.'

'No, I mean, that's nowhere near damning enough.'

'But you don't understand. Rob bought her a one-thousand-pound coffee machine. Harrods is the only place in England to sell them, but she has *never* used it. She doesn't even know how. She has to hide her Kenco in the biscuit tin.'

Laura wrinkled her nose. 'Small fry.'

'And she's addicted to chocolate,' he tried.

'Show me a woman who isn't,' Laura challenged.

'The cheaper, the better.'

'I'm liking her more by the second,' Laura sighed disappointedly.

'She has ice baths before she goes out to big events.'

'*Why?*'

'It makes the skin tighter,' he shrugged.

'Tch, that's just plain daft,' Laura said dismissively, looking away.

'Hmmmm. You are a hard customer.'

A red button buzzed on his phone and his face fell as he checked his watch. 'Oh, I'm sorry. I have body pump now. My ladies are waiting.'

'What? But we've only just started,' she protested.

'I'm so sorry. One of my teachers is sick and I'm standing in for him.'

'Can't anyone else take the class? I've travelled nearly three hours to get here.'

He gave a big, hopeless shrug. 'I'm so sorry. The schools break up next week and all the ladies are in, trying to drop weight for their Christmas parties. We are stretched to the limit.'

'Aren't we all?' Laura responded. '*I* need to get the necklace finished in time for Cat's birthday. I have to get all the interviews done asap so that I can get on with actually making it.'

He arched an eyebrow. 'But you are coming to Verbier, no?'

'I don't know. I have to talk to my boyfriend about it,' she sighed.

Orlando stared at her for a moment, obviously wondering who, in this day and age, required *permission* from their boyfriend to take a work trip. Resting a light hand on the small of her back, he led her along the corridor and back down the stairs. They reached the reception area. 'Okay, so then if not Verbier, why do you not come here next time you are in the area? Then we could have lunch and I promise you can have me as long as you like. In the meantime I will think of something hateful about Cat that will make you like her,' he said conspiratorially.

Laura grinned. 'Well, in that case . . .'

He kissed her happily on each cheek. 'Good. Now I must pump, and you must see Kitty.'

'Kitty?'

'Yes. She has your mobile phone. Did I not tell you?'

Laura shook her head.

He smacked his forehead as he walked away. 'It's lucky my mother put a pretty face on this empty head.'

\*

Keeping to the far side of the lane as she drove past Sugar's field – windows up – Laura spotted Kitty coming home in the opposite direction. Samuel's buggy was bouncing so alarmingly over the potholes that the poor child looked like he was trampolining.

'Laura!' Kitty cried, giving a happy wave as Laura parked Dolly on the grass verge opposite the cottage. 'How super to see you.'

Laura opened her door and stood up, arms resting on the roof. 'Hi, Kitty. Apparently I left my phone here?'

'You did!' Kitty called back across the lane. 'Did Orly pass on my message? He's such a poppet. I spoke to your girl and she said you were seeing him today. Golly, aren't you just racking up the miles? Here Tuesday and again today.' She leant down and unbuckled Samuel, who jumped out and promptly tripped over one of the ducklings. 'Come in, come in. It's just on the kitchen table. We can have a cup of coffee. I've made a splendid coffee and walnut cake.' She lowered her voice into a stage whisper. 'It was supposed to be for the Christmas fete last Saturday, but I decided it was *far* too good to give away.' She flicked a hand as though batting away protests.

'Thanks, but I really should head straight off.'

'I insist. Besides, I've been thinking about you since you came and I've thought of some more cracking stories to tell you about Cat.'

Damn. She checked her watch. It was just gone twelve.

'Well, okay then,' Laura replied, reluctantly shutting the door and crossing the lane. 'But I really mustn't stay for long. The traffic will be shocking if I leave too late.'

'Understood,' Kitty nodded, a delighted smile plastered all over her pretty pink face.

*

Two hours later, half the cake was gone, along with all of Laura's resolve. Samuel had made out like a bandit and was charging round the yard on his caffeine high, in direct contrast to Pocket, who'd been foraging underneath the table and was now, like any good libertine, sleeping it off.

'I'd offer you a proper drink if you weren't driving back,' Kitty sighed, pouring the last of the coffee from the cafetière. Laura didn't have the energy to put her hand across the top of her mug. She had rapidly learned that resistance was futile with Kitty. 'I've drunk so much coffee, Joe will think I've been at the gin anyway,' she giggled.

Laura stiffened at the mention of his name. She had forgotten all about him. 'Where is he?' she asked, casually tapping the side of her mug.

'Still cutting back the hedges. He's got nearly eighty linear miles to do, but the days are so short now he can't even stop for lunch.'

Laura thought it was frankly a shame that he stopped at the eighty-mile mark and didn't just carry on going until he hit the Scottish border. Quite what somebody as lovely as Kitty was doing with a man like Joe, she didn't know.

'So tell me what Orlando told you,' Kitty said, half slumped on the table and stacking the sugar cubes into a tower.

'Not a huge amount yet, to be honest. I'm going to need a lot more time with him at the next interview.'

'He's fun, though, isn't he? Such a scamp.'

Laura nodded. 'He was very amusing.'

'And *so* handsome! It's a shame he's gay.'

'Yes. He and Cat must make a beautiful couple. Platonically speaking, I mean.'

'*Gor*geous. In fact it's as well he is gay, or I don't think Rob would let him near her.'

'Is Rob the jealous type? He's hardly a slouch to look at either,' Laura said mildly.

Kitty leaned in, a wicked look in her eyes. 'Do you think he's attractive, then?'

'Who? Rob?'

Kitty nodded.

'He's my client. I tend not to eye up my customers – especially the married ones making grand, sweeping declarations of love to their beautiful wives.'

Kitty sat back, disappointed to have been knocked back in her girly gossip. 'Does your boyfriend get jealous?'

'Jack? No. He's so laid-back he's practically horizontal.'

'And you're happy together?'

Laura folded her hands, one on top of the other. 'He's a good man.'

'Like Joe, then,' Kitty said, taking a slurp of lukewarm coffee.

Laura smiled, disagreeing vehemently in her head. She let her eyes wander around the rambling, dark cottage. It was so chaotic and cluttered, she half expected to see a little old lady living in a shoe in the corner. She thought of the light, minimal perfection that she'd just come from at the Cube, the very embodiment, Orlando had said, of Cat's own vision, and it seemed increasingly hard to believe that a woman who cared about mood colours and clean lines would want to spend any significant amount of time here, dodging low beams and dog hairs.

'Do you see much of Cat these days?'

Kitty looked at her, alarmed, her cheeks a rising pink. 'Why do you ask?'

'I was just wondering,' Laura replied, surprised by her

defensiveness. 'I mean, people change all the time and you've got your hands full with five children . . .'

Kitty sat rooted to the spot. 'It doesn't matter how little or often I get to see her. I'll be her best friend for ever, no matter what, no matter how busy or different our lives become.'

Laura nodded. It was like some kind of mission statement. 'Great.'

There was an awkward pause and Laura shifted uneasily, having hit such a raw nerve. Her suspicions were confirmed: Kitty had been dumped.

# Chapter Eleven

It was late on Friday afternoon, the end of a hard week, and Laura smiled as she rounded the corner and saw Fee already waiting for her, piles of Argos and Accessorize bags fanned out on the pavement around her ankles.

'You've got your Christmas shopping sorted, then?' she asked, stopping six feet away, the nearest she could get.

'Oh yeah,' Fee smiled. 'I'm on it this year. No more Christmas Eve panics for me. Mum was not happy with her iTunes gift card last year, I'm telling you.'

'I did tell you she didn't have an iPod.'

Fee bit her lip and looked at Laura guiltily. 'Anyway, what have you had going on that was so interesting you couldn't come with me today? We always do our Christmas shopping together.'

'Can't you guess?' Laura asked, striking a pose. She'd been so excited walking down the old high street.

Fee narrowed her eyes. 'You do look different. What've you done?' she demanded, grabbing Laura's hand and checking her nails before scanning her teeth like a pushy parent. 'Have you had your teeth whitened?' she accused, then stood back to get a better look. 'No, don't say it's a fake tan. Never thought I'd see the day!'

'I've had layers put in my hair!' Laura said, amazed that her friend hadn't clocked the dramatic new shaping around her face. She checked her appearance in the window. Was it too subtle?

'Aaaah! Uh-huh. Uh-huh,' Fee murmured, stepping over her bags and taking long, slow steps round her, appraising the cut. 'I like,' she said finally, crossing her arms with satisfaction. 'Very classy. At least now you don't look like one of those protestors camping outside St Paul's.'

'Good. So it gets the official Fee Tisham seal of approval, at least,' Laura said, starting off towards Tom's.

Fee gathered her bags together hurriedly and trotted after her. 'So what prompted it?' she asked, swinging the bags so that they just clipped Laura's legs.

'I caught sight of myself in the mirror the other day and thought I looked a bit . . . drab?' She looked over questioningly at Fee, who was the official fashionista of the two. She was glad Fee hadn't been with her and clocked the glamazons leaving the Cube the other day or she'd have been busted right away.

'Good. I'm glad you're finally listening to me and beginning to take care of yourself a little. You're so pretty, Laur. You ought to make the best of yourself. You won't be thirty-two for ever, you know.'

'Jack doesn't care what I look like.'

Fee was quiet for a bit.

'Well, it's a good start, but it's not the cut that really matters. I keep telling you, it's the colour. Your hair pretty much matches your eyes.'

'My hair is *not* grey,' Laura said sulkily. 'Most people in Britain are mouse.'

'Mouse? You should be so lucky!' Fee raised an eyebrow. 'I saw a colour in Homebase on the Farrow & Ball chart that was exactly your colour: wanna know what it was called?'

'Not particularly,' Laura muttered, already wincing.

'Elephant's Breath.'

'Oh, thanks! So now you're saying I've got hair like an elephant with halitosis?'

Fee cackled mischievously. 'Has Jack seen it yet?'

'No. And from your rubbish reaction, he might not even notice – you know what men are like.'

'Are you *mad*?' Fee wheezed. 'He notices whether you've changed deodorant. He notices when you've plucked your eyebrows. Hell, I bet he knows your monthly cycle better than y—'

Fee's voice trailed off and Laura shot her a sidelong look. It was supposed to be withering and dismissive – her preferred form of riposte – but there were times when she was almost blind-sided by the astute accuracy of her whimsical friend's observations. It was true – he did know her cycle better than she did. She bit her lip nervously as she realized she might not be the only one who'd woken up suddenly in the middle of the night, counting off days.

Fee walked beside her in silence, no doubt thinking the same thing. How long could Laura keep her secret for? Other men might not notice, but he would. He was *too* considerate, that was the problem. She felt Fee's questioning glances coming her way, but she kept her eyes dead ahead. The subject was out of bounds.

The town was busy. School was out for the weekend and scores of children with daisy-printed wellies, bobble hats and duffle coats were cluttering the pavements, mittens dangling from strings beside their red-cold hands as their flustered parents queued outside the butcher to place orders for the turkey and ham, and then did it all again at the florist, agonizing over holly berries or cinnamon sticks or dried orange rings to go in their holly wreaths.

Laura side-stepped them briskly as Fee swapped admiring glances with an eleven-year-old girl who was dressed almost identically to her in faded skinny jeans, padded gilet, long-sleeved purple T-shirt and chunky sheepskin boots.

'Did you see that?' Fee chuckled as Laura strode on. 'My very own mini-me.'

'You probably shop in the same stores,' Laura replied, throwing an eye over Fee's sinewy frame.

Laura flung open the door to Tom's and walked straight through to their usual table overlooking the veranda at the back as Fee threw her bags behind the counter. An over-sized, twinkling Christmas tree had been erected since their last visit and stood quietly in the corner like a dutiful waiter, with tiny green plastic champagne bottles hanging off it instead of baubles, and white fairy lights wrapped around the clipper pictures. It was still quiet – it was far too early for the Friday-night regulars yet.

'This is on you, right?' Fee asked, fluttering on to the chair like a wind-blown leaf.

'You make it sound like there's a multiple-choice answer to that question.' Laura looked out through the enormous windows. The sky was bleached with just a single drag of red slowly bleeding through the air, like a silk scarf in the hot wash, and she felt her body instinctively relax as she tracked the breeze rippling over the water. She hadn't been in the studio at all today – before going for her hair appointment, she'd done some shopping for the beach hut – and her body felt stiff and tense. The view from her keep was like a meditation for her, and she felt it when she missed a day.

Fee sighed. 'Not all of us have prosperity staring us in the face.'

'Neither do I now I've blown it all on a heap of firewood.' Laura rubbed her eyes and suppressed a yawn.

'You look tired.'

'I am. I was up till one o'clock last night.' And awake again at four, but she didn't add that.

'Oh, you didn't get stranded again!'

'No. No. I was at home, writing up the notes from my interviews with Orlando and Kitty.'

'Kitty?' Fee mused, closing her eyes as she tried to remember the list of names. 'Oh yes – Kitty Baker, Quinces Cottage.' She shot Laura a crafty look. 'She sounds like she does the gardening in pearls.'

'Actually she has a camel with an ASBO.'

'Oh!' That shut Fee up for a moment. 'And Orlando – which one's he?'

'Her personal trainer and business partner. She helped him set up the business.'

'Oh, I remember. Sexy accent. Is he good-looking?'

'Very,' Laura nodded.

Tom came over with their chilled bottle of Prosecco. 'Ladies,' he said in greeting.

'Thanks, Tom,' said Laura as he half filled their glasses.

'You can fill mine to the top,' Fee winked. 'We were just getting on to the man of my dreams.'

Tom rolled his eyes. 'And how many times have I heard that before?' he replied, walking off.

Laura patted Fee's hand. 'He plays for the other side.'

'What makes you think I'm talking about your fella?' Fee

asked, clinking Laura's glass loudly – it was just as well they weren't crystal – and taking a hefty slug.

Laura watched her in surprise. 'Spit it out!' she sighed, rolling her eyes. Fee's adventures always had to be accompanied by a drum roll and moody lighting.

'I've met someone.'

'Well, I gathered that! Who?' Laura asked, peering at her curiously.

'His name's Paul,' Fee said, swallowing hard. 'Paul Weston.'

Laura spluttered on her drink and the bubbles went up her nose, making her cough noisily. '*PC* Weston?' she managed.

'Yes, that's right,' Fee replied, looking nervous.

Laura laughed. 'You are kidding?'

'No. Why would I be?'

'Because he's as thick as two short planks and looks like a potato, that's why!' Laura guffawed.

'He does *not* look like a potato!' Fee replied indignantly. 'He used to play prop in rugby, that's all. That's why he's just a bit—'

'Mashed up!' Laura cried, beginning to shake with laughter.

'Not all of us can go out with James Blunt, you know!' Fee said stroppily. 'If you must know, I personally think Jack is too pretty. He looks *effeminate*.'

She practically spat out the last word, and Laura stopped laughing. They each looked away, both knowing they'd gone too far, their eyes pinned on the horizon.

'So it sounds like you're really keen on him,' Laura said more quietly after a moment.

'Yeah, well, he's a good kisser.'

Laura tried not to grimace. Her only direct interaction

with PC Paul Weston had been at the fireworks night last year when a ground-cracker had sent her into an immediate freeze – Jack had been off getting hot dogs – and Paul had lifted her, fireman-style, out of the crowd. It hadn't been an inconspicuous exit and she'd felt totally humiliated, the open scars she lived with plain for everyone to see. Clearly she held a grudge. 'Well, that's a good start,' she murmured.

'And he's really strong. If I get cross with him, he bench-presses me until I laugh and forgive him.'

Laura frowned. 'Just how many times have you seen him?'

'A couple of weeks now.'

'But this is the first I've heard of it.' Laura was hurt.

'Yes. Because I knew precisely how you'd react when I told you.'

Laura blew out through her cheeks. 'I just think you can do better than him, that's all.'

'He makes me happy, Laur. He makes me laugh.' Fee shrugged. 'That's good enough for me.'

Laura shot her a sideways glance. 'You're twenty-three. It's not like you have to settle for any old bloke, you know.'

'I'm not *settling*. I really like him.' She stared at the bubbles rising in her glass. 'In fact, I think I might even be able to . . . love him.'

Laura looked at her in alarm. 'No, you couldn't! You'd have told me about him before now if you really thought that.'

'I really wouldn't have. I *knew* you'd be like this.'

'Like what?'

'Jealous. You like keeping me all to yourself.'

'I do not!'

'Yeah, you do. You get to mess about being superior to

me all day long, then go home to Mr Perfect who's walked the dog and made your dinner for you.'

Laura gasped in shock. Fee didn't really think like that about her, did she?

'I am not being superior about him. Nor do I want you to be alone. I'd be delighted if you found your Mr Right.'

'Well, I reckon I might have.' Fee bit her lip, her eyes down.

'But . . . but *when* have you been seeing him? I mean, you still spend every Saturday night with us!' Laura protested, scarcely able to believe that all this had been happening to her very best friend in front of her and she'd deliberately kept it a secret. 'Are we seeing you as usual tomorrow night?'

'Yes. He works shifts and he's been on weekend duty the past month. But that'll change.'

Laura watched her friend closely. Something was up, she knew it was. There was no way Fee would have kept this from her if she was a hundred per cent certain Paul was the man for her. 'There must be something about him that drives you mad. There always is, with you. One little thing that niggles away in your head.'

Fee shook her head. But slightly too hard.

'I knew it! Come on, out with it. Tell me his fatal flaw.'

'Actually, it's not a deal-breaker,' Fee said, drumming her fingers on the tabletop.

'I think I'll be the judge of that,' Laura said, refilling their glasses.

'He pretends he can speak Korean.'

Laura frowned at her. 'Why on earth would he do that?'

'He has to learn bits for his tae kwon do. You know, just phrases, but he always makes out he's fluent. I think he wants to impress me that he's got another language.'

'French would be more useful,' Laura replied, her voice heavy with sarcasm.

'Well, it doesn't bother me,' Fee replied defensively.

'You just said it did.'

'No! I said . . . *you* said . . . you asked what irritated me. That's different. Completely. I never would have brought it up.'

'Yes you would. You know you would.'

'Tch!' Fee tutted tetchily, fidgeting in her seat. 'Can we just drop it, please? I *knew* you'd be like this,' she muttered more quietly.

Laura's phone rang quietly on the table.

Fee frowned at it. 'Why is that ringtone back on your phone? I put "Single Ladies" on for you.'

'Jack replaced it with "Pachelbel's Canon". He read that its alga-rhythms chime with the brain, or something, and he says you're *not* to change it. My startle response is high enough as it is.'

'Oooh, get you and your startle response,' Fee muttered, as Laura picked it up.

'Hi, Jack . . . Yes, I'm at Tom's . . . Uh-huh, with Fee. We're just chatting about . . . Oh . . . uh-huh . . . But I thought you had to finish that Howard chair . . . I see . . . Okay, well, I'll head back now, then . . . No, it's fine . . . Yup, see you in a bit.'

Laura disconnected and gave Fee an apologetic grimace.

'Don't tell me, you've got to go,' Fee said flatly, her eyes on the horizon as she watched the light of a ferry motoring back from Belgium.

'I'm sorry. He's made dinner,' she said, tipping back her glass and draining it.

Fee shrugged as Laura stood up, the chair scraping painfully on the floor. "Course he has.'

Laura looked down at her. 'Really, Fee, I thought he was working late tonight.'

'Sure. You've gotta go. I'll stay here and finish the bottle. Tom can come and join me.' She looked around the still-deserted bar. 'It's not exactly heaving yet.'

'I'll make it up to you next time, I promise,' Laura said, waving behind her as she marched towards the doors.

'Yeah. That's what you say every time,' Fee murmured to herself, as the swing doors closed and she was left with only the stars for company.

# Chapter Twelve

'She can't *still* be away, surely?' Laura protested huffily down the line.

'Well, she's not responded to any of my messages, and I must have left, what – four now?' Fee's voice had risen an octave, a clear indicator that she was stressed, although whether that was because of Laura's bad mood or the queue of ADHD kids in front of her wanting to go on the water flumes was open to question.

'But I need to get on. I've seen two people on the list now and I was supposed to see her first,' she argued, jumping as an HGV whistled past the lay-by she was sitting in, causing Dolly to rock like a boat.

'Jeez, where are you?' Fee complained. 'It sounds like you're sitting in the middle of a runway.'

'I'm near Slough, looking at futons for Urchin. There's a factory clearance sale.'

'Mmm, well, I don't know what to tell you,' Fee murmured. Laura could hear her opening the till and handing over fifty-pence pieces for the lockers. 'I can't ring the woman incessantly. I'll get done for harassment.'

Things still hadn't quite returned to normal between them since their argument at Tom's the week before and she knew Fee was sulking because she'd called Paul a 'potato'.

'Look, can you just text me the address? I may as well see if I can talk to her in person whilst I'm over this way.'

Two minutes later, her phone beeped and Laura looked up the village on the Surrey map she'd bought at the service station last time she'd been here seeing Orlando. Brampton Oakley appeared to be close to Kitty's village. Just a few miles away, in fact.

Leaving it spread out on the passenger seat beside her, Laura pulled out of the lay-by and headed west towards Guildford, determined to pin this woman down once and for all.

Dolly sat idling as Laura looked up at the elaborate wrought-iron gates from the far side of the road. *The Parsonage* was carved into stone slabs set in each of the tall, dusty brick pillars on either side of the drive, and although she couldn't see the house from here – the drive swept around and away from the road – she had glimpsed an impressive stack of chimneys beyond the fir trees on her approach. So far, so imposing.

Turning the engine off and getting out of the car, Laura crossed the road and pressed the button on the keypad. She took a step back, expecting a voice to bark back at her. Instead, a low whirr of motors started up somewhere nearby and the gates – with stately slowness – began to open.

Laura turned back towards Dolly in surprise. She wouldn't be able to pass through the gates before they closed again. Clutching her bag closer to her, she stepped on to the private property.

The lawn spread out like a sheet, flat and smooth, before her as she followed the gentle meander of the drive up to the main approach. It wasn't a long drive, maybe six hundred yards or so. From the street it looked as if it could have extended for half a mile, but the house was standing before her almost prematurely.

It was tall and reasonably narrow, built in a plum-coloured brick with high sash windows and a porticoed front door that was reached by a short sweep of steps. In the window above the door, she could see an antique bow rocking horse, and all the curtains appeared to be drawn and draped to exactly the same degree.

Laura shivered as she looked up at it. For all its desirable symmetry and impressive ceiling height, it looked forbidding, cold and reproachful. She could just imagine secrets lurking within it, trapped in the corners by sticky cobwebs and heavy locked doors.

She walked up the steps and rang the doorbell. Far inside the cavity of the house, she heard the jangle of a small brass bell, wall-mounted in the old servants' quarters, no doubt. She waited.

But no one came. She tried again.

Nothing.

Bending to the side, she peered in through the front windows. A stack of boxes stood at the back of one of the rooms, a velvet wing chair the only piece of furniture in there. In the room on the other side was an oval dining table with eight chairs around it and an intricate candelabra with the remaining stumps of six mulberry-coloured candles.

Laura walked back down the steps and sat on the bottom one, pulling her notepad out of her bag. She thought for a moment about what to say.

## The Perfect Present

*Dear Mrs Tremayne,*

*I dropped by hoping to arrange an appointment for an interview with you, regarding the charm necklace Rob Blake has commissioned me to make for your sister's birthday. Please would you call my studio on 01728 662490 at your earliest convenience.*

*Yours sincerely,*

*Laura Cunningham*

She folded the sheet of paper and dropped it through the letterbox. She was just starting back down the drive, eager to leave the deserted house, when a sudden noise came to her ear.

Laura stopped and listened. It had come from the side of the house, in the gardens.

She walked tentatively around the building, almost tiptoeing. Part of her wanted to jump in Dolly and get on the motorway and back home. The sun had barely got out of bed today and it was bitterly cold. But '150 miles' kept blinking in her brain, and if she could just get this meeting over and done with, it would mean an extra day in the studio with Old Grey for company and the tides as her clock.

Laura passed an old lean-to glasshouse with several broken panes, rounded a corner and stopped abruptly at the sight of a long shadow moving ahead. She inched forwards. A woman was kneeling by a flowerbed at the edge of the lawn, weeding the bare, hard-crusted beds vigorously. Laura watched her, transfixed. Her hair was beautiful, a true golden blonde that shone in the late-afternoon light, her thin frame visible beneath her pansy-patterned needlecord dress and jumper as she grabbed, pinched and pulled the weeds from the soil. Oversized suede gardening gloves emphasized her thinness further.

'Excuse me,' Laura said.

The woman twisted round to look up at her, her pale face visibly draining of colour at the sight of Laura.

'I'm sorry, I didn't mean to alarm you,' Laura said quickly. 'I rang the bell but no one answered. I've just dropped a note through the door. I was leaving when I heard you back here.'

The woman stared at her in silence. Her face was plain and devoid of make-up, and she looked nothing like the slick, body-con, sexualized women at the Cube. She was nothing like Laura had imagined Cat Blake's sister to be.

'You are Olive Tremayne, aren't you?' Laura asked. 'My name's Laura Cunningham. I'm a jeweller. Your brother-in-law has commissioned me to make a necklace for your sister's birthday . . . I've been trying to contact you for a couple of weeks now.'

The woman continued staring at her, and Laura wondered whether she had understood. Maybe she was just a worker here, or perhaps she was foreign?

Slowly, the woman got to her feet and walked towards Laura, her palest-blue eyes pinned on her visitor like a sparrow hawk hovering above an unsuspecting mouse.

'Did you . . . did you get any of my messages?' Laura asked, repressing the urge to step back from the woman's intense scrutiny and the small fork in her hand.

The woman stopped twenty feet away. 'Go.' She swung her arm out like a hinge towards the gate. Laura followed the point with her eyes.

'But if you could just let me explain,' Laura began. 'I didn't mean to trespass. But I live awfully far away and as Mrs

Tremayne hasn't returned any of my calls, I just thought I'd try to make contact directly.'

'Go,' the woman repeated in a lower voice. Her chin was dipped down towards her chest and Laura could see tremors rippling across her dress like wind over water. 'You are not welcome here.'

'But Rob ask—'

The woman silently repeated her gesture towards the gates.

Laura sighed. 'Fine. I'm going,' she said, holding her hands up and beginning to walk backwards. 'I'm sorry to have disturbed you.' She turned away, marching quickly down the drive. It felt so much longer on the way out than on the way in. As she passed the sensor and the gate's motors started up, Laura turned round. The woman was watching her, and her arm was still up, pointing the way out. She looked like a statue in her eerie stillness.

Freaked out, Laura began to run through the opening gates and back to Dolly. She started the car up immediately and pulled away from the kerb with a squeal of tyres, the vision of the woman's stony stare still chasing her down the street like a hound.

Not until she was back on the motorway did her pulse settle down enough for her to begin to realize what this meant. If that woman *had* been Olive Tremayne – and it seemed more than likely that she was – she clearly had no intention of contributing to her sister's gift. Rob Blake was going to have to go back to the drawing board on this. His big romantic idea wasn't going according to plan.

# Chapter Thirteen

'You're exaggerating,' Fee said, sitting back and admiring her black metallic toenails. 'Like?' she asked, waggling them.

Laura grunted at her workbench, huddled over her parallel pliers as she gently bent the gold thread to shape. 'I am not. You didn't see her. She was like some kind of Medusa woman – all mad hair and cold eyes and witchy fingers. Jeez, she's about as far from Cat Blake as I expected her to be.'

'Well, why should they be alike just because they're sisters? Loads of sisters hate each other's guts. They're probably complete opposites.'

Laura considered the comment – one of Fee's frighteningly astute ones – and remembered something Kitty had said about them being closer than sisters, than twins even. Laura had taken it as a harmless boast, just a turn of phrase. But what if she'd actually been referring to an estranged relationship between Cat and her sister Olive?

'Yes, well, she's shot her bolt with me, I can tell you, throwing me out like I'd done something wrong. I'm not going to work with her after that. She's off the commission as far as I'm concerned.'

Fee raised her eyebrows. 'And have you told Rob Blake that?'

Laura shook her head. 'Not yet. No doubt the mad harpy will get to him first and tell him I've been snooping around the grounds or something.'

'Oh, I doubt he'll be sympathetic to her. After all, he's the one desperate to make all this happen for his beloved wife, remember. And he did say he'd got everyone lined up for you.'

'Whatever. I'm moving on,' Laura muttered stroppily. 'Next charm, next name on the list.'

Fee looked up at her. 'As your manager, it's probably worth reminding you that you're getting two thousand four hundred pounds per charm. You might want to suggest he chooses someone else for the charm rather than just drop it altogether.'

Laura shot her a look.

'What? I'm just saying,' Fee protested, the nail-polish brush in one hand, the bottle in the other. 'It's not your fault she's been uncooperative and weird. Why should you miss out on that extra cash just because of her strange behaviour? You could buy a car from that one charm alone.'

'One without an engine maybe,' Laura argued, wrinkling her nose as she gently tapped her brass hammer, forcing the gold in her hand to yield and bend. 'But you might have a point,' she conceded after a while.

'I most certainly do,' Fee replied, no doubt relieved her commission wasn't going to be cut further. 'So who's next on the list, then?'

Laura put down her blowtorch and reached for some papers just off to her left. 'Uh . . . Alex. Alex Windermere.'

'Want me to set up the appointment now? I can talk with wet toes you know.'

'Wow! Multi-tasker *extraordinaire*. What men could learn from you!'

'Cheeky,' Fee laughed, chucking a used cotton-wool ball at her. Too light, it barely got to the end of the sofa.

'No, there's no point. He's the one in Milan. I'll have to talk to him in Verbier.'

'Oh. So you are going, then?'

'I think I'm going to have to. Kitty's the only one who's been any use so far. Rob's about as confiding as a spy, I've not had more than ten minutes with Orlando, I can't get Olive Tremayne to even talk to me, and they all live over *here*. God knows how I'd pin down the two living abroad,' Laura sighed.

'What charm have you decided on for Kitty?'

Laura hesitated. 'I haven't yet. She has shared some good stories from their childhood together, but I'm slightly worried she's been glossing them up – making the two of them out to be BFFs when actually I'm not sure they even see each other that much any more.'

'Does that matter? So they were friends as kids. That's fine. That's what you show.'

'I know, I know . . . I just need to make sure that what she's telling me is actually rooted in the truth and not fantasy. This is practically a twenty-grand necklace, Fee – it needs to be right.'

'Well,' Fee said dubiously, beginning her top coat, 'at some point you're just going to have to make a decision and commit to it. Time and tide wait for no woman.' She burst out laughing as she looked out of the window. 'God knows you know that better than anyone.'

Laura rolled her eyes at her friend's amusement, just as they heard a shout below them.

'Anybody home?'

'Jack?' Fee replied brightly as he stomped noisily up the steps. 'Oh, say you've brought lunch!'

He stopped in the doorway, two brown paper bags in his hands, grinning at the sight of the two of them – Laura frowning in her goggles at the bench, Fee sprawled on the sofa, nail polish in hand and feet on the coffee table. 'I should have known – a hive of industry in here.'

He walked over, kissing Laura softly on the mouth. 'How are you?' he murmured gently.

Laura nodded. 'Yup. Just pushing on with these orders.'

Jack turned to Fee, who was hobbling across the floor – loo roll woven between her toes – to answer the phone.

'Hello?' she asked. 'Yes, just a sec . . .' She held the phone out towards Laura. 'For you.'

'Who is it?' Laura asked.

'Didn't say,' Fee shrugged. 'What's in the bags, Jack? You must have read my mind. I'm starving.'

'You're supposed to ask who's calling,' Laura muttered, taking the handset from her. 'Hello?'

'Laura, it's Rob Blake.'

'Oh, hi.' Laura watched Fee peering in the bags, her eyes widening at the sight of the saveloy inside.

'I haven't heard back from you about the trip, and I need an answer. My secretary's booking the flights at the moment, and it makes sense for us all to travel together.'

'Yes, of course.' Laura looked at Jack handing Fee a can of full-fat Coke, teasing her by threatening to shake it.

'So?' Rob asked into the silence. 'Are you coming?'

'Uh . . .'

She heard a small sigh whistle down the line. 'There's not much time left, and this is by far the most efficient way of speaking to everyone you need to. Laura? Are you still there?'

His voice sounded far away to her. She was watching Fee and Jack sitting on the arms of the sofa, chatting away comfortably, and she knew he had no idea yet – his manner was too relaxed. It had been remarkably easy managing to avoid spending time alone with him. She was working late most evenings on the pretext of her seasonal rush, and he was busy too, of course, in the run-up to Christmas; everybody wanted their sofas ready for the post-turkey collapse.

She watched as Jack gallantly ripped open the ketchup packet for Fee with his teeth. This was how it always was – the three of them together, their tight unit closer than any family, bonded by a tie stronger than blood. Safety in their number had worked for them all, but right now, the fit was wrong: one on one with either of them felt too intense for her at the moment and she was bickering with Fee almost constantly. But the three of them together felt too distracting, overwhelming. She needed time and space to think. And in spite of Fee's bullish logic, she might not want to be a mother, but that didn't mean she could easily live with the alternative open to her. She couldn't bring herself to take the test yet, either, for as soon as the pregnancy was confirmed, she would be obliged to act one way or the other. Denial had been her chosen path up till now, but Rob wasn't the only one running out of time: not making a decision would soon *become* the decision, nature would do the rest.

'Laura? I need an answer – are you coming to Verbier or not?' Rob pressed impatiently.

Time and space . . . She hadn't mentioned the possibility of the trip to Jack yet, but it suddenly occurred to her that Verbier could offer her both those things. It was exactly what she needed. 'Tell her to go ahead.'

'Good. That's good. It'll simplify things enormously.' The

relief in Rob's voice was evident. 'Can you get back to Claudia within the hour with your passport details?'

'Okay.'

'Great. She'll give you all the information then. See you Friday.' And he hung up.

Laura rolled her eyes. She *hated* that he kept doing that to her.

'Who was that?' Jack asked as she replaced the handset and walked back over to him. He handed her a latte bought from the café at the top of the shipyard and a thickly buttered bacon bap.

'The client for this charm necklace I'm working on.' She took a deep breath. 'I've got to travel for some of the interviews.'

'I thought you already were. You've been up and down that motorway like a rat up a drainpipe.'

'Well, one of the interviewees is in Milan, and—'

'Milan?' Jack's jaw dropped open.

'And the other one's in Frankfurt.'

'What? You've got to go there for a necklace?'

'No. I'm going to Verbier instead.'

'What?'

'They're all going to be out there together. It's someone's birthday, blah, blah, and they reckon it's simpler if I just catch them all under one roof.'

Jack stared at her open-mouthed. 'But you *never* take holidays.'

'This isn't a holiday. It's work, Jack. Very lucrative work.'

He shook his head, baffled. 'But . . . I mean, when is it?'

'It's this Friday and I get back Monday.'

'This weekend? But we were going to do the Christmas tree together.'

She suppressed a sigh of frustration. 'And you still can. It'll be lovely for me to come home to find the house all decorated,' she shrugged.

'It won't be the same without you.'

'Fee will help, won't you, Fee?' She forced a smile and shot Fee a 'help me' look.

'If you like,' Fee mumbled with her mouth full.

'But what about . . . I mean, there's that band playing in the pub on Friday night. I got tickets for you as a surprise – Smack Doris. You loved them last time.'

Laura kept her smile fixed. She really hadn't. 'It's just a few days, Jack. Over and done with by this time next week.'

He stared at her for a second as he heard the finality in her voice. 'And if I hadn't been here just now, when were you going to tell me? Send me a text as you boarded the plane?'

'Jack, don't be daft – of course not!' she said dismissively, wandering back to her bench.

'It's nowhere near as implausible as you want it to sound,' he muttered to her back, scrunching the bag up in his hand and tossing it through the open door of the wood burner.

Fee looked between them nervously as the bag instantly ignited. 'Me and Paul will come with you to the pub, Jack.'

'Isn't Paul working then?' Jack asked, looking down at her.

'No. Not this weekend.'

'You know about Paul?' Laura asked him.

'Of course. Why wouldn't I?'

Laura swallowed and shook her head. She was the link that connected them, and yet sometimes she felt like the spare part in their threesome. 'No reason.'

'So it's all booked, then, is it?' he asked, throwing his arms out. 'I don't get any say in it whatsoever?'

Laura sighed. 'I don't see what the big deal is.'

Jack stared at her sadly, his cheeks flushed. 'No. I guess you wouldn't.'

# Chapter Fourteen

Laura clutched the ticket tightly in her hands as she moved through the security scanners. There were only twenty minutes to go till departure, and she was beginning to worry she might have left it too late after all. She had actually arrived at Heathrow two hours earlier, allowing for delays on the motorways, but not wanting to spend any longer with this group of strangers than was necessary, she had spent ninety minutes of that time sitting in Dolly in the short-term car park. Now she realized she'd underestimated the queues at check-in, and getting through the security checks was taking an interminable time.

Picking up her leather satchel from the conveyor belt and slinging the strap across her body, she walked out into the departure hall. Her eyes scanned the jostling, noisy space, looking for the champagne bar Claudia had told her about. It was opposite Harrods and below Garfunkel's, 'probably next to a Lamborghini'.

Laura found it easily, even without the giveaway £100,000 car revolving next to it. The group of people standing around drinking champagne and chatting animatedly were catching everyone's eyes. They were glossier and shinier, somehow, than the average travellers in elasticated waist-bands and trainers.

Laura took a series of deep breaths and rolled her lips together anxiously as she drew nearer, annoyed with herself for feeling so nervous about meeting Cat at last. She felt it confirmed the aura of 'specialness' that Kitty and Orlando had conjured up about the woman – her great taste! Her staggering beauty! Her selfless kindness and off-the-scale emotional intelligence! When probably, in all reality, she told herself, they were embellishing the truth and flattering Cat artificially. After all, being asked to contribute memories and thoughts about someone for a gift automatically implied a rose-tinted perspective. Still, Laura was undeniably intrigued to at last meet the woman who had the mighty Rob Blake in her thrall. She'd give her that, at least.

'Laura!' Kitty cried, spotting her first and careering over.

'Hi, Kitty.' Laura smiled as Kitty enveloped her in a soft, talcumed hug.

'We were just wondering where you were,' she said, planting a champagne flute in Laura's hand. 'She's here, everybody!' Kitty cried, holding Laura's arm up as if she was a lost toddler.

Everyone turned and Laura felt herself shrink an inch as four pairs of eyes swivelled over to her. She shifted her weight nervously, aware of her tummy growling at her. The drive down meant she had skipped breakfast.

Rob came over to her, still in his business suit, although his tie had been fractionally loosened. 'Laura, you cut it fine. I was beginning to think you might miss the plane. We're leaving for the gate in a moment.'

'Traffic,' Laura replied, trying to smile, aware of a hawk-eyed redhead watching her with keen interest. 'I've had rather further to come than you.'

He nodded, but with an expression that almost made her

feel he knew she'd been hiding away in the car park, delaying the start of this weekend for as long as possible.

'Let me introduce you to the others.' He swung an arm around to enclose the group. 'This is Sam Radcliffe and her husband David.'

The redhead offered a slim, scarlet-manicured hand. She had a strong oval face with a small, thin-lipped mouth and hazel eyes. But it was her hair, a magnificent mane of titian brushed-through ringlets that did all the talking about her.

'Hi, Laura,' Sam said in a deep, almost mannish, voice. 'Just been hearing all about you.' The inflexions in her voice made it appear that the conversation had been interesting, which Laura found hard to believe.

'Pleased to meet you, Laura,' her husband David said, shaking her hand. He was tall and slightly balding, with dark hair just on the turn and an easy smile.

'These guys have just come in from Frankfurt,' Rob explained.

'Well, I have,' Sam corrected him coolly. 'David's been here since Wednesday. Playing.'

'Shooting,' David corrected her. 'Corporate necessity.'

'Oh,' Laura said interestedly. 'And what do you do in Frankfurt, Sam?'

'I'm a lawyer at Deutsche Bank.'

'Oh.' That hair plus lawyer plus bank. It was hard to think of a more intimidating combination.

'And I believe you've already met Orlando,' Rob continued.

'Briefly,' Laura smiled, offering a polite hand, but Orlando, looking very European in a snug lilac cashmere V-neck and jet-black jeans, ignored her hand altogether and kissed her exuberantly four times on her cheeks.

'Oh! My!' she gasped as she was swung from side to side.

'This woman,' Orlando grinned, wrapping an arm around her shoulder. 'She is so funny. And *so* wicked.' He winked at her.

Laura blushed, wishing Orlando hadn't just said that, aware that Rob and Sam were now staring at her intently as though waiting for the entertainment to begin. She looked around at the small group. Where was she?

'Uh . . . where's Cat?' she asked.

'Duty-free,' Rob replied. 'She'll be back any second. Now remember, she thinks you're here as Orlando's plus one, okay?'

Laura nodded as Orlando winked at her. 'We make a beautiful couple.'

'Oh look, here she comes now,' Kitty smiled.

Laura followed her gaze and saw a woman walking towards them, her shoulder-length platinum-blonde hair curled under itself like a fox's tail. She was tall – maybe five foot nine – and slim, small-breasted but with a hip-waist ratio that would have Jessica Rabbit reaching for a tracksuit. She was wearing mocha-coloured skinny jeans and a neatly fitted jumper with a deep rolled-over collar in some sort of honeycomb pattern that was repeated on the cuffs of her sleeves. Cream. Designer. Her plush, extravagant boots – a warm-honeyed fur that swayed with her steps – came to her knees and she was wearing a matching hat that from a distance obscured her eyes, emphasizing instead high, slanted cheekbones and a full mouth.

Laura realized she was holding her breath. Here was the woman who had raised over £20,000 for charity, who'd saved a lamb, harpooned a squirrel and had a bridge defaced in her name. The woman who was going to wear a £20,000 necklace round her neck – and it would be worth every penny, because a life like hers surely had to be recorded.

'Oh good, there you are,' Rob said, placing his hand lightly on the small of his wife's back (which was very small indeed). 'Cat, meet Laura Cunningham, Orlando's guest.'

Laura held out a faintly trembling hand, knowing that in the gilded haze she looked like a shadow – her grey hair, grey skin, grey eyes and grey jeans were enlivened only by an ice-pink puffa, which now seemed slightly too shiny and slightly too puffy. 'Hi.'

Cat shook it warmly. Her skin was smooth and soft – lavender-scented, no doubt – and up close, Laura could see her beautifully shaped green eyes beneath the fur hat. 'Laura, I'm so glad you could join us this weekend.' She dropped her voice and leaned in closer to Laura. 'Although you must be mad. This lot are certified loonies.' Her smile was wide and engaging, and Laura knew she was grinning back like a loony herself.

'Well, we'd better make our way to the gate,' Rob said briskly, putting his glass down and picking up the briefcase by his feet. 'They started boarding ten minutes ago and we're all here now.'

Everyone drained their glasses.

'Drink up, Laura,' Kitty encouraged her. 'You need to play a bit of catch-up.'

Laura drank the champagne in one go, although she didn't need it. She already felt a faint euphoria.

She fell into hurried step with Kitty at the back of the group, her eyes trained on the Blakes – Cat's hand enclosed in Rob's, their chins up, long legs striding out. It was fascinating just to watch them. Their combined effect was universally acknowledged – men, women and children of all ages and nationalities turned to stare as they passed – and Laura knew she would have run the marathon herself if she'd been put behind Cat in shorts. She quite literally couldn't take her eyes off her.

'This must be what it's like travelling with the Beckhams,' Laura murmured, making Kitty laugh.

'So what do you think?' Kitty asked her as they swerved round a cart with flashing lights that was transporting an elderly lady to her gate, a walking stick resting on her knees.

'Stunning. It's like being in the presence of . . . I don't know – a model, a celebrity, a royal . . . all wrapped up in one.'

'Grace Kelly.'

'Yes,' Laura grinned. 'Exactly.'

Kitty nodded proudly and Laura suddenly understood why she couldn't let go of the friendship they'd shared as children. Laura already knew she would dine out on this weekend for years to come . . . if she ever started to dine out, that was.

'You look great, by the way,' Kitty said, beginning to pant as they tried to keep up with the others. The Blakes were setting a brutal, Amazonian pace, marching ahead to ensure they kept the gate open. 'You've had your hair done since I saw you last, haven't you?'

'Yes. Thanks for noticing,' Laura smiled, running her hand self-consciously through her hair. 'By the way, where's Joe?'

'Not coming. He can't leave the farm, sadly; although, to be fair, he's not a skier anyway. My mother's come to look after the kids for me. Do you know this is my first holiday away from them all *ever*?' She shook her head. 'I hope I can cope.'

'I'm sure you'll be fine.'

'Mmmm . . .' she said anxiously as they started speed-walking along the travelators. 'So what are you wearing for Orlando's dinner party tomorrow night? You know it's a surprise, right?'

'Yes, Rob told me. Um, I've just packed trousers and a top. Nothing special.' She wished now that she'd done some shopping before coming away this weekend, but Jack had been so quiet all week with her that she had put it out of her mind as much as possible.

'Oh. But you do know it's black tie?'

'No!' she gasped. 'Claudia didn't mention it.'

'Oh . . . Well, don't worry. I'm sure we can sort something. I've packed a couple of extra things.'

Laura looked at her to see whether she was joking – there were at least three dress sizes between them – but apparently she wasn't. 'Thanks,' she murmured uneasily.

They reached the gate where the others were waiting. They were clearly the last to embark and Laura could already imagine the glaring looks the other passengers would shoot at them as they did the walk of shame, searching for their seats.

'Where are you sitting?' Laura asked Kitty as the group formed a short queue.

Kitty checked her ticket. 'Six D. How about you?'

'Ten B.'

'Oh, shame. It would have been fun if we could have sat together.' Kitty leaned in to her conspiratorially. 'I hope that doesn't mean I'm sitting next to Sam,' she whispered.

'Why not?'

Kitty made a tipping motion with her hand to her mouth as they handed over their tickets to the gate official, who scanned them and pressed lots of buttons on her keyboard.

'Oh.'

The woman handed back their tickets and they jogged down the tunnel together. 'I bought a load of magazines in WH Smith earlier. Have you got anything?'

'Afraid not. I wasn't thinking ahead. It's, uh . . . been a while since I've been on a plane.'

'No worries. You can read some of mine.'

The plane was only three-quarters full. Kitty found, to her relief, that she was sitting next to Orlando, who was already poring over the duty-free aftershaves and turning down the corners of anything that featured Calvin Klein. Laura continued down the plane, determined not to catch anyone's eye, and was relieved to find there was no one in the seat next to her.

She was no sooner sitting than the hostess went past doing a final numbers check and the doors closed. Laura looked ahead of her. She could see one of Cat's gargantuan boots just straying into the aisle as she leaned across to talk to someone. A toss of red hair shot above the seat like a flare and she knew it was Sam.

'Pssst!' Kitty was twisted in her seat, holding out a couple of gossip magazines.

'Thanks,' Laura smiled, taking them gratefully from the man in front, who passed them over to her. The doors had been sealed now and the plane began to move away from the gate. She started flicking through the pages, wondering to herself who would really wear gold sequinned leggings and why pictures of celebrities with cellulite were considered of national interest. By the time she was reading her horoscope (having had to find her sign by checking the dates first), the seat belt signs were off and there was a buzz of conversation above the noise of the engines. At one point she saw Sam disappear off to the loos and half wondered whether any alarms would go off – she seemed the type to sneak off for a furtive cigarette in the toilet; later, she saw David and Cat swap seats with each other and Cat and Sam becoming engrossed in conversation, their silky heads together. Poor Kitty, she thought.

'Hi.'

She looked up to find Rob staring down at her.

'I just wanted to check you're okay down here?' he asked.

'Oh, sure,' she said, just as the hostesses appeared with the refreshments trolley and started moving down the aisle towards him.

'Excuse me, sir,' one of them said, a flirtatious smile on her lips as she anticipated squeezing past Rob.

He looked down at Laura. 'May I?'

'Oh yes,' she replied, unbuckling her belt and hastily shifting into the next seat.

The hostess gave a disappointed smile as Rob escaped unmolested. 'A drink, sir?'

Rob looked over at Laura. 'Thirsty?'

She shrugged. 'Yes, I suppose so. If you . . . I mean, only if you're having one.'

'Two champagnes, then,' he said to the hostess, who would clearly start walking on the wings if he asked her to.

'So,' he said a little awkwardly as they watched her pull the foil off the mini bottles. 'How's the beach hut coming along?'

'Getting there,' Laura replied. 'The plumber's been and gone so there's running water now, and the carpenter should be in and out this weekend, weather permitting. He's a friend of Jack's, helping me out so that I can get it done in time for Christmas. Hopefully all I'll have to do when I get back is paint and furnish it.'

'That's all, huh?' She didn't need to look at him to know he was amused. 'Well, I'd love to see it when it's done.'

'You can, next time you're visiting your client in nearby Glasgow.'

'Norwich.'

'If you say so,' she quipped, and she heard him chuckle, a surprisingly buoyant sound from a man who was usually so brusque.

'Does your boyfriend know about it?'

'Heavens, no. It's got to be a surprise.'

'What does he do, your boyfriend?' Rob asked after a moment.

'He has his own business,' she said grandly, instantly regretting it.

'Oh? What's his field?'

'Upholstery.'

He nodded, just as the hostess handed him the two glasses of champagne. 'There you are.'

'Thanks.'

'So what do you think of everyone so far?'

'They seem very . . .' Terrifying? Intimidating? '. . . friendly. Aren't we missing a few people, though?'

'Alex and Isabella are meeting up with us at the chalet. It's easier that they travel direct from Milan.'

'And who is Alex again?'

'Cat's first love,' Rob said tightly.

'Oh. And you're all . . . ?'

'Friends? Yes. I suppose so. How modern of me, right?' His eyes twinkled.

'Cat's, uh . . . very beautiful. I mean, she's really . . . wow.'

He smiled and shook his head. 'I know. She has such an incredible impact on people. We've been together five years and yet whenever she walks in the room I still feel the same as I did the first time I set eyes on her.'

'You're really lucky,' Laura said quietly, watching him as he gazed at his wife's long leg, which was slung casually across the aisle. They were a perfectly matched couple: successful, charming, she as beautiful as he was handsome, both kind and generous. Laura already knew about Cat's charity work, and Kitty had told her that Rob had paid for her flight here too, not just Laura's. They tallied up completely.

'Tell me how you met,' she said. Rob looked over at her warily and she smiled. 'You have to tell me sooner or later, and it really would help to have some background knowledge going into this weekend. I don't doubt I'm going to hear lots of wonderful and interesting stories about your wife, but no one knows her like you do.'

He paused for a moment. 'It's strange really to think that by the end of this month – this weekend even – you're quite possibly going to know more about my wife than I do.'

'That's not possible,' Laura argued.

'No? By the time you've interviewed everyone, you'll know her life story from three hundred and sixty degrees.'

'No one can know another person more intimately than their spouse.'

'Well, it would be wonderful to think that could be true,' Rob said, looking out of the window, and Laura thought she caught a glint of sadness in his tone, like sunlight on a wave.

Laura looked sidelong at him. His profile was angled down, his skin washed gold in the setting sun like a honey glaze. She watched his Adam's apple bob firmly down in his throat, noticed the first flecks of late-in-the-day stubble and saw that his full mouth was set in a firm, stressed line.

'I saved her life,' Rob said after a moment. 'I very nearly lost her the moment I met her.'

'What happened?' Laura asked, taken aback.

'It was July. I was having lunch with my girlfriend. We were sitting outside in this pedestrianized square, and there was some banal sponsorship event going on, with traders wrestling in sumo suits. I noticed this girl sitting on the steps on the other side. She was on her own. It was a really hot day and she was wearing this silky polka-dot dress that kept catching the breeze. I couldn't take my eyes off her.' He gave a small grin. 'I kept hoping the wind would blow her skirt up so I could see her legs.' He shrugged as Laura's eyes widened at his candidness. 'What can I say? She was the most beautiful thing I'd ever seen. I was completely transfixed. I didn't hear a word my girlfriend said to me.'

'Had you been with her long? Your girlfriend, I mean.'

'Eight years. We'd been at uni together.'

'Ouch. Where were you at university?'

'Trinity College, Cambridge, reading classics.'

'Oh.' She'd been expecting something like economics or maths.

He smiled at her expression and she knew he was probably used to it. 'Anyway, when Cat stood up to go, I got us to stand up too, pretending I wanted to go for a walk before returning to the office. I know it sounds terrible to Lisa – my ex – and it was, but I couldn't let Cat just disappear into the crowd and risk never seeing her again. I had to find out where she worked. So I followed her.'

'Like a stalker,' Laura deadpanned.

'Exactly,' he said, giving it back.

'Did either of the girls notice what you were doing?'

'No, thank God. We were just a few steps behind her when her phone went in her bag.' He shook his head, his voice slowing down. 'She reached into her bag to answer it, just as she stepped off the kerb. And it was like I *knew* what was going to happen before I even saw the lorry. Everything just happened in slow motion. A cement truck was heading straight for her but she wasn't even looking. I grabbed her by the arm and pulled her back into me, really hard. I mean, her feet left the ground; it must have hurt her. But the truck missed her by a hair's breadth.'

Laura turned in her seat so that she was facing him. 'She would have been killed outright.'

He nodded. 'Even now I dream about it sometimes – how close I came to losing her.'

'She must have been completely shaken up.'

'More so by the fact that I then proceeded to kiss her, I think.'

Laura's eyebrows shot up in surprise. 'Right in front of your girlfriend?'

'Right in front of the world – I didn't care. Whether it was shock or . . . or, I don't know, realizing that I'd met the girl I wanted to marry. I just kissed her until she kissed me back.' He grinned at the memory. 'I didn't know her name, didn't know if she spoke English. But that was our hello.'

Laura straightened up and stared at the headrest in front. 'I am so depressed now,' she muttered.

'Why?'

'Because that's only, like, the ultimate love story. It makes everybody else's suck next to yours.'

'Tell me yours. How did you meet your boyfriend?'

'No, I don't think so.' She shook her head. 'Trust me, it's a very dull story by comparison.'

'I told you.'

'Yes, because you're paying me to get this information from you.'

'Hmm, cute,' he replied, sitting back in his seat and clearing his throat. The gesture alone told her they were back to business. 'So, by the end of this weekend, then, you should know what you're doing for the charms for me, Kitty, Orlando, Sam and Alex?'

Laura nodded. 'I don't see any problems with that.'

'So who does that leave? Olive, Min—'

'Ah, about Olive. You have a problem there. She doesn't want to do it. She didn't return any of our phone calls, though Foo must have tried four or five times, and when I stopped by the house to try to arrange an appointment with her directly, she threw me out.'

'She did *what*?' His voice was hollow with shock.

'I'm afraid it looks like she doesn't want anything to do with this commission, and I don't see how I can do anything more without harassing her. If you'd like to think of someone else to replace her . . . ?'

Laura bit her lip, hoping he wouldn't just drop the charm altogether. As Fee had so shrewdly pointed out, it was worth nearly two and a half thousand pounds.

'And when you say she threw you out, you mean . . .'

'She properly threw me out, yes.' Laura nodded.

'I'll speak to her and get her to apologize as soon as we get back, Laura.'

'No, please. I'd rather you didn't. It really makes no difference to me.'

153

'Well, it makes a difference to me. You can't work together until this is resolved.'

Laura's heart sank. 'You still want her on the necklace, then?'

'It's imperative that she's on it. How can I possibly give Cat her life story and not include her sister? I know it'll be a tough interview for you. Olive's not easy. She and Cat have always had a very tense relationship. More has gone unsaid than said between them, that's the trouble, But I was rather hoping this might go some way towards reversing that.'

'Well, if you can get her to meet me, I'll do my best,' Laura shrugged.

'Great.' He pulled himself up to standing. 'And listen – don't try to sweeten the relationship into something it's not. Every charm has got to be true.'

Laura squinted at him. 'Are you sure?'

Rob nodded his head. 'Don't edit to be kind to me or anyone else. I want you to discover all Cat's sides and flaws and strengths, and then choose the stories that, in the balance, show who she really is. That's how you'll capture her, by showing the warts and all.'

Laura stared despondently at the headrest in front of her. 'If there is one thing I can be absolutely certain of already, it's that your wife is *not* warty.'

Laura watched as he returned to his seat, chuckling, slowly becoming aware of a familiar telltale ache in the pit of her stomach. She had missed breakfast and absent-mindedly dismissed it as hunger pangs, but this . . . this wasn't hunger. She clasped her hands over her tummy and felt the warmth there and faint swelling that came every month. Had it been a false alarm, after all? The sleepless nights had been for nothing? Relief flooded her and she began rifling in her handbag for her emergency supplies. Wait till she told Fee. Now she could stop with the worried, haunted looks she kept throwing when she thought Laura wasn't looking.

Laura took a celebratory sip of her champagne before getting out of her seat and heading off to the loos. Just like that, her life was back on track.

# Chapter Fifteen

The minibus Rob had hired to transfer them from Geneva to the chalet was ready and waiting as they trooped out of the arrivals hall, and everyone piled on noisily, sprawling themselves across both seats in each row in unspoken agreement. Laura made a point of sitting – or was it hiding? – at the back of the group. Sam, sitting up front, had pulled a couple of bottles of Dom Pérignon from her suitcase before they'd boarded, and the group were drinking it steadily as they made their way through the mountains, swapping stories of their summer holidays and which runs they wanted to make.

Rob and David were sitting separately in the front two rows, talking in low, serious voices and doing lots of earnest nodding at each other's comments. Laura was much more interested in getting a handle on the rest of the group. From what she could tell, peering inconspicuously over the head-rest, Cat was the queen bee of the set, Sam was the party animal, Kitty the mother hen, and Orlando the chameleon, able to camp it up singing along to Adele with Sam one moment, and commiserate over rampant mint in the strawberry beds with Kitty the next.

It was clear everyone was up for a party, drinking happily without worrying who was going to be 'designated driver' or whether they had to be up early with the kids the next morning. Interestingly, they were much more imposing as the sum of their parts. Laura had met both Kitty and Orlando separately and been intimidated by neither, but here, amidst the ready laughter and insider repartee, they fulfilled all her nervous expectations of what she'd envisaged the Blakes' glamorous social set to be – even Kitty, now that she was out of her crooked cottage and pinny, looked imposingly grand without children hanging off her. She had blow-dried her hair and was wearing a spot of make-up, and she now perfectly embodied Fee's observation: 'She sounds like she does the gardening in pearls.'

Laura wondered for a moment what Fee would make of them all. At twenty-three, Fee wasn't just significantly younger, she was infinitely less sophisticated too. The conversations that Laura kept picking up on – spending Easter on Lake Como (Sam); the numbers being paid at Mat Collishaw's new exhibition (Cat); the long-term returns of investing in wine (Orlando); hosting the Boxing Day meet (Kitty) – were so far out of her orbit, they might as well have been conducted in Latin, and it saddened Laura to realize that her own dearest friend would be dangerously out of her depth here.

And what about Jack? How would he fit in? Laura's eyes flitted back to Rob and David, appraising the sleek cut of their expensive suits and the discreet thickness of their seven-fold silk ties, the way they made bullet points in the air with fingers that didn't boast wedding rings. He would flounder here too, she knew. The few suits he did own had the shine to them that was the downside of being washable, not dry-clean, and his voice lacked the bass timbre of theirs that came from years of public-school debating and corporate pitches. Nor did he do irony or sarcasm of any kind; he was unapologetically straightforward and sensitive, and perfectly happy to wear his heart on his sleeve. Even his face was wrong somehow – too fine-featured and clean-cut, as if he hadn't started shaving yet. He was a boy to their men.

'. . . Laura?'

'Huh? What?' Laura turned to find Cat, Kitty, Sam and Orlando staring at her.

'You were miles away!' Kitty smiled. 'Sam asked whether you ski.'

Laura's heart sank. There it was. The single question that pinpointed to them all whether or not *she* fitted in here. Even if she could look the part in her new clothes and keep up with the broader strokes of the conversation, could she do what they could do? Backwards? Drunk? In the dark? In their sleep?

'No,' she replied quietly. 'I don't.'

An embarrassed hush fell over the party and Laura felt the humiliation rain down upon her. She felt a quiet fury gather inside her. She had been sitting quietly, tucked away at the back, determined not to bring attention to herself or intrude in any way on this intimate gathering. She hadn't asked to be here; she wasn't trying to muscle her way in to their oh-so-exclusive clique.

'Oh,' Sam said, with a certain archness.

'Don't worry,' Cat said quickly. 'We've got a fantastic instructor out here. He'll have you flying down the slopes in no time.'

Laura felt Rob's eyes on her and looked at him for help. But he said nothing. 'Thanks so much,' she replied. Cat couldn't know she was here to work.

'In the meantime, have another drink,' Orlando said, filling her glass to the brim so that bubbles sloshed on to the carpeted floor.

Laura accepted it with a tight smile and looked out into the darkness of the Alpine night. The point had been made and everyone knew where they stood now. Kitty's, Cat's and Orlando's friendliness notwithstanding, she wasn't one of them.

'So this is it!' Orlando grinned, holding Laura's hand as she alighted from the steps.

'It's not much, I know,' Kitty quipped as Laura took in the low, rather small, stone chalet with shallow casement windows and top-heavy pitched slate roof that sat upon it like an oversized hat. It was tiny and there were going to be nine of them here. Rob hadn't mentioned anyone sharing a room.

'Finally! What took you so long?' a male voice boomed from the beam of light that spilled out through the front door.

Laura took a deep breath. Here was the next one to contend with, then – and he didn't sound shy.

She hung back, fiddling with the extending handle on her bag, as Cat, Sam, Kitty and Orlando – particularly Orlando – swamped him with affectionate, drunken embraces. David was behind her unloading the rest of the bags and Rob was tipping the driver. The others, forgetting all about their luggage, raced into the house, 'dibbing' particular rooms.

'Bagsy I get the sheep!' Kitty shrieked.

Laura sighed, knowing that as 'the staff', she had no say whatsoever on the matter and would probably be doing well not to be sleeping on a sofa. Pushing her suitcase on to its wheels, she stepped into the light towards the stranger who was standing watching her.

'Hello, I'm L—' she began, but her voice failed as though all the breath in her body had been snatched out of her by a sprite. His skin was darkly golden, his hair more blonde than brown, he had a dimpled chin like that Hollywood actor with the sex problem – what was his name? – and blue eyes that were double-ringed so darkly they were like stop signs.

She couldn't move.

'Sorry. I missed that.' His eyes were as steady as her pulse was not.

'Laura. Laura Cunningham,' she mumbled. 'I'm the jeweller.'

'Hello, Laura-the-jeweller,' he replied, his gaze grazing over her. 'I'm Alex-the-ex.'

Rob drew up alongside them both, a leather holdall under each arm and wheelie cases in each hand. 'Make yourself useful, Alex,' he muttered in an unfriendly tone.

Alex flashed an amused grin at her as Rob stalked into the house. 'Guess I'd better get the rest of the bags,' he said, releasing her finally with his eyes. 'See you in there, Laura-the-jeweller.'

Laura shot into the chalet as if she'd been prodded with a red-hot poker and walked through a roomy porch, banked on both sides by deep bench seats with at least half a dozen pairs of ski boots sitting on racks and various skis and poles pinioned to the walls. She didn't see the stray shoe that someone had kicked off in their race for the best bedroom and lurched into the main body of the house inelegantly, falling straight into Orlando, who was talking in a low voice in rapid Italian with a sensational-looking woman.

Orlando caught her by her elbow and straightened her up quickly before anyone else saw.

'Thanks,' she said gratefully, looking back to the porch and seeing a solitary python stiletto that she'd clocked Sam wearing earlier.

'Laura, here you are! Let me introduce you to Isabella, Alex's fiancée.'

'Hello,' Laura nodded, shaking her hand briskly and taking in her laughing brown eyes – the chocolate counterpart to Alex's – and lithe, angular figure. Laura didn't need to see the two of them side by side to guess at the chemistry between them.

'*Ciao*,' Isabella smiled, doing her own visual sweep.

Alex followed her in with the remaining bags, dropping them dramatically in a heap, arms outstretched.

'Hey!' Orlando cried, rushing to rescue his pale blue leather Connolly bag. 'Mind my duty-free!'

'You should have carried them in yourself, then. What else are all those extra muscles for?' Alex quipped, wandering over to a tray of glasses and handing one each to Isabella and Laura. 'Ladies.'

Laura sipped it tentatively as she began to look around her. The chalet wasn't anywhere near as small as she'd thought from outside. In fact – she wandered over the stone floor to the balustrading and looked down – they were on a mezzanine above a double-height sitting room.

'Come on, let's get you settled,' Alex said, leading her over to a wide stone staircase in the right-hand corner that, gently and in no rush, took them down to the main living areas.

Laura rotated several times at the bottom, taking in the vast exposed stone chimney wall and the pale, limed wood walls that appeared to have been cut and laid like bricks. The floor was wooden but barely visible beneath a massive pale grey evenly patchworked ponyskin rug, and acres of plum velvet sofas were blanketed with taupe cashmere throws.

It was all Laura could do not to take her clothes off and rub her skin against the sumptuous textures like a horse in hay.

'Got it! Got the sheep,' Kitty called, panting as she emerged from another staircase that apparently led to yet another floor below and coming to stand by Laura. 'Like it?'

Laura nodded. What words were there to describe this? 'It's very nice' wouldn't really cut it.

'Sorry. I tried to get you the cow, but Sam beat me to it. And I really thought I had a chance against her in those shoes, too.'

'I kicked them off,' Sam crowed, appearing behind her.

'How many bedrooms are there?' Laura asked, just as Cat and Rob reappeared, wondering if this meant she was going to be on the sofa after all . . . Rob had changed out of his suit into jeans and a grey cashmere jumper. It was the first time she'd seen him not wearing a suit and he looked a lot more rugged, his curls untamed and flopping forward at last, and a distinct five-o'clock shadow across his jaw.

'Ten,' he said, walking past her towards the kitchen. Laura turned, taking in the glossy seal-grey units and row of five burgundy oversized drum lights hanging from the ceiling. Two uniformed women were busily and silently arranging canapés on long silver platters.

'Oh.'

Cat smiled at her as she wandered over to the sound system and turned Coldplay on to blare through the chalet.

She had taken off her sumptuous fur accessories but her pedicured feet looked just as expensive on the ponyskin rug. She had a jade-green polish on her toes that on anyone else would have looked tacky, but against her honey-brown skin and contoured jeans it looked high-fashion edgy.

Laura felt clumsy just standing up, compared with the easy, oiled way Cat moved, wiggling her shoulders and hips unselfconsciously to the music. 'It's so kind of you to let me come along this weekend.'

One of the maids came over with a tray and Cat took a drink from it. 'Nonsense! *I'm* so excited to get to meet one of Orlando's new friends. He's one of my favourite people in the world, you know,' she shrugged. 'You must be pretty special. He hasn't stopped telling me how witty and funny you are.'

Laura gulped her drink, feeling woefully unwitty.

Rob came over and Laura watched the way his eyes lingered on Cat's face as if they were taking a rest there.

'Have you had this chalet very long?'

'Three years this Christmas?' Rob replied, his intonation indicating he couldn't be sure exactly. 'I bought it for Cat as a surprise.'

'You bought Cat this chalet as a *Christmas present*?'

'Why do you sound so shocked?' he asked. 'You've bought your boyfriend the beach hut.'

Laura tried not to laugh at his sincere expression. As if the two properties could be remotely compared to each other!

'Ooh, tell me about your boyfriend, Laura,' Cat said, her green eyes keen and interested, as the beats of '*Viva La Vida*' made the floor vibrate beneath their feet. 'I want to know all about you.'

The maids began wandering around with the canapés and

Laura accepted one enthusiastically. She was surprisingly hungry, and realized she'd only had half-glasses of champagne to drink since arriving at the airport – not that Sam or Orlando were showing any signs of slowing down. If anything, they were only just getting started, their bodies beginning to move to the music. Isabella was standing by the fire with Alex, one arm slung languidly over his shoulder as she spoke quietly in his ear. Laura watched as Alex smiled and kissed her lightly on the lips, then took her by the hand over to the others, his eyes flitting briefly over at Laura, Cat and Rob.

'There's not much to tell,' Laura shrugged uneasily. 'His name's Jack. We live in a tiny fishing village called Charrington in Suffolk.' She ran out of information. 'We have a dog called Arthur.'

'I love dogs,' Cat sighed. 'I'm desperate for one, but Rob won't let me.'

'Don't make me out to be the bad guy,' Rob protested. 'You know perfectly well we could have animals if you chose to stay at home. But you're always so busy flitting between Surrey and London and here and God only knows where else. We're never in one place long enough to eat, much less keep pets.'

Laura saw Alex flop on to the velvet sofa next to Sam, pulling Isabella down on to his lap. She watched as Sam tucked her legs beneath her, her flaming hair clashing gloriously with the sofa as she regaled them all with a story that made Orlando slap his thigh with laughter. She could almost see the group rebonding, tightening like a knot.

Cat's sigh pulled her attention back and she saw that Cat was shooting her a conspiratorial look. 'See what I have to put up with? He's so unreasonable.' Her hair swished silkily around her shoulders with every shake of her head and Laura resolved to practise with her own in the mirror later. 'So, do you work?'

Laura nodded, her eyes meeting Rob's briefly as she wondered how much to leave out. 'I'm a jeweller, actually.'

'You mean you actually *make* the jewellery yourself?'

Laura nodded.

'I can barely make a sandwich.' Cat smiled. 'Or the bed!'

'Laura's been featured in the *FT* magazine,' Rob added.

'So then you're talented as well as shockingly pretty and witty!'

'Oh no I'm not . . .' Laura faltered.

'I *knew* that would make you blush,' Cat grinned. 'You are crazily modest. Do you have anything I can see?' Her eyes flitted over Laura's hands and face and neck, looking for rings, necklaces, earrings. But she was wearing only a watch.

'No, I . . . I never wear jewellery myself.'

'But why not?' Cat puzzled.

Laura shrugged.

'But you could be your brand's best ambassador,' Cat pushed, echoing Fee's sentiments entirely. (Oh, Fee would be so proud if she knew!) 'Do you have any sketches I could look at?'

'Everything's in my studio.'

Cat smiled, determined not to be brushed off. 'Well then, I'll just have to come to your studio, won't I? We could go for lunch.'

'That would be lovely,' Laura said quietly, overawed by the interest Cat was taking in her.

'Hey, Cat!' Orlando called over. 'Why are you hogging Laura? She's my guest, you know.'

'Tch, look at that! We're fighting over you already – it's far too exciting to have some new blood in the group!' Cat winked, sashaying over to them.

Frangipani wafted behind her as Rob and Laura watched her go.

'Well, it doesn't look likely that I'm going to get to interview anyone tonight. They all look like they want to unwind, and I'm pretty tired,' Laura said quietly as Cat stretched out on Orlando's lap. 'If you can just let me know where I'm sleeping, I'll head to my room and get out of everyone's way.'

Rob frowned at her. 'Don't be ridiculous.'

'I don't want to intrude—'

'You're not intruding.'

'Okay, but this is a gathering of your closest friends and I'm here to work. It's only natural that—'

'Laura, you are a guest and as welcome here as anyone else – you don't have to hide yourself away this weekend. It might make Cat suspicious.' He cracked a wry smile. 'But I'll show you where everything is, anyway.'

He turned, leading her towards the stairway she'd seen the others come up from. It was significantly smaller than the one at the entrance and led down to a wide corridor with arched doors running along at ten-metre intervals on the left-hand side.

The first door was open and David, sitting on the edge of the bed, a BlackBerry in his hand, looked up sheepishly. 'Ah! Do you need me? I won't be a sec. Just got to dash off a quick—'

Rob held up his hands. 'No rush, David. I'm just giving Laura the tour.'

Relief washed over David's face. 'Super,' he said, looking back down at his screen.

'So this is the cow room,' he said briefly, giving Laura only just enough time to clock the chocolate-coloured quilted velvet bedspread and thickly padded curtains that puddled dramatically on to the leather floor. Laura spotted a heap of silk, chiffon and sequinned evening dresses already upended on the bed and felt a quiver of panic shoot through her. Exactly how formal was this weekend going to be?

Rob led her along to the next room. 'And this is the sheep room,' he said, opening a door to reveal a similar room in a creamy palette, this time with ivory sheepskin rugs everywhere.

Laura looked at him questioningly. 'Cow? Sheep?'

He gave an embarrassed cough. 'I made the fatal error of allowing my six-year-old niece to name all the rooms.'

Laura couldn't help but smile – a multi-million-pound chalet named after farmyard animals? 'I see. This should be interesting, then.'

'Yes,' he replied, not meeting her eyes. 'So Kitty's in here, and Orlando's in the next one.'

He opened the next door to reveal a butterscotch and cream colourway with gingham curtains at the windows. Laura looked at him quizzically. She couldn't work out how this fitted into the theme.

'Palomino pony,' he sighed.

'Very specific,' she giggled.

'Mmm,' he said, closing the door quickly. 'So that's this floor. All the rooms are en suite, of course.'

*Of course*, she echoed in her head, following him down another flight of stairs.

'And this is the spa,' he said, motioning towards a vast pool bordered with huge slate tiles and replenished by a flat, minimalist chute at one end, with wall-to-wall picture windows on the far side. Behind the pool was an arrangement of sofas with magazines – fashion, economic, current affairs – fanned across a low table.

'So down here there's a steam room, snow room and sauna, jacuzzi and a massage room. Both Sasha and Gemma, the house staff, are fully trained in shiatsu, Swedish, Thai, hot stone, reflexology . . . whatever you like. Just try to let them know the morning you'd like a treatment so they can order their schedules accordingly.'

'Okay,' she managed. She had absolutely no intention of indulging. She was here to work. 'What's a snow room?'

'It releases snow on you. It's like a steam room, but cold.'

'But *why*?'

'It reduces inflammation, amongst other things – helpful if you pick up a niggle on the slopes.' He pointed to a narrow corridor beyond the treatment rooms. 'The cinema's back there, and the staff's bedrooms are just beyond it, so I ask guests as a courtesy not to wander back there unless we've scheduled a film night.'

'Of course. Is my room down there?' she asked, thumbing the way.

Rob frowned at her. 'Of course not.' He turned and led her towards a door in the corner. He pressed a button on the wall and the doors pinged open. A lift!

She stepped in after him, aware of how tiny the space was. It couldn't really fit more than four people at a time and she kept her eyes up, away from the mirrors, as they sped up through the house.

'This is the top floor,' Rob said when the doors opened, and they stepped into a thick-piled carpet that almost swallowed her feet. Further along the corridor, she could see the stone floor and balustrade of the entrance hall. 'There are three suites up here.'

'I'm in a suite?'

'Yes. Well, you're going to need to work, aren't you, and there's more room in these. Plus they're quieter for the interviews.'

'Oh.'

He opened a door into a large room that was a symphony of dusty pinks. She couldn't help but smile. 'The Pig room?' she asked, arching an eyebrow.

Rob smiled back. 'I prefer to call it the Old Spot suite.'

'I'm sure you do.'

Rob pointed towards a door to their left. 'Cat and I are in the Leopard suite on the corner there.' Then he pointed to the right. 'And Alex and Isabella are in the Drake at the other end.'

'I think I can probably guess what they look like.' From the sounds of their room she wasn't sure she wanted to see it. *Leopard* suite? It sounded more Vegas than Verbier.

He walked further into the pink room and Laura followed him in, seeing her bags had already been brought up and deposited beside the wardrobe. The same muted pink velvet had been used for both the bed coverings and curtains, which had four rows of tiny pleated mushroom silk ruffles running down the centre panels, and a deeply pocketed slipper seat was positioned at the end of the bed. Laura walked over to the windows and peered down over the valley. The lights from all the other chalets twinkled beneath her like a starlit sky reflected in water. She could scarcely wait for morning to come and the view with it.

'There's a place for you to work at, obviously,' Rob said, indicating the antique George IV desk alongside the wall, 'and the bathroom's just over here,' he continued, pressing a button that looked nothing like a light switch but the lights came on anyway, revealing whisper-pink marble and a steam shower. 'And that's it. That's everything,' he shrugged. 'So at least you know where you are now.'

'Yes, heaven on earth,' she smiled, just as her mobile buzzed in her pocket. 'Oh, that'll be Jack.'

'Right,' Rob said. 'Well, I'll give you some privacy. Come back down when you're ready.'

'Actually, if it's okay with you, I will just turn in for the night, now I'm here. I've been working long hours recently and I'm really tired.'

Rob looked sceptical. It was barely nine o'clock, but she desperately wanted a warm bath, a painkiller and to curl up in bed. The first day 'on' was always the worst.

He looked at the phone still ringing in her hand. 'Fine. Breakfast is anytime from seven. The first lift opens at eight forty-five a.m.'

'Oh, but I don't . . . ski,' she said, but the door had already closed on her. Natch.

She pressed connect. 'Hi, Jack.'

'Hi! How's it going over there?'

'Fine. We only got here half an hour ago.'

'How was the journey?'

'Fine. On time.'

'Where are you? It sounds like you're in a club. I can hear Chris Martin from here.'

'I'm in my room. Everyone's up for a party downstairs, so I thought I'd have an early night.' Rejoicing, she didn't add.

'Uh-huh. Is it nice there?'

'Oh, you know . . . so-so.' Her hand brushed the silk velvet beneath her. 'How're things over there?'

'Yeah. I'm just waiting for Fee and Paul to swing by and we'll head off to the pub together.'

'Great. Send them my love.'

'I will.' A small silence bloomed. 'Bit chilly here tonight,' Jack murmured.

'Put another dog on, then.' Their house was so cold and draughty, it was their favourite joke. He forced a laugh for her sake.

'Arthur's looking at me as if I've done something to you.' His voice changed and she knew he was talking to the dog. 'Aren't you? Why are you looking at me like that? She's fine. Go and lie in your bed.' He came back again. 'He's missing you.'

'I'm missing both of you.'

'Are you?' His tone took her aback. Why would he doubt it? Of course she was missing them. But he'd been quiet all week since she'd presented this trip as a *fait accompli*, as though she had in some way thrown him over.

She heard the lion's head knocker rap sharply on their front door.

'Oh. That'll be them,' he murmured. 'I'd better go.'

'Sure. Have fun.' She heard Fee's distinctive laugh in the background as she used her own key to get in.

'Hey, Jack! You're so never gonna guess what just happened to *me*,' Fee screeched.

'I'll call you tomorrow,' he said quietly.

'Okay. Bye.'

Laura threw the phone on the bed, vividly imagining Fee blowing through the house excitedly in her Friday-night 'pulling kit' – skinny jeans and a scoop-neck red top with a

sparkly silver belt and vertiginous ankle boots. Almost immediately the vision of Cat downstairs – barefoot, languid and
creamy – swam before her eyes. She pulled off her socks
and looked down at her own toes sinking into the thick
carpet. They were as pale as porridge, the nails a bleached
albino that hadn't seen any kind of colour since her twen-
ties. It was lucky for her that Jack didn't care about things
like that. She wiggled them, wondering how they'd look in
jade green. Gangrenous probably.

She sighed, stripped down to her underwear and turned
the bath taps on before wandering back to the windows
again. She couldn't help it, even though she knew all she
would see would be the black of night. Just knowing the
view was there was enough to accelerate her pulse. She didn't
need to see it to feel it.

Her eyes began to make out the shadows of the mountains and she knew that being a spectator was going to be
the hardest thing about this weekend. Everything about this
place was a feast of the senses – the as-yet-unrevealed view,
the purer-than-pure air, the heady textures, the music pulsing
faintly now beneath her. It all felt strangely intense, as though
the colours were stronger, the tastes sweeter.

She was usually so meticulous about never putting herself
in the way of any kind of temptation, but this had been
unavoidable. The interviews wouldn't be completed otherwise, and with the money already spent . . .

She took a deep breath and exhaled slowly. She would be
fine. It was just a few days and then she'd be—

The door burst open and she looked up with a gasp. Alex
was standing there.

'Oh!' he said slowly, his two-toned eyes taking in the sight
of her in just her bra and knickers. 'Sorry – wrong room.'

'Th-that's okay,' Laura stammered, immediately pulling at the tawny-pink velvet curtains and wrapping them around her.

A couple of beats passed. 'Well, sleep tight, Laura-the-jeweller,' he said in a low voice.

'Yes,' she whispered.

He shut the door, but she didn't dare move, didn't dare drop her cover. Only when she heard a door close further down the corridor did she run across the room and lock herself into the bathroom. She told herself not to panic, but how could she not? Rob had told her on the plane that Alex and Isabella had arrived here last night. Which meant he knew perfectly well where his own room was. There'd been nothing accidental about it at all.

# Chapter Sixteen

The view was worth the wait. When Laura opened her eyes nine and a half hours later, she felt her soul shift at the glimpse of Alpine majesty that could be seen through the gap where she'd parted the curtains. She padded over the carpet and opened up the panorama, drawing back the curtains as if she was rolling back a world map. Below a deep blue sky, a scooped-out bowl was crested with jagged peaks, its sides streaked with miles of vertical runs.

To her delight, Laura saw she had a balcony and she grabbed the bathrobe from the end of the bed. Wrapping herself in it tightly and pulling on a pair of red- and navy-striped fleecy bed socks, she unlocked the doors and stepped out.

The cold was as breathtaking as the scenery and she shivered, pushing her hands deeply into her pockets as her eyes soaked up the view. It was as different from the flat, grey Suffolk landscape as it was possible to be, and it looked like the snow forecasts had been correct – there was foot upon foot of fresh powdery snow.

She looked down and saw that beneath her balcony was another that spanned the width of the chalet outside the sitting room, and a further three smaller balconies on the level below that. And to think she'd thought this place poky when they'd arrived!

She turned and leant back against the verandah to get a better look at what was, for a few short days, anyway, home.

'Morning.'

Startled, she looked to her right. Rob was sitting at a small table reading his paper on the neighbouring balcony, which appeared to wrap round the corner of the building, ensuring he got the sun from the east and the south. An espresso was steaming before him, sending tiny tendrils of warmth into the cold December sky, and he was already wearing his ski kit – gunmetal-grey trousers and a black thermal top.

'Hi.'

'Did you sleep well?'

'Like you wouldn't believe,' she said as it hit her for the first time that she hadn't woken once. She frowned. 'In fact, I don't think I moved,' she said, puzzled.

'Well, that's got to be a good thing, right?' he asked, watching her baffled expression.

'I'm just . . . not very used to it, that's all.'

'Poor sleeper?'

'The worst.'

'Me too,' he nodded.

Laura shook her head. 'I bet my insomnia's worse.'

'Is it a competition?' he asked wryly, going back to his paper.

Laura turned back to face the view again. 'It looks like you're going to have an ideal day for skiing,' she said, searching vainly for clouds.

'Yes. Chilly, though. We'll have to watch for ice.'

Laura looked back at him. 'You must know the runs here really well.'

'Like the back of my hand,' he said, looking up at the

frosted horizon. 'That's my favourite over there – Les Attelas. It's got some couloirs that are pretty extreme.'

She felt a shiver ripple through her. 'Do you do blacks?'

He chuckled, amused. 'Yes.'

'Off piste?'

'Mainly.'

'Oh.' She looked over at the balcony on her other side. Alex and Isabella's. The curtains were firmly shut and she wondered whether they were still sleeping or just not getting out of bed.

'So, what's your itinerary today?' Laura asked, wondering when she could grab people between skiing sessions.

Rob put down his paper, folding it in half. 'Well, we'll do a couple of the local runs first thing, just to let everyone find their legs. Then we're going to take the helicopter round to some of the drops on the back.'

'You've got a helicopter?'

'No,' he smiled. 'It's just a charter. Three hours' heli-skiing.'

*Just* a charter. She thought she was being flash when she hailed a cab.

'Then ski back, pop into town if we need to, get here late afternoon and allow everyone some R&R before Orlando's dinner tonight.'

'Does he know yet?'

Rob shook his head. 'We'll keep it quiet till we're all dressed and having drinks. Sam thought it would be fun to do Secret Santas as well.'

'Oh?'

'We're pulling names out of a hat at breakfast and it's confidential who you get. Also, you're not allowed to spend more than five euros,' he said, shaking his head in dismay as though he didn't think it possible to spend so little money.

He pushed his chair away from the table and stood up. 'Anyway, you'd better get dressed. You'll freeze out here in just that. I'll see you downstairs.'

'Sure,' she said, watching him disappear into his room and feeling no more enlightened as to the structure of her day than she had a few minutes ago. When was she supposed to grab everybody for their interviews? And would they really want to talk about Cat when they'd spent the day jumping out of helicopters and bombing down mountains? This might not be as easy as he'd led her to believe.

Everybody was already seated at the long table when Laura came down forty minutes later. Half that time had been spent trying to turn the shower on, the other half convincing herself to finally come out again. She'd have stayed in for hours if she could. After her complete night's sleep and the deep steam clean, she felt positively glowing.

She self-consciously pulled her belted cardigan tighter into her waist as everyone looked up at her approach.

'Morning,' David said in a jolly voice as he reached over for the freshly squeezed orange juice, his BlackBerry next to his water glass.

'Laura, I saved you a place!' Kitty called, patting the empty seat next to her.

Sam shot Kitty a look.

'Morning, everyone,' Laura mumbled as she sat down, aware of Alex opposite her, staring.

'Sleep well?' he asked, passing her a glass of juice.

Laura nodded without meeting his eyes.

'Honestly, I was tempted to sleep on my floor,' Kitty said through a mouthful of porridge sprinkled with sesame seeds, honey and chopped banana. 'Have you seen the sheepskin rugs in my room? I could lose one of the kids in them – like a gateway to Narnia or something. Actually, there's an idea . . .' she chuckled, making Cat, who was sitting next to Sam, shake her head fondly.

'You look like you slept well, Laura,' Cat smiled, spearing a slice of kiwi fruit.

'So well, thanks.'

'Can you pass the butter, Kit?' Rob asked.

Sam, dressed in a black all-in-one ski suit that she had rolled down to her waist, held a solitary cup of black coffee in her pale hands. Her hair flamed dramatically against her clothes, although she looked washed out and had dark circles under her eyes. Orlando was sitting next to her, looking just as bad, although just as chic in navy.

'What time did you two go to bed last night?' Isabella asked, merriment playing on her lips.

Orlando groaned. 'Four.'

David rolled his eyes and began scrolling down through his BlackBerry with a thumb, spooning his Frosties in with the other hand.

'You're not going to make us do Les Attelas, Rob?' Orlando pleaded. 'Tell me you will be kind.'

Rob shrugged. 'If you want to come all this way to play on the nursery slopes, Orlando, it's up to you.'

'You and I could *chat*, if you're not up to skiing yet,' Laura said hopefully, trying not to get Cat's attention.

Sam looked at Laura, then placed a hand on Orlando's arm. 'Stick with me, Orly. We'll get round together – somehow.'

Orlando shrugged back at her. 'Later, definitely, Laura – okay?'

Laura nodded and reached for the kiwi fruit.

'Right, well, seeing as we're all here, it's time to pull names out of hats,' Kitty said, reaching behind her and putting a small cardboard box on the table. 'I've put everyone's name in, so just pass it round and pull one out. Obviously, if you get your own name, put it straight back in, please, and take another.'

'Yes, Mum,' Sam said as Kitty passed the box to David on her other side.

Laura waited for it to go round the table. She would be the last to pull a name out and she hoped to goodness she got Orlando or Kitty. At least she knew them a little.

*Sam.* Dammit. Tucking it into her pocket, Laura reached for a croissant.

'Aren't you skiing today?' Isabella asked Laura from the other end of the table, her eyes flicking down to Laura's jeans.

'I don't ski,' Laura replied briskly before Sam could say it for her.

'Actually, I've arranged for you to have a private lesson this morning,' Rob said, sitting back as Gemma, the older maid, refilled his tea. 'You really can't come all the way out here and not even give it a go.'

'But . . .' She only just stopped herself from saying she was working. 'I don't have any kit with me,' she said lamely.

'You can borrow some of mine,' Cat offered. 'I keep loads of kit out here. Half of it I've never even worn.'

'No, I couldn't,' Laura cried, dismayed.

'Laura, it's fine. They're just clothes. I wear them a couple of times a year and we're about the same size.'

Laura didn't know how else to keep protesting without appearing rude. She could see Sam shooting 'get her' looks at everyone across the table.

'I've booked Mark for you,' Rob continued. 'He's excellent

– we always use him. He'll be here at nine o'clock. You usually have to meet at the Médran lifts, but seeing as you don't know the area, he's going to come here to get you.'

'Thank you . . .'

Kitty nudged her with her elbow as conversation around the table resumed. 'Lucky you,' she murmured. 'Cat's told me about him. Apparently, he's *gorg*eous.'

Laura nodded miserably. She didn't care what he looked like.

A ring at the door had Rob, David and Alex out of their seats in a shot. 'Right, that's our driver,' Rob said, throwing down his napkin as Sam and Orlando dropped their heads into their arms. 'Come on, look lively.'

Kitty and Isabella pushed their chairs out, and Kitty squeezed Laura's arm conspiratorially. 'Enjoy!' she whispered, her eyes glittering excitedly.

Rob looked across at Laura. 'We'll see you back here later. Mark will come and collect you in about half an hour, as I said.'

'Grab whatever you want from my room,' Cat smiled, rising like the sun to reveal chocolate-brown silk leggings and a matching polo neck. 'Honestly. It's better it gets worn than not.'

'Thank you,' Laura murmured, wondering how Cat managed to make knee-length socks look so good as she made out the lines of a tiny thong on her retreating bottom. She listened to the stomp of ski boots being stamped on in the porch and watched Sam slide her arms into the rest of her suit. It had a belt and fur collar on it, and she controlled her unruly hair with an extravagant wide fur headband. She looked just like a Bond Girl. Laura looked over at Isabella, who, in a matt silver belted jacket and skinny white trousers,

looked like a model, and at Kitty in her royal blue and orange
. . . Well, Kitty looked like a farmer's wife – on planks.

'Don't do anything I wouldn't do,' Sam said archly.

'Well now, that doesn't leave very much *to* do, does it,
Sam?' Kitty said, pushing her through the door.

'*Ciao, bella,*' Orlando sighed wearily.

'Take it easy, Orlando. You really don't look so good,'
Laura said sympathetically

'Why do I do it to myself?' he asked, throwing his hands
up in the air and stomping towards the door. 'Is not like I
am young any more. You know, this is what it is to grow
old, Laura! The body decaying—'

'Your body is *not* decaying, Orlando!' Laura chuckled. 'It's
the most undecayed body I've ever seen.'

'You?' he asked hopefully.

Laura nodded. 'Really.'

'No! You are being kind. You don't—'

'ORLANDO!' Sam bellowed from outside. 'Get your arse
in here now or we're going without you!'

Orlando heaved a sigh of regret and, saluting her, left.

Laura smiled. Poor Orlando – he really was a lover, not
a fighter. She listened to the sound of the car pulling away,
wondering how to get out of the mess she was in. Skiing in
Verbier was just about as bad as it got.

# Chapter Seventeen

The bedroom door closed with a discreet click, and Laura leant back against it, her eyes scanning the room in anticipation of the homage to Versace – but everything was a soft winter-white: the linen-hung walls, the huge eight-foot-wide bed, the curtains, the sofa along one wall. It was the muted, almost faded leopard-print carpet that gave the suite its name, and it was stunning, completely unlike the French–Swedish looks Laura was always seeing in the interior decoration magazines that she and Jack had scoured so reverently when doing up the cottage.

Light poured in from the dual-aspect floor-to-ceiling windows and she saw the fur yeti boots – one standing, one on its side – positioned in the sun like basking cats, the matching hat tossed casually on the seat of a tub chair.

The furniture in here was as fine as in her room, but the surfaces were cluttered with antique perfume bottles, and an enormous baby-pink powder puff had dusted the glass top of the dressing table slightly. Laura peered closer, inhaling the subtle scent. It was completely Hollywood, completely, contrarily Cat: when everyone else was wearing mousse foundation, it appeared she was using old-school, high-glam powder puffs.

Laura's eyes fell upon a silver-framed black-and-white

photograph of Cat and Rob on their wedding day and she picked it up. It had been a winter wedding, and the shot was a close-up: a white fur hood encircled Cat like celestial light, her emerald eyes were flashing, and her laughter was almost audible to her as Rob, so handsome in his morning coat, gazed at her with a smile on his lips and adoration in his eyes. Laura remembered the story he'd told her of how they'd met: a kiss had been their hello; a passionate, life-affirming kiss that had precluded everything and everyone – even the woman who had spent the previous eight years with him and must have all but picked out her ring. Laura swallowed at the thought of such an all-consuming love. It excited her a little, but it terrified her more.

She put the photo down again, and her eyes flitted quickly over the other silver framed snapshots. Cat and Rob leaning back in a Riva speedboat, water glistening behind them; Cat in a bikini, standing on a swing on a beach, her hair blowing behind her; Rob lying back on a picnic blanket, his arms behind his head as he stared sleepily at the camera . . . Laura could tell Cat had taken that one from the way he was staring into the lens.

She moved away hurriedly, unable to look such unadulterated happiness in the eye any longer. It made her feel like a snoop. Ski kit. That was what she needed. Cat had told her – practically ordered her – to get some from here.

She crossed the exotic carpet determined not to look at anything else – bedside table: water carafe; Berocca; reading glasses; baby names book, oops! – and flung open the wardrobe. Its contents glittered back at her like jewels in a box – extravagant evening dresses, many full length, shimmered lightly in the draught, sequins and embroidery catching the light; a fur jacket jostled for space; ten or more pairs of jeans in varying shades were folded in cubby holes, and more deluxe jumpers than Laura could count had been colour-coded for easy access. The ski-wear was at the far end of the wardrobe and looked like a one-stop ski shop – there were all-in-one suits (of the type Sam had been wearing), shiny padded coats – a few belted, others fur-trimmed – and skinny twill salopettes. How did Cat ever decide? What could the elimination process possibly be? Everything looked brand spanking new, and very expensive.

Laura's eyes were immediately drawn to a red all-in-one, but she just as quickly pulled them off it. The last thing she wanted was to stand out. She was just pulling out a discreet pale blue and white jacket and some white trousers when she heard the doorbell ring.

She dropped her head in despair. Her moment of reckoning had come.

Mark was standing on the mezzanine, leaning against the wall, texting, as she came out, still tying her hair back in a ponytail.

'Hi,' he smiled, taking in her designer get-up. The fit was perfect, the colours infinitely flattering. 'I'm Mark, your instructor.'

'Laura,' she nodded, shaking his hand.

Kitty had been right. He was crazy hot, with a ski tan she reckoned was probably year-round, day-old stubble and an all-American-type smile. He couldn't have been more than twenty-four; perfect for Fee, she mused. Far better than that Paul, anyway.

'So, Rob says you're a novice.'

'Not quite.'

'You're not a novice?'

Laura took a deep breath and shook her head. 'No.'

'Oh. How much skiing have you done before, then?' he asked, clearly puzzled.

'Quite a lot.'

'So . . . '

'Rob misunderstood. I used to ski. I don't any more.'

'Right. A bad accident, was it?'

Laura paused. 'You could say that.'

'So you lost your nerve?'

Laura didn't reply. She hadn't lost anything.

'Well, look, we'll start slowly. I'll treat you as though you're a beginner, and try to see where the lack of confidence shows – it might come out in the turns or whatnot – and we can take it from there. That sound okay?'

Laura nodded.

'Have you got your own boots?'

'No. I never would have come if I'd thought there was any chance of me skiing this weekend. I'm supposed to be working. That's why I'm here.' She bit her lip. 'I shouldn't be doing this.'

Mark paused, puzzled by her reluctance. Who didn't want to ski in Verbier? 'What shoe size are you?' he asked, walking into the porch.

'Thirty-eight.'

He crouched down and looked at the row of boots arranged in descending order by the benches.

'Okay, thirty-eight – let's try these. Sit down.'

Laura relaxed. They were red – an auspicious sign. She let him put the boots on her, quite prepared to curl her toes like a geisha if need be to make them fit.

'How do they feel?' he asked, snapping the last clasp shut around her ankle.

'Heavy.'

'Can you wiggle your toes?'

She nodded.

'What about round the leg? Do you feel like your legs can move?'

'No, they're pretty snug.'

He stood up. 'Right, now for the skis,' he said, eyeing the remaining pairs left on the racks. He picked up a set of carvers. 'We'll start you on these,' he said, opening the door and letting the cold air rush in. 'A hundred and thirty pounds?'

'What? The lesson?' Laura asked, patting herself for cash, even though she knew full well she hadn't put any in her pockets. She couldn't. Everything was too slim-fit, even for a fiver.

'No,' he grinned. 'Your weight. For the bindings.'

'Oh.' She shrugged. 'I'm not really sure.'

He nodded and went out. Laura followed him.

Mark fiddled with the skis using a small screwdriver, threw the skis on to the snow and held out his hand. 'Right, if you just step in,' he said, helping her to balance.

Laura slid her feet in and, as she felt the boots click into place, a feeling – old, familiar – stirred deep within her. She closed her eyes. 'Just go through the motions,' she told herself.

'Lean forward,' Mark ordered, holding her up. 'And to the side . . . Right. We're good to go.'

'Excellent,' Laura whispered sarcastically, eyeing the undulating terrain. The slope of the land circling the chalet was gentle, as though the gardens sleeping beneath the snow had been levelled and landscaped, but a hundred yards further on the ground dropped away and the wide open expanse fed in rivulets into the trees before connecting further on with the piste she could see from her balcony.

'Now, before we go anywhere, I want to see your posture and natural balance, so I'm not going to give you your poles just yet,' Mark said, tucking them under his arm.

Laura eyed them as she might eye up water in the desert.

'I want you to bend your knees and bring your weight forward . . . that's it. Now, twist from here,' he said showing her how. 'You use turns to control your speed on the descent. When you make a turn, always turn your upper body into the mountain, like this . . . very good. Use your shoulders to finish the shape . . .'

Laura followed his lead effortlessly through changes of weight and position.

'Okay. Now we're going to have a go at making our way over to the trees there,' Mark said, pointing with his pole. 'Don't worry! I won't expect you to ski through them. We can walk that bit. I just want you to slowly point your skis gently towards that tree over there. Try to think about keeping your skis straight so that the tips don't cross. And on my mark, you're going to come to a stop by doing a snowplough. Weight forwards, bend your knees inwards and push your heels out so that the tips of your skis make a point. Think you can do that?'

Laura nodded, determined to let him patronize her. It made it easier.

'Okay. When you're ready, then . . . I'll be at your side the whole way,' he said kindly.

Laura looked down at her skis, then towards the tree Mark had pointed out. In truth, she knew the gradient here was so gentle you could roll a baby down it, but she was still scared. She knew the second she moved, no matter how slowly, it would all come rushing back – the love, the passion, the thrill.

She tipped the skis forwards and to the side slightly, feeling the snow instantly slide beneath her.

'How's that feeling, Laura?' Mark asked as she glided smoothly over the powder.

Laura nodded, trying her best not to feel anything. The wind slipped over her skin and ran through her hair like water as she carefully turned her body one way then the other. She tried to concentrate on the cold in her toes instead.

'Okay,' Mark said after a while. 'Now begin to push your heels out. You'll feel the resistance against the snow and it'll slow you down to a— Oh! To a stop. Just like that. Well done.'

Laura looked around them. They had travelled maybe five hundred yards and were at the treeline. The paths weren't as narrow as they'd appeared from the chalet, but they weren't wide runs either.

Mark looked at her, considering. 'Do you think you'd be comfortable going through the trees here? Or would you rather walk? A lot of people get nervous on the narrower paths. It's not far to the piste. Maybe half a mile.'

'I'm happy to carry on,' Laura nodded solemnly.

'Okay, well, let's do the same again, then. Control your speed with your turns and move into a snowplough whenever you feel you're going too fast. I'll go ahead this time, and I want you to ski in my tracks, okay?'

Laura nodded and they set off again, moving into the shade of the trees and out of the wind. The firs were like giants, shooting up to heights of six metres or more, all fighting for the sunlight, which fell on to the forest floor in dappled spots. Everything felt enchanted; nothing could be heard except the swoosh of their skis. She sniffed and tried to think about the red tip of her cold nose.

Laura kept up with Mark easily, double-imprinting his S-bends with her own, never too wide or shallow, always on his line.

Mark turned to face her as they reached the side of the piste, his eyes noting the accuracy of her turns upon his. 'Right. We're at the highway now, so there are other people to think about. The first rule is that you always give way to the person—'

'Downhill from you – yes, I know.'

'Do you want to go into parallel turns?'

Laura shrugged.

Mark handed her a set of poles and ran her through the mechanics of the more advanced turn. She pretended to watch him closely, trying to quell the enthusiasm that was beginning to surge up in her. All she had to do was go from the top to the bottom. Top. Bottom. Up and down again. For one hour. And just not feel anything.

'Check it's clear uphill, then push yourself off. I'm going to follow you from behind, this time, to see how you're doing. Use a snowplough if the parallels feel too much, and don't worry, I'll be right behind you all the way. Just call if you want me to pull ahead, okay?'

But Laura didn't even pause to nod. Having sighted a clearing in the piste, she pushed herself off, sweeping on to the run in wide arcs, her body instinctively, gracefully moving in and out of the pull of the mountain.

'That's fantastic, Laura!' Mark called out behind her. 'Just keep going!'

But she scarcely heard him. The second she built up any

kind of speed, she had lost the fight. Nothing could stop her – she was free again, untrammelled, undamaged; so weightless she almost felt she could fly, just take off and feel the wind under her body.

All around her, other skiers were winding and weaving, bobbing and rising – feeling the same rush. For the first time in years, she felt part of something; felt part of the club again. She laughed with delight, feeling the strength in her muscles kick in as she worked them – *really* worked them.

But before she knew it, too soon, she ran out of mountain. She was too fast, too good. The slope levelled off and she and Mark slid to an easy stop at the back of the queue for the chairlifts.

'Wow, Laura!' Mark said, grinning and slapping her matily on the shoulders as she giggled delightedly. 'That was incredible.'

'I can't believe it,' she panted, looking back up at the piste, where the skiers looked like ants from this distance. She dropped her face in her hands. 'I can't believe I did it.'

'And with some serious style, too. Come on, out with it! What's your background?'

Laura hesitated as they reached the front and the chairlift scooped them off their feet and lifted them into the blue sky. 'I skied for my university.'

Mark narrowed his eyes. '*And . . . ?*'

Laura snuck a glance across at him.

'There's something else too, isn't there? I can feel it.'

She looked ahead. 'I was invited into the British Juniors.'

Mark's mouth dropped open. 'And you let me demonstrate a freaking *snowplough*? Man!'

'I didn't join, though,' she said hastily, rebutting his admiration. 'So where are we going now?'

'I'm taking you on to the best runs on this mountain.' He winked at her. 'You just became my favourite client!'

Two hours later, Laura's thighs were burning and her cheeks were hot pink, but she didn't want to stop. She'd lost the fight spectacularly. Up there, in the virgin snow, the passion had rushed down on her like an avalanche, burying her resistance, and she'd given herself up to it completely. It was too late now; it had been too late this morning when she'd glimpsed the peaks through her curtains. It wasn't just because it was a pretty view; the mountains were part of her. Something in her physical make-up, her DNA, remembered what her conscious mind would not allow: that she was happy here.

Faced with the off-piste, she'd made her deal in a heart-beat. she would ski this weekend. She would ski her heart out, pounding, carving, slicing and scarring the snow; she would write her signature on skis; she would bounce over the moguls like a buggy on the moon. She would give herself up to this exhilarating happiness, this unadulterated passion, here in the midst of strangers who knew nothing about her. She would stop being Laura Cunningham this weekend. She would be simply Laura-the-jeweller. For once, she was prepared to pay the price when the joy turned to torment and she had to parcel this up and hide it somewhere deep inside her.

'Look, still no white bum!' she laughed, showing off her spotless, snow-free suit as she and Mark readied themselves at the top of a black run. They had gone across to the far side of the Four Valleys ski area where it was quiet and hard core, and she'd taken everything he'd thrown at her in her stride – bump fields, woods . . .

'See you at the bottom!' she called out, pushing herself off and pointing directly downhill. She had no fear. She trusted her body's instincts on this in a way that she didn't on anything else.

'Hey!' Mark called, setting off after her and racing in her tracks. She only just beat him to the bottom, laughing so hard that she did, finally, topple over when she was almost at a stop.

She lay there, spreadeagled in the snow, her hands across her stomach as she laughed and laughed and laughed. She couldn't remember when she'd last been so happy.

'What have I created?' Mark chuckled, sidestepping over to her to pull her up. But a sudden wave of snow obscured Laura from his sight as another skier came to a dramatic stop between them.

'Do my eyes deceive me?' the skier asked, looking down at her. He pushed his goggles back and Laura found herself looking into those distinctive blue eyes again.

'Alex!' she exclaimed, propping herself up on her elbows.

'You said you couldn't ski.'

'No, I said I didn't,' she sighed. 'There's a difference.'

Alex shook his head. 'I've just watched you bomb down that run like a pro. He couldn't catch you,' he said, indicating to Mark.

'How did you know it was me?'

'Looking like that?' he asked, holding out a hand and pulling her up. 'Who else could it have been, Laura-the-jeweller?'

He held her hand for a beat longer than was necessary. 'So where are you off to next, then?' he asked, looking round at Mark.

'Well, actually, we're heading back to Médran. I've got

another lesson in a quarter of an hour.' He looked over at Laura. 'Unfortunately. I could ski with you all day.'

'I'll bet. Call this a job?' Laura teased as Mark grinned and Alex looked on.

Alex slapped him on the shoulder. 'Well, tell you what, you get back to your next lesson and I'll take Laura from here.'

Mark looked from Alex over to Laura. 'Are you sure? You're a great skier, but you don't know the runs yet.'

'No. But I do,' Alex insisted. 'The rest of us are meeting at Chottes for lunch, so I'll take her with me.'

'Is that okay with you, Laura? I'm very happy to take you back to Médran.'

Laura didn't hesitate. *As if* she was done for the day. 'Yes, it's absolutely fine. My legs are up for a bit more.'

'Aaah!' Alex grinned, slapping a hand over his chest. 'A woman after my own heart.'

Laura giggled as she shook Mark's hand. 'Thanks for everything. You've been brilliant.'

'No,' Mark argued. '*You* have. That was seriously fun.'

They watched him hop on the ski lift that would take him back to the resort.

'So,' Alex said, turning back to Laura. 'Alone at last.' A wicked smile crept on to his berry-red lips 'What *are* we going to do with ourselves?'

# Chapter Eighteen

Although it was only the first full week of the season, the heavy snow had drafted in plenty of skiers, and the restaurant was filling up by the time they got there. Laura had never been so happy at the thought of sitting down. If she'd pushed herself skiing with Mark, she'd practically skied for her life against Alex. They had taken five runs to get here, and on each one Alex had weaved round her, giving chase, recognizing in her the thrill of speed and knowing she couldn't resist the challenge. And she couldn't. Each time, against her own better judgement, she'd taken the bait, sometimes beginning her descent with a bluff, arcing across the plain in languid sweeps before suddenly pointing her skis downhill and crouching down to improve her aerodynamics. Other times she was off and speeding away before he'd got his goggles back on. But every time, she'd known that, for all her skill, he could still just about take her. He liked chasing her, but he liked catching her more.

Sticking their skis in the snow and unbuckling their boots, they walked into the restaurant, a traditional Savoyard-style chalet with rows of pine tables set out on various levels. Laura swept the room, looking for Rob, Kitty, Orlando and the rest. And Sam – where was she?

'Table for two,' Alex said to a waiter as they walked in.

Laura turned back to him. 'For two? But you said we were meeting everyone for lunch.'

'So I lied,' Alex said, his eyes challenging her as they had on the slopes.

The waiter, standing at their table, gestured for them to join him.

'Of course, if you want to ski the five runs back to where they're meeting, we can,' he shrugged.

'Back? You mean we were already there when you saw me with Mark?'

'I was just about to join them. But then I saw you laughing in the snow and what was I supposed to do? Share you with everyone else?'

They sat down. 'You know I'm living with someone,' she said as the waiter handed her a menu.

'I'd prefer not to think about it, actually.'

Laura couldn't help but laugh, enjoying his humour. She felt positively euphoric with the afterglow of her morning's exercise – her skin was glowing, her heart was still pumping double-time, and this badinage was uplifting and fun. 'Poor Isabella. I hope she knows what she's letting herself in for. When's the wedding?'

Alex motioned for some drinks. 'Yet to be decided. Summer, probably.'

'And how did the two of you meet?'

'Through work.'

She dropped her menu down and gave him an exasperated look. Blood. Stone. 'And what is it that you do?'

'I'm a sports broker.'

'Ooh. I bet you're popular with the lads in the pub, then.'

Alex agreed. 'I get to do what every little boy dreams of.'

'And Isabella? Is she a broker too?'

Alex shook his head. 'She's a marketing executive for Nike, Ronaldo's sponsor. Ronaldo's one of my clients.'

'Oh wow. So you're a *power* couple,' she said.

Alex sat back to let the waiter set down their drinks and a bowl of warm bread rolls. 'Hardly.'

'No? If I wanted tickets to the World Cup final, could you get them for me?'

'Sure, although it's not for ages.' He placed his elbows on the table and leaned in towards her. 'But is this really what you want to know about me? My job and my fiancée?'

'No,' Laura said, shaking her head, playing the game. 'What I really want is to know about you and Cat, Alex-the-ex.'

Alex sat back in his chair and studied her. 'Must we?'

'It's why I'm here,' she said, beginning to pick at a bread roll.

'I brought you here so that I could get to know more about *you* and how you learnt to ski like the devil. It makes me wonder what else you can do.'

Laura met his eyes and a zip of electricity flashed between them. 'I make killer jewellery.'

'You must do, if the rumours are right about what Rob's paying for this necklace of yours.'

'It's not merely decorative, Alex. It's going to tell Cat's life story.'

'You'd better give me an extra-big charm, then. I feature pretty heavily.'

'Oh, I'm sure,' Laura nodded, an amused smile on her lips. 'You're her first love, the boy who broke her heart. It makes you unforgettable.'

He slumped back in his chair, his eyes pinned on her. 'I want to know why you didn't say you could ski like that. You could have joined everyone on the heli-ski earlier.'

Laura shrugged. 'I'm not here to play.'

'So what are you doing out here now, then?' He gestured to the chalet they were sitting in, positioned halfway up the piste.

'Being polite.'

*'Polite?'*

She burst out laughing. 'What else could I do? There was no one at home for me to interview. Rob had arranged for Mark to give me a lesson so I couldn't keep protesting I'd be holding you all back, and Cat told me to wear her clothes so I couldn't plead that I didn't have any kit either. If I'd kicked up a fuss about still not going out in the face of all their hospitality, Cat would start wondering exactly what I *was* doing out here, and this necklace is supposed to be a surprise, remember.'

He shook his head. 'No. It's not that. There's something else. You're different. Something's happened to you since we left you at breakfast this morning.'

She leaned forward, pressing her weight on to her elbows. 'Ah, I see you're a conspiracy theorist,' she grinned, puncturing his truths with teasing jabs, her eyes sparkling.

He paused for a beat. 'I'll get it out of you, Laura.'

Laura held his gaze for a moment before looking down at her menu. If he persisted in staring at her like that, he might get more than just plain talking from her. 'Well, while you're busy giving me an exotic past, I'm going to order. I'm starving.'

He cracked a tiny smile. 'Then we must not delay. Appetite is like desire.'

Laura lowered the menu. 'Huh?'

Those eyes were pinned on her again. 'The only way to overcome it is to satisfy it.'

'I'm glad we're just in time, then!' a familiar voice snapped next to them. Laura looked up to find Rob clicking his fingers at the waiter to bring over another table. He looked down at Laura. 'And he's quoting Somerset Maugham, by the way. Don't be fooled into thinking the words are his own.'

'The sentiments are,' Alex muttered tetchily, sitting bolt upright as Cat, Isabella, Orlando, Sam, David and Kitty rocked up behind Rob.

'So this is where you're hiding!' Kitty grinned, grabbing the chair next to Laura.

Laura smiled at her, relieved to be rescued from Alex's attentions. She watched as Cat, looking particularly feline, unzipped her caramel-coloured suit and every pair of eyes in the restaurant swivelled over to her.

Rob practically threw himself on his seat, looking furious. 'What are you doing here, anyway? You knew we were all meeting at Marmotte.'

Alex shrugged. 'Hello, darling,' he said as Isabella came over and leant down to give him a kiss. 'I don't see what you're making such a fuss about, Rob. I ran into Laura on the way over and decided to take her to lunch.' He lowered his voice, throwing a discreet look over at Cat to check she wasn't listening. 'She does have to interview me, after all.'

Laura marvelled at how easily he told the lie. They both knew he hadn't had interviews on his mind.

'How did you know where to find us?' Alex asked.

'We ran into Mark. He said you were taking Laura to have lunch with us here.'

'Well, it's all turned out fine, then, hasn't it? We're reunited for lunch after all.'

'Give us another five minutes,' Rob said to the hovering waiter. 'And bring over some more *vin chaud*.'

Sam's eyes skidded over Laura's light blue ski-bunny outfit and pink cheeks. 'Had a fun morning?' she asked, still pale in spite of the day's exercise.

Laura straightened up and looked her straight in the eye. 'Yes, thanks. Fabulous.'

'Bully for you,' Sam muttered, lunging at the bottle of wine that Alex and Laura had already ordered.

'Orlando? Was it fun?' Laura asked, turning her attentions to him.

'Two wipeouts.'

'Oooh, ouch!' She placed a sympathetic hand on his arm. 'Poor you.'

'My own fault. I am never drinking again. As you are my witness.'

'Not God as your witness, Orly?' Kitty asked from Laura's other side, smiling indulgently.

'Let us not be hasty,' Orlando said, a smile growing on his lips. 'I say "never", but I mean . . . "until tonight".'

'We'd better not make this a long lunch,' Sam sighed wearily, lighting a cigarette. 'We've got to get Laura back now. That's going to take some time.'

'Oh, don't worry about me, please.'

Sam snorted, arching a plucked eyebrow at Laura's newly assertive behaviour. 'You think you can keep up, do you?'

Laura fixed her with an even stare. She was actually going to enjoy this. 'You know, Sam, yes, I think I just might.'

By the time they'd skied back – everyone almost falling over as Laura zipped past them effortlessly – and stopped off in town to buy their Secret Santa presents, it was getting dark.

They fell through the front door, laughing, pink-cheeked and half drunk, unzipping their top layers and unbuckling their boots in the porch. Sam – first through – was surprised to find a large Christmas tree set up by the windows in the sitting room, a box of decorations sitting alongside it. 'A delivery for you, Rob!' she called.

Laura hung up her jacket carefully as Cat stripped back down to her thermals. 'Cat, I just want to thank you again for lending me this kit. It's amazingly kind, and completely unexpected.'

'If I had known you were such a great skier, I might have thought twice,' Cat smiled. 'You made us all look bad out there today. And my bum doesn't look half as good as yours in those trousers,' she chuckled, patting her lightly on the bottom. 'No fair,' she winked.

Laura laughed, not taken in that Cat thought *she* looked good, and kept her trousers on as she walked down the stairs, unlike the others, who had stripped down to catwalk-ready thermals. Cat looked lean in chocolate silk long-johns, Isabella cosy-cool in pale grey ribbed leggings, and Sam was in a Dolce & Gabbana knitted reindeer-print playsuit that was almost inducing an on-the-spot heart attack in Orlando – she was wearing a pair of navy opaque tights over white knickers. Not a good look. The fact that Kitty was also staying covered up suggested she felt she had just as much to hide as Laura.

Laura joined Kitty by the sixteen-foot tree and peered into the box of decorations, curious to see how the Other Half decorated Christmas. She was guessing it wouldn't feature tinsel or plastic reindeer.

'I thought we could all decorate it later, when we have drinks,' Rob said, leaning over the mezzanine and addressing them both. Laura looked up. He had stripped down too and was wearing a black cotton vest that revealed muscles that were clearly primed to cope with more than just off-piste skiing. He hadn't shaved from the day before and the two-day-old stubble glinted like metal filings. From this distance – with his hair dishevelled and the delight of a hard day's skiing reflected in his eyes – he looked more like a logger than that stiff, polished businessman who'd knocked at her studio door and Laura found herself thinking this rugged look suited him better. If she was Cat, she'd keep him here all year round, so that he'd stay looking like that – vital, strong, happy. 'It's something of a tradition,' he added.

Laura realized she was staring and nodded quickly. 'Great.'

He smiled and headed off to his bedroom.

'A sixteen-foot Christmas tree? It seems rather extravagant for just a weekend jolly,' Laura murmured, turning back to Kitty, before remembering that if he didn't count a chartered chopper as an extravagance, a non drop blue spruce was hardly going to cause him any sleepless nights.

'I know,' Kitty sighed, reaching into the box and twirling a Lalique crystal snowflake on the end of her finger. 'He doesn't realize, of course. He's not trying to be flash.'

Laura looked around them. Things had gone surprisingly quiet – at least for the moment. David and Alex were drinking beer and watching the Inter Milan versus Juventus match on the fifty-inch plasma screen; Cat must be in her room with Rob; and Orlando and Isabella had gone off to have the side-by-side facials they'd booked at breakfast.

'Hmm, I wonder where Sam is? Now would be as good a time as any to try to interview her,' she said quietly, just in case Cat should be approaching.

'Good idea. She'll either be in her room or in the spa, I should think. Drinks aren't till seven-thirty. I'm going to ring home. I'm dying to speak to the kids.'

'See you later, then,' Laura smiled, padding towards the smaller staircase.

It was quiet on the lower levels and Laura hesitated at the Cow-room door. It was firmly shut, and for a moment Laura worried Sam might be sleeping. She'd had scarcely any sleep last night, a morning's arduous exercise and a skinful of *vin chaud* at lunch. If she was resting, she would not be happy to be disturbed by Laura for a chat about Cat.

On the other hand, Laura was here to work, and in between skiing, massages, drinks and meals, exactly when was she supposed to get hold of everybody?

She knocked, weakly at first. Then, when there was no reply, harder.

'Sam?' she asked into the thick wooden door. 'Sam? It's Laura.' Gently she pushed the door open. 'I wondered if we could have our . . . talk.'

The bedroom was empty. Was she in the spa? Laura was just turning to go when Sam appeared at the bathroom door, dabbing her face with a towel and swaying ever so slightly, a glass of water in her hand.

'Oh. I thought I heard the door.' She was deathly pale and looked more like she'd spent the day sleeping in a coffin than skiing in the Alps. She took a sip of water and walked further into the room.

'Sorry, I didn't mean to intrude.'

'I suppose you want to talk about Cat?' she sighed, grabbing a hairbrush from the shelf next to her and bashing down her hair.

'Yes. But I can come back if this isn't a good time.'

Sam dropped her hands down and leaned heavily against the wall. 'No, no, let's get it out of the way,' she said, finishing her drink and throwing the brush on to the floor ready for David to step on later on his way to the bathroom.

'Come in and shut the door, then. Drink?' Sam asked, walking over to a table by the window and screwing the cap off a bottle of vodka and pouring it into her glass. Not water, then. Laura shook her head. It was too early for her.

'No, thanks. I've, uh, got a massage in an hour so . . .' she fibbed.

'God, yeah! There's nothing worse than drinking before one of those.' She added tonic water to the glass and took a sip. 'Remind me not to book one!'

Laura couldn't help but smile – Sam was nothing if not consistent – and she scanned the room discreetly, looking for somewhere to sit. It was very definitely a room of two halves. On David's side, his suits were hanging on padded hangers, his trousers were pressing, and the latest Robert Harris was sitting bookmarked on the table. On Sam's side of the room, savage heels poked out of perilous mountains of clothes, the make-up on the dressing table looked as if it had been thrown there, and copies of *Grazia* and German *Vogue* were tossed on top of a tower of plastic-coated files.

'Is it okay if I sit here?' Laura asked, pointing to a chair that was covered in a shaggy Mongolian fur jacket – the designer version of the type she'd been considering for Fee – and six pairs of jeans.

'Just shove all that stuff on the floor,' Sam said, flinging herself on to the bed and lighting a cigarette.

Laura lifted it all up in an armful and carefully placed it in an artful heap on the floor.

'So how does this work, then?' Sam asked, blowing out a puff of smoke and staring at Laura through the grey haze. 'Are you going to take notes?'

'I will later.'

Sam's eyes narrowed. 'Is that accurate enough?'

Laura ignored her. They were hardly legal documents. 'Tell me how you and Cat met.'

'We were at Manchester together. Shared a room in digs. Hated her on sight.'

'Why?' Laura asked, hoping she wasn't going to answer every question in bullet points.

Sam hiked up her eyebrows. 'You've seen her. I was totally determined to hate her,' Sam smiled, flicking ash into a cup beside the bed. 'Make her life a living hell. Why should I give her an easy ride? I thought.' She gave a sudden devilish laugh.

'Why did you want to do that?' Laura asked mildly, resisting the impulse to fling open the door and sprint away from this insanely competitive woman.

'Ugh, I can't bear these pretty-pretty girls who waft around simpering and being decorative.' She shot Laura a contemptuous look. 'I thought Cat was one of them.'

'But she wasn't?'

Sam's eyes met hers, fierce and shining. 'She was a soulmate. Up for anything. "No" wasn't a word that was in her vocabulary.'

Laura watched her take another sip of vodka. 'It sounds like you had a wild time.'

'Oh yes,' Sam said, retreating further into the memories. 'I reckon if you went back to Manchester now and mentioned our names to the students, they'd know who we were. We *ruled* that campus.'

Big claim. Big ego, Laura mused. 'What was your crowning moment together, would you say?'

'Flying our knickers from the flagstaff on graduation day,

definitely,' Sam replied without hesitation. 'Knickers were our signature back then – well, knickers and *lack thereof*. We had set up a little business on the side making them out of old scraps of Liberty fabric. They had tied ribbons at the sides that pulled apart. Every girl on campus wanted a pair. It made us some pocket money,' she shrugged, swinging a toned leg restlessly. 'Of course, every other blonde you meet is making them now, but we were the first. Agent Provocateur even took them for a while.'

'Really? So has the business continued?'

'Hell, no. There's no money in it. No serious money, anyhow. We jacked it in as soon as we graduated.'

Laura wondered what qualified as 'serious money'– her yearly income as a day rate? 'You said you shared a room in the first year. Did you live together after that?'

'Yes. We got a house near campus, shared it with some rowers. The rugger buggers wanted us too, but we weren't stupid.'

'Because they'd have wanted to sleep with you?'

Sam shrugged, cradling the glass. 'We'd pretty much slept with them all anyway. Except for the tight-head prop. Bad skin.' She shook her head. 'No, the problem was, we couldn't cook. Literally. One of them had to show us how to make pasta with Dolmio. "See the bubbles, girls? That means the water's boiling. Now, pour in the pasta . . ."' She giggled. 'It was a tactical decision to keep us fed. They were so into their diet and shit.'

'Did they know you were using them?'

'We would throw occasional benefits their way,' Sam said, her eyes flashing provocatively as she continued emptying her glass in increments.

Laura tried not to react – it was exactly what Sam wanted

– but it was hard to reconcile this portrait of Cat with the one she'd heard from Kitty and Orlando, or indeed with the woman she'd met upstairs. From what Laura had seen so far, Cat was charming, generous and understated. She had gone out of her way to make Laura feel comfortable here, complimenting her and opening up her house, her wardrobe . . .

Sam took a drag of the cigarette and held it in front of her as though assessing it. 'Man, we were useless. If they were away, we scarcely ate . . . We served toast at a dinner party once.'

'No. You didn't,' Laura protested, dragging her attention back to Sam's recollections again. It was likely that Sam was guilty of the same mistake as Kitty – ramping up the past into a higher-voltage version of itself. In Kitty's case, it was a sisterly nostalgia. In Sam's, wistfulness for bygone wildness.

A hint of a smile threatened to splinter Sam's face. 'We'd made everyone dress in black tie too. It was hilarious.'

'What did you both study?'

'Cat did economics. I did French and German.'

'So you didn't have any lectures together?'

'No, thank God,' Sam drawled. 'That was the only time I got any sleep.'

Laura chuckled. She might not like Sam, but she had to admit she had a certain dangerous allure.

'You have to go abroad if you do languages, don't you?'

'Yes, in the third year. Six months for each country.'

'It must have been hard for the two of you being apart when you'd been so close.'

'We made sure we kept in touch. I was staying in Méribel for the French component, autumn through to Easter. Cat came over in the holidays and we worked as chalet girls together.'

'But surely you have to be experienced cooks to work as chalet girls?' Laura asked, watching as Sam swapped hands and drank from her vodka glass.

'In theory. But our housemates taught us six recipes the week before we left – ham omelette, carbonara, chicken cordon bleu . . . a different meal for every night – and we just put cereal, yoghurts and croissants from the bakery out on the breakfast table every morning. No one ever sussed we didn't even know how to mash a potato.'

'Did you remain close after university?'

Sam took a deep drag, closing her eyes as she let slip a ribbon of smoke. It was her final puff and she dropped the stub into a water glass beside the bed – there were already four butts in there – and let her arm drop heavily down the side of the bed. 'We moved to London together and shared a flat for three years until Cat met Rob.'

'Where were you living?'

'Putney. We lived in the same street where *Mr Ben* was set, actually. D'you remember that TV series? It was about a bloke going into a fancy-dress shop and whichever outfit he put on, he'd be magically transported to that particular world. Well, we called ourselves the Bennies. Every party we had there was fancy dress.'

Laura straightened up excitedly. This could be good for inspiration.

'What themes? Do you remember?'

Sam closed her eyes, thinking, and for a moment Laura wondered whether she was going to sleep. 'One was called "Come as something beginning with P"; another was "I can't believe you're wearing that!" They were the best. All-nighters. The police got called out every time.'

'What did Cat go as?'

'Oh, man . . .' she sighed. 'She was a pilchard at the P party – wrapped herself in tin foil for that one. And she was . . . um, a . . . oh God, yes! It was classic! She was a diver at the other: wetsuit, snorkel, mask, flippers, the lot. It was a nightmare every time she had to go back to the kitchen to get refills. She worked out that walking backwards was best,' Sam chuckled, taking another slug of her drink.

'Random.'

'Funny!' Sam insisted.

'Did you go on holidays together too?'

'A couple of times. We went inter-railing around Europe together the first summer at Manchester. We had to wash in train terminals and eat—' She pulled a face.

'Oh no,' Laura squirmed. 'Please don't say out of bins.'

'No. But we'd go round the cafés in the evenings, sweet-talking the waiters into giving us the sandwiches they were going to throw out. Even now I can't look a prawn sandwich in the eye.'

'It sounds hard.'

'It was excellent! The first time in our lives we were both completely and utterly *free*,' she exclaimed vehemently, punching the word out so that her shoulders lifted off the pillows. 'Pity it didn't last,' she murmured, staring sightlessly at the far wall.

'Are you still as close?'

Sam gazed down sadly at her hands. 'I live and work in Frankfurt. What do you think?'

'Oh. You must miss her.'

'More than *you'll* ever know,' Sam said, her eyes fluttering up to Laura's and back to the far wall again. Laura flinched at the sudden aggression in her voice and she noticed Sam's eyes were glassy and unfocused. Laura glanced over at the vodka bottle – it was half empty. How many had she had since she'd been down here?

'Well, I am trying to know,' Laura said in a conciliatory tone. 'That's the point. Rob wants it to—'

'Tch, Rob wants, Rob wants,' Sam mimicked. 'And Rob always gets what he wants, doesn't he?' She held up her glass, staring into the clear liquid as if it showed her the future. 'Well, not this time, if you ask me,' she murmured.

'What won't he get?' Laura asked, confused. It was clear Sam was drunk.

Sam stared over at her. 'That's for me to know and you to find out,' she taunted.

Laura sighed. 'I think I'd better leave you to rest,' she said, getting up from the chair. She got to the door, stopped and turned back. 'Can I just ask you one more thing?'

'Ssshoot,' Sam slurred, waving her drink dangerously about.

'What three words would you use to describe Cat?'

Sam's eyes narrowed like a cat's. 'Ooooh, good one!'

Laura waited as Sam stared intently at the opposite wall. 'When you're ready.'

'Wild, definitely.'

'Uh-huh.' Another long pause.

'. . . Fearless.'

'Yes.' There was another minute's procrastination. 'Wild, fearless. What else?'

'. . . Angry,' Sam mumbled.

'*Angry?*' Laura echoed. 'What is she angry about?'

But her only reply was the sound of the glass tumbling on to the leather floor as Sam finally, thankfully, passed out.

# Chapter Nineteen

Laura pressed her forehead to the glass window, enjoying the feel of the cold seeping into her skin. It was already dark outside – the only colour in the sky a streak of magenta back-lighting the mountains – and she was watching the lights switching on in the valley one by one.

Cat. Angry. She kept running the two words together in her head, but they just didn't fit, repelling each other like two magnetic norths. From everything she'd seen of Cat – relaxing with friends in her own home – she seemed anything but: she was languid, chilled-out, gracious.

There was a quick knock on her door.

'Come in,' she called, turning.

Cat came in, smiling. Talk of the devil! Or rather, angel. She was wearing a bathrobe – her waist looked tiny in the tightly cinched belt – and her hair was twisted back in a casual chignon. 'It occurred to me that you might not have any swimwear with you,' she said, holding up a small white bag. 'I've never worn this. It's still got the tags on, so you can have it if you like – if you don't think it's a bit "eww" to wear another woman's swimwear, that is.'

Laura chuckled. 'God, you really are the consummate hostess. You think of everything! Thank you so much. I didn't have anything with me, no.'

'Well, bless Orlando. He's great on advising which mois-
turizer will help with chapped skin out here, but an actual
packing list? Hmmm.' She walked towards the bed, looking
at the clothes Laura had laid out ready for dinner. 'Is that
what you're wearing tonight?' she asked.

Laura looked over at her outfit: jet-black skinny Gap cords,
a scoop-necked silky T-shirt from Next with black bead
details, and a new pair of fabulous red-heeled shoe-boots
that she'd been hiding from Jack for about two months at
the back of the wardrobe. They were open over the foot,
with large, looping semicircles meeting and lacing in the
centre – far too dressy for the rest of the outfit, but she didn't
care. She didn't have anything else that would go with them
and she'd been so desperate for an opportunity to wear them.
She knew it wasn't an ideal outfit for tonight, if Sam's cornu-
copia of satins and chiffons was anything to go by, but it
was the best she could cobble together, given that Claudia
had omitted to mention the dress code for Orlando's party
plans.

'Yes.'

Cat looked back at her, a diplomatic smile on her beautiful face. 'It's black tie.'

'I know, but . . . well, I haven't got anything else that's
suitable,' she shrugged. 'It's the best I can manage.'

Cat nodded kindly, but Laura could tell this best wasn't
good enough. 'Well, I'll leave you to get ready for the pool,'
Cat said. 'We're all going down to the spa for a bit before
we get ready for drinks. Come down if you fancy it.' She
put a knowing hand on Laura's arm. 'Please don't hide away
in this room. I know it's hard coming into a noisy group like
ours, but we're all really glad you're here – especially now
you've shown yourself to be an Olympic-standard skier. Poor

Sam's spitting nails!' She laughed. 'And Rob's so excited. He's just been raving about your technique on the moguls, actually. He gets so frustrated skiing with me – I'm happiest on blue runs, you see. He calls me Scaredy Cat.' She rolled her eyes. 'Anyway, see you downstairs, maybe.'

'Okay. I'll be down in a minute, then,' Laura promised.

She waited for the door to close and peered inside the bag, pulling out the red bikini with mounting horror. It had a tiny triangular top and skimpy side-tie bottoms and wasn't much bigger than her hand. And she had little hands.

Laura's bare foot touched the slate floor and she hugged herself protectively in the bathrobe. The first person she saw was Isabella, wearing a leopard-print bikini and reclining on one of the loungers, a folded towel over her eyes. Beside her was Cat, doing the same in a white bandeau bikini that showed off a tummy that was not only enviably toned but also tanned, paying no respect whatsoever to the fact that it was the middle of December and most people's tummies – in both colour and muscle tone – resembled bread sauce.

Laura sat down next to them, wordlessly sucking her tummy in and deploring Jack's generous helpings, which meant her ribs didn't show. She was just arranging a towel to place over her eyes when Kitty raced past in a low-leg, muscle-back navy Speedo.

'Hey! Where are you going?' Laura asked her.

'Into the snow room. Alex and Orlando have promised to buy one each of Joe's pigs next Christmas if I manage five minutes in there.'

'Oh well, if it's for the pigs . . . a noble cause,' Laura quipped.

Kitty laughed. 'I could buy the kids' stocking presents

alone from the proceeds. Want to join me? I could do with the moral support.'

Laura did – it sounded a laugh.

'Actually, Kit, I was hoping to take the opportunity to get to hear a bit more about Laura's jewellery business,' Cat said, peering from under her towel and placing a hand on Laura's arm. 'You don't mind, do you?'

The disappointment in Kitty's eyes was only evident for a moment before it was blinked away and replaced with a careless smile. 'Sure thing,' Kitty shrugged, running self-consciously towards the snow room and leaving Laura behind with the cool girls.

An hour later, there was a knock at Laura's door. She had just finished painting her toenails, having bought some red polish in town earlier – as much as she was inspired by Cat's edgy green, she didn't fool herself that she could pull that look off – and was wondering how to achieve a 'smoky eye' with a four-year-old Rimmel kohl stick and some Avon eyeshadow which was damp from the steam in the bathroom. She usually didn't bother with make-up at all, but tonight . . . well, tonight she felt different. She had completely stepped out of her own skin today and it was as if she had champagne flowing through her veins. She felt enervated, fizzy and giggly all at once, perpetually ready to laugh and smile, to chat, to flirt even – she'd held her own against Alex earlier and was revelling in Cat's attention. And she didn't want to give these feelings up. At least, not yet.

'Come in,' she called, sitting on the stool by the dressing table.

Rob popped his head round the door. 'Hi. Cat wondered if you could just nip in to her for a moment?'

Laura nodded, but before she could get up, he checked the corridor was clear and stepped into the room, quickly shutting the door behind him. 'Before you go, have you managed to speak to anyone yet?' He leant against the wall looking immaculate in his dinner jacket, his eyes glittering with excitement at the surprise he was planning.

'Well, I managed to get some time with Sam.'

'Ah, and how was our quiet friend? Soft and fluffy, obviously.'

'Yes, exactly.'

'You've heard her nickname, I assume?'

Laura shook her head.

'The Blazing Assassin.'

'I didn't think it was going to be the Easter Bunny! Well, she was very forthcoming. She told me all about her and Cat's time at Manchester, inter-railing, moving to London together . . .' She pulled a face. 'It sounds like they were pretty scary, to be honest.'

'They were quite a force to be reckoned with. If I'd met Cat when she was out with Sam, I'm not sure I'd have approached her.' He was silent for a moment. 'Actually, no, that's not true. I'd have walked through fire to get to her.'

Laura stared at him in amazement as he realized what he'd said and looked away in embarrassment. She hadn't ever met anyone who was so clearly as besotted with his own wife as he was. Other people's, certainly . . .

'Cat must be a strong character herself,' she said. 'To be able to take on a woman like Sam.'

Rob considered for a moment. 'She is. But Sam's not really as tough and scary as she makes out. A lot of it's an act.'

'Oscar-winning act.'

'What else did she say about Cat? I'm intrigued.'

'Well, it would appear your wife was an atrocious cook. I can only assume the way has been up since then?'

'In that we have a cook.'

'Oh!' Laura giggled. 'Well, as a chalet girl, she had a repertoire of just six recipes – pretty much all ham and cheese.'

'You mean like raclette, omelette, fondue . . . ?'

'Something like that – and those were the glory days! Toast kept her alive up until that point, I gather.'

'She still loves hot buttered toast.'

'But did you know she served it once at a black-tie dinner?'

Rob's face crumpled with laughter and again she saw exactly how he had looked as a twelve-year-old boy, just like she had that first day in her studio. Most of the time he came across as so bluff and buttoned-up, but occasionally she glimpsed this other side to him – relaxed, witty, playful, teasing . . . Rob-lite.

'It sounds like it went really well, then.'

'. . . Yes.' She had survived at least.

He smiled, looking around the room casually. 'And are you comfortable in here? Is there anything you need?' His eyes fell upon the red bikini drying in the bathroom and she saw him notice that she had made up the bed with hospital corners, the towels were hanging as she'd found them, and all her make-up was still packed in her bag, not strewn across the counters like Sam's, which had looked more like an explosion in a flour factory. A baffled expression registered across his features at how little she had settled herself in.

'It's like being in a five-star hotel. It's amazing. I can't believe you live here,' she said nervously.

'Huh, I wish. I'd stay here all winter if I could.'

'But you come out for weekends and holidays, don't you?'

'Yes, as much as possible. It never feels enough, though.

I love the mountains,' he said, walking across to the windows and looking out. The curtains were still open and Verbier sparkled back at them like diamonds on velvet.

'Me too.'

He looked back at her. 'So what's the story on you, then? I'm curious. Why did you lead us all to believe you couldn't ski?'

'I didn't mean to mislead anyone. I just genuinely didn't think that *I* would be skiing this weekend. It was very much a work trip in my mind.'

'And now?'

'Still a work trip. I'll get it all done, I promise.'

He laughed lightly. 'No, I mean . . . I don't know. You just seem completely different out here,' he said, his words echoing Alex's at lunch. Was the distinction really so obvious?

'Well, so do you. We're all off-duty and relaxed now,' she continued, trying to close down the conversation and stop the questions before they started. 'But look, I'd better go and see what Cat wants. I don't want to keep her waiting.'

Rob looked disappointed that the conversation was being cut off so obviously, but he followed her as she got up and walked to the door.

'See you downstairs, then,' he said, bounding athletically down the stairs.

Laura nodded and knocked on the door of the Leopard suite before opening it. Kitty was sitting on the tub chair, looking lovely in a greeny-grey chiffon dress, which had puffed sleeves to show off her freckled arms and a gold lace detail at the bust. Her gold sandals had been kicked off and she was hugging her knees.

Cat, who had been peering into her wardrobe, walked over to the bed and held up a dress. It was black lace with a slash neck and sleeves that stopped at the elbow. There was a pronounced waist and a skirt so tight it looked like castors were going to be the only way of getting about in it.

'Oh wow,' Laura breathed reflexively, feeling infinitely flattered that Cat was asking for *her* opinion. 'Yes. Whatever else you were going to show me – yes. It has to be that one.'

'I'm glad you said that,' Cat laughed, winking at Kitty. 'Because it's got your name on it.'

There was a moment's delay as Laura realized Cat's intention.

'It's got someone called Dolce & Gabbana's name on it,' she protested, and Kitty threw her head back, giggling like a schoolgirl. Laura watched her, amused – she was sure the snow shower had gone to her head. Brain freeze?

She looked back at Cat. 'It's gorgeous, Cat – and I really do appreciate the thought, but I couldn't possibly. That dress is worth more than my house, and I've already worn quite enough of your clothes today. I'll get by with what I've got . . .'

Cat stared at her evenly, all friendliness suddenly gone. 'Laura. This is Orlando's fortieth-birthday dinner. He's been on the brink of a breakdown since he turned *thirty*. The absolute only thing that's going to get him through this crisis is if we, his girls, dress top to toe in Italian labels – basically his porn – and dirty-dance with him till dawn.'

'Do it for Orlando,' Kitty pleaded.

'Orlando, the pigs . . .' Laura muttered at her. 'Tch, talk about a pound of flesh.'

Cat took a step closer to her, swinging the dress ever nearer.

'I'll try it on,' Laura said finally, reaching out for it. 'But it probably won't even fit.'

'Oh, it will,' Kitty said, as though the dress wouldn't *dare* not to.

'Well, thank you,' Laura said, turning to go.

'Not so fast.' Cat planted her hands on her hips. 'We're not done yet.'

A small shiver danced up Laura's spine. She looked down at Kitty – dear, sweet, gentle Kitty – who merely shrugged. 'We're not?'

Cat swept an arm towards the bathroom, and Laura spied Gemma in there, her sleeves rolled up and towels in her hand.

'What's she going to do?' Laura mumbled.

'Don't worry, Laur,' Kitty smiled, jumping off the bed and propelling her along. 'There's actually nothing she can't do. She's got more strings to her bow than Gwyneth Paltrow's nanny.'

Laura swallowed hard as Cat and Kitty shoved her into the bathroom with Gemma and shut the door behind her. She shrugged at Gemma helplessly. 'I didn't know Gwyneth Paltrow's nanny played the violin.'

# Chapter Twenty

An hour later, Laura wandered back into the corridor, bouncing into the walls as she turned the dress in her hands through all angles as though it was a riddle that had to be solved. It was too beautiful. She'd feel too conspicuous in it. She steadied the towel turban Sam and Kitty had insisted she wear back to the room, even though Laura was sure it would undo all Gemma's excellent work. And it was excellent. Flawless.

The towel fell, lopsided, to the side of her head, and she had to rebalance it in one hand. She could already hear the men chatting in the sitting room below the mezzanine. Alex and Isabella's door opened as she passed, and they wandered out, stony-faced.

'Hi,' Isabella muttered in a distinctly frosty tone as she passed by, looking glorious in a skimpy gold lurex knitted dress that clung to her like a prayer. Alex said nothing, just gave the merest shake of his head, as if to say, 'Don't ask.'

'See you down there,' she said quietly to their backs.

The dress fitted like a dream. It clung and curved and positively kissed her body, and the red shoe-boots gave it a modern edge that was more like Scarlett Johansson than Anita Ekberg. Laura smoothed her hair nervously as she turned the final curve of the staircase and stepped into view.

Everyone was dressing the tree. Kitty had accessorized herself with a length of thick purple tinsel wrapped round her neck like a feather boa. 'I never get to do this at home. The kids always hog the tree in our house,' she trilled, artfully draping a particularly bushy length of silver tinsel.

'*Tinsel*, Rob?' Sam asked, wearing a tiny hot-pink strapless dress that was so tight it was more like a compression suit, and spike heels that doubled as weapons and had no doubt left dot-to-dot pinpricks on the leather floor of their bedroom. The memory of her slurring and waxy on the bed a couple of hours previously was like a distant dream.

Rob shrugged. 'My niece insists. She says it's not a proper Christmas tree without tinsel.'

'That's the lovely thing about Christmas,' Kitty said. 'Everyone's got their own rituals. I've started up a tradition of making gingerbread stars with the children to put on our tree, even though every single year, Pocket and the ducks eat them all. I tell myself I won't bother next time and yet come the first weekend in December I still find myself elbow-deep in golden syrup and cookie-cutters,' she sighed, blowing out through rosy cheeks. 'Here, Isabella – can you pull this round? Try and get it to go in and out of the branches.'

Isabella began weaving the tinsel to Kitty's instructions, whilst Sam looked disapprovingly at a bunch of glitter-covered laminated snowflakes that were clearly home-made. 'You know, there's such a thing as giving kids too much power, Rob,' she drawled.

It was Orlando who saw Laura first, and his jaw dropped open with a Latin appreciation of the female form that completely disregarded whether he wanted to sleep with her or not.

'*Bella!*' he whispered, causing the others to turn too, their glasses in their hands. They all looked so imposing in their tuxedos, like one of those group shots of impossibly good-looking men in Ralph Lauren ads. The room fell silent. Except for Sam.

'Fuck me!' she hollered. 'Who the hell did that?'

Laura instantly turned to race back up the stairs and hide under her duvet, but Cat – laughing delightedly in her red silk wisp of a dress that gave less coverage than lipstick – ran over and grabbed her. 'Doesn't she look amazing?' she asked, tugging Laura towards them all.

The entire group was open-mouthed – even Kitty, who had been in on Cat's plan. The combination of the new hair and dress was dazzling.

'Well . . .' David blustered, breaking the silence first. 'Blonde s-suits you.'

'*Suits* her?' Cat repeated, rotating Laura on the spot. 'Look at her! She's a goddess.' She nodded proudly, squeezing Laura's arm in her own. 'My work here is done.'

Laura glowed happily, delighted by Cat's response.

Sasha came over with a drink for Laura and Cat handed it to her. Laura looked at the glass in her hand and at the same time the other small badge of belonging – the grey Chanel polish that Cat had insisted was painted on her fingernails – shone under the lights.

'Thanks.' She looked up hesitantly at the others, keeping her eyes off Isabella. She could feel the chill six feet away. The men were all gathered in front of what appeared to be a giant box that had been shrouded in red velvet. Some present!

Rob nodded. 'Stunning, Laura,' he said chivalrously, but with a look in his eyes that suggested he wasn't merely being polite. 'And the, uh . . . . dress, too.'

'Thanks to Cat,' she murmured, sending her mentor another grateful smile. Looking at everyone gathered here, she only now realized how woefully underdressed she would have been in cords.

She felt Alex's eyes on her and turned to look at him, intrigued to know *his* reaction – she bet he was a man who loved blondes – but he walked away and started fiddling with the stereo system with his back to her. Inexplicably, her spirits dived.

'Nice shoes,' David commented.

Laura bit her lip. 'Yessss . . . Something of a weakness. My boyfriend doesn't strictly know about these yet,' she smiled.

'Oh, you're one of those! You buy something and hide it for a few weeks, and then, when your other half asks if it's new, you reply, "What? This old thing? I've had it for ages, dear."'

Laura held her hand up. 'Busted!'

'Yes. We have one of those in our house,' he said, glancing over at his dramatic wife, who was delicately – with one hand – placing stripy Murano-glass baubles on the tree, completely unprepared to put down her drink, even for a minute. 'Here you go,' he said, handing her one of the Lalique crystal snowflakes.

Laura took it nervously, hoping it was insured. It didn't matter quite so much when a bauble slipped off the tree at home – their decorations were from Debenhams.

'Well,' Rob said after a while, once the tree was as decorated as the guests, 'there's a tree in my house and snow on the ground. But neither Christmas, nor – and I can't believe I'm going to say this – skiing are the real reason we're here.' He took a step closer to the red velvet box and put his hand on the cloth. 'We've had to keep this a secret or we knew he'd never come, but Orlando – happy fortieth, buddy!' And with a quick tug, he pulled away the velvet to reveal an ice bar, sculpted into the shape of the Eiger, with a luge funnelled through the middle.

'What? No!' the big man gasped, as everyone cheered and burst into a spontaneous round of 'Happy Birthday'. 'I am so old,' he wailed, real tears sliding down his cheeks as he touched a finger to the ice.

'Yes, but so handsome,' Kitty smiled, patting him on the arm.

'And so buff,' Sam drawled. 'I'd so do you if you weren't gay.'

'You promise?' he sniffed.

'Totally,' she grinned, and Laura caught the mischievous glint in her eyes. Was this what Rob had meant earlier, when he'd said a lot of her outrageous behaviour was an act? She was playing for laughs? Or gasps?

'Anyone in the mood for some games? Let's play charades!' Kitty half asked, half ordered. A murmur of easy assent rose up.

'So long as you go first,' Cat said, tucking herself into the corner of a sofa.

Kitty stood patiently in front of the fire, whilst everyone settled themselves on the cushions. The flames leapt behind her excitedly, trying to compete with Sam's hair.

Laura sat down – perched on one buttock, the skirt was so tight – squeezing herself between Isabella, and Rob and Cat. Sam, David, Orlando and Alex were on the opposite sofa. Alex kept staring at the floor, clearly lost in thought. He looked stupidly handsome in his dinner jacket and appeared to be brooding about something. He had mimed the rendition of 'Happy Birthday', she'd noticed. She looked at Isabella, next to her, and saw the same scowl on her pretty face as his. No doubt ferocious arguments were part and parcel of their passionate relationship – the making up would be so much more fun. Laura sighed as she looked back at Kitty. She and Jack never argued. Ever.

'Book,' Rob said beside her as Kitty mimed the signals. '. . . and film . . . three words.'

'First word . . . *The*,' David cried, and Kitty stabbed a jubilant finger in the air at him.

'I can see *you've* got a degree, darling,' Sam quipped.

'Second word,' Orlando murmured. 'Third syllable.'

Kitty pulled a stroppy face and slumped her shoulders.

'Moron!' Sam cried.

'Zombie,' called Cat.

'*The Hunchback of Notre Dame!*' Orlando shouted, jumping to his feet.

'That's five words,' Isabella reminded him.

'Oh.' Orlando sat back down again dejectedly.

'Teenager,' Alex muttered.

Kitty began stabbing her finger at him.

'Teenager?' Alex repeated, surprised to have got it right.

Kitty pushed her hands together, leaving just a small gap between them.

'Teen?' Rob asked.

Kitty nodded vehemently. It was clearly an agony for her to keep so quiet.

'. . . Second word, second syllable . . . ' Sam murmured, sitting on the edge of the seat, her competitive spirit well and truly awakened.

Kitty got down on all fours and began padding around, panting.

'Dog,' Isabella called out.

Kitty lifted her left arm and held it like a paw.

'Sick dog! Poor sick dog! Lame dog!' Rob called out, not pausing for breath.

'Amputee dog!' Sam hollered.

Kitty quickly stood up again and put on a serious face. She pretended to put something in her ears and then held an imaginary thing in front of her, moving it around and cocking her head.

'Vet!' Orlando shouted so loudly it could have set off avalanche warnings all through the resort.

Kitty, pointed at him delightedly.

'Vet . . . teen . . .' Rob murmured.

'*The Velveteen Rabbit*!' Laura blurted out.

Everyone looked at her in amazement, and then back at Kitty, who let the sounds explode out of her.

'YES!!!!!' she cried, running over and hugging Laura tightly as though she'd successfully answered the riddle from the troll who was going to eat her babies.

'What is it?' Sam asked Alex. 'I've never even heard of it.'

'It's only, like, the most perfect children's book ever,' Kitty cried. 'It completely defines my childhood. Cat and I used to read it together all the time, didn't we?'

Cat nodded enthusiastically.

'We liked the bit about him playing in the garden with the real rabbits best, remember?' Kitty continued.

Cat held her breath, desperately trying to think back and recover the details, but it was fairly obvious that she couldn't remember it. Kitty's face fell.

'Yeah, well, like I said – never heard of it,' Sam drawled.

'That's because you were *born* twenty-one,' Kitty muttered, taking a seat on the sofa. 'Right, your go, Laura.'

Laura froze. Now *she* had to stand in front of all of them and mime? In The Dress? Oh, why had she answered? Why couldn't she just have kept her big mouth shut?

She shuffled up to the fireplace, staring at the flames for inspiration. It had to be something literary and clever. She couldn't come up with that Jilly Cooper she'd read in the Peak District last August, even though that was the last thing she'd read . . .

Sam was pouring herself another glass; David was pointedly covering the top of his glass with his hand; Isabella was talking to Orlando – who had crossed sides and was now sitting in Laura's place – in what appeared to be furious Italian; and Cat was miming something to Alex. Only Rob was watching her intently, ready to play the game.

She turned to him, but Rob looked down at his feet as she did so. As Alex looked up, though, he met her gaze this time, and she felt her stomach flip as his eyes held hers. Something had changed. The chemistry between them had been obvious from the second she'd stepped off the coach, and he'd not squandered a single opportunity that had come his way to flirt with her. But this was different. The playful teasing had gone. Manners could hide a lot of things, but not desire, and somewhere she knew a clock had begun to tick.

'Get on with it,' Sam said restlessly.

Laura looked away, her pulse rocketing as she sensed the shift between them. Quickly she held up five fingers, feeling all her defences kick in.

'Five words . . . song . . . ' Kitty cried, enjoying herself immensely. 'Second word . . . *The.*'

'Fourth word . . . small word,' Sam said through narrowed eyes. '*The, and, if, of, me, you, it* . . .'

Laura pointed at her suddenly.

'*It!*' Rob called.

Laura shook her head.

'*You,*' David tried.

Laura pointed to him, nodding.

'Blank *the* blank *you* blank,' Cat murmured.

'Fifth word . . . small word again . . .' David said, watching her hand movements keenly.

'*The, and, if, of, me, you, it, is, are, yes, no* . . . *No!*' Kitty cried as Laura pounced on her.

'So blank *the* blank *you no*?' Isabella asked Orlando. 'I don't understand this game.'

'Me neither,' Orlando shrugged. 'The English.'

'*I've* got it,' Alex drawled, looking straight at Laura and reading her secret message clearly. '"Better the Devil You Know."'

Laura nodded, clapping him feebly.

'What? *Kylie?*' Sam sneered snobbishly.

But Laura ignored the dig. Isabella was still in her place and she had to sidestep over Alex to take his place as he got up for his turn. There wasn't much room between the sofas and the coffee table, and he placed his hands on her arms to steady her, gripping her with slightly stronger pressure than was needed so that she looked at him as he passed only inches away from her. She willed her eyes to clearly back up the point she had just made, but his stopped her with such giddying intensity that it made her heart gallop. Before his eyes had said, 'Stop.' Now they said, 'Go.'

She sat down on the sofa, trembling, her eyes on her hands as everyone else started to decipher Alex's own efforts: another song . . . five words . . .

Laura knew it just two words in: 'Take a Chance on Me.'

# Chapter Twenty-One

Dinner was formal, but the people eating it were not. Orlando, Kitty, Alex and Sam were fast getting screaming drunk at the far end of the table, playing a chaser drinking game with shots from the ice bar, and David was making Cat and Isabella laugh by wiggling an After Eight off his forehead and into his mouth without using his hands. A thin smear of chocolate down his face traced its progress like a snail's track.

'Do you have a party trick?' Rob laughed, turning to Laura, sitting next to him, as it fell off David's cheek and he had to begin all over again.

Laura hesitated.

'You do!' Rob cried.

'No, I—'

'The fatal pause,' he argued. 'It's proven that when we're about to lie, we inhale deeply to buy more time and get the story straight.' He picked up his wine glass and drained it. 'Come on, out with it. I'll tell you mine.'

'Promise?'

'My word is my bond,' he said solemnly, thumping his chest with a fist.

'Mmm,' Laura hummed, unconvinced. They had all been drinking for hours. In fact Sam and, to a lesser degree, Orlando had scarcely stopped since they'd got here, and there was hedonism in the air. The bass from the Arctic Monkeys was making the crystal glasses vibrate, and everybody was talking faster and louder, arms were gesticulating wildly, hair was being tossed like hay.

She felt emboldened. 'Well, when I was at university, I could drink from a glass without using my hands.'

Rob shifted position, intrigued. 'Show me, then.'

'*Show* you? No! You said to tell you.'

'Show me,' he insisted firmly, and she wondered how she'd ever won that first argument in her studio.

Laura shook her head.

'Don't force me to play the "sing for your supper" card,' he said slyly. 'It wouldn't be gracious.'

'Oh God . . .' Laura's shoulders dropped. The pink velvet bedroom and private spa weren't coming for free after all. 'Well, I'd need a beer glass or high-baller.'

'Gemma!' Rob called.

Gemma, who was clearing the dishes in the kitchen, looked up.

'*Oui, Monsieur Blake?*'

'Could you bring over a beer glass, please?'

It was in front of Laura in under a minute.

'What shall we fill it with?' he asked. 'Beer, cider, mulled wi '

'Beer.'

She watched as he filled the glass carefully. Then she positioned the glass on the inside of her right elbow, bringing her forearm in but keeping her hand arched back, so that the glass became wedged between her lower and upper arm. Slowly, she raised her arm. The glass wobbled precariously a few times and then tipped just enough for her to drink from it.

'Ha-ha, bravo!' Rob cheered as she drained it. 'Very impressive.'

Laura burst out laughing, relieved to have pulled it off. It had been years since she'd done it last. 'God, I've gone straight back to being a student!' she moaned.

'Not looking like that, you haven't,' Rob remarked.

The comment appeared to take him by surprise as much as her. '. . . Right, well, your turn,' she said quietly, trying to cover their mutual embarrassment.

Rob stared at her intently and she wondered whether he was just trying to get used to her being blonde.

'Go on!' she said bossily, feeling herself begin to blush.

'I just did,' he grinned.

'What? What did you do?'

'Watch.' He stared at her again.

Laura scowled. 'You aren't doing anything.'

'Aren't I? Watch my ears,' he instructed, thoroughly amused by her indignation.

Laura looked at his ears and realized they were pulling backwards and forwards, without a muscle in his face moving.

'Oh my God!' she tittered. 'That's hilarious! How do you do that?'

He shrugged.

'More to the point, how did you ever discover you could do it? How do you *accidentally* twitch an ear?' she teased.

'Prep school,' he sighed, draining his glass. 'A wonderful institution. Equips you with so many vital life skills.'

'Hmm. Well, I can do better than that.'

'Oh really? I find it hard to believe anything can beat my ears.'

Laura stood up, chuckling. 'Watch this.' Kicking her shoes

off, she laced her fingers together so her hands were clasped behind her back. Then she curled herself forwards, shimmying her shoulders left and right, so that – slowly – her arms began to inch past her hips, over her bottom and down her thighs so that she was crouched into a small ball. Carefully, checking her balance, she lifted one foot, and then with a triumphant smile stepped back over her hands and brought them up to her tummy. 'Ta-da!'

'Right!' Rob laughed, clapping at her enthusiastically. 'It was a good effort. And I applaud your spirit, really I do. But it's obviously time to bring out the big guns.'

He unlaced his shoes and stood up in his dress socks, shrugged off his jacket and threw it over the back of his chair, then took off his cummerbund too.

'I'm not playing strip poker with you, Rob!'

He doubled over with laughter. 'That's later.' Clasping his fingers together, he stretched his arms up; Laura was able to see the riff of his abs through his shirt but tried not to look. Then he rolled his head and pressed each ear down to each shoulder a couple of times as if he was warming up for a race.

'Tch, in your own time,' she muttered, inwardly dying to see what he was going to do.

He shot her a glittering look as he reached his right hand down to his left foot and brought it up so that his leg and arm looped diagonally across the front of his body like a loose strap.

He paused and looked up at the ceiling for a second.

'What's wrong? Chickening out?'

'Just trying to remember the excess on my insurance.'

He inhaled slowly twice, and then, with a sudden burst of explosive power, jumped in the air, keeping his hand and foot connected but bringing the right leg through them.

Laura screamed with delight, jumping up and clapping wildly. 'The human skipping rope! I tried to do that for *years*! I almost knocked a tooth out trying once.'

'You need to be a prime athlete to do that.'

'Oh! Like you, you mean?' she giggled.

'Exactly,' he nodded, sitting down again, his thighs splayed wide on the chair as he relaxed, a freshly refilled glass – thanks to Sasha – in his hand.

'As if! You're just a namby-pamby broker boy.'

'I'm not a broker,' he said. 'I'm a fund manager.'

'Whatever. You're still City soft.'

He glared at her in outrage. 'Touch that!'

Laura looked down at a flexed thigh.

'No, thanks,' she said with a convincing look of distaste, but Rob grabbed her hand and planted it on his leg. It was indeed not soft. 'And?'

He sat back, regarding her. 'You don't rise to the bait, do you?'

'Huh?'

'I just taunted you about not being a prime athlete. When actually you and I both know full well that you were.'

She froze. 'And how do you know that?'

'Mark told me.'

'Mark's got a big mouth, then.'

'As well as a way with the ladies.' He watched her closely.

Laura shrugged. 'Has he?'

Rob leaned in closer. 'Why would you tell him and not me?'

'It was relevant to the moment. He'd tried to teach me how to do a snowplough. There have to be limits.'

Rob grinned. 'Tell me about your skiing. I want to know. I *demand* to know,' he added dramatically.

Laura looked at him for a moment. Why not? She'd already told Mark. 'There's not much to tell. I skied for my university—'

'Which university?'

'Bristol. I did well and was invited to try out for the British Juniors.' She shrugged. 'But I never got round to it.'

'Never got round to it? How does that happen?' he asked, incredulous.

'I graduated, got a job and ran out of time. Work took over my life and I just couldn't get the hours in on the slopes.'

'You gave up a place in the British ski team to *work*? You must really love making jewellery,' he said, sitting back and drumming his fingers on his glass.

'Actually, I wasn't a jeweller back then.'

His eyes flashed up at her. 'No?'

'I worked in corporate finance at Goldmans.'

Rob stared at her. 'Corp. . . So then how have you ended up making *charm bracelets* for a living?'

'They are very beautiful, very expensive charm bracelets,' she murmured. 'And I'm very proud of them.'

'Indeed. But . . .'

'I just wanted a life change, that was all.'

He shook his head. 'And I thought my wife was enigmatic. You've got more secrets than Whitehall,' he said, tapping the table between them.

Kitty suddenly launched herself into their orbit, landing on Rob's lap with a thud. 'Is this a private conversation or can anyone join in?' she beamed, red-cheeked from necking vodka with Orlando at the luge.

'Are you aware of the double life Laura leads?' he asked Kitty.

'It's not a double life. I live one life at a time, thank you very much.'

'Yes, right. So currently you're a jeweller in Suffolk who lives with her boyfriend and does up beach huts on the side.'

'Pretty much.'

'And she's got a dog,' Kitty added helpfully.

Rob nodded. 'I don't buy it. That seems a little too *quiet* in my opinion for a woman who was an extreme skier and took on the biggest boys in the City.'

'Life change, like I said. Tried it, it didn't work out. I much prefer my life as it is now, thanks.' She looked down at her watch. 'Talking of which, I'd better go check it's all still running in my absence. I need to call Jack. I'll be back in a bit.'

She walked over to the stairs, aware that the dress and drinking combined were making her wiggle, wondering if she was just imagining the weight of Rob's stare on her. Or was it someone else's entirely? She couldn't forget the loaded look between her and Alex earlier either. Was he going to 'accidentally' burst in on her tonight too?

Skipping up the steps, she let herself into her bedroom.

Nine missed calls. She rang home, wandering over to the windows and staring out at the full, promising blackness. She opened the doors as the dial tone beeped in her ear and stepped out on to the balcony, welcoming the sobering blast of coldness on her skin.

It was a still night. Barely a ripple of wind rustled the trees and the snow lay where it had fallen. She leant on the railings, just making out the strains of music coming from the town over the bass beat from downstairs.

'Laura?'

'Hi, darling,' she smiled, straightening up.

'Where have you been? I've been trying you for hours!' His tone was panicked and she picked up on his anger immediately.

'I'm so sorry. I meant to call before dinner, but I managed to fit in an interview with someone, and then it's been Orlando's birthday party so it's all been pretty full-on.'

'*Whose?*'

She could well imagine what Jack would make of a name like Orlando.

'You sound drunk,' he added. It was more of an accusation than an observation.

'Do I?' she asked, enunciating with extra care and giving herself away completely.

'You said this was a work trip!'

'And it is. But it's Saturday night, it's someone's birthday, and the interviews have to be a secret. The woman has no idea I'm speaking to all her friends about her. I have to make an effort to blend in, Jack.' She heard the pleading whine in her own voice and winced. When had *she* ever whined?

'Well, from the sounds of you, she'll have no suspicions.' Sarcasm wasn't his strong point and was therefore all the more shocking when he did employ it.

Laura rolled her eyes impatiently. 'Well, I don't see why it has to bother you. I'll bet there are a couple of beers on the table in front of you right now.'

He was silent. She knew he was right. She thought back to Alex and Isabella and how she'd imagined their arguments to be passionate and exciting. But this just felt soul-destroying.

'Jack, what is it? What's wrong?' she sighed. 'You've been off with me for days.'

'Nothing.' There was a long pause. 'I . . . Look, I'm tired and you're drunk. I'll speak to you tomorrow when we're both feeling better.'

'Okay,' she replied quietly.

'Night,' he said curtly.

She pressed 'disconnect', feeling frustrated, smaller and less blonde again.

The doors on the balcony below her slid open and she saw everyone pile on to the terrace, laughing and shrieking as they kicked off a midnight snowball fight. They were always playing, this group, always finding fun and the lighter side of life. She felt ten years younger when she was with them all. Laura watched unseen above them, her eyes on Alex's back as he aimed a perfect hit at Orlando's head. She watched the way Rob crept up behind Cat, snaking his arms around her slender waist as he planted a surprise kiss on her neck that didn't have quite the desired effect and made her leap away. She watched as David grabbed a handful of snow and shoved it down the back of Sam's dress, making her howl with rage.

Laura stayed where she was. She felt the pull to go down there and join them, but she knew that was exactly why she shouldn't. Speaking to Jack had been the reminder she needed. She had given herself a day out from her own life, but that was all it could be. Nothing more. She wasn't like any of them, no matter how much she might wish it to be true. She might be staying in a multi-million-pound chalet, but playfulness was a luxury she couldn't afford.

# Chapter Twenty-Two

The music was on max by the time she reappeared fifteen minutes later – loud, thumping dance tunes that were more redolent of Ibiza in August than Verbier in December.

'Where've you been?' Kitty asked her as she jived to David Guetta, heaving her very ample bosom up and down.

'Sorry. I was talking to Jack.' She smiled, taking in the parcels that had been put on to the coffee table, all in the same-sized boxes and wrapped in identical paper. Sam had been adamant that anonymity must be preserved, and Laura, for one, had been more than happy to stick by that rule. She didn't want Sam to know that she was her Secret Santa.

'Right,' Kitty said, motioning at everyone to come over so she could read the names on them – written in capitals to disguise handwriting – and dole them out.

'Okay, we'll open in a clockwise direction,' Sam ordered.

'Not that you're OCD or anything,' David joked, earning himself a slap on the arm.

'Isabella, you go first,' she went on.

Laura looked to her left, watching Isabella gasp and pull out a tiny red mesh thong that she twirled on her fingers, one eye arched suggestively at Alex. Laura looked away, knowing Isabella was beginning the first tentative moves towards rapprochement and suspecting she'd probably hear them through the walls later.

'Good God!' Kitty exclaimed, shocked. 'That would fit my daughter's Barbie!'

David was next, pulling out a glow-in-the-dark cock-ring. 'Uh . . . uh . . .' he stammered, blushing beetroot as Sam grabbed it in hysterics, crying, 'Oh no, it's far too big!'

Orlando opened his with trepidation, but he needn't have worried. Inside was a vintage collection of VHS fitness videos by Jane Fonda, Elle Macpherson and Cindy Crawford. He clutched them delightedly to his chest. 'You guys . . .' he beamed.

'Kitty, your go,' Alex said, sitting on the arm of the sofa.

Kitty took a deep breath.

'You don't have to inflate the box, Kits,' Sam said, making Kitty instantly splutter and blow the air back out again.

She pulled out a big red cape with a distinctive 'S' logo on it. 'Superman?' she said, puzzled, putting it on over her dress.

'Or Supermum,' David suggested, giving away his identity and earning himself, this time, a big lipsticky kiss on the cheek.

'Who's next? Right, Rob, your go,' Orlando said, picking up the MC duties.

Rob raised an eyebrow as he opened his, obviously worried that he too was going to find something that glowed in the dark. 'A magnum of Moët? This did not cost less than five euros!'

'But you're such a generous host,' Kitty blurted out before slapping her hand over her mouth and shooting a frightened look at Sam.

Rob laughed, leaning over and giving her a big hug. Kitty

wrapped her arms around his neck tightly and patted his back fondly.

'Ugh! You lot are bloody useless!' Sam shouted. 'That's two of you who've messed up now! What's the point of me putting all these rules in place if—'

'Shut up and open your present, dear,' David said calmly, eliciting a titter of giggles.

Sam rolled her eyes dramatically and started opening her box. 'So long as it goes, "Glug."'

Laura held herself dead still, scared to do anything at all that might give her away, such as breathing, blinking . . . Sam pulled out a battered copy of the book *How to Win Friends and Influence People*. Sam did not smile. 'Who in this room thinks I can't be charming?' she demanded in an ominously quiet voice. 'I am perfectly charming. Totally. Never a problem making friends. Never.'

'I think it's supposed to be ironic,' David said in a placating tone.

'I think it could well be meant to be instructive, actually,' Alex chipped in.

'Was it you?' Sam gasped, glaring at him, but Alex just held his hands up. Laura had a feeling he'd bought the red thong.

'You're the one insisting on this being a classified exercise, darling,' David riposted with infuriating calm.

'Alex, your turn,' Isabella said, smiling sweetly. She was definitely on the path to forgiveness – whatever it was she had to forgive.

Alex's face fell as he pulled out a silver-plated golf tee. 'Oh! It's, er . . . it's very . . . Wanna swap, David?'

'Absolutely!' David cried, almost throwing the luminous aberration at him. 'What a result!'

'Indeed,' Alex grinned.

'See? I wasn't lying,' Sam drawled. 'He knew it wouldn't fit eith—' But before she could finish, David had walked over to her and pulled her back by the hair, silencing her with a kiss that made everyone fall silent. Even Alex, who was getting ready to strut around like Cock o' the North. Maybe he and Isabella didn't have the monopoly on passion after all.

'Who's . . . who's left?' Kitty asked, fanning herself with the edge of her cape, no doubt shocked to have glimpsed that side of David. Everyone looked around, counting heads.

'Oh, Laura,' Orlando said.

Hesitantly, Laura opened hers, hoping to God her Santa hadn't found the same shop as David's and bought tassels or something. A hush descended as she peered in.

An envelope was lying inside. She opened it. What could it be? A book token? An iTunes voucher?

'FWQ one-event licence,' she read out, her eyes instantly meeting Rob's. He was the only one here who knew. And Mark had told him at lunchtime. There'd been plenty of opportunity for him to buy it for tonight. Plus it cost bang on five euros.

'What's that?' Kitty asked, baffled.

'Freeride World Qualifier,' Laura sighed. Now they would all know. 'It's a joke.'

'Is it?' Rob challenged. 'Or maybe it's a dare.'

Laura's eyes flashed at his words.

'I still don't get it,' Kitty whispered to Orlando.

'Freeriding is extreme off-piste skiing,' Laura explained. 'You basically walk up a mountain and push yourself off. There's a start gate at the top and a finish gate at the bottom. You make up the bit in between yourself.'

'Oh well, I'll join you tomorrow morning, then,' Sam muttered sarcastically.

'The closing tournament's in Verbier on the twenty-eighth of March,' Rob said provocatively. 'It'll go to France and Russia before coming here for the finals.'

'I don't know why we bothered making this secret!' Sam spluttered crossly. 'I mean, the lot of you are useless.'

'Are you sure *you* wouldn't like it?' Laura said, holding the licence out to Rob and ignoring Sam completely.

'I'm not good enough. Besides, it's got your name on it,' he shrugged. Laura looked at it. Sure enough, it had.

She pocketed it silently, wanting the subject dropped. Any second now the others were all going to start asking about the full extent of her skiing experience. *Extreme off-piste, Laura?* She could feel Rob was watching her and was itching to tell her story for her.

'Is it my turn?' Cat asked, and all eyes swivelled back to her, their default resting place.

She opened her box delicately. 'Oh! I haven't seen one of these for years.' She pulled out an old second-hand Polaroid camera. 'Who bought me this?'

'No! Don't say a fucking word!' Sam hollered, pointing at them all accusingly. 'Any of you.'

Everyone shook their heads. They wouldn't dare.

'Come on, let's dance,' Orlando said, putting down his DVDs and shuffling through the Spotify playlist to Pixie Lott. 'I want all you girls in a line. I am going to show you some moves to follow.'

'This is a party, not a Zumba class, Orly,' Cat scolded lightly, but Orlando just picked her up and spun her round, causing her to flash a glimpse of champagne La Perla.

'You girls shall be my backing dancers,' he said.

'Just a sec, Orlando,' Rob interrupted, taking Laura by the elbow and leading her away from the line. 'I wanted to run something by you. While you were upstairs I booked the helicopter for two hours tomorrow morning. Seven o'clock. I want to do the north face of Petit Combin. I've never done it before. It's rocky in parts and pretty dangerous.' He looked at her intently. 'I want you to come with me. No one else has the experience.'

'You're mad!' she exclaimed punchily.

'Probably.'

'I'm here to work, Rob. You have flown me out here to interview your friends, not—'

'Yes, but that was before I knew you can ski like a ninja.'

'Do they ski?' she asked, puzzled.

Rob burst out laughing, a sudden unexpected sound that made her shiver and she felt an urge to brush her palm over his stubbly cheeks. She knew she shouldn't have done that party trick and necked that beer. 'No idea!' he grinned.

'What makes you think I want to spend my Sunday morning bombing down a treacherous cliff where I could be killed by an avalanche or fall off a rock face at any—?' But before she'd even finished the sentence, the gleam in her eyes matched his.

He grinned at her devilishly. 'I know. It sounds good, doesn't it?'

# *Chapter Twenty-Three*

The clouds had fallen to earth during the night, blanketing the ground with another half-foot of snow and leaving the sky a clear, rinsed blue. Laura winced as the sub-zero temperatures hit her sleep-coddled body, still rosy from sleep. Rob helped the driver attach their skis to the car roof.

Everyone else was still sleeping, of course. The party the previous night had gone on till four, with Orlando hosting dance-offs all night. Cat, it transpired, moved like Beyoncé with silky hips and shimmying shoulders. Kitty appeared to specialize in ska; Isabella had a Shakira hip action that had practically hypnotized the boys; Sam seemed to be more influenced by Jessie J – all foot stomps and fierce faces. Alex had showed off his breakdancing skills, including a terrifying-looking head-spin that made a mess of his beautiful hair. Laura had laughed like a drain when he'd gone into the 'worm'. What looked cool in an underground car park with a pack of teenagers looked somewhat ridiculous among a bunch of thirty-somethings in black tie. She'd stopped laughing pretty abruptly, though, when Alex had caught her eye and thrown her a look of such simmering intensity she had thought he was going to chase her up the stairs there and then.

Laura climbed into the car and turned on the heated seats,

blowing on her hands. She watched Rob packing the rest of the kit – a rucksack with emergency supplies, poles, boots . . . She could see from the way he moved how excited he was – his body was taut and moving rapidly, already on high alert. The adrenalin was pumping through him – that and last night's vodka.

'Let's go,' he said with bright eyes, sliding into the seat beside her.

Strange, she thought, how they'd gone from being stiff and formal with each other in their business relationship to provocatively daring in a social one.

The car purred up the drive (well, as much as a car can purr with snow chains on) and they left their exhausted, toxic housemates behind them as they fed into the virgin snows. Only the snow-packers were about, orange lights flashing, as they bashed and compacted the fresh falls. They were pulling up at the heliport within eight minutes.

Laura looked at the helicopter sitting in its circle, the pilot inside running through his tests. She felt a stab of fear as she realized the enormity of what they were about to do: attack one of the most notorious mountain faces in the region on two and a half hours' sleep and a hangover. Usually she couldn't even do the laundry on a hangover. She looked over at Rob as he shook hands with the pilot. He'd been as half cut as everyone else last night, although that had only been apparent by how he *hadn't* behaved. Unlike the others, who stumbled over their own feet (David) or slurred their words (Orlando, disintegrating into an appalling Italian-English hybrid language that was as undecipherable to Isabella as to the others), Rob had been given away only by the brightness in his eyes and an unrestrained vigour that wasn't characteristic of his usual reserved manner. Out of his suit, out here, he was an entirely different man: an adrenalin junkie, an athlete pushing himself to his limits.

She fastened her helmet as Rob waved to her from the helicopter to climb in. The blades were starting up and she had to crouch low to run past. He buckled her into her seat with a speedy ease – betraying just how much this wasn't his first time in one of these – before sitting opposite her, staring at her intently. He was as finely tuned this morning as a Ferrari.

She tensed as the helicopter lifted up, pushing her head back against the seat for a moment before daring to turn and look out. Verbier shrank before her, iced and pristine like a Christmas cake.

'So, how do you want to do this?' Rob shouted across at her.

'Do what?'

'Get out of this thing.' He gestured to the helicopter they were sitting in.

'Through the doors, please. Not the ejector seat,' she shouted back.

He laughed, so thoroughly amused that she started giggling too.

He leaned in towards her and she met him halfway. There was a gleam in his eyes and it thrilled her to think she had put it there. 'I mean, do you want us to land first? Or do you want to hit the ground skiing?' he asked.

Laura looked into those copper eyes. She could see what he wanted her to say. He thought he'd found a kindred spirit in her – someone whose skill could match his appetite. 'I don't think I can jump, Rob.'

'I think you can. I think you just don't want to.' His voice was velvety, coaxing her on.

'Okay, I don't want to, then. I'm worried enough about my survival as it is.'

'I wouldn't have suggested it if I thought it would put you in danger.' He smiled and took her hand in his. 'I'll look after you, Laura. I promise.'

Laura stared at him. Rightly or wrongly, she trusted him. She nodded.

Rob gave a thumbs-up sign to the pilot and slid her skis over to her. She fastened her boots with shaking hands.

'Can you carry one of these?' he asked, holding up a small black rucksack.

Laura nodded, slid her arms through the straps and checked the chinstrap on her helmet.

'Okay, do you want to go first, or shall I?' he asked, placing a hand on her arm. Laura hoped he couldn't feel her quaking with fear through her jacket. It was official. She was clinically insane. She had thought it was bad enough to be off-pisting one of the most extreme faces in the Alps on two and a half hours' sleep; now she had gone and made the scenario *so* much worse by agreeing to jump out of a helicopter first! What was wrong with her? What would Jack say? Actually, she didn't want to think about it. Not right now. What she was about to do was so far removed from the Laura he knew and loved, he simply wouldn't believe it.

'You first. I'll follow.'

'Okay,' he nodded as the helicopter began to drop height, circling over a shallow plain just below the rocky outcrop of the summit.

Rob slid open the door and straightened himself up. Getting ready to go.

'Wait!' Laura clamped a hand on his arm suddenly, struggling against the icy winds, which broke over her like waves. 'Don't we . . . don't we need a guide or something? I mean, how will we find our way down from here?' she gabbled, panicking.

He slid back into the helicopter. 'I've been coming here since I was three. I know these mountains better than most of the guides. I pay a discretionary premium *not* to have one come with us. Don't worry, I know what I'm doing.'

'But . . . but what if there's an avalanche?'

'There's an avalanche probe in your backpack.' He shrugged. 'Or just ski faster.'

'*Ski f—?*'

He put both his hands on her arms, squeezing her and looking straight into her eyes. 'Trust me.'

She nodded dumbly.

'Count to three after I go, then jump. Okay?'

He winked at her, turned away and in the next instant was gone. Just like that. Laura gasped as she watched him land a second later, perfectly balanced, easing straight into wide, meandering S-bends, keeping his speed down as he waited for her and looking back to check that she actually was going to follow him out.

Three. She thought of Jack.

Two. She thought of Fee.

One. She thought of . . .

Nothing at all. For she was airborne, her body tucked and tight, as she felt the wind above, below and all around her. It was so cold she could almost feel the friction of the minute crystals in the air as she sliced through them, and then she was down and off, travelling at thirty, forty miles an hour within seconds, the pristine snow immaculate beneath her skis.

Rob held his poles up in jubilation as he saw her weaving down towards him, her ski tracks and his the only signs of life on this cold, hard mountain. He whooped at her and she screamed back with delight. She let instinct take over – her body knew this made sense. Her body knew what her mind did not: that there's a tangential difference between existing and living – and this was living.

She followed him easily, letting him lead, feeling no compunction to catch up or overtake as she had with Alex. Today she wanted to enjoy the ride. She laughed as they zipped down wide motorways, disappearing into the shadows thrown down by the rocky walls, slicing cleanly through the blue light of icy cols before emerging into the wide, sun-drenched vista of a glacier.

They jumped three times – becoming almost blasé about the military procedure – before Rob showed some mercy and stopped for breakfast. Laura slowed down her approach behind him, buying herself a little more time for the tears to drop from her lashes and sink into the cushioning of her goggles. After years of silence, her soul was singing again and its sweetness was almost more than she could bear. She felt closer here – to herself, to them.

'Nice place to stop for breakfast, don't you think?' Rob asked with deadly understatement, his eyes lingering on her a moment when he saw the wet tracks on her pink cheeks as she removed her goggles.

'It'll do,' she quipped, looking back up at their tracks, overlapping, intertwined, mirrored.

He chuckled as he took off his backpack. 'You've got the cheese. Stinking Bishop.'

'Eww! And there I was thinking you'd put a pair of your

socks in here to force me down this mountain quicker,' she joked, swinging the bag over to him.

They settled on a small exposed slab of rock, sitting side by side and smearing the incredibly Stinking Bishop on their baguettes as they watched a snowboarder far, far below on the south face of the Grand Combin opposite.

Rob poured them each a hot chocolate from a thermos made by Porsche. 'So, glad you came?'

Laura nodded. 'I can't believe how beautiful it is up here.'

'Feels like sitting on top of the world, doesn't it?'

'Mmm . . .' she agreed, lacing her fingers around the enamel cup and letting the steam warm her cheeks. 'Oh look! A balloon!'

Rob followed her pointed finger to see a red hot-air balloon drifting towards them from Evolène.

'I've never been in one. I bet Cat would love it. I ought to book a trip for next time we're out.' He looked over at her. 'Have you ever ridden in one?'

Laura nodded. 'Once.'

'Was it good?'

She nodded again. 'Terrific.'

'Where did you do it?' he asked, intrigued.

'Tanzania. An air safari. It was amazing – we saw a lion kill right beneath us,' she murmured, smiling wistfully as she watched the balloon drift higher above the crags and over towards France.

'What?' she asked after a minute or so when she realized that his eyes were still trained on her.

'I don't know,' he shrugged. 'I'm just trying to work you out.'

'I'm not a sudoku.'

'I tend to think I'm a pretty good judge of character, but you're not at all who I thought you were.'

'Huh,' she breathed, content not to pursue the line of conversation.

But Rob was persistent. 'When we first met, you were really uptight and defensive and . . . kind of sad.'

'Gee, thanks. As I recall, you weren't exactly showing your best side either.'

'I meant sad as in unhappy, but you're different out here. You're funnier, friendlier, prettier . . .' His eyes slid over her hair.

'The altitude's getting to you,' she muttered.

'No,' he grinned. 'I'm perfectly sane. You're being defensive, and you're only being defensive because you know I'm right. You were desperate last night that no one should know how accomplished you really are. I was watching you. I thought you were going to bolt for your room again. I don't get why you'd want to keep something like that a secret.'

Laura hiked up her eyebrows. 'You've got to get over the skiing thing. It was just an invitation to try out.'

But he shook his head, making her groan. Why couldn't he just give it up?

'I ask whether you can ski and, eventually, no thanks to you, discover you were one of the top young skiers in the country. I ask whether you've been in a hot-air balloon and learn that yes, an air safari over Africa, Rob, thanks for asking . . . Are there any other epic life experiences you want to share? Do you go potholing in Staffa? Do you go deep-sea diving and wrestle great whites?'

'Not quite,' she snorted.

'Not *quite*?'

She looked at him sideways. 'I am a qualified diver.'

250

Rob rolled his eyes. 'I don't believe this. I was joking.'

'It wasn't anywhere near as exotic as you're making it out to be.'

'Tell me the gritty truth, then,' he said, turning himself slightly on the rock so that he was facing her.

Laura sighed. 'I volunteered on a marine conservation project in the South Pacific. Twenty weeks on an island called Gau during my gap year. We had to explore the mangrove forests and inter-tidal areas, as well as do visual censuses of the reefs, assessing algal and coral cover.'

He stared at her, fascinated and baffled all at once. 'Christ, scratch the surface with you . . . Why are you so determined to hide yourself?'

'Hide myself?' she scoffed. 'I am out here this weekend to work, not to pursue my own personal happiness agenda. My life is just the way I want it. You're not the only one living the dream, you know.'

'You think I'm living the dream?'

'Hello? Deluxe chalet, helicopter on standby, the most beautiful woman in England as your wife . . . Do I need to go on?'

Rob stared at her. 'Nobody's life is perfect.'

'You have to admit yours is pretty damn close.'

He was quiet for a moment. 'It's all just stuff. It doesn't mean anything.' He looked out over the valley, his eyes on a distant helicopter that was ferrying another set of privileged skiers to the mountain's VIP area. 'Money's great not because of what it allows you to buy, but because of what it allows you to do. Stuff like this. It's not about being flash in a chopper. It's about having breakfast on the glacier,' he shrugged. 'What can beat that?'

'I hear you,' she sighed, watching the snow being blown off the eastern escarpment like icing sugar.

'And anyway, there's plenty money can't buy you.'

'Love?' she asked ironically, prompting him to reach down and throw a well-aimed snowball at her shoulder.

She shrieked, trying – and failing – to get out of the way and falling off the slab they'd made their seat.

'I was going to say time, you cheeky mare,' he remarked, watching her sit up, giggling, in the snow in front of him.

'Oh, so Orlando's got company in his midlife crisis, then, has he?' She blew a lock of hair out of her face and looked back at him, relieved the focus was off her at last. 'You're not even forty yet, are you?'

'Thirty-six. And not getting any younger.'

'Well, I think everyone would probably agree that you've proved yourself,' she said, wrinkling her nose unsympathetically, angling her face up to the sun.

He watched her basking and shook his head. 'You're missing the point. I'm the youngest of five,' he murmured.

Laura opened her eyes. '*Five?*'

He nodded.

'Don't tell me. The youngest of five brothers. That's why you're so alpha.'

'Four sisters.'

'Ah, so that's why you're so in touch with your feminine side.' Her highly sceptical tone prompted another snowball, which hit her on the other shoulder. 'Hey! What am I? Target practice?'

'Yes, if you're going to carry on with the sarcasm. Something of a speciality for you, I notice.'

Laura let the observation pass and sat forward, resting her chin in her hands, her elbows on her knees. 'Four sisters, huh? I bet you've seen it all.'

'More than any man should ever have to see,' he agreed,

a smile on his lips. 'It was great, actually. Never a dull moment – or a quiet one!' He looked over to the crenellated horizon. 'I always assumed that I'd have a big family too. I thought it would have happened by now.'

Laura fell silent, all teasing gone as she remembered the baby names book she'd seen on his bedside table yesterday morning.

'Well, I'm sure it will. You're both young and healthy,' she faltered. It was an assumption based on Darwinian theory – the human race didn't get any fitter than the Blakes.

He shrugged. 'Cat isn't as bought into it as I am. She didn't have a particularly happy childhood so she's not in the same rush to do it all herself . . . But she's getting there.'

Laura nodded. It was no wonder he hadn't wanted to have this conversation surrounded by other commuters in the café. At least three and a half thousand metres up this mountain splendid isolation was their only witness.

'How about you?' he asked, looking across at her.

'You know I don't have children. I told you when we first met.'

'I mean, what about your family? Growing up?'

Laura swallowed. 'It's just me.' She saw the pity clamour in his expression. 'What? Don't look at me like that. I don't need your sympathy. I've got a great boyfriend, a dog I love, a best friend . . .'

Rob pulled a face. 'Shouldn't that have been the other way round?'

'What?'

'Shouldn't it be that the dog's great and you love your boyfriend?'

'That's what I meant.'

'It's not what you said.'

Laura stared at him. 'An error, then.'

'Or a Freudian slip. Maybe you're not really living the dream after all, Laura Cunningham.'

He didn't stand a chance. Within a fraction of a second, the snowball she lobbed hit Rob square in the face, and she fell back in the snow, laughing with her hands across her stomach, her eyes closed in the sun. The valley was still in shadow and she'd only been awake a few hours, but this was fast shaping up to be one of the best days of her life.

# Chapter Twenty-Four

Kitty and Orlando were sledging in the garden when they returned later that morning. Miles of swirling, parallel tracks, punctuated by heavy splodges where they had fallen off, marked the once-pristine snow, and the two of them were weak with laughter and over-oxygenation from the immaculate air.

Rob and Laura stopped on their way from the car – skis over their shoulders – to shake their heads and chuckle as they watched the two of them hurtling down the garden, shrieking like toddlers on roller skates.

'Having fun?' Rob called out as they trudged back up to the top of the lawn, nattering away to each other, sledges bumping behind them.

They looked up the drive. 'You're back!' Kitty beamed. 'Have fun?'

'We *scarred* those slopes!' Rob quipped, prompting Laura to groan.

'I officially object to you talking like a dude,' she riposted as Orlando and Kitty arrived, panting, in front of them. 'And, Orlando, you are mine! Sam's not here to save you now. You can't get away from me this time.'

'I would never try to,' Orlando flirted, winking a dreamily long-lashed eye.

'My room? Half an hour?'

'Aaaahhh, my favourite words,' he joked, placing one hand across his heart. Then he pulled a sad face. 'But I must have a massage. I cannot have all this lactic acid staying in my muscles.'

'All this *what*?'

Orlando's eyes widened as an idea came to him. 'Let us have massages together. We can talk on our tummies!'

'O . . . kay,' Laura said slowly. 'So long as the towels stay on.'

'Baby! We shall be Adam and Eve *before* the apple. Innocence and beauty and joy.'

'Towels *on*, Orlando,' Laura said firmly, following him into the chalet.

Orlando turned and squeezed her hard around the shoulders so that her feet almost left the ground. 'You English roses!' he cried. 'Such puritans! What you need is a little Latin passion in your life.'

'Thanks, but I'm perfectly happy with my life.'

'Hmm, she said the same thing to me too,' she heard Rob say with devilment in Orlando's ear as he passed through the porch. 'But I'm not buying it either.'

Twenty minutes later, they were as naked as babies and Laura had never felt safer with her clothes off. Gemma and Sasha had moved the two tables into one room and were synchronizing their movements, poor Sasha having to work double-time to cover Orlando's considerable muscle-mass.

'Maybe this wasn't such a good idea,' Orlando mumbled. 'Is making me sleepy.'

'Wake up, Orlando!' Laura barked at him. 'I've waited all weekend for this.'

'Okay, okay,' he moaned, forcing open his eyes and staring at her with hugely dilated pupils.

'You promised you would think of hateful things that would make me like Cat. And also some more stories.'

'You like her anyway. She won you over without my treachery. But I do have a story for you.' He grinned lazily. 'You will love it.'

'I'm listening,' she said, flattening her hands together under her cheek.

'We had gone to Milan together for a few days.'

'To see Alex?'

Orlando shook his head. 'No, no. We were in the design stage of the Cube and Cat wanted to go to this trade show. She had read about the coloured glass and someone was exhibiting there . . . You've seen it yourself.'

Laura blinked yes.

'Anyway, *I* had heard about a club, very famous for its beautiful dancers. Some friends had been, and . . . I mean, I was excited about the glass, of course, ' he added guiltily.

'Did you go to the club?'

His eyes twinkled. 'I just assumed Cat would go to bed early when I told her.'

'Assumed?'

'She insisted on going with me.' He nodded sombrely.

'What's wrong with that? Women go to gay clubs all the time.'

'Not this one, they don't. Strictly no women, not even the lesbians.'

'Oh.'

'Do you know what she said?'

'Not a clue.'

'She told me to *man her up*.'

There was a brief pause.

'You mean . . . ?'

Orlando nodded. 'Well, you don't argue with Cat, especially when she has *that* look in her eye, so we strapped her chest with some bandages and bought her a suit.'

Laura gasped. 'But what about her hair? Her face? There's no way she'd get away with it. How could she possibly be mistaken for a man?'

'Her hair was shorter back then, so we slicked it back. And she is good with make-up, so she did . . . you know, something on her brows to make them heavy.' He shrugged.

'You're not going to tell me she actually got away with it?'

'She did!'

'But she *can't* have looked like a man!'

'No. You're right, she didn't. She didn't look like a man, no. But she was the most perfect, beguiling, effete boy. They went wild for her, I tell you. No one could take their eyes off her. And we danced, danced all night.' He lowered his chin, looking up at her conspiratorially. 'I think maybe, at the end, some people knew. She took off her jacket, and her arms and shoulders – you know, they are women's, so slight. You cannot fake that. But no one cared by then.'

'What did Rob say?'

'I don't think she told him. It was our secret,' he whispered.

'Cat Blake dressed as a man in a gay club in Milan,' Laura murmured. 'Well, that certainly wasn't what I was expecting.'

Orlando's eyes gleamed. 'She is wild. Do not underestimate her. There is so much more to Cat Blake than most people know.' He winked.

Laura thought for a moment as Gemma worked on a knot

by her left shoulder blade. 'It's funny you mention this wild side to Cat. Sam talked about it too, whereas Kitty and Rob seem to hold a more romantic view of her. She seems almost to be a woman of two halves.'

'We all have our dark sides, our secrets.' He looked at her intently. 'You too.'

Laura kept quiet. It was the light side she didn't have.

'It is strange this job of yours, no? You are more like an undercover reporter than a jeweller.'

Laura felt hurt. 'I'm not interested in digging up dirt, Orlando, and I'm not making a judgement on anything people are telling me. Cat's life is what it is. Pretty damn amazing from where I'm lying, admittedly, but it's not like I think she's perfect either. Who is? And Rob feels the same. He loves Cat in her entirety: the good, the bad, the not remotely ugly.'

Orlando grinned.

'He doesn't need you to be kind or protective about his wife and he doesn't need her to be perfect.' She continued, 'All he wants is for this necklace to be honest and reflect her life. Nothing more, nothing less.'

Orlando stared at her for a long moment, one eye closed as he lay his head on its side.

'How did you start doing this, Laura? No one else makes jewellery like this. I have a friend – very beautiful, very rich. She wears a diamond cross because she thinks it is pretty, but she's Jewish. Half the women in my club are cheating on their husbands, but they all still wear their wedding rings. Whereas you are making jewellery that really means something to the person wearing it.'

'I suppose because I believe that it's memories that are the gift.' She propped herself up on her elbows, her cheek resting in her hand. 'It feels worthwhile, somehow, to cast devotion and adoration and friendship and everlasting love into silver and gold and platinum, because it means those memories and stories can be remembered for always and passed down like the treasures they are. Memories *have* to be remembered, Orlando. Above all else, they are what ultimately define us.'

A beat passed between them and Laura felt suddenly embarrassed to have climbed on to her soapbox. Had she said too much? Revealed her scars? But she needn't have worried. Orlando looked back at her, visibly moved by her passion. 'Well, that and size-twenty-seven jeans,' he said with the utmost, endearing, seriousness.

# Chapter Twenty-Five

'Hey, Laura,' Kitty said, her hands laced around a steaming mug of tea, as Laura wandered distractedly back up the stairs. Orlando had fallen asleep on the table and Sasha was covering him with towels, putting several bundles on the floor for good measure, just in case he should roll off. 'How's Orlando?'

'Sleeping off his lactic hangover,' Laura smiled, coming over and leaning against the worktop, looking at Kitty in dawning horror as she took in her outfit – a blue and yellow romper suit.

'Cuppa?'

Laura could only nod as she watched Kitty – looking like Andy Pandy – pour a cup of boiling water straight from the tap. 'How are you feeling this morning?'

'Oh dear, I have to admit I'm missing the babes like mad today,' Kitty mumbled, dunking the Earl Grey teabag several times. 'Typical, isn't it? I have the opportunity to sleep till noon and what happens? I wake up after four hours' sleep, completely unable to drop back off. I'll be kicking myself on Tuesday.' She paused, very un-Kitty-like. 'I do hope Joe's being polite to my mother.'

'Kitty, I have to ask: what the devil have you got on? Have you been raiding the kids' wardrobes?' she asked.

'D'you like it?' Kitty asked, delighted, doing a twirl. 'It's a onesie. I got it in town yesterday. All the kids are wearing them this season.'

'Yeah, the *kids* . . .' Laura quipped, just as Cat padded up the lower staircase.

'Hey, the very person!' Cat beamed, catching sight of Laura. 'I was wondering where you were.'

'Oh!' Laura remarked in surprise. Cat had been looking for her? 'I just had a massage. My muscles were pretty sore from this morning.'

'How was the skiing?'

'Ummmm,' Laura pulled a face. 'Terrifying!'

Cat laughed. 'I did feel for you. I almost died when I heard Rob getting up. It felt like the crack of dawn.'

'It did to me too.'

'How did you find the energy?'

'Adrenalin did it all for me. I expect I'll crash and burn big time now.'

David, Alex and Isabella burst in through the porch upstairs, dropping snow in their wake. 'Where were you?' Isabella called down.

Cat cocked her head apologetically. 'This morning's been a bit of a struggle.'

David looked at Kitty. 'What's your excuse?'

'Orly and I didn't have the co-ordination to stand on skis. We decided we'd be better off sitting on the sledge. Sam not with you?'

'Still sleeping.'

'I know I ought to hit the slopes seeing as we're going home tomorrow, but . . . ugh!' Cat slid her arms along the worktop, resting her head on them so that all that could be seen of her was her hair and legs. 'I think I'm only capable of stretching out on sofas today. We could put a film on.'

'You can do that anytime,' Rob scolded, jogging down the stairs in fresh jeans and a blue shirt.

'Oh, don't be mean, Rob,' Cat pouted. 'We can't all be hard core, you know.'

'But I thought we'd get the skidoos out today,' Rob said.

Cat groaned, Isabella sagged in her fiancé's arms, and Kitty and Laura just smiled quietly at each other. A world where it was tedious to ski/skidoo/frolic in the snow on a hangover wasn't their world.

'Sasha and Gemma have organized a hog roast to be ready for us in Smez.' Rob slung his arm round Cat's shoulders, easily pulling her into him. 'Think that can whet your appetite?'

Cat scowled prettily. 'Not really.'

'You'll love it when we're there. You know you will.'

'I'm not the only one who's tired, you know. Poor Laura's shattered. She's had hardly any sleep, thanks to you.' Cat caught Laura's eye and winked conspiratorially.

Laura looked from Cat to Rob. She actually loved the idea of going on a skidoo, but Cat was clearly asking her to back her up in this. Cat was asking her to be a friend. 'I am pretty tired,' she agreed.

She saw the disappointment glimmer instantly in Rob's eyes. He saw her, if not as a friend, then certainly as a comrade. They'd broken new ground – quite literally – this morning. Breakfast had been a revelation of many sorts – personal, emotional, spiritual – and she knew that her siding with Cat was a slap in the face to all that. But what else could she do? She was indebted to them both.

'Fine,' he nodded, stiffening immediately. 'So it can just be the men, then.'

'Well, I'm afraid, boys, that there is no way I can join you even if I wanted to – which I do not,' Isabella said, smiling coquettishly. 'I ran into an old friend at Médran on the way back. I've arranged to see her in her hotel this afternoon. I'm sorry. I did not know there would be fixed plans,' she shrugged.

'Nothing's fixed,' Rob replied as Isabella plucked a cherry from the fruit bowl and sauntered off upstairs to change. 'I just want everyone to have a good time,' he said frostily, wandering over to the fridge.

Cat arched an eyebrow. 'Oh, baby, don't sulk,' she murmured, following after him and rubbing a hand across his shoulders.

'I'm not sulking, Cat,' Rob muttered irritably, staring unseeing at the contents of the fridge.

She heaved a weary sigh, throwing all sorts of looks back at the assembled troupe. 'Fine, we'll go, then. Won't we, Laura? When are they expecting us?'

'Two hours,' he replied stroppily.

'Two hours!' Cat exclaimed. 'In Smez? Rob! Why didn't you say so? We need to go now!'

'What's the point? I'll just cancel it.'

'Baby! I was only stringing you along. You know how I like to make you beg.' She cupped his face in her hands, kissing him lingeringly on the mouth and arching her body into his. Laura saw how instinctively he drew her into him – forgetting them all – and she quickly looked away.

'Guess we'd better get dressed, then,' Alex said brusquely.

They all dispersed to their rooms to change. Laura ran up the stairs feeling disquieted somehow. She quickly checked her phone – no missed calls from Jack – and climbed back into her thermals. She was just shutting her door when Rob came out of his room.

He looked at her coldly. 'Where do you keep going to?'

'I just came up to get change—'

'I mean when Cat and the others are around – what happens to you? She says, "Jump," you say, "How high?" The person I was out on the slopes with this morning just completely disappears, and you become so . . . *meek*.'

'I-I don't know what you mean,' she stammered.

'No?' he asked, marching past her.

She watched him go, her heart pounding as wildly as it had on Petit Combin this morning. There had been a connection between them, alone up there – so strong it was almost visceral – but just like that, they were back to square one. Strangers again.

Everyone was already suited up and waiting – Orlando and Kitty throwing snowballs at each other in the garden – by the time she worked up the nerve to come outside. All her excitement about doing this had evaporated. She shuffled outside, keeping her eyes down, noticing how the violet light made the snow appear to glow even more brightly against the shadows.

Sam was up – finally – and in full roar. It was almost as if she had an On/Off switch: she was either completely comatose, or full-throttle, bossing everyone around and issuing orders. Currently, she was organizing the skidoo 'teams'. She was with David; Rob was with Cat; Orlando was with Kitty. That left her with Alex.

Laura watched as Cat slid into the seat behind Rob, resting her head on his back and hugging his torso with her arms.

She looked at Alex, who was fastening his helmet, his eyes still, like an eagle's, upon her.

'What took you so long?' Sam demanded, as though it was Laura who'd been sleeping in all morning and she was the one who'd already done several hours' off-piste skiing.

Laura took the helmet Sam was holding out to her and put it on.

'Ready?' Alex asked, coming to stand in front of her. 'Have you done this before?'

She shook her head.

'Jet-skied?'

She nodded.

'It's not dissimilar to that. Don't worry,' he said, smiling with his eyes. 'I'll look after you.'

Laura nodded. The words didn't sound as reassuring coming from him as they had from Rob.

He swung a leg over one of the glossy black machines lined up in front of the chalet. 'Sit behind me, like you would on a motorbike.'

Laura swung her leg over and slid into the seat, trying at the same time not to touch him.

He turned, an amused smile on his lips. 'You're going to need to get a whole lot closer than that if you don't want to come flying off,' he grinned.

Laura slid forward an inch.

'More,' he insisted.

She slid another inch.

'More.'

She tried again.

Alex sighed, grabbed her behind the knees and slid her into him so that their bodies were rammed together. She gasped as he found her arms and wrapped them around him tightly so that her cheek was pressed against his back. 'Much better,' he said, turning his head back as far as he could.

Laura saw Rob and Cat watching them and she gave a nervous smile. Rob looked angry with her still and she knew he felt she'd let him down.

'Hold tight, everyone, and just follow me,' Rob commanded.

Everyone started up their engines. Cat gave an excited whoop, Sam punched her fist in the air, and Kitty copied them both, almost falling off in the process as Orlando suddenly pulled away.

Laura heard Alex laugh as he revved the engines a couple of times as if warning her before seamlessly accelerating up the drive and into the trees. The cold air ripped over them like a tide and Laura wished she was wearing a balaclava under her helmet. She shivered, squeezing her muscles instinctively to promote blood flow, and felt Alex's body react next to hers.

The power of the machine they were sitting on was intimidating. Laura was used to moving fast over packed snow, but it was a different feeling entirely with 120 horsepower beneath her. The roads were perilously narrow, with the steep drops on one side protected only by a token meshing that would simply break a fall rather than stop it. But Alex was a masterful driver, and after ten minutes or so she began to relax, trusting in him after all and working with him. If he leaned left, so did she. Their wind resistance dropped.

After a while, they emerged from the trees on to an open, flattish area, and drew up alongside Rob, David and Orlando, who had come to a halt. The men were clearly squaring up for a flat race. Sam, Kitty and Cat began screaming at their backs with delight, and Laura couldn't help but submit to the adrenalin rush. She had never experienced the mountains like this before – she was completely and utterly hooked. The urge to give in to hysterical giggles was overwhelming, and a fight that Kitty had clearly lost.

She tightened her arms around Alex's waist. On Rob's nod, the men revved the handle gears and the bikes accelerated wildly. Laura screamed happily, catching Rob's attention and appearing to encourage Alex to go faster.

David drew in front immediately, he and Sam crouched low, Sam's hair streaming behind her like the Olympic flame as she looked back at the stragglers triumphantly. But neither Rob nor Alex was the type to accept defeat without a fight. Rob's machine began to nose ahead as Alex and Laura pegged level with David and Sam. Ahead, in the distance, Laura could see a new treeline emerging. It looked to be a good few miles away, but at the speeds they were travelling – surely up to seventy miles per hour now – they'd be there in minutes.

Laura felt Alex dip himself lower, so low that he was almost lying on the seat, his hands reaching above his head to the handlebars. She pushed herself down on to him, her body contoured to his completely, and they accelerated faster. They were in front now and she couldn't help but look across at Rob and Cat, her cheek pressed to Alex's back, as they pulled away definitively. It was like flying. It was like lying on a broomstick and letting magic do the rest.

They were upon the trees first, Alex refusing to brake until the last second, determined that neither Rob nor David should steal a march on him in the dying moments. The skidoo skidded to a halt and Laura jumped off giddily, punching the air with her fists and doing a little snow dance. In the next instant, Alex – howling his victory – had leapt off too and was swinging her round, her feet off the ground as they cheered victoriously. Rob and David, despondent in defeat, were parking up their skidoos as Alex put Laura back down again. But as she slid down him, she caught the look in his eyes and knew instinctively what was going to happen. Without a word he wrapped his arms around her and kissed her.

Everyone fell silent. The only thing to be heard was the sound of snow falling off the pines as squirrels jumped from tree to tree.

Laura pulled away, looking up at him breathlessly, realizing they had an audience. She saw Kitty's shocked expression first, then Sam's narrowed eyes, Cat's impassivity, David's embarrassment, Rob's anger. More anger.

Alex winked at her. 'You're my lucky charm, Laura-the-jeweller.'

'Alex, you prick!' Sam shouted, stomping over to him and thumping him on the arm. 'What the bloody hell about Isabella?'

'What? It was a winner's celebration. It's allowed,' Alex laughed, rubbing his arm.

'That had nothing to do with the race and you know it!' Sam bellowed. 'You've been sniffing around her all weekend. Don't think we don't all know what you and Isabella were fighting about last night! Just you keep away from her! She's got a boyfriend, all right?' Sam ordered. Laura was stunned to realize that Sam was actually on her side. 'Are you okay?'

Laura nodded, dumbstruck.

'It was just a kiss!' Alex protested.

'It was not going to stop there as well you know!' Sam shouted, turning back to him. 'I'm keeping my eye on you, understand? You might not like your fiancée very much, but I do. Got it?'

Alex rolled his eyes.

'Here. I'll go on the skidoo for the rest of the way with Alex,' Cat said calmly. 'You go with Rob, Laura.'

'I'm not some kind of sex pest who has to be segregated from her, you know!' Alex argued as Cat vaulted on to his skidoo.

'Sure about that?' Cat asked, giving him another punch on the arm for good measure.

'He's such a randy sod,' Sam muttered, stalking back to David, who was looking very disapproving of the whole episode.

Rob sat impassively as Laura walked over, unable to meet his – or anyone else's – eyes. She slid on to the seat as innocuously as she could, but body contact was inevitable. Compulsory.

'We'd better get a shift on if we're going to get there in time for lunch,' Rob said to everyone, starting up his engine. Laura felt the vibrations travel through her as she miserably laced her arms around him, as rigid as a tightrope. For a day that had started on the top of the world, it was rapidly, both literally and proverbially, going downhill.

# Chapter Twenty-Six

Laura hunkered down on the log next to Kitty, a generous helping of apple strudel in her bowl. She needed the sugar rush. Breakfast on the glacier had been hours ago now, and her body felt utterly depleted. She was also desperate to lie down and go to sleep. The paltry two and a half hours she'd snatched from the night were making themselves known.

'Blimey, that was a turn-up for the books, wasn't it?' Kitty murmured to her, helping herself to a second slice. She nodded towards Sam, who was talking intently to Rob and David.

'Mmm. An unexpected ally.'

Kitty paused a second. 'Was he good, though?'

'Who?'

'Alex . . . I mean, obviously I've known him too long to have those kinds of feelings about him, but I've always sort of wondered in the back of my mind . . .'

Laura shrugged. 'He just got carried away. There wasn't any kind of emotion behind it other than triumphalism.' But that was a lie. The heat that had surged between them in those few moments had practically left scorch marks in the snow. He was a phenomenal kisser.

'I mean, don't get me wrong,' Kitty said quickly. 'Joe's my man and I love him to pieces. I just can't help wondering

271

sometimes, that's all,' she sighed. 'There's never been anyone but him, you see.'

'Alex is trouble, Kit. End of story. He didn't give two hoots about his fiancée or my boyfriend back there.'

'Are you going to tell Jack?'

Laura shook her head quickly. 'There's honestly nothing to tell. It meant nothing. He may as well have bitten me.'

Kitty laughed. 'You're no pushover, Laura Cunningham, I'll give you that . . . I need more custard. Save my place.'

Laura watched her go. She knew she had put on a good show, but she didn't feel anywhere near as confident as she sounded. Alex was her last interview out here – how could she shut herself away in a room with him now? She watched as he said something to Sam, making her laugh and throw a raisin at him. They were friends again.

'Hey,' Cat said, noticing her sitting alone and coming to sit beside her in Kitty's seat. 'Having fun?'

'Absolutely.' Laura smiled quickly.

'Don't let Alex freak you out. He's just a teenager, really.'

'It's fine. I can handle him.'

Cat nodded, twirling her spoon round her bowl distractedly. 'So, I've been thinking and I wanted to run an idea past you.' She took a nervous breath. 'How would you feel about me throwing a cocktail party for you when we get back? You know, to showcase your designs. I've got so many friends who I know would just love your stuff, and I'd love to help if I could.'

'But you haven't even seen my work yet.'

Cat shrugged. 'I know, but Orlando and Rob have been raving about it, and, I mean, if they're excited . . .' She put a hand on Laura's forearm. 'Oh, tell me you'll let me. It could be your official launch. We'd have such a scream.'

'I don't know what to say,' Laura replied. 'I'm so flat-tered.'

'Say yes.'

'. . . Yes. Please.'

Kitty came back with her fresh custard, her face falling as she saw Cat settled in her seat. 'What are you two plotting?' she asked, sitting cross-legged in the snow instead.

'Laura's domination of the London accessories scene. I'm going to throw a party for her when we get home and invite all my best and dearest and *richest* friends,' Cat replied, eyes gleaming. 'By Easter we'll have made Laura the hottest jewellery designer in London.' Her opal eyes opened wider suddenly. 'Oh, Rob!'

Rob, who was sitting on the parked skidoos with David and Orlando, looked over.

'Don't you know Bertie Thingamabob?'

'*Who?*'

'You know, he's on the BFC. You met at that Asprey's dinner last summer.'

'Bertie Penryn?'

'That's the one!'

'I've met him once, Cat.'

'Yes, but couldn't you make an introduction for Laura? To get her into the tents at London Fashion Week.' She looked back at Laura, grasping her hand eagerly in hers. 'That's where you need to be if you want to get the international buyers.'

Laura looked over at Rob, her eyes hopeful.

He shrugged petulantly.

'He can,' Cat assured her. 'He *will*. I have my methods of persuasion,' she winked.

Laura beamed as Cat gave a squeal of excitement

and Kitty started drilling her feet in the snow like a drum roll.

'New dress, new dress, new dress,' Kitty chanted.

'God, the tents . . . That's, like, the centre of my universe. I'm just so overwhelmed,' Laura murmured, shaking her head. Wait till she told Fee!

'We'll make you a star, baby,' Cat laughed. 'We'll organize the party for you as soon as we get back – it's vital we catch everybody before Christmas, because straight after they shoot off to the Caribbean. And I'll ask my friend Jinny to come too – she's the jewellery editor at *Harper's*. And we must ask . . . ooh, what's her name, the new diarist at *Tatler*?' Cat asked Kitty, clicking her fingers as she tried to remember. Kitty looked at her blankly. 'Araminta Pitt! She'll take one look at all the women clamouring for your stuff and that's it. You're in!'

Laura shook her head in amazement. A society launch party in London? An introduction with the British Fashion Council? The *FT* feature had been a lucky break that had inadvertently come through Fee's well-intentioned meddling, but this was another league altogether. Cat was finding ways to position her with the fashion elite *and* bring her face-to-face with a cash-rich, sophisticated clientele. The ripple effect from those women alone would probably span three continents.

She'd need a logo and proper packaging. A website and a studio that wasn't in the middle of a creek. She should be in London, and . . .

She stopped herself. No! What was she *doing*? Laura felt the familiar ambition begin to throb inside her. This was everything she had told Jack and Fee she didn't want – she'd told them she wanted to keep everything small, local, bespoke – but already she could feel her brain beginning to engage, the ambition that she struggled to subdue leaking out.

Let Cat host the party. It was just a party. Nothing else had to change.

The light was fading by the time they got back, and energy with it. Everyone was shattered, Laura most of all, but she couldn't hightail it up to her room to rest. She might have been welcomed with open arms into the fold and played with the rest of them, but her brief was still different from theirs. They had been invited as friends; she had been invited to work. Orlando hadn't been so far from the truth after all when he'd likened her to an undercover reporter. Somehow she had to get an interview in with Alex without Cat noticing. Tomorrow he'd be driving back to Milan and she would be flying home, and it was Cat's birthday in twelve days' time.

'Laura,' Cat said as they pulled their boots off in the porch. 'Would you mind flinging the black lace dress back in my room tonight? Sasha's going to take it in with the rest of the dry-cleaning tomorrow.'

'Of course. And I'll pay to have it cleaned, naturally.'

Cat smiled kindly and simply shook her head. Laura felt instantly foolish.

She padded down to her bedroom and immediately started running a bath before flinging herself backwards on to the bed like a felled tree. She felt fatigue tiptoe up her body, leadening her muscles, slowing her breathing down, the radiant heat of being indoors again beginning to sedate her.

Her phone rang quietly on the bedside table and she knew it would be Jack, but she was too tired to pick it up, even though she knew she should speak to him. She needed just a little more time to regroup before she reconnected with him and her real world. She felt so far away from him right now – not just geographically, but within herself, and she knew he would hear it in her voice instantly. She could do without the questions and puzzled pauses. She wanted to be left alone.

She closed her eyes, listening to the water running in the background. Everyone was chilling in their rooms for an hour or so before reconvening for a film and pizza downstairs at seven. But Alex – she must fit him in somehow. Bath, interview, film? It worked for her, but what was he doing? Swimming? Sleeping? Making up with Isabella again?

With a weary sigh, she pushed herself up off the bed and retrieved the dress from her wardrobe. Cat was just skipping towards the lift in a thin, white cotton bathrobe as she stepped into the hall.

'Oh, Cat! I've got the dress,' she called after her.

Cat turned back to find Laura holding it up. 'Thanks, Laura. You're a star! Just throw it on my bed, will you? I'm going down for a facial.'

'Sure.'

Laura heard the lift doors trill open as she stepped into the Leopard suite and took in that marvellous carpet again. It really was a thing of beauty and testament to Cat's exquisite taste that it didn't come across as remotely tacky, but as high end and sumptuous.

She walked quickly across the room, turning the neck of the hanger round so that it would hook on to the wardrobe door, when the bathroom door next to her opened suddenly.

Rob, towelling his hair dry and with only a towel over his hips, stood stock still at the sight of Laura – and not his wife – in his bedroom.

Laura gaped back at the sight of him. 'Oh God! I'm so sorry. Cat asked for this dress back for the dry-cleaning and I . . . She told me to put it on the bed, but I thought I'd better hang it up because it's so expensive . . . I assumed no one else was in here. I would have knocked otherwise. I'm so sorry.' She was gabbling.

'Stop it,' he said tersely.

'What?' she asked, taken aback, as he strode past, resuming his towel-drying.

'Stop being sorry. All I ever hear you saying is fucking "sorry".'

Laura stared at him, stunned, as he walked over to the balcony doors, the muscles in his back clearly delineated as he towelled his head vigorously. Silently she ran over the carpet, catching Rob's eye in the mirror as she left.

'Shit. Laura, wait! I—'

The door clicked behind her and she ran into her room, shocked, angry tears streaming down her cheeks. She leaned back against the door, wondering why Rob was being so persistently aggressive to her. He'd been in a cold fury all afternoon, ever since she'd sided with Cat about not skidooing. Was that really such a crime? She *had* just jumped out of a helicopter with him. That more than sang for her supper.

'Laura?'

She blinked her eyes open in fright. Alex was leaning against her bathroom door, watching her.

'What's wrong?'

'What are *you* doing in here?'

A knock on the door behind her made her jump again, and she moved away from it. Rob came in, flustered and urgent.

'Laura, look . . .' His voice died away as he saw Alex in the bathroom. 'What's *he* doing in here?' he demanded, just as he clocked her wet cheeks.

'I could ask you the same thing, mate,' Alex remarked.

Rob looked down at himself, half dressed.

Laura looked back at Alex and he held his hands up in a gesture of appeasement. '*I* came to see whether you wanted to interview me for the necklace,' he shrugged. 'We're running out of time. I knocked, no one answered, I could hear water running, so I came in. And it's just as well I did – the bath was about to run over.'

Laura rolled her eyes heavenwards, annoyed with herself. Water damage on the top floor of the chalet? That would have been just precious.

'Thanks. I forgot. I just went to return Cat's dress, and . . .' Her voice trailed off.

Alex looked questioningly at Rob. Everyone was accounting for their movements. What was *he* doing here?

But Rob had settled into another stony silence, and Laura saw again how very little the two men actually liked each other.

'The film's at seven,' Rob muttered, turning to go.

'We knew that, didn't we?' Alex asked her before looking back at Rob. 'We knew that. Why are you *really* here?' he smiled. It was so clear what he was doing – tarring Rob with his brush. He had kissed Laura, so therefore Rob must be chasing after her too.

Rob threw him an icy glare and slammed the door behind him.

Laura and Alex stood in awkward silence for a moment. 'Shall we do this now, then?' Laura asked curtly, wiping her cheeks dry with the back of her hand and walking over to the bureau, where her notebook and pens were. 'I'm tired and I'm sure you must be too. I'd really like to have a rest before this evening.'

Alex watched her cross the room, taking in her fresh anger. 'I also wanted to apologize about this afternoon,' he said. 'I was bang out of order.'

'Yes. You were.'

'Do you hate me?'

'I don't have any feeling about you,' she snapped, thumbing through her book to the next new page.

Alex looked like he'd been slapped. Telling him she hated him would have been far preferable to utter indifference, she guessed.

She sat down in the chair, hoping he believed her, and dug her toes into the carpet like an axe into ice. 'Do you want to sit down?'

He looked around. The pretty chair was too small to accommodate his shoulders. 'On the bed?' he asked, looking at her.

'Of course,' she shrugged with a casualness she didn't feel.

He sank on to the edge of the bed, his knees wide apart and his arms draped loosely on them. 'So.' He fiddled with the gold signet ring on his left hand.

Laura inhaled deeply, trying to focus on the job in hand. She looked down at her notebook, knowing the answers to the questions weren't in there, but she didn't want to meet his eyes. 'Tell me about you and Cat,' she said quietly, more gently, as she pushed her finger over the silky-smooth paper. 'Rob said you were her first love.'

'I'll bet he did.' He shrugged as he took in her quizzical expression. 'What? It keeps me nicely boxed up, doesn't it? I'm just the first love but Cat's the love of his *life*. I got the Once-Upon-a-Time, but he's got the Happy-Ever-After.'

Jesus. If he was going to be this chippy all the way through . . . 'How did you and Cat meet?' she asked wearily.

Alex's expression changed at the memory. 'At sixth-form college. I can even remember the day I first saw her. She walked into the economics class wearing white jeans and a red and white striped jumper. The sun was shining behind her at the door, making her hair all, like, bright. Like a halo.'

'*Was* she an angel?'

'Oh yeah,' he murmured. 'Top three in the class. I only passed because of her. There was nowhere else to sit except next to me, and so that was that. I could hardly talk to her for the first term, and it was another term after that before I could look her in the eye. She was so beautiful.'

This was better. 'So what changed? How did you get her to fall in love with you?'

'By making her an offer she couldn't refuse. I bought tickets for Take That at Wembley. Had to sell my bike to do it, but it was worth it – an early lesson in speculating to accumulate,' he chuckled. 'Everyone was so jealous. Her friends because they wanted to see Mark Owen. Mine because they'd have sold their mothers to be with her. After that, we were inseparable. The chemistry between us was insane.'

'What's your best memory of her?'

'Easy.' He smiled so that his eyes shone. 'Skinny-dipping at midnight on the summer solstice, the night after our last exam. God, she looked breathtaking,' he murmured, his eyes moving as though they were even now skimming over her figure, the image burnt on to his retinas. 'It was her idea.'

'Oh.' There it was again – that wildness. 'Was it just the two of you?'

'Thank God,' he nodded. 'It was a memorable night for other reasons too.'

'You mean . . .'

'Yes.' He watched her, the way her eyes slid away from his, the way she pressed the nail of her index finger against her thumb. 'Aren't you going to ask me about it?'

'No. It's none of my business.'

'You don't think that something as seminal as Cat losing her virginity to her first love is relevant to this project? I'd have said it was a central story in her life.'

Laura bit her lip, her eyes still on the carpet. 'Fine. But leave out the gory details.'

Alex grinned. 'Well, like I said, it was the day of our final exam. Everyone had been messing about afterwards at the Rec on their bikes and boards. Someone had brought along a boom box and we were all lying about on the grass, smoking and drinking beers. Kitty and Joe were there too, snogging each other's faces off.' He chuckled. 'It was just one of those days when everything felt right, y'know? It was hot, there was a glorious sunset, the entire summer was stretching out before us . . . Cat was wearing a little pink dress, like a tennis dress, with no sleeves and one of those flippy pleated skirts . . . such great legs,' he murmured. 'Anyway, we were there for hours, just singing and watching the sun go down, when suddenly one of the lads – Tom Anderson, I think it was – pitched up with some bags of flour, and before we knew it, everyone was having a massive flour fight. It got in our eyes, our mouths, our hair, up our noses. And our clothes were covered. We looked like ghosts by the end of it.'

Laura smiled at the vision of their teenage antics.

'It got really bad when someone started chucking the beer around too, though. That's when everything got lumpy and sticky. Cat said there was no way she could go home looking like that, that her mother would kill her. I told her to come back to mine for a shower, but she just . . . she just gave me this smile. I'd never seen her smile like that before. Sometimes, I've almost thought she planned the whole thing somehow.' He shook his head. 'Anyway, she took my hand and said we should go down to the mill pond at Tipper's Brook.' He looked straight at her. 'I swear to God that was the most terrifying moment of my life, that one. Because I knew then what was going to happen.'

'Was it your first time too?'

'No. But it might as well have been. It changed us both. She was the first girl who had ever meant anything to me.'

'What made you split up?' she asked.

'We never really did. It was just a series of longer and longer breaks. The first one was when we went to university, and, looking back, my biggest mistake. I had a place at Manchester too, but I didn't want to seem like I was trailing there after her, so I went to Durham. She, uh . . . went off the rails a bit.'

'You mean she cheated on you?'

Alex looked directly at her. 'Sam was a bad influence.' He forced a smile. 'But fun. I've forgiven her since, clearly.'

'Go on.'

'Well, once I knew the score, I made a point of playing around too. There was no point moping after her a hundred and thirty miles away, knowing she was off with . . . well, God knows who. But back home in the holidays we just couldn't stay away from each other. We ended up coming to a sort of unofficial agreement that we'd see who we wanted in term time and get back together at home.'

'And you were happy with that?'

'I had to be,' he shrugged. 'In theory it was the ideal scenario. My mates couldn't believe it – whichever girl I wanted at Durham, and Cat back at home?' He looked up at her from under his thick lashes. 'It never really felt as good as it sounded.'

'What happened when she moved to London?'

'Pretty much the same. I hung out at her and Sam's flat a lot, but we were fighting more. She wanted her freedom. I represented home to her, and home was everything she wanted to escape. She didn't want to even think about it.'

'What? Even Kitty?'

'Yes. Even her.'

'But why did she want to escape from home?' Laura asked.

'Her parents had had a bitter divorce. It really screwed with her head,' he said. 'Anyway, things got steadily worse between us – a real "couldn't live with each other, without each other" scenario. It messed us both up.'

'So what was the final nail in the coffin?'

'Rob. He literally met her and married her within months. It was one of our "off" times and the first I even knew of him was when the invitation dropped on to the mat.' He jumped up off the bed and began pacing, the tone of his muscles sharp beneath his skin.

'And by then it was too late?'

He looked out into the blackening night and nodded.

'Did you go to the wedding?'

'Of course not. There was no way I could watch her walk down the aisle to another man. That's when I moved to Milan.'

'So you left the country because of her.'

'Distance just felt better. It made it easier to move on. A completely fresh start.'

Laura stared at his back. 'When did you next see her after the wedding?'

He turned back to her, pressing his skin against the cold glass without a wince. 'I opened my door one morning two years ago and there she was, on my doorstep.'

'In Milan?'

He nodded and she felt another stab of pity for him. He had left the country, tried again with another woman, but Cat haunted him like a ghost. Did she even know how he felt about her still? Did *he* know how he felt about her? The way he behaved, flirting with everyone – her, Orlando, Sam – Laura could almost believe the truth was still a secret to him.

'What about Isabella?'

He looked at her sharply. 'What about her? She's fantastic, and Cat's married. What am I supposed to do? Live like a monk? Let my life pass me by just because Cat ran off with another guy on a whim?'

'It's hardly a whim, Alex. They've been married for over four years.'

He shrugged and looked away. Laura felt sorry for Isabella, but to her surprise she felt even sorrier for him.

Laura exhaled slowly. 'Well, I think we're done,' she said quietly, standing up.

'What? But we've only just started.' He came and stood by her, his default setting back on – flirt.

Laura shook her head, no longer flustered by his proximity. She couldn't be safer with him. 'What I needed was to understand the essence of your relationship, Alex-the-ex, and I've got it. I know exactly what I'm going to do for your charm.'

'What?'

But Laura shook her head. 'It's Cat's surprise. Not yours. I'm sure you'll know soon enough.'

Alex stared at her for a second, almost deflating as he gauged the lack of response from her. Before the air between them had crackled and fizzed; now it was as flat as week-old champagne. His heart was shackled to Cat and they both knew it. He left the room without a wisecrack or loaded look, all the cocky grins gone; he was only half the man who'd walked in.

Laura walked to the glass doors and pressed one hand against the cold glass. She felt a poignant sadness for him – the Romeo undone by his own teenage dream; she knew only too well what it was to present a brave face to the world. She remembered what she'd said to him at lunch yesterday. *You're her first love, the boy who broke her heart. It makes you unforgettable.*' Who'd have thought it had been the other way around?

A slight movement to the left of the window made her start, but it was too dark to see clearly. She opened the doors quickly and stepped out on to the balcony. No one was there. The Blakes' balcony was deserted too, but the curtain was swaying slightly as though it had just been moved. They had probably been enjoying the night view as she was, but she had a funny feeling that she and Alex had been watched.

But that was ridiculous. Neither Rob nor Cat could possibly care about what she got up to in a locked room with Alex.

# Chapter Twenty-Seven

Laura sat on the sofa in the back row of the cinema room, wondering how it was that Cat made even slobbing-out look chic. She was wearing a winter-white cashmere tracksuit with baby-blue and white striped cashmere socks. Laura looked down at her own ensemble: dark green Jack Wills trackie bums bought in the sale and a navy and green flannel lumberjack-type shirt that had already lost a button and so had to be either closed up to the neck or left flopping open and dangerously close to exposing her M&S bra.

Laura dragged her eyes back to the screen and watched dispassionately as George Clooney performed a masterclass in being handsome and funny at the same time. He usually did it for her, but tonight she was more interested in the men who were busy being handsome and funny in this blacked-out room. Since her revelatory interview with Alex, and the contretemps with Rob, she felt like she was on shifting sands. She didn't understand Rob's persisting anger with her, any more than she understood why Alex was going to marry a woman he didn't love.

Alex, sitting in the middle of the three rows, had started a popcorn fight and kept landing perfect aims on Orlando, but more particularly Rob. David didn't stop texting, driving Sam to despair as his bright screen interrupted her concentration until eventually she confiscated it from him altogether.

'On the naughty step, David?' Alex chuckled, lobbing a piece of popcorn at him so that it landed in his beer.

Laura watched in silence, happy to be protected by the darkness. Now that she had some context, Alex's behaviour was easy to read: the joking, happy-go-lucky, inveterate flirt – they were all modes that kept attention on what he was doing and deflected attention from how he might be feeling.

Isabella snuggled into him, yesterday's fight already forgiven and forgotten. Maybe she knew what she was dealing with. Women were intuitive in these matters. Perhaps she accepted the off-screen role that Cat played in their lives. Cat was married, after all, and posed no direct threat to their relationship. It was Alex's fantasies and memories she had to contend with, not the woman herself.

Laura's eyes drifted over to Rob, the man living Alex's dream. Cat was stretched out on him, her head in his lap, and she kept intermittently feeding him. Occasionally, Laura would see Cat's arm snake up to his neck, bending him down to her for a kiss, even though he seemed more interested in the film.

A wave of loneliness broke over her in the back row, closely followed by exhaustion, and she wasn't sure she could manage several more hours of keeping a smile on her face. She had to go to bed. She'd already seen the film they were watching anyway. Quietly, she rose to go, placing a finger on her lips as Kitty looked across at her questioningly. Laura put her hands to the side of her cheek, indicating she was going to bed. Kitty nodded and winked as Laura tiptoed along the back row.

The spray of light as she opened the door into the hall was only momentary, and she ran lightly up the corridor towards the spa and lift. She stepped in, pressing the 'up' button and leaning against the back wall. Would it be wasteful to run another bath?

The doors were just closing when a hand suddenly shot between them and Rob followed in after her.

'Rob!' she said in alarm.

'I need to talk to you,' he panted as the doors closed behind him.

She sank against the back wall with no desire to do anything of the sort after his sharp words earlier. 'I've done all the interviews, if that's what you're worried about,' she sighed. 'I've spoken to everyone I need to here and I'll talk to Min and Olive when I get b—'

'No. I don't mean that.' He coughed into his hand and she knew now that meant, *Cue real emotion.* 'I have to apologize for the way I spoke to you earlier in the bedroom. It was unforgivable. A complete overreaction. I'm not even sure why I was so—'

'It's fine. You don't have to explain!'

'Yes I do! I was harsh on you,' he insisted vehemently. He shifted his weight, staring at her in bafflement. 'Why do you do that? Why do you think it's okay for people to treat you badly?'

A long moment passed as Laura tried to find a way out of this conversation. 'Is this some kind of corporate team-bonding thing where we're all supposed to pull together and increase our self-esteem?'

She tried to pass it off as a joke but her sarcasm angered him. 'Don't try to fob me off this time. Why don't you think you're worth more than that?' he demanded.

The doors opened and she went to move out, but Rob barred the way with his arm.

'Rob!' she laughed nervously.

But he just stared back at her.

'T-This is ridiculous!' she stammered.

Another awkward moment passed between them and she found she couldn't hold his stare. 'Where did you jet-ski, then?' he asked.

'*What?*'

'On the skidoo earlier, you told Alex you'd jet-skied. Where?'

She held out her hands questioningly in a WTF gesture that only infuriated him further.

'In the British Virgin Islands,' she said finally. 'Why?'

'What were you doing there?'

Laura tipped her head to the side, feeling her own temper beginning to surface. 'We were closing on a deal with a client, Okay? Is that enough for you?' she asked huffily. 'Do you want to know what I was wearing too? What I'd had for breakfast that day? What is this? Why do you even care?'

'I don't care, I just don't understand how the woman who skied with me on the glacier today can be the same one tiptoeing around like she wants to be invisible. I watch you with everyone here and you're so supplicating and submissive, as though what *you* think or feel doesn't matter.'

'Because it doesn't.'

'How can you think that?' he demanded angrily, taking a step towards her.

'I don't understand why you're shouting at me,' she said quietly, shrinking back. 'You said you wanted to apologize, but now you're angry with me. *Again.*'

'Because I want to understand why you're so determined to deny the fact that you're talented and brave and daring. I mean, you're just . . . you're . . .' His voice broke and his eyes roamed her face, hungry for the answers to his questions. 'You're incredible.'

His words appeared to stun him as much as her as they stood together in the tiny lift, their reflections mirrored back to them a hundred-fold. Neither of them dared breathe, blink, speak . . . The very air between them felt combustible, as though words would ignite into flames in here. He looked away first, his breath coming fast and Laura willed herself to move. She stepped to the side to get past him as he stood stock still, hands on his hips, his head dropped – in shock? Embarrassment? Shame? She didn't know what – when she felt his hand grip her arm and swing her back into him. The coppered glass of the lift was cold against her back, but his lips were hot as he kissed her with a passion that made all the colours and noises and desires she'd drained from herself spring like a riot. That tangential difference between surviving and living hit her again like a punch, and for one moment – two – three – she went with it. She couldn't not. Every impulse in her body was fighting for it as if it was the breath that sustained her.

But it couldn't last. She couldn't let it. She pulled away from him violently, feeling the vitality that he made rise in her ebb instantly. It was like moving away from a fire, the heat falling with every step. 'No,' she whispered, edging past him, her hands feeling for the open doors and the space she needed to escape him. This.

'Laura,' he implored, his chest heaving with the effort it took *not* to grab her again, but she shook her head, desperately.

'No . . .'

'Laura, I'm sorry . . . I didn't mean to . . . Just talk to me!'

But the woman she knew he'd glimpsed in their kiss had already gone. The woman he was so intent upon finding, she was equally determined to hide.

# Chapter Twenty-Eight

It was only two in the afternoon, but already Laura had jam-packed frenzied activity into every minute of the day. Being too damned busy to think was her master plan and it had got off to a great start: a dawn flight and rush-hour traffic on the motorway had kept her concentrating all the way home. And when she'd found the house empty, she hadn't tarried there either – wolfing down a ham sandwich as she threw her clothes into the washing machine, she had marched straight back out again, calling Fee from the car. Twenty minutes had been allocated to choosing paints in Homebase and now she was ready to throw herself into some hard labour and pick up her own life where she'd left off. Verbier had never happened.

Laura lifted the enormous paint pots out of Dolly's boot and staggered haltingly back over the sand towards the hut. She set them down carefully on the new veranda, determined not to create a single dent or chip in the carpenter's handiwork. He'd done her proud – the rotten shiplap boards had been replaced, new felt put on the roof, a new floor laid and triple-glazed safety glass cut to size for the windows that would hopefully help with insulation. She patted it triumphantly.

Laura had asked Fee to go via the studio to get some clean

cups and fresh milk for them both, and when she came back, they'd be set to start; all that remained now was to decorate the inside and out, and furnish the interior.

Laura looked down the beach for her, agitated, not wanting to be still for a second, but there was no sign. She cupped her hands together and breathed hot air into them, scrunching up her toes in her wellies to keep the circulation flowing. The temperature had dropped significantly over the weekend – bizarrely it felt colder here than it had done in Verbier – and storms were heading in from the North Sea. She could see the waves in the distance being whipped up like meringues, and the shore boasted a dirtied white froth on the sand like a moustache.

Laura hopped inside the hut to take shelter, shutting the new half-glazed door behind her and muffling the roar of the sea. The carpenter had fitted a deadbolt on to the door to maximize security, but you still couldn't leave anything worth more than a biro in here. God only knows what security measures Jack would install when she gave it to him – lasers? Armed patrol?

She crouched down, levered open a paint pot with a butter knife and began to stir fast, a few splatters dotting the new floorboards.

'Dammit,' she muttered, smudging them hurriedly with a J-cloth.

'I'm back!' a reedy voice called, and Laura jumped up and opened the door. Fee was climbing the steps, her eyes to the ground as she carried a stack of letters wedged beneath her chin and two steaming cups of tea in her hand.

'What on earth are you doing?' Laura cried, taking the letters from her.

Fee groaned and stretched out her neck. 'Ooh, that's better.

I was getting so stiff walking all that way like that. I felt like a swa—' She faltered and her mouth dropped open as she took in Laura's new blonde look.

'I cannot believe you made the tea and walked half a mile with it, Fee!' Laura said, panicking at her dumbstruck expression and trying desperately to divert her with anger, the best form of defence. 'I meant for you to get the cups and milk and we'd make it *here*.' She pointed towards the shiny red whistling kettle perched expectantly on the new white melamine worktop.

Fee just gaped at her. 'You went *blonde*?'

'Not my idea. Cat and Kitty's,' Laura mumbled, smoothing it nervously with her hands. 'What do you think?'

'What do I think? You know perfectly well what I think! I've been telling you to dye it for years! But what does my opinion matter? Three days with the posh girls and you're putty in their hands! And talking of your—' She picked up Laura's hands and stared at the grey polish. 'You *never* paint your nails.'

'It's Chanel.'

'Oh, is it?' Fee asked, unimpressed. 'Well, they make your hands look like they're dead.' She dropped Laura's hands disgustedly. 'I can't believe . . . I mean, you were gone for three days and you've come back looking like a completely different person!'

Laura held her breath. She had felt like a completely different person. Out there.

'Has Jack seen you yet?'

Laura shook her head. 'It's only a wash-in hair colour, Fee. I can always change it back if he doesn't like it.' Laura rolled her lips together, trying not to cry. Her emotions were alarmingly close to the surface.

Fee softened, knowing her too well. 'Well now, don't be hasty. It looks a lot better, like I always told you it would. I'm just upset you trusted some strangers' opinions over mine, that's all.'

'But they're not strangers, Fee . . .' Laura began, before catching sight of Fee's face.

They fell silent.

'Anyway, this looks great!' Fee said, pointedly steering them into safer waters.

Laura nodded. It was a million miles from being a deluxe chalet in Verbier with leather floors and . . . She squeezed her eyes shut. No. 'Well, when it's all painted up, it'll be, uh . . . yes,' she faltered.

'You'll have to put up some hooks for your wetsuits,' Fee said quietly, crossing to one of the side walls and patting it. The pat marked the spot. 'And you'll need a shelf or more hooks for towels.'

'Yes, and I've just bought a basket for shoes and flip-flops. Wellies too in the winter.'

'Yup. Storage. I like it.'

'And I thought I'd have a go at making a curtain to pull along under this counter so we don't have to look at that ugly great gas canister.' Laura kicked it lightly with her foot. It was a long way from the sushi grill in the chalet.

They stood looking at the tiny, unpainted space together, their half-full cups of tea steaming in the cold air.

'Jack's going to love it, Laur. And he'll be so touched when he hears all the trouble you've gone to to make it like this for him,' she said quietly, looking across at her as though still trying to absorb the transformation. 'You've got a bit of a tan.'

'Really?' Laura touched her face, remembering how this

time yesterday she'd been flying across the mountains, holding on to Rob for dear life on the back of that skidoo. She still remembered how his muscles had contracted beneath her touch as she held onto him. 'Wind-burn probably,' she said, her voice thick. She quickly turned away, crouching down and stirring the paint.

Fee watched her. 'Is everything all right?'

'Of course. Why wouldn't it be?'

'I dunno. You just seem a bit . . . subdued.'

'I'm fine.'

She heard Fee inhale deeply. 'Well, you're not the only one with stuff going on. Paul and I broke up.'

'What?' Laura asked, toppling backwards off her feet and landing on her bottom with a thump, splattering yet more paint on the floor. 'That's—' She stopped herself only just in time from saying 'great'. 'That's a shame. You seemed keen.'

Fee shrugged awkwardly.

'Was it the incessant Korean?' Laura asked, trying to raise a smile. But for once it didn't work and this time it was Fee who turned away. 'Well, I met a guy in Verbier who'd be perfect for you. His name's Mark, he's a ski instructor, and he's totally drop-dead gorgeous,' Laura said, doing her best impression of the teenage speak that Fee still used.

'Oh right,' Fee said, tapping her foot. 'Well, I'll just get the next flight out, then, book a lesson and we can get on with choosing names for our babies.'

Laura rolled her eyes. 'Don't be like that. Even Kitty thinks he's gorgeous, and she's very circumspect.'

Fee's eyebrow jogged at the mention of Kitty's name. 'Well, if Kitty thinks so . . .' she said, employing Laura's trademark sarcasm.

'Fee! I'm just trying to cheer you up.'

''Course you are. Because now you've got your new flash friends to run your life for you, we'd better all bow down to them. They know best, right?'

Laura bit her lip in the face of her friend's jealousy. Suddenly, she didn't know how she was going to bring up the topic of Cat's launch party.

'I care about you and want something more for you, Fee, that's all. You could live such an interesting life. I don't want you to just settle like – ' She stopped.

'What? Like you, you mean?'

'I wasn't going to say that.'

'Yes you were.'

'No! You and I both know that Jack's Mr Perfect. You're the one always telling me how lucky I am, and I am. I know I am.'

Fee narrowed her eyes. 'Oh yeah? Then why's your voice gone all funny?'

'I'm tired, Fee!' Laura cried, throwing her hands up in the air. 'I was up at dawn today.'

'You weren't supposed to be. You were supposed to be coming back this evening,' Fee said calmly, watching her closely.

'Yes, and I realized I had far too much work to do to lose half a working day to packing and drinking freshly squeezed papaya juice in Switzerland.' She swallowed hard, wondering what they had all said when they came down to her note on the kitchen table this morning:

*Family emergency, so sorry, have to catch first flight. Thank you for a lovely weekend. I'll never forget it, Laura.*

If she was lucky, only Rob would know the real reason she had fled and no one would think any more about it.

'You're crying,' Fee whispered.

'I'm just tired,' Laura half said, half sobbed, pressing the heels of her hands to her eyes. 'I slept badly again last night.' After two nights of deep, dreamless sleep, she had been punished for it with her usual nightmare, only with three times more menace than usual – a shadow covering her till she was blind and breathless, crushing her until her bones snapped, reasserting itself as the black shroud she must wear at all times. What had seemed so bright, so possible in the sunlight in Verbier had slipped out of reach again: passion, adventure, accomplishment, friendships . . . plain bloody *fun* – they were never supposed to have been hers. She belonged to the fringes, the shadows.

Fee stared at her strangely 'Well, this hut's not going to paint itself,' she murmured. 'Come on, let's put on some music to get us going,' she said, pulling out her iPod and scrolling through to some Tinie Tempah. She placed it on the windowsill, turned it up so loud that the panes vibrated, and the two of them immersed themselves in the job in hand, both grateful not to have to talk any more. For the first time in their friendship, a problem shared was a problem doubled.

They let themselves into the studio four hours later, speckled with paint like mistle thrushes, arms aching.

'Aahhh!' Laura sighed as Fee flopped dramatically on the sofa. 'That was harder than it looked. I can't believe we still haven't finished it.'

She stopped in the middle of the room as she clocked the miles of warm-white fairy lights Fee had stapled around the vast windows over the weekend. The studio twinkled like a fairy's grotto and Laura clapped her hands delightedly. 'Wow! This looks great, Fee! Very festive. Maybe we should have Christmas in here.' She noticed a tiny potted Christmas tree on the small table near the wood-burning stove. 'Fee?'

Fee had been unusually quiet all afternoon. Once they'd got going, Laura had done most of the talking, but they were significantly down on their usual quota of words per minute and she sensed Fee was taking the break-up with Paul harder than she would admit – or at least admit to Laura.

'Huh? What?'

'Tea?' Laura asked, walking straight over to her bench.

'Love one,' Fee replied quietly.

'I meant, would you *make* one, you daft nana,' Laura chuckled, trying to josh her along. 'I've got work to get on with. I've chosen the charms from the interviews this weekend. Just got to . . . oh, *make* them now. Seven charms in ten days, and I've still got two interviews remaining.' She shook her head. 'Honestly, I must have been mad taking all this on.'

'Well, think of it this way – you're giving Jack his dream for Christmas, and you got a free holiday out of it,' Fee replied flatly.

Laura kept her eyes down and her back turned as she arranged her tools in descending size on the bench. She couldn't help but feel she had lost more than she had gained on that holiday. Yes, she had given herself a 'lost weekend' – fifty hours out of her own life to indulge in her every desire (and how!) – but it had come at too high a price. She'd been naïve to think she could take it. From the moment she'd stolen away at dawn this morning, she'd felt like she was rolling in glass, every achingly familiar step through her own life today making her heart contract sharply. She'd been robbed of the peace of mind that had made her life here bearable before.

She pressed the answerphone button, irritated by the flashing red light.

*'Hello . . . this is a message for – muffled cough – Laura Cunningham. This is Olive Tremayne speaking . . . I . . . I would like to invite you to the house for the interview on Wednesday, one o'clock . . . Don't call back. I'll assume you're coming unless I hear to the contrary. Goodbye.'*

Laura listened to the recording twice. The woman's voice was clipped and incredibly strained. What had Rob said to her to force this change of heart? She closed her eyes, feeling her nerves rising already.

She pressed for the next message.

*'Hello? Anyone there?'* Laura instinctively smiled at the sound of Kitty's voice. *'It's me, Kit. Just checking in on you, hoping everything's all right with your family emergency.'* Laura shut her eyes, knowing Fee was already frowning at her. *'All's well here. I got back two hours ago and had to go straight into lopping trees in the orchard. Back to reality, huh?'* An image of Kitty swinging from a harness with a power tool in one hand made Laura burst out laughing, prompting further furrowed brows from Fee. *'Anyway, I just wanted to say, please do pop in whenever you're in the area next. Verbier was such fun! Missing you already, sweets. Byeee.'*

'She's pally,' Fee said coolly, sitting up on the sofa.

'Yes, I guess so.'

'You need to be careful, Laura.'

'Why?'

'"Be friendly, not familiar" – that's what my grandpa always used to say. Wise words too. They're only clients, remember.'

Laura looked over at her. 'You sound jealous, Fee.'

'I'm not jealous.'

'No?' Laura arched an eyebrow.

Fee shot Laura her most innocent look and a short silence passed between them. Things had been changing recently, Laura could feel it. Other people were coming between them – first Paul, now Kitty and the others, breaking the seal on their cosy little vacuum. There seemed to be an almost constant undercurrent of tension in their conversations.

'So, tea was it, m'lady?' Fee asked, hoisting herself up off the sofa with a pained expression.

'Don't worry, I'll do it,' Laura sighed, crossing the room.

'Have you spoken to Jack since you got home?' Fee asked, watching her.

'No. But that's a good point. I'd better try him again. There's no reception on the beach. I'll call him now.'

'Oh, leave it – let's have our tea first.'

'I should just let him know I'm back.'

'He can wait a bit longer. You're always going off after talking to him. He'll tell you he's already home making some romantic supper and I won't get my cup of tea. And then what'll I do?'

'Make it yourself?' Laura smiled, relieved to see some of Fee's usual dramatics return.

'Meh!' Fee said, swiping the suggestion away and falling back on the sofa.

Laura rolled her eyes as she walked over to the kitchenette, catching sight of her reflection in the bathroom mirror. She looked noticeably younger and healthier. More vital. She stopped and stared at her new image, trying to see herself as Jack would see her tonight. Would he like it? What would he say? What would she? Would he see the other changes in her too?

She gave a small resolute nod to her own reflection, like an officer to his sergeant. It was only a hair colour. It didn't mean anything. She was still Jack's girl, the girl he chose to love – in spite of all her meekness and small-mindedness and sarcasm. She blinked hard, banishing Rob's harsh words from her mind. That was already the past. Unreal. She was home now and back on a safe path once more, no net required.

# Chapter Twenty-Nine

None of the lights were on inside the cottage as she parked Dolly at the back and walked down the garden path, her eyes scanning for the usual ice patches. She let herself in, wondering if Jack had splurged on the tree and where he'd put it. The position of the Christmas tree constituted one of their three annual rows, the other two being Valentine's Day cards are not romantic (her position), and the first day of the Ashes should be a bank holiday (his).

She silently bet herself he'd put it in the back corner of the sitting room, even though he knew she preferred it in the small bowed window that nudged into the street. It looked prettier and more festive from outside, and acted as a screen for nosy passers-by looking in on them, but Jack felt it was too close to the door there and made him feel like he was walking into a hedge.

Laura switched the lights on and hung up her coat in the porch before opening the sitting-room door, to see whether her hunch was right. She stared in dismay at the pristine sight before her. Nothing had been done apart from the hoovering. There was no tree, no tinsel, not a card nor plastic angel to be seen. Even the candle on the coffee table was a lily-of-the-valley scent from the summer. It could have been July.

Feeling disproportionately flattened by the revelation, she moved into the kitchen, kicking off her shoes by the table and staring, bewildered, into the fridge. Carrots, mushrooms, a pot of chicken liver pâté, hummus, some tenderstem broccoli and mint jelly. She racked her brain, wondering what meal Jack was planning to make out of those ingredients and whether she could make it first.

'You're home.'

Jack's voice was quiet behind her.

Laura spun round with fright. '*Wha—?*' she shrieked, holding on to the fridge door for support, one hand trying to steady her hammering heart. 'Jack! What are you doing sneaking up on me like that? You almost gave me a heart attack. Jesus! I didn't hear you come in.'

'That's because I wasn't out. I was upstairs,' he replied in a subdued voice, his eyes on her hair as if it was moving of its own accord. If he was as shocked as she was, he was doing a better job of hiding it.

He'd been upstairs in the dark? Laura swallowed nervously. 'Like it?' she asked, plastering a hopeful smile on her face and bobbing the bottom of her hair with her hands.

'When were you going to tell me, Laur?'

'Well, I thought it would be better to show you than tell you over the phone. I thought you might freak out and think I'd done a Marilyn or something. But it's not bright blonde, is it?' she asked rhetorically. 'It's just a few shades stronger than my natural colour.'

He gave a tired sigh and walked up to her at the fridge. Laura puckered up for a kiss, but Jack simply reached past her and pulled out a beer.

'Jack?' she asked, as he turned and walked out of the room again.

Laura stared at the spot where he'd been standing, trying to make sense of what had just happened. She followed him into the sitting room, where he had thrown himself on the sofa and was flicking through the sports channels at lightning speed.

'Jack? What's wrong?' she asked, resting her cheek against the edge of the door.

His eyes flicked up to her. 'I asked you a question. If you want to waste my time and yours gabbling on about your hair, then be my guest. I'd rather hang out here.'

'But I thought that's what you were talking about.'

'Did you now?' Sarcasm oozed from his words. Everyone was at it.

'Yes. What *are* you talking about?'

'You really can't guess?'

Her heart lurched and Laura sank on to the arm of the sofa. She could now. His eyes – bitter and disappointed – told her exactly what he knew. He'd had the realization in the middle of the night after all.

'Oh God, Jack. It's not what you think. I can explain. I wasn't trying to—'

'What? Hide it from me? Get it taken care of before I could do anything about it? No, of course not!'

'I mean it, Jack. I was going to tell you. I just needed time to think. It was a shock, that was all.'

'That's why you couldn't get on that plane fast enough, wasn't it?' He wouldn't look at her.

Laura swallowed. 'It's true I thought the change of scenery would do me good. I thought it would help me get some perspective.'

'And did it? Did partying with a load of hedge-funders in Verbier help you decide whether to keep our baby?'

She looked down, his words hitting hard. 'You know it's not a straightforward decision for me.'

He was quiet for a long time. 'You know what I think, Laura? I don't think your concerns were about whether or not to have a baby. I think they were about whether or not to have *my* baby.'

'Jack, no!' Laura gasped, collapsing on to the sofa next to him. 'That's categorically not true.'

'No?' His eyes followed a bobsleigh hurtling down a luge.

She shook her head frantically. 'It just wasn't a decision that I could take lightly.'

'But you could take it alone, that's what you're saying?'

'I would have told you, Jack – I promise!' Laura cried, stretching across the sofa so that she was now sitting on his lap and obscuring his view of the TV screen that he was so determined to focus on. 'I just needed to discover what I thought first before I told you. I already knew what you would say,' she said softly, stroking his cheek.

'Did you?' His eyes met hers.

She nodded. 'I know you'd love a baby more than anything. I know how badly you want us to be a proper family. But having children isn't something we've ever talked about and I just didn't know that I could do it. I'd be so frightened all the time and what kind of mother would that make me? I'd be neurotic and smothering . . .' She kissed his temple lightly. 'And I knew that if I told you, you'd talk me into it with that ruthless, gentle persuasion of yours.'

Laura rested her cheek against the top of his head, her fingers stroking his shaggy hair. Sweet, darling Jack, so dependable and safe and familiar, like worn slippers; he was everything she wanted. He didn't change with the wind; he didn't push her to be someone she didn't want to be; he didn't make her jump out of helicopters or slam her against walls to kiss her; he didn't hold her heart in his hand and leave her breathless and terrified that he might crush it with whimsical caprice.

She closed her eyes. If Verbier had shown her anything, it was how fragile her world was without Jack, how quickly she had succumbed to her own passions in his absence, sampling danger and desire with reckless abandon. She needed Jack's quiet steer and gentle guidance.

'But Verbier gave me the time I needed, Jack, and I think maybe we *should* have a baby.' She waited for the light to reach his eyes, but it didn't. He pulled away, silent and unresponsive. 'Jack?' she asked, watching the Adam's apple in his throat bob up and down. 'Did you hear what I said?'

He got up, moving her so roughly to the side that she practically fell back on to the sofa. He walked over to the window, where the Christmas tree wasn't.

'I can see that you're trying, don't think I can't,' he said quietly. 'But I can always see it; that's the problem.'

Laura looked at him in confusion. 'What?'

'You try so hard all the time to love me.'

'I do love you, Jack.'

He shook his head. 'No. You love what I represent, and that's not enough any more. It hasn't been for a long time.' He looked into the deserted street. The cottage opposite was empty – owned by Londoners who only came on summer weekends – and shrouded in darkness. 'I told myself that I could love you enough for the both of us, but every day I watch you trying to live my life with me and every day it breaks my heart.'

'It's *our* life, Jack.'

'No. It's mine. I belong here. I have a business, friends—'

'So do I.'

'You live on the surface, Laura. You could pick up your tools and leave tomorrow and the only people who would notice would be me and Fee.' He looked at her sadly. 'I see you trying to mould yourself into the person you think you should be for us. If I didn't love you so much, I'd hate you for it. It's so patronizing seeing you fold into smaller versions of yourself – but I'd have put up with anything so long as you stayed.'

'But I'm not going anywhere, Jack. I want to be here, with you. I don't understand where all this is coming from. I'm sorry that I didn't tell you I thought I was pregnant, but I really did just need to get my head straight.'

'And so did I, because you weren't the only one with a decision to make.' His tone was final. 'If you'd only asked, I'd have told you I can't bring a child into the world either. Not when I know in my heart that its mother doesn't love its father.'

'That's not true,' Laura protested. She wanted to stand but wasn't sure her legs would support her. She'd told him she wanted his baby. Why were they having *this* discussion?

'We've shuffled along up till now because you've tried and I've tried to be blind. But a baby changes everything. And we owe it to the baby, if not to ourselves, to face the truth – we're not going to make it.'

Tears blinded her and she dropped her face into her hands, shaking her head and trying to block out his words, but like the tears, they kept coming.

'As much as I love you – and I really do fucking love you, Laura . . .' He choked, his voice ragged and torn. '. . . I can't spend my life apologizing for not being more than the man I am. We both gave it our best shot, for all the right reasons, but we've run out of road. You can't have this baby.'

Laura looked up at him desperately. 'But I'm not!'

'What?'

'I'm not pregnant. I never was. I was just late.' Hope bloomed again. 'Don't you see? Nothing has actually changed between us at all. We can just carry on as we were.'

He went grey before her eyes. 'But Fee said you were—'

'*Fee* said?' Laura echoed, shocked. 'Fee's the one who told you?'

She'd thought he'd guessed. Fee had been spot on when she'd quipped that day, in town, that he knew her monthly cycle better than Laura did. If ever she wasn't sure, she checked her dates with him.

'She thought I should know. She's done nothing wrong, Laur,' he said quietly after a moment.

Laura looked at him sharply, instantly on the attack. 'Why are you defending her?'

'I'm not, I—'

'Yes you are. You're protecting her. My best friend has betrayed my confidence and *you're* defending her.'

'This is beside the point, Laura. It changes nothing. Whether Fee told me or not, whether you're even pregnant or not, our ending is still the same.'

Laura's brain began to race as she thought back to Fee's subdued mood. 'You said a minute ago that I patronize you and Fee,' she murmured. 'But what's Fee got to do with any of this? We're talking about having a baby. Why did you bring *her* into it?'

'I didn't mean anything by it.'

'Yes you did. You see you and her as the same and I'm an outsider all of a sudden? *I'm* the one who brings us all together.'

'No. You've always been the outsider, Laur. That's what

I'm trying to tell you. You're lying to all of us by pretending that this is enough for you, and it's only something as real and for ever as a baby that's giving me the strength to say this.'

'Oh my God,' Laura whispered, not even hearing him now. 'You're in love with her.'

'No. I'm in love with you.' The rims of his eyes were reddening.

Laura stared at him. Fee's muted behaviour this afternoon made more sense by the moment. She wasn't cut up about Paul. She had felt guilty for what she'd said, for what they'd . . . Laura gasped. 'Did something happen between the two of you while I was gone? Is that why there's no Christmas tree – you couldn't get out of bed this weekend? Is that it? Is that why she's broken up with Paul?' Her voice was shrill and rising.

Jack shook his head, but fractionally too late. The fatal pause Rob had told her about.

'Laura . . .'

But she simply held up a single, shaking hand. 'Don't . . .' she whispered. 'Just don't. You've told me everything I need to know.'

# Chapter Thirty

Laura pressed the tile to the wall and held it for a few seconds, reaching down with the other hand for the plastic X pegs that set the spacing. She felt it bond and slowly released her hand from it. The tile held.

Stepping back, she admired her work. Dimpled and rustic in a matt sandy pink with starfish and winkles indented into them like fossils, they had come from a small batch of seconds a local artist had been offering in a box outside her studio. They looked lovely around the sink. Fresh.

Tomorrow, she could apply the grouting and the hut would be ready for . . . well, for what? Hardly the grand Christmas unveiling she'd bought it for.

She shook her head, trying to make the memory of last night disappear before the tears could gather. She must buy a small tree, she reminded herself, digging her nails into her hand – preferably one that was potted. And she needed to stop by B&Q at some point and get a peg rack, and some wicker baskets.

Pulling on her puffa coat and wellies, she locked the hut behind her. The dark pigeon colour she'd chosen for the walls looked great next to the vanilla windows and veranda. In the space of three short weeks Urchin had gone from being the scruffiest hut on the beach to one of the smartest.

It had started to rain and she marched quickly down the sand to the water's edge, walking into the mercurial shallows. The water was anthracite grey today with rolling white surf, the sky a molten gold with blowsy black clouds gliding slowly across like galleons. The metallic colours brought the necklace back to mind – not that it was ever very far away, given the hours she was putting in on it. She'd worked for six hours solid when she'd gone back to the studio last night – desperate to do anything other than think, as she heated and melted, annealed, shaped, hammered and fired the happiness in another woman's life – before falling into a fitful sleep on the sofa at two a.m.

Work was the best therapy she knew. Talking was a waste of time; she'd learnt that lesson long ago. Life would go on she'd lived through worse than this and she know what she had to do. Gary, the locksmith, was booked to come in tomorrow whilst she interviewed Olive and Min, so neither Fee's nor Jack's keys would work and she could stay at the studio without worrying about them turning up unannounced, determined to talk – as she knew they would. Both of them had tried calling her. Fee particularly had left tearful messages, protesting innocence and begging her to call back, but Laura had simply switched off her phone. Soon, Fee would ball up her courage and make the trip face-to-face, risking Laura's white-hot anger, and Laura was determined to deny her the chance. She wanted the silence between them to be as impermeable and slow-moving as ice, to grow thicker by the day. There was simply nothing to say. Jack and Fee – her only family – were lost to her.

Laura looked out to sea, watching raindrops pinprick the surface. She felt numb and defiant. There were things to love about her newfound freedom – like eating microwave meals

KAREN SWAN

for one at ten o'clock at night, getting up at dawn and not having to explain it, deleting AC/DC from her iPod and singing Florence & the Machine songs at the top of her voice.

Plus she was blitzing her workload. Kitty and Orlando's charms were now finished; Sam and Alex's were nearing completion. Of the interviews that had been done, only Rob's charm remained – he had unwittingly opened up enough on the glacier to give her more material than she could have hoped for in a formal interview – and she'd been avoiding starting work on that for the simple reason that it forced her to do precisely what she was trying *not* to do: think about him. But with Cat's birthday not much more than a week away, and two interviews to do tomorrow, she knew she couldn't put it off any longer.

The water came to just an inch below her boots as she waded across the channel, but it was rough and spilt over the tops of her wellies, soaking her jeans and socks. Pulling them off at the bottom of the steps, she ran up barefoot, her hair dripping fat splodges of water down her back.

Her Skype was ringing when she unlocked the door, and she ran, skidded and lunged for it, pressing 'connect'. The first thing she saw was Rob, peering so near to the screen that he looked like he might fall in – or kiss her again. Her eyes fell upon his in close-up, so close she could see the golden specks that dotted them like freckles; she saw the surprise register in his face at the sight of her before him so suddenly, the quick spread of his pupils against their copper beds, the breath-holding silence as they each relived the mutual bewilderment of that last moment in the lift.

'So you just press that button there – and off you go,' he muttered, moving back, and Laura could see Cat sitting behind him, staring quizzically at the screen. She was wearing a pistachio-green cashmere polo neck, and tufts of blonde hair fell wispily around her face.

'Laura!' she exclaimed excitedly when she saw Laura staring back at her, sopping wet and bedraggled, through the screen. 'Oh my God! I can't believe I did it. I've never worked this before! How are you?' she beamed, before frowning. 'Is it raining over there?'

Laura nodded back, trying to look at least okay – it was beyond her to pull off 'happy' today – as she raked her hands through her wet hair. 'Yes, great, thanks. Did you all get back all right?'

Cat tipped her head to the side and pulled a sad face. 'We so missed *you*. What happened?'

'Oh, you know . . . the dog . . . had a temperature . . . Jack panicked.' She rolled her eyes, keeping her voice steady as she said Jack's name, aware that Rob was still in the room. She could see him behind Cat, flicking awkwardly through a magazine, no doubt worried Laura was going to drop him in it.

'But it's okay, the dog?' Cat asked, concern tattooed all over her face.

'Yes. False alarm. I'm sorry if anyone was worried. I didn't want to cause a fuss.'

'Do you hear that, Rob? It's all okay.' She leant in closer to the screen so that Laura swore she could pick up notes of frangipani. 'He's been so worried. It's so sweet!'

'Aaaah!' Laura kept her eyes dead ahead, determined not to look at him behind Cat. Her peripheral vision told her they were in the bedroom – it was all very pale and milky from what she could gather, and she wondered whether there was another expensive, exotic carpet on the floor – zebra perhaps? Without moving her eyes a fraction, she saw him throw down the magazine and start to pace. Even across the country and through a screen, she could see the tension in his movements.

'Well now, listen – I have got some great news,' Cat confided breathlessly. 'I must have phoned half of London since we got back yesterday, and I can confirm: The. Party. Is. On! We'll have it in London at a friend's flat – I'm not sure exactly where yet, so many people want to help – but it's definitely going to be Friday week, six o'clock to seven-thirty. We'll start early because it's the day before Christmas Eve, obviously, so everyone's just rammed.'

'But isn't next Friday your birthday?'

'How did you know that?' Cat gasped, delighted. 'Who told you? I bet it was Kitty! It was Kitty, wasn't it?'

Laura nodded, aware that Rob had stopped pacing in the background and was standing, motionless, his hands in his pockets. She wished he would go away. She wished she had never met him. 'Yes. Kitty told me.'

'Well, listen, we'll do the party early evening and then whatever Rob's got organized for me – and I know it'll be something fabulous,' she squealed, half turning towards him, 'we'll go on to it together.'

'Oh no, Cat, I couldn't possibly intrude in—'

'Enough already! You're one of the gang now. So listen, I'll email you the address, but just bring everything you've got and aim to be in High Street Ken for four p.m., okay? We'll need to set up properly. And the dress code's cocktail.'

Laura nodded nervously. 'Okay.' She didn't have anything here at the studio that would constitute cocktail; she barely had anything here that constituted 'dressed'. She would have to go home to raid her wardrobe – but what if Jack was there? Or worse still, Fee?

'See you next Friday, sweetie,' Cat winked. 'I can't wait. And Rob's going to make that call to Bertie, aren't you, Rob?'

Rob muttered something unintelligible in the background.

'Baby, how do I turn this off?' Cat asked, lifting her hands in the air delicately as though afraid the keyboard would give her septic shock.

Rob came to the laptop, leaning over Cat so that she was lost from Laura's vision again.

'I'll do it,' he said, his eyes on Laura, his finger hovering over the button for several seconds before he cut the connection between them.

Laura sat back, her heart pounding. She told herself it was from the brisk walk over the beach; she had run up the stairs; she was excited about the party Cat was throwing for her next week . . .

She stood up, agitated, and got the fire roaring so that an orange glow lit up the studio like a beacon. Once she had pulled the duvet out from under the sofa and snuggled under it, she grabbed her laptop and checked her in-box.

The name that flashed up in it left her in no doubt as to the real reason her heart was pounding. She clicked it open.

*'It was a mistake. I apologize. Clearly it won't happen again.'*

Laura took a sharp intake of breath at the curt message. That wasn't what his eyes had said.

# Chapter Thirty-One

The next day didn't start well. After her usual 2 a.m. jolt awake, she had struggled to drop back to sleep again – her mind kept running over various images of Jack and Fee together – and when sleep did return, it was like ether, sending her into a black, dreamless void that didn't register outside stimuli such as alarm clocks. As a result, she was fifty minutes behind schedule by the time she did open one lazy eye, and it took another five before she could summon the will to move and start this next day alone. Traffic was particularly bad on the way into London, and by the time she had located the gallery, driven round the block nine times trying to find a parking space and then squeezed Dolly into it, she was over an hour late for the appointment with Min.

She overfed the meter and darted through the perfumed crowds in ill-chosen bootcut jeans, red Converse and an itchy grey rollneck that matched her eyes. She had forgotten her jacket, typically. Yesterday's rain had turned Arctic and it was sleeting lightly, covering the pavement with a subtle sheen that made her run on her toes as she wove a zigzag path down Holland Park. The gallery was easy to spot, even from a distance, as a tubby sculpture of a naked man rendered in metal coils was squatting outside the huge plate-glass windows. Laura felt an overwhelming urge to plonk an elf's hat on his head.

She stared in through the windows. Inside, she saw a short-haired woman with even shorter legs talking on the phone. She was wearing a cream silk shirt and chocolate trousers, and a burnt-orange polka-dot scarf was tied elaborately round her neck.

The woman looked up and saw her and, without breaking stride in her conversation, beckoned for her to come in. Laura pushed open the glass door, leaving behind her a greasy handprint.

The woman's voice was strident and imperious as she carried on with her conversation, seemingly giving directions to a warehouse somewhere in Florence. Laura stood placidly in the middle of the gallery and looked around, trying to muster an expression of interest. Vast pretty canvases of landscapes rendered in cherry-pink, apple-green and cobalt-blue oils lit the space. They were idealized and naïve – some of the scenes even sparkled with touches of glitter, as though fairies had tiptoed across in the night – but the application was so bold and vigorous that their appeal was immediate. Except to her. She couldn't feel anything right now.

'You're Laura,' the woman said, finally finishing her conversation and advancing towards her, but stopping just out of reach of a handshake.

Laura nodded. 'Yes. You're Min, I take it?'

The woman didn't feel the need to confirm. 'You're late.'

'Yes. I'm sorry. Traffic's shocking. I've come in from Suffolk.'

'I'm very busy,' Min frowned, clearly wanting rather more grovelling than Laura was giving.

But Laura didn't have the energy or the time. She was going to have to get what she needed quickly if she was going to be out of here and on time for her next interview – and she really didn't want to be late for that one.

'So. This is for Cat's latest birthday surprise, is it?'

'Yes, a gold charm necklace. It's very good of you to give me some of your time. You're obviously busy. I'll try to keep the interview as brief as possible for you.'

'To tell you the truth, I'm at a loss as to why Robert Blake wants me to be included in this . . .' She waggled her fingers as she reached for the right word. Not finding it, she let the statement hang, unfinished, in the air. Her eyes flicked up and down Laura as though assessing her for likelihood of robbery or assault. 'Come on, then. You'd better come through to my office.'

She walked through the gallery to a narrow corridor that ran off to the left at the back. From what Laura could see as she passed, there was a smart marble-decorated bathroom, a kitchenette, a tiny storage room and Min's office. This was reasonably sized and very bright, with a recessed light well cut into the roof, two pale leathers chairs the colour of cappuccino foam and a desk with bronze legs shaped like duck's webbed feet at the bottoms. Canvases were stacked five deep along the walls, and there was a tower of taped-up boxes in the far corner.

'Sit,' Min commanded as she marched to her seat behind the desk. Like a good Labrador, Laura sat.

'Some mineral water?'

Laura shook her head at the meagre offer. It was trying to snow outside. This was the kind of day hot chocolate was made for.

'Let's get down to business, then.'

Laura reached down and pulled out her digital recorder, saying nothing but asking permission with enquiring eyebrows. Min nodded.

'So when did you first meet Cat?' she began.

'When she came to work for me here. Although I knew her by reputation before that.'

'And what was her reputation?'

'Attractive, good taste, highly social. Invited to all the best parties and married to a rich husband. My target customer, basically.'

'She lives in Surrey, though,' Laura said, puzzled. 'Surely you couldn't have "heard" about her from there?'

'This was several years ago. They used to live around here, on Aubrey Walk, back then.'

'Oh. Why did they move, do you know?'

'She said they were talking about starting a family.'

Laura nodded, remembering Rob's face on the glacier. 'And was she one of your clients before she started working here?'

Min thought for a moment. 'No. But I was aware she was very well connected and knew a lot of my clients. When I finally met her myself at a party, I could tell she was bored of the housewife parade, so I offered her a role here, at the gallery.'

Laura nodded. That tallied up with Kitty's comments about Cat wanting to prove herself in ways beyond her looks. And hadn't Orlando said they'd each realized an ambition, teaming up together to open their own business? Alex had said she was intelligent – top three in economics, which she later read at university. Laura could see Cat was constantly trying to break out. 'Tell me what you thought of her when you first met. You said you knew her by reputation beforehand . . .'

'Yes. And she pretty much confirmed all my assumptions – blonde, bored, pampered and spoilt. Surprisingly clever, though,' Min added graciously after a moment.

'It sounds like you didn't like her very much,' Laura suggested carefully.

'Not to begin with.' Min's frankness was surprising.

'So then why hire her?'

'Where Cat Blake leads, others follow. If she had her nose pierced, I can guarantee everyone else would do the same within the fortnight. My turnover doubled within her first four months here.'

'Was she aware of this?'

Min snorted, crossing her arms. 'Oh yes.'

'Did you become friends?'

Min slowly straightened, like a cobra rising from a basket. 'Yes, I would say so. I think I quickly came to see the *real* Cat Blake, and she came to rely on me in her own way. Not that we ever discussed it in such explicit terms, you understand, but when you're working closely with someone day after day, you're bound to see the truth of their lives.'

Laura nodded, recognizing the territorial pride she had noticed everybody took in their friendship with Cat. She understood it now, maybe even felt it herself. Even taking her formidable beauty out of the equation – which it was such a cliché to admire – Cat was the pinnacle of everybody's personal ambitions: intelligent and driven; kind and generous; compassionate, delicate, feminine and fashionable.

'What's she like to work with?'

'You want the truth? Maddening. She's like a dog with a bone when she's got an idea in her head. Never takes "no" for an answer. Not many people say "no" to Cat. I expect you've already found that out yourself.'

Laura nodded. It was true – she hadn't said 'no' to her, even though the launch party was everything she'd once told Fee she didn't want. Much like blonde hair and painted nails.

'Can you give me an example?'

Min pursed her thin, rouged lips together. 'Well, the most obvious is a gala show we held for the local hospice a few years ago. There was an artist Cat had come across at a party, and she kept badgering me to host an exhibition for him. He was a fellow called Ben Jackson, based in a bothy somewhere in the Highlands. Don't misunderstand me – it wasn't like she'd discovered him or anything. He had been lauded for his graduation show at the Slade years earlier, but he was very much of the artistic temperament. You know, he'd rather live on moss and dew than make any money from something substantial or, God help us, commercial.' Min rolled her eyes. 'He wouldn't play the game, and even the art world can only cope with so much eccentricity. But Cat kept plugging away at me to let her try. Eventually – just to shut her up, to be honest – I told her that if she could convince him to produce some new work for us, I'd put together an exhibition for him.' She shrugged. 'I mean, there was no way she – an inexperienced, uneducated art world part-timer was going to be able to talk him into it.' She dropped her chin.

'And yet you're going to tell me she did,' Laura murmured, knowing that the woman who provoked men to graffiti marriage proposals on railways bridges would also have inspired a reclusive artist to paint for her. 'How did she do it?'

Min shrugged. 'Batted her eyelash extensions? I don't know. But she travelled up to see him on a Tuesday and came back a week later with nine canvases and a further eleven promised for delivery eight weeks later.' She shook her head, as if still in disbelief at the coup. 'It was simply unheard of. As soon as word got out, we had offers on the spot for the entire collection from four Mayfair galleries, a couple in Paris and one in Manhattan. Of course, Cat insisted I turn them down. She was adamant the event should be held for "local people".'

That compassion again. 'What was the exhibition called?'

'Exposure. It explored the boundary separating space, solitude, retreat, from isolation – a glorious interplay between shadow and light. It was all very intense and moody. Sold out within hours, of course. *The Times* ran a lead on it, and people were buying simply what was available. Most didn't even look at the canvases first. We had to hire some security to control the numbers. People were left standing on the pavement trying to get in. Some particularly crafty sorts actually abseiled down from the flats above and came in through the back door.'

'A triumph, then,' Laura said, wondering how on earth she could represent all that on a charm.

'Yes, and it was purely Cat's. I take no credit for it. It's purely thanks to her that Ben's a bona fide star now.'

'Do you still represent him?'

She shook her head. 'He's got a contract with Lehmann Maupin Gallery in SoHo. There was no way we could compete with the terms they were offering.' She gave a small snort. 'He's changed a lot since his Highland seclusion days. Put it this way, he doesn't live in a bothy now.' She inhaled sharply. 'But it's served us well, being his launch pad. We get a lot of new artists fighting for our patronage. And people coming to us know they're getting in early on future names and that they'll get a good return on their investments.'

'Would you say Cat has a good eye for art, then?'

'One of the best I've come across. She could have had a glittering career as a dealer, in my opinion. Half the job's what you know; the other is who you know. She's blessed in both departments.'

'Have you ever shared that opinion with her? From what I've learnt from her family and friends, she's ambitious.'

Min shook her head. 'She never took it seriously enough. Once she'd nailed Ben Jackson, she seemed to lose focus. Maybe doing this was only ever a rich girl's whim after all.'

'What do you mean?'

'Well, she just lost all interest in pushing for any recognition beyond making the tea. I hired her as a publicist-slash-ambassador, to leverage her contacts and increase footfall through the door, but that all just stopped and suddenly she was pulling her hand up to do menial things like the photo-copying. I mean, I get eighteen-year-olds on work experience in here who shoot me death stares for even suggesting they photocopy something. She stopped chatting up the customers, too, making a big thing instead about standing by the window and looking for the warden or feeding the meter.' She shrugged. 'I couldn't go on justifying her salary when she was basically a glorified tea-girl.'

Laura's eyebrows jumped up. 'Sorry? Are you saying she doesn't work here any more?'

Min shook her head. 'No. Not for about two years now.'

*Two years?* Laura frowned, confused, as she tried to recall Rob's words about her in the café. He'd given no indication she had left her job – or lost it. 'I'm sorry, but that's . . . that's just so strange. When Rob asked me to see you, he said that you were her boss and that she works here several after-noons a week. He definitely used the present tense.'

'You mean he thinks she still works here?' Min looked as surprised as Laura.

Laura sat back in her chair. Was Cat too ashamed to tell Rob she'd been sacked?

'Do you still see Cat in a social capacity?'

'No. I do often see her around and about, but she never comes in.' Min's lips set into a flattened line. 'I expect it's sour grapes on her part.'

'You see Cat around *here*?'

'That's right. She's a regular at the Italian on the corner over there. I see her at least once a week hopping in and out of taxis.'

'But she never stops by?'

'Not once.'

Laura hesitated, then turned off the digital recorder. 'Well, thank you for sparing your time. I'm going to need to go back to Rob on this. I'm as baffled as you are as to why he's included you in the project. I think perhaps he's misunderstood your relationship with Cat. Each charm is supposed to be a homage from the closest people in her life, and if you'll forgive me for being so blunt, you're clearly not.' She stood up and let Min lead her to the door. 'If it's okay with you, I'll speak to Rob and come back to you if I need any further information.'

'Fine,' Min replied, holding her hand out this time. 'Please do send Cat my best if you see her. It's sad to lose contact altogether.'

'Yes, of course. Goodbye.'

Laura walked quickly down Holland Park, lost in thought. It had begun to snow properly now, the sky a toxic grey with a lime shine to it. All around her, the wealthiest denizens of London swept past in 4x4s and furs. She checked her watch: 11.44 a.m. That gave her just an hour and a quarter to get to Brampton Oakley. She had lied to Min about the traffic, but in these conditions, the motorways really would be slowing down and snarling up – there wasn't time to call Rob now. It would have to wait till later. And besides, she'd prefer to send an email explaining the situation rather than hear his voice in her ear.

She saw a traffic warden stop at Dolly up ahead. Oh great! Just what she needed. She could tell from the telltale flashing halfway down the street that the meter had expired and she saw him pull out his electronic bookings pad. Laura broke out into a run.

'You're over,' he said aggressively as Laura wordlessly ran round to the driver's side. 'Oi, wait!' he said as she opened the door 'I've started writing out your ticket.'

'Yep, but you've got to get it on my windscreen to validate it, haven't you?' she shouted back to him, turning on the ignition noisily and throwing Dolly into reverse.

The warden started typing faster, but he was no match for Laura's haste and he could only watch as she manoeuvred out of the parking space.

'Merry Christmas!' she shouted, pulling out into the traffic and heading west for the Surrey Hills. It was only a mini victory, but it was the first thing that had gone her way in days.

# Chapter Thirty-Two

The door opened with a creak. Suitably, Laura thought as she braced herself for entering the tall, dark and creepy house at last. She took a deep breath before she was in Olive's line of sight and forced a weak smile. Ironically, Olive Tremayne had become, in the wake of Monday's events, her ideal interview candidate: brittle and recalcitrant, she matched Laura's mood perfectly. Even Min's 'spiky' demeanour had been preferable to wide smiles and polished conversation – they would have finished her off before she'd begun. It had been enough of an achievement just getting dressed today. Left to her own devices, she would have sat on her studio window-sill in her pyjamas, looking out on the sea as a meditation.

'Laura,' Olive said, looking an inch past Laura's left ear so that Laura's new look was only in her peripheral vision. 'Won't you come in?' Her behaviour made no reference to their previous meeting.

'Thank you,' Laura said quietly, smoothing her jumper down as she passed by, her Converses squeaking slightly on the highly polished black and white tessellated floor. She followed Olive past an old-fashioned coat stand that had a mac and an umbrella hanging from it, and a gothic staircase that turned on itself in sharp ninety-degree angles.

Olive led her into a large room with burgundy silk-papered

walls, a dramatically swagged marble fireplace, ornate plas-
terwork on the ceilings and a dusty chandelier that looked
as heavy as a car. A bottle-green tartan carpet stretched from
skirting board to skirting board, but other than two patched
velour wing chairs by the fire, a battered chesterfield opposite and a leather-topped round coffee table, there was no
other furniture in the room. It was like the visitors' room in
an old people's home, Laura thought as she sat in one of
the wing chairs – its purpose felt transient, the decor half
baked.

Olive sat opposite her, the fire crackling between them.
Her wild, frizzy hair had been plaited back into a blonde
rope, and she was wearing navy trousers with a lemon silk
blouse and a canary-yellow V-neck jumper. Her face was
delicately made up, and Laura found it impossible to guess
how old she might be. She could be in her thirties, but the
way she dressed – as if she shopped from the back of weekend
magazine supplements – she could have been twenty years
older than that. There was none of Cat's easy charm or grace,
effortless style or inherent sexiness. She was like a dowager
aunt and seemed different from Cat in every way it was
possible to be.

'So, you want to discuss my sister with me,' she said quietly,
looking at Laura for only the briefest of moments before
shifting her position so that her long legs were pointing
towards the fire.

'Yes, please,' Laura said, reaching down to get her digital
recorder out of her bag. 'Do you mind if I . . . ?'

Olive gave a vague gesture of consent. 'How does this
work, then?'

Her voice was so quiet, Laura had to strain to hear her.
'Well, I wonder if you could start by telling me a little about

your childhood together. Your strongest memories of growing up with Cat.'

The door opened and a woman carrying a tray came in. She nodded at Laura as she set the tray down on the low table. It only had coffee, scones and biscuits on it, even though it was 1 p.m. and Laura hadn't eaten lunch. But she wasn't hungry anyway.

'Would you like me to pour, Mrs Tremayne?'

'Thank you, Mary,' she replied. 'This is Mary, my woman who . . . does,' Olive murmured.

'Pleased to meet you, Mary,' Laura said. She was rewarded with a smile from this woman, at least.

Mary served the coffee to the two women, who sat waiting for her in silence. She passed Laura a small plate with biscuits on it.

'Thank you,' Laura said again, feeling absolutely no appetite for the food in her hands.

Mary nodded at Olive and left the room.

'Where were we?' Olive mumbled, as though they'd been in full flow when Mary had entered. 'Oh. Yes. Childhood . . .' She sighed heavily.

'Are you the elder sister?' Laura asked, taking a tiny, polite nibble of the biscuit.

Olive fixed her with a chilly stare. 'By four years.'

'And your parents. Can I ask a little about them? I haven't heard anything about them yet and Rob hasn't—'

'They're dead. Died within six months of each other, eight years ago. Cancer, both of them.'

'I'm so sorry.'

Olive looked at her hard for a moment, as though assessing whether she looked suitably sorry, before staring back into the fire.

'So then you and Cat—'

'What? Have each other?' She gave a low snort. 'No. We have our own families.'

'Right.' It seemed hard to believe. Laura's eyes skated around the room, but there wasn't a single photograph or toy in evidence. She remembered the rocking horse she'd seen through the window on her first visit here.

'I noticed the rocking horse on my way down the drive,' Laura ventured. 'Is that your children's?'

'I don't have any children. It's just my husband and me here.' Bitterness that she was having to divulge all this clung to every word. 'That rocking horse belonged to me and Cat as children. This house was our childhood home.'

'Oh, I see!' Laura said, looking around with renewed interest. As a childhood home – with noise and bustle and some mess, perhaps – this house might come to life. Perhaps that was what it was missing now. A noisy, busy soul. 'Was the rocking horse a favoured toy?'

Olive's lip curled slightly. 'Hardly. I've kept it because it's a valuable antique.'

'It doesn't sound like you were close.' Laura paused. 'Would that be accurate to say?'

'Why would you want to say it? I thought this was just about a piece of jewellery?'

'It is . . . yes,' Laura said haltingly. 'Each charm is supposed to be representative, that's all, of the key people in your sister's life.'

Olive snorted again. 'Well, God only knows why Rob's got such a bee in his bonnet about including me in this thing. He practically begged me to talk to you.'

Laura frowned. 'But Cat's your sister. There must be some happy memories that you look back on?'

Olive stared at her for a long moment before picking up her teacup wearily, almost painfully. 'Our pony, Truffle,' she said finally. 'A Welsh cob our father bought for us both. I was almost eight; Cat was four. We shared him – the only thing we ever shared. ' She rubbed her lips together, contemplatively. 'I would sleep with his brushes under my pillow so that I could smell him while I slept. Our mother had to confiscate our alarm clocks in the end. We were getting up before five o'clock at one point to muck him out and feed him.' A ghost of a smile hovered above her. 'It didn't stop us, though. We loved that pony more than anything.'

'Do you ride still?'

'No. Not since Truffle.'

'Oh. Does Cat?'

'She did for a bit. Purely decoratively, though.' The ghostly smile had been replaced by a sneer.

'What do you mean, decoratively?'

Olive shrugged. 'She looked good in jodhpurs. I imagine she liked the image more than the actual horses.'

'But she'd loved Truffle?'

Olive nodded. 'Yes. She loved him.'

Laura cleared her throat. It seemed no topic was safe. 'Can you think of any other fond memories?'

Olive's eyes swivelled back to the flames. Utter concentration was needed.

'Cornwall. We took a holiday there the summer I turned nine. My mother took us down on the train and it was everything you might expect – rounders on the beach, ice-cream cornets, playing in the rock pools, beachcombing.' She looked up suddenly, although only at Laura for a moment. 'Beachcombing was a shared interest. I'd entirely forgotten.'

'Tell me about that,' Laura encouraged her, resisting the urge to shout for joy.

'The guest house we were staying in overlooked the beach, and if the tide was going out, Mother would let us go down in our pyjamas and wellingtons before bed. There was one night when we found a conch shell, sitting there, just waiting to be plucked from the water. It was the biggest shell we'd ever seen, like those ones people have in their bathrooms nowadays as some type of *ornament*. We ran back to the guest house with it, but Mother wouldn't let us bring it into the house. Something had died in it, I think, and the smell of rotting shellfish was . . .' She pulled a face. 'I can almost smell it now. It was ghastly. Cat was convinced that if we washed it through with some bleach or washing-up liquid or disinfectant, we would clear it. She's nothing if not persistent, my sister. For days we tried, pouring one poison after another on it. But in the end we had to admit defeat. There was just no way we could travel home with that smell accompanying us.'

'So what did you do with it? Throw it back into the sea?'

'No. There was a small fishpond in the back garden of the guest house. We put it in there. Nobody knew about it. It was our secret. We always said we'd go back for it one day and could smuggle it home safely.'

'And did you?'

Olive stared at her. 'Of course not.'

'It might still be there, then.'

'I sincerely doubt it. The owners probably threw it back in the sea a week after we left.'

'Well, if they didn't know about it . . .' Laura shrugged.

'Even if they didn't find it then, there are now so many health and safety regulations for anyone wishing to open their house to the general public that I'm quite sure the pond would have been filled in years ago.'

Olive was clearly determined to kill that dream. 'Well, did you make any other wonderful discoveries?'

'Yes. We also found a spider crab in a rock pool just behind our favourite lagoon that summer. It was enormous – the size of a dinner plate. I'm not exaggerating,' she added sternly. 'There was a café just up the beach, and someone said they were going to tell the owners about this crab for fresh sandwiches. So Cat and I stood on guard for the rest of the day. We were too scared to pick it up, but we took turns standing up to our knees in the freezing water, hiding it from people and protecting it until the tide came back in.'

A slow satisfaction crept across her face, and her hands opened like flowers on the armrests. 'That was a good day. It was the first time we had ever worked together on anything as a team. It was the first day that I really understood what it was to have a sister.'

'So it brought you closer together, then,' Laura commented, filled with hope that here was her story.

But Laura's voice appeared to interrupt her reverie and Olive drew her breath in sharply. 'No, not really. It was just a freak day. Nothing changed.' The shutters came straight back down.

The fire made all the noise for a few moments as Laura tried to think of a new inroad into Olive's memory bank. So far, she had a pony called Truffle, a stinky conch shell and an endangered crab to work with, which was great – far better than she'd dared to hope. All of those stories could be transposed into graphic charms. But was that really it – the only vestiges of the sisters' childhood?

'Can you think of any other stories like that which

show your relationship with your sister? It would help enormously.'

'I'm afraid not,' Olive replied unapologetically.

They sat in silence for a minute or two. Laura sipped at her tea, which was so hot it was burning her lips.

'Well, is that it? Are we done?' Olive asked, encouraged by the protracted silence and gathering herself to stand.

'Uh . . . yes, okay,' Laura managed, switching off her digital recorder and following suit. 'You've been very helpful. Thank you.'

'I was expecting that to be a lot worse,' she said, her demeanour approaching a shade of cordial now that Laura was on her way out.

She opened the front door and the blue December day rushed into the dark house like a wind. 'Well, goodbye.'

'Oh, just one last thing, if you don't mind?' Laura said, turning back on the step. 'I wondered if you could sum up your sister in three words for me?'

Olive's eyes shone at her. 'Easily,' Olive replied after a short pause. 'Dead. To. Me.'

And with that, the door closed and there was a quiet, but resolute, click.

'Door's open!' Kitty yelled from inside the house as Laura rapped the knocker. 'Come through.'

'It's me, Kitty! Laura.'

Laura pushed the front door off the latch and walked through the small, dark hallway. Compared with the vast proportions of the Parsonage, it felt like burrowing through an underground tunnel. Tucked in the far corner of the hall, by the staircase, was a modest Christmas tree covered in green and silver tinsel, with a 1970s fairy on top and the nibbled, rather forlorn gingerbread decorations Kitty had mentioned in Verbier that the children had made. Multi-coloured paper chains were Blu-tacked to the ceiling in shallow swags and jugs full of holly were sitting on every surface. Christmas had come to Quinces.

She walked into the kitchen, where Kitty was crouched in front of the Aga, her arms stretched deep into one of the ovens. She looked like she was being devoured by it.

'Damned thing!' she cried as she caught sight of Laura. 'Went cold this morning and I think there's a block in the control-valve filter. If I can just . . .' She puffed, twiddling with something out of sight before dropping her arms and head in defeat. 'No. It's too stiff. Joe will have to do it when he gets back.'

She extracted her arms from the cavernous cold oven and wiped her hands on her apron as she came over to Laura with her arms opened wide. 'How excellent that you're here!'

Laura felt herself droop as Kitty embraced her, biting her lip to stop the physical contact from making her emotional.

'Well, I was just over seeing Olive, and after I got your message . . . I mean, I hope it's not inconvenient,' she said awkwardly.

Strictly speaking she should have hightailed it back to Suffolk the second she'd finished at Olive's. The sky had darkened ominously and London's dithering sleet was falling as crisp, plump snow across the North Downs. It was going to take hours to get back; she had to get on with making these final charms to free up some time to make some new pieces for Cat's party too, but the knowledge that Kitty and some tea and sympathy were only three miles away had been too much to resist. Just an hour. Then she'd be gone.

'As if!' Kitty bellowed with a laugh. 'Especially as I made a plum cake yesterday. Trust me, it's amazing.'

'Oh, I'm sure,' Laura agreed quickly, even though she'd had all the appetite of a chair since Monday. 'You're an incredible cook.'

'Thanks! But I can't take credit for the recipe. I got it off my allotment growers' website.'

'Oh.'

'Do you grow anything?'

'Afraid not,' Laura grimaced. 'I've only got two settings when it comes to growing stuff – flood it or starve it to death.'

Kitty burst out laughing as she switched on an electric kettle and rooted in a cupboard for a cafetière. 'So. Olive.' Kitty pulled a face. 'Was she civil?'

'Just about, although if she'd had a choice between that and water-boarding . . .' Laura watched Kitty shovelling heaped spoonfuls of coffee into the glass container. 'Do you get on with her?'

'I didn't ever know her that well.'

'Well now, I don't believe *that*,' Laura argued. 'You and Cat were practically one person growing up. You couldn't have avoided her.'

'We did, actually. It was perfectly easy. What with being at different schools and living apart, we hardly ever saw her.'

'What do you mean, different schools?'

'You know – Cat went to the local primary with me, whilst Olive got sent to the private girls' school at Bridgestock. Lady Olive we used to call her.' She looked at Laura's shocked face. 'Surely she told you that?'

Laura shook her head. 'No. She never mentioned it. Why

335

would her parents have done that – sent one daughter but not the other?'

'They couldn't afford it. They were financially devastated after the divorce. They had to sell everything – the house, the car, the—'

'The house?' Laura interrupted. 'You mean the Parsonage?'

'That's right. She's bought it back now, but it was the first thing to go back then.' Kitty wrinkled her nose. 'Cat said she never liked it there anyway. It reminded her of when her parents were always fighting. Things got pretty hairy, I think. Vases thrown, that kind of thing . . .'

'Poor kids.'

'She and Olive used to spend all their time hiding in the garden or in their bedrooms. Sometimes they didn't see their parents from one end of the day to the next. They were looked after by a nanny.' The kettle boiled and Kitty filled the cafetière with tumbling water.

'Mary?'

'I can't remember,' she shrugged, watching the coffee swirl with the water. 'Anyway, you can imagine why Cat loved it so much when she and her mum came and lived in the cottage up here.'

Laura remembered. Kitty had told her that the first time she'd come here. 'So if Cat and her mum came to live here after the divorce, where did Olive live? With their father?'

'God, no! He was a raging alcoholic. There was no way she could have gone with him. She went to board at Bridgestock instead.'

'Bridgestock was a boarding school?' Laura shook her head. 'But I just don't understand that. How on earth could they have justified sending one daughter away and keeping the other at home with them? Why didn't they keep them both at home?'

Kitty looked at her. 'You're making it sound like Olive got the poor end of the stick, being sent to boarding school. What about poor Cat? She missed out on a first-class education and all the privilege *that* brings.'

Laura ran this scenario through her head. Seen from that perspective, Kitty was right to see Cat as the victim. 'I guess you're right. Why was Cat overlooked in favour of her sister, then?'

Kitty leaned forwards. 'Well, I've always had a theory – although Cat would never accept it, and I sincerely doubt you'd have got an adult to admit to it either – but I reckon it was because Cat possessed something her sister didn't.'

'And what was that?'

'Looks. Cat got them all.' With enormous satisfaction, Kitty pressed down on the plunger.

'But Olive's attractive.'

'Yes, but compared to Cat?' Kitty shrugged. 'Everyone always knew that Cat had that fallback. What did she need a fabulous education for when she was clearly going to marry a rich man who'd worship and look after her? Olive, on the other hand, needed every advantage she could get.'

'But that's just awful,' Laura cried. 'It victimizes them both.'

Kitty shook her head and sighed, pouring out the coffee. 'I know. And it definitely affected Cat more as she got older. I think she felt she had to prove that there was more to her than just her looks.' Laura thought back to Cat's excitement when she was relating her idea for the launch party. More than just a rich woman's whim? 'But Olive was the one who lost out ultimately,' Kitty said sadly.

'How? You just said she was the one to get all the privileges.'

'I think she suspected what I did – that her parents judged her against her sister and she came up short. It's such a shame. By trying to compensate for her, they confirmed her worst fears.'

'Oh God! No wonder she hates her,' Laura said, slumping against the back of a chair as Kitty handed over her mug. 'And I've just forced her to recount that not-so-happy childhood, all for some over-the-top romantic gesture by Cat's—'

'Rich, handsome, besotted husband? Yes, it's hardly surprising she didn't want to be part of it, really. Anyway, it's done now. And I'm sure she would much rather have been included in the project than not. Her pride would have demanded she be counted in her sister's life story if nothing else. What stories did she tell you? There can't have been many,' Kitty asked, slurping her coffee loudly.

'She told me about their pony.'

Kitty tutted sympathetically. 'Oh, poor Truffle. They were both broken-hearted when he went.'

'Was he sold after the divorce too?'

'No. Well, not directly. The girls managed to persuade their father to let them keep him. He hadn't been gelded, so we stabled him on the farm here and he was put to stud a few times. That brought a bit of money in. But then he fell lame with sinking laminitis – it's curable, but time-consuming and expensive, and their father refused to pay the vet's bills to save him. Instead, he . . .' Her voice trailed off. 'Oh, it's an awful story.'

'Tell me.'

Kitty sighed reluctantly as she heaved an enormous square cake out of a tin. 'He sold him to the knacker's yard. That way he got some money back on him.'

Laura couldn't respond. Olive and Cat's father had sent his daughters' beloved pony to its death to make back some *money*? No wonder Olive hadn't been on a horse since.

'Oh, why didn't I know any of this going into the interview?' Laura moaned. 'It throws a completely different slant on things.'

'Sorry,' Kitty apologized. 'I figured it was Olive's story to tell, not mine. I just picked up Cat's life once she came to live here.'

'No, no, I'm not blaming you,' she murmured. 'So Cat's was a childhood of two halves, then. Before – big house, pony, alcoholic father, warring parents. After – you, chickens, no father, sister at boarding school.' Something occurred to her. 'How old was Cat when her parents divorced?'

Kitty inhaled slowly, deep in thought, the cake knife hovering above the first cut. 'Five-ish? I remember being told that this girl my age was coming to live in one of the cottages, and I sat on the gate waiting for her. She was coming back from a holiday, and Mum had said to me to be extra kind to her because this girl didn't know that she wasn't going back to her old house and it might all be a bit of a shock. But we took one look at each other and . . . ' Kitty shrugged. 'We just smiled. That was it.'

'Where had she been on holiday?'

'Cornwall, I think, just with their mum. Their father stayed behind to clear out the house.'

'So then Cornwall was the last week that Cat and Olive knew as a family,' Laura murmured, thinking of the two little sisters standing guard over the giant crab in a rock pool. 'When they came back, everything had changed – their father had left, Olive was sent away . . .'

'I know. It was an almighty mess,' Kitty said, shaking her head sadly. 'The entire family torn apart because of one sliding-doors moment. I mean, how do you live with that?'

'Sliding doors?' Laura frowned.

'Yes.' Kitty looked at her, quite still. 'Oh, *please* tell me someone's told you about Daniel.'

'Who's Daniel?'

Kitty looked shocked. 'Their brother.'

'They've got a *brother*? But why didn't Olive or Rob say anything? Is he estranged too?'

'No. He's dead. He died when he was eleven months old.'

Laura's hands flew to her mouth.

'He choked on a grape in front of Olive. She was only about three at the time.'

'But where were their parents?'

'Upstairs, *making up* after one of their rows,' Kitty said. 'Conceiving Cat, as it turned out.'

'Oh God,' Laura whispered, understanding the fatal fissure between the sisters immediately: Olive had witnessed her brother's death and felt she was to blame, whilst her pretty little baby sister was born with a clean slate and the promise of making things good again.

Laura thought about her parting words: *Dead to me*. They made perfect sense now. Olive couldn't forgive – she couldn't forgive herself for not saving him; she couldn't forgive her parents for neglecting them; but most of all she couldn't forgive her sister for being born whilst their brother had had to die.

'Those girls never stood a chance of being sisters,' Laura said. 'Not a chance.'

'No,' Kitty sighed, putting a saucer of plum cake down in front of her. 'But enough of other people's worries. How are things in your neck of the woods? I was so worried when you left in such a hurry. Sam's convinced Alex did something to scare you away.' She dropped her voice. 'He didn't try anything on, did he?'

Laura shook her head. 'No, no! Nothing like that. Jack was worried about Arthur, that was all,' she replied, keeping her voice steady as she said Jack's name. 'He, uh . . . had a temperature.'

Kitty didn't look entirely convinced. 'Everything's okay, though?'

'Absolutely.' She nodded vehemently, keeping her eyes down as she picked at the cake. The impulse to tell Kitty about Fee and Jack was overwhelming. She knew that if she told her, Kitty would hug her again, probably cry with her and feed her more cake. But how *could* she ask for a shoulder to cry on when she was guilty herself of betraying Kitty's own best friend? She had kissed Rob and would become the enemy in an instant – irrespective of whether or not she had 'started' it – and Laura wasn't sure she could cope with losing Kitty's friendly face too. She'd come to rely on her more than she wanted to admit. 'Mmm, delicious,' she murmured instead.

'We all missed you – even Sam! It wasn't the same without you.'

'Really? But it was only a few hours.' Cat had said the same thing, but it seemed so hard to believe they'd have missed *her*.

'Well, once the dynamic changes, even just a little bit . . . Everyone was furious with Alex. No one believed he hadn't tried it on with you. We all saw that kiss on Sunday – it was a real smacker. Even Rob was fuming, and you know how mellow he is.'

Laura simply nodded, remembering how the last time she'd seen him he'd been as far from mellow as it was possible to get. Shame flooded through her as she recalled the white-hot silence that had paralysed them both in the lift. It wasn't even the kiss that made her feel so guilty – that had clearly come as a surprise to them both. It was the way it had made her feel about him afterwards, pushing forward thoughts and feelings she would never have dared acknowledge otherwise. And the way she'd reacted at the sight of him yesterday made her panic. Rob had called it a mistake; he was trying to draw a line under it and move on. But whatever had been stirred up between them in Verbier, it wasn't gone, she knew – not yet.

# Chapter Thirty-Three

'I *must* go,' Laura said an hour later, forcing herself into a standing position. 'I've got so much work to do it would make your eyes boggle.'

'Boggle! Great word!' Kitty chuckled, high on caffeine again.

Laura tramped to the front door reluctantly, dreading the three-hour journey back, and stared out at the unfamiliar landscape. Dolly was disappearing into the snow like a toddler's welly in mud.

'Oh no! How the hell did that happen?' she cried, looking up at the snow tumbling down from the great black sky like feathers from a pillow fight. Several inches had fallen during her foray into Quinces Cottage and was shin-deep already.

'Oh dear,' Kitty murmured over her shoulder.

'This is going to be a long drive home,' Laura sighed. 'I don't suppose you've got a shovel?'

Kitty looked across at her in surprise. 'Don't tell me you're going to try to drive back in this?'

'Well, of course.'

'Laura! Look at the snow!'

'It's just a shower,' Laura said uncertainly. 'It'll thaw in a bit. It never settles in this country.'

'Didn't you see the weather forecast?'

'No. I've been staying at the studio since I got back. Working,' she added hurriedly as Kitty frowned. 'I don't have a TV there.'

'Heavy snowfall's been forecast – up to a foot. This is earlier than they said it was coming, but you won't get back tonight. You'd end up sleeping on the motorway. There's no question of driving back.'

'But . . . but . . .'

Kitty placed a hand on her shoulder and steered her back in. 'Come on. In with you. You're white as a sheet. I wouldn't be surprised if you're coming down with something. Come on. We'll run you a bath while I make up the spare room.'

'Kitty, no, really, I'm—'

'In! Joe will be back with the kids any second and then it'll be all hands to the pump.'

'I don't want to be in the way,' Laura moaned.

'Trust me, you won't be.'

'Well, at least put me to use,' Laura said as Kitty shut the door and trapped the honey-coloured light back inside the cottage.

'Just relax and take some time out. You look so stressed.' Kitty placed a concerned hand on her shoulder.

'I'm not stressed,' Laura said, shaking her head far too many times to be believable.

'Well, I am. I need to get supper on the table and I don't have an Aga.' Kitty chewed a lip thoughtfully. 'I'm tempted to give them plum cake.'

'I could help you make . . . ' Laura faltered. What could you cook if you didn't have an oven? 'Toast?'

'Upstairs. You'll only get me nattering again if you're anywhere in earshot, and then we'll never get the kids to bed. And you do *not* want to be around Joe if the kids are up past eight.'

Laura nodded politely. She did not want to be around Joe full stop. Oh, how had this happened? She had no clothes here, no toiletries . . .

Kitty bounded up the stairs and into the bathroom, expertly dodging a couple of potato guns and accompanying potatoes left lying on the steps. Laura followed, hearing the water pipes clatter into life one by one behind the walls as Kitty began running her bath.

She looked in on one of the bedrooms as she passed. *Toy Story* curtains threw a blue intergalactic light into the room, and a bunk bed was strewn with dressing-up costumes. A lava lamp had been left on on the desk, and the carpet was almost completely obscured by toys. How did they get to bed? Laura wondered. Hover over? Perhaps she could be defiantly helpful and colour-code the Lego?

'You're in here,' Kitty called. Laura identified where she was from the creak of the floorboards and peered round the door, smiling, taking in a bald maroon carpet and a set of 1940s curtains printed with blowsy blackish-purple blooms. Very Agatha Christie. A vintage teal velvet dress was hanging from a wire hanger on the wardrobe.

'It's not Verbier, I'm afraid,' Kitty said, blushing slightly and quickly making up the bed with an antique linen mono-grammed sheet and padded comforter.

'Thank God for that,' Laura laughed. 'I was all opulented-out by the end of the weekend. This looks fab.'

Kitty straightened up, beaming, as she looked around proudly. 'Well, it's home,' she shrugged happily.

The slam of a door downstairs alerted them to the return

of her brood. 'Oh God! They're back,' Kitty said. 'You'd better get in the bathroom quick before they start playing battle-ships with the shampoo and use up all the hot water.' She shoved a clean lilac towel into Laura's arms and pushed her into the bathroom. 'Oh, and I apologize in advance for their behaviour.'

The smile slid off Laura's face. 'Why? What are they going to do?'

'Who can say?' Kitty shrugged helplessly. 'But I'm sorry anyway.'

Even under water, she could hear Kitty's little menagerie. The hum of shouty conversations and mischievous, teasing laughter vibrated through the floorboards and into the pris-tine white enamel beneath her bare bottom. Kitty's voice threaded through it all like a loving kiss, alternately reproving – someone throwing carrots? – and soothing as another fell off a chair. Family life.

Feeling her eyes sting, Laura slid under the bubbles, still able to hear them practising carols. She wondered how long she had to stay up here for. What would be a polite absence? Reappearing after they'd all been put to bed? She looked around the bathroom as though trying to unearth its family's secrets. The walls were mint green with white tongue-and-groove boarding on the lower half. A looped bath mat was clean and springy – clearly freshly washed – but the legion of towels hanging on pegs along the back of the door were rather more . . . limp. All the shampoos on the side of the bath were 'no tears' varieties except for a slim bottle of Head & Shoulders; there was a series of half-used emollient bath lotions, and a pot on the side of the basin was the place where toothbrushes clearly came to die. There must have been twelve in there, with three different types of toothpaste. A yellow plastic step was placed around the base of the basin pedestal, and a red potty had been pushed back against the wall.

It was the nitty-gritty of family life exposed, the bare bones of lives shared and lived together. Something of which she knew nothing. Her bathroom was like a spa by comparison, with limestone-replica tiles, fancy chrome waterfall taps and his 'n' hers electric toothbrushes charging side by side. The bath gleamed so brightly she could practically put her make-up on by looking in it. Her bathroom was beautiful and ordered and hygienic. Or sterile, if you wanted to be bald about it.

She heard a creak and turned to the side. A little round face was peering at her and she instinctively covered herself with her hands, even though there was enough bubble cover in that bath to hide a submarine.

'I need a poo,' the child said.

'Oh, okay,' Laura replied, instantly flustered. 'If you just give me a minute, I'll get out of the way for you,' she said, understanding that *this* was the moment to reappear to Kitty. She went to rise.

'Or not,' she said, sinking back down. The little girl just walked into the room, staring at the floor. She took the yellow stool from the base of the basin and put it in front of the loo. Then, pulling up her dress, she sat down.

Laura watched her colour change, with rising alarm, from tender blush pink to fuchsia to crimson to royal purple.

'Uh . . . what's your name?' she asked, pretending to study the ceiling.

The little girl didn't answer.

'I'm . . . I'm Laura.'

347

Still nothing, just more straining. She shut up. The poor child clearly needed all her breath.

'Oh, there you are!' Kitty said, and Laura almost capsized as she turned in alarm and then tried to cover herself again. Kitty laughed. 'Sorry, Laura! Please . . . pretend I'm not here,' she said, coming further in and helping the little girl off the loo. 'Come on, Martha. Let Mummy clean your bottom,' she sighed, grabbing a wet wipe.

Martha! Martha! Laura repeated to herself. Must. Not. Forget.

Laura froze as Martha bent double, wondering how on earth it could be that she was lying in a bath in front of near strangers. Well, okay, not complete strangers. Laura had seen Kitty in a onesie – that automatically assumed a certain level of intimacy – but they were hardly friendly enough to be naked and wiping bottoms together!

'Right, there you are, madam. All done. Now back to your bedroom and take your clothes off. It's bathtime.'

Laura looked up in outright panic. They were all coming in *here*? All of them?

'I'm just getting out, actually,' Laura said, not making any move. It was one thing being naked in front of a five-year-old . . .

'Great,' Kitty beamed as the thunder rolling up the stairs suggested the rest of the herd was on its way. 'Well, would you be a love and leave the water in?'

Laura waited for Kitty to leave, then jumped out of the water as if she'd been torpedoed and wrapped herself like a bandage in the fat lilac towel Kitty had given her. She was just securing the knot when the door burst open and the bathroom was flooded by little people looking up at her curiously.

# The Perfect Present

'Kids! This is Aunty Laura! She's having a sleepover with us,' Kitty hollered across from the airing cupboard on the landing. 'I'm afraid you'll have to put up with the prefix, Laura. It's either "Aunty" or "So-and-So's Mummy".' She staggered over beneath a pile of old towels and dumped them on the floor, then planted her hands on her hips and did a headcount to make sure all were present and correct, completely oblivious to the look of sheer terror on Laura's face as the children swarmed around her. She clutched her towel tighter. 'Anyway, just so you know – in descending order – Tom's the oldest, he's just turned eight,' Kitty said, pointing to the highest-up head. 'Then there's Lucie, she's seven; that's Martha, she's five; Finn's four; and of course you remember Samuel.'

Laura nodded. How could she forget him? At least some of her trauma at the prospect of a child could be attributed to this little horror.

'Nice to meet you all,' she nodded.

'Right, you lot. In!' Kitty said, swiping all towels from the back of the door and replacing them with fresh ones.

The children charged for the bath and Laura gingerly tiptoed around the tangle of knees, elbows and bottoms, clutching tightly to her towel lest anyone should snatch it. She breathed a sigh of relief as her bare feet met bare carpet and she was back in the safety of the hall again. And there and then she swore a solemn oath that – come what may – she would never, ever own a bathroom with a latch door.

# Chapter Thirty-Four

The clock chimed eight times and Laura heaved a sigh of relief – she had officially survived. The rumbling thunder that had all but shaken the house from its foundations was steadily replaced by the whistling wind of five sets of baby snores. Laura had managed to make herself useful at last, reading a bedtime story to the two older kids. Tom and Lucie had been laughing over a cartoon book depicting bunnies committing suicide when she first walked into the room, instantly making her doubt her chosen book, *The Velveteen Rabbit*, as a suitable choice. But as Laura had settled herself nervously in the squashy armchair positioned in the corner of their bedroom and begun to read, Tom and Lucie had abandoned their positions on the floor and slid down each of the arms of her chair so that they were squashed together on her lap. The physical proximity had completely disconcerted her at first, but as they wriggled themselves carelessly into comfy positions and rested their heads against her chest, she felt theirs and *her* breathing change, almost as though a rope that had been compressing her breath had been allowed to slacken. By the story's end, Tom had fallen asleep and Lucie had thrown her arm up around Laura's neck, twirling her index finger round the hair at the nape of her neck whilst she sucked her thumb. They had sat like that in silence until Kitty looked in and rescued her.

Rescued wasn't the right word, though.

'Ah, wine o'clock,' Kitty sighed as they came downstairs. She strode straight over towards the Aga – which, thanks to Joe, was now slowly warming up like a basking bear – and grabbed the bottle of Cabernet Sauvignon he'd placed at the back.

Laura followed her into the kitchen, self-conscious in the oversized flannel pyjamas Kitty had sweetly left out for her. But what else was she going to wear?

She stopped at the sight of Joe sitting on the sofa, still in his boiler suit, a beer in his hand. With one hand he was idly patting Pocket's docile head.

'Hello again,' she nodded.

Joe looked up at her and grunted as if to say, 'You again?'. 'I've towed your car off the lane. It's in the barn,' he muttered after a moment.

'Oh. Thank you,' Laura remarked, pleasantly surprised by his consideration.

'Although I wouldn't be surprised if you find half of it scattered along the path. Seems to me like it's Sellotaped together.'

Or maybe not. 'Well, it's very good of you and Kitty to let me stay here tonight. The weather closed in so quickly—'

'It *was* forecast.'

'Not in Suffolk, it wasn't,' she replied quickly, her eyes flicking anxiously towards Kitty lest she should pick up the hostility between the two of them. 'They're just getting rain over there.'

Joe looked back to the TV, switching channels with the

remote. 'Well, you'll be able to get back on your way tomorrow.'

'Yes.'

Kitty set the bottle and glasses on the worktop. 'Here, Joe, put those on the table, please. Laura, on a scale of one to ten, how hungry are you?' she asked, holding a ladle above a brown electric slow-cooker that looked like it had been purchased in the 1970s.

*Eight*, her tummy growled. She realized she had missed lunch altogether getting from Min's to Olive's to Kitty's, and the plum cake seemed like a long time ago now. 'Ooh, six,' she said politely.

Kitty ladled up a man-sized portion of beef stew regardless, and they each took their plates over to the table. Joe began eating in silence, chewing every mouthful at least fifty times.

'The children settle to sleep so well,' Laura said, searching for a topic of conversation that wouldn't ignite Joe's ire.

'I know. They fall into bed like they've been clubbed. It's keeping them asleep that's the tricky part,' Kitty sighed. 'The three littlies will all end up in with us by the morning.'

Joe rolled his eyes in silent suffering, indicating through the gesture that they all ended up on his side of the bed, but continued to eat. Laura wondered what on earth Kitty saw in him.

'You must get so tired,' Laura sympathized.

'Yes, but that's just how it is in this period of our lives, isn't it? I keep telling myself I'll look back on all this in twenty years when they've gone to university or whatnot, and the house is quiet and tidy and clean, and . . . ' Kitty gave a small shudder and Laura noticed Joe give his wife a quick, reassuring wink.

'How's Sugar going to be coping with this weather? It's hardly her indigenous climate.'

'Camels are adaptable,' Joe replied. 'It's what makes them such good survivors.'

Laura looked at him. What did he know about surviving?

Kitty touched his arm. 'By the way, did Tom tell you his latest joke?' Her voice was lower, more intimate, and Laura remembered what Alex had said about them, that first day of the summer holidays, lying on the grass 'snogging each other's faces off'.

He shook his head, and Laura noticed they were sitting so closely together, he had to keep his left arm immobile in order not to knock Kitty with it. He could easily shuffle over to the right a little, but he appeared to be choosing not to.

'How do you make Lady Gaga cry?' Kitty asked, the giggle already in her eyes.

He shrugged. 'I don't know.'

'Poke 'er face.'

There was a moment's delay as Joe struggled to get it – Laura didn't imagine he listened to dance music in his tractor – before he suddenly burst out laughing. It was a deep, goose-honking sound, and replaced his omnipresent scowl with crinkly laughter lines around his eyes.

Laura, to her utter surprise, responded in kind and Kitty joined in too, the three of them giggling harder every time they made eye contact before they eventually subsided into a bemused, slightly self-conscious silence.

Kitty broke it first. 'Seconds? There's plenty.'

Laura hesitated, letting Joe push his plate towards his wife first, before responding, 'That would be wonderful. If you're sure there's enough.'

'You need feeding up, lady,' Kitty said, carrying the plates towards the sink just as there was a knock at the front door. 'Get that would you, Joe?'

He scraped his chair back noisily along the floor.

'It's good to see you two getting to know each other better,' Kitty said diplomatically, returning with the extra helpings. 'He's not so bad, you know.'

Laura was mortified that Kitty had read the situation so accurately. 'Oh no, no. I never thought he was,' she lied as the distant bass of voices started up in the hallway.

'I think probably you're just too alike, that's all.'

What – dour, miserable and sullen? Was that how Kitty saw her? Laura felt her spirits dip at the realization. She over-piled her fork with food and started chewing, cheeks full as globes when the kitchen door opened and Joe came back in.

'Look who I found!' he said, instantly falling into the role of mine host and crossing the room to pour their guest a glass of wine.

Rob sauntered in a second later, shrugging off his over-coat and shaking snow out of his hair. He was wearing a navy suit and pale blue shirt, the tie loosened and his top button undone, ready for home. Laura froze.

'I'm under orders to collect the Christmas pudding and cake, Kit. Cat's convinced we're going to be snowed in till Christmas now,' Rob laughed, kissing Kitty on each cheek before catching sight of Laura. 'Oh.'

Laura felt herself cringe all the way down to her toes as she swallowed her food hurriedly. 'Hello,' she mumbled, a hand over her mouth, feeling layers of embarrassment clamber upon her as she remembered she was also wearing Kitty's pink flannel pyjamas.

A beat passed.

'Laura,' he said, walking over and putting one hand lightly on her shoulder, kissing her politely on the cheeks for appearance's sake. 'This is a surprise. I didn't know you were here.'

'I-I'm an interloper who's rather thrown herself upon their mercy for tonight,' she said, looking at the floor. 'I hadn't realized snow was coming and I stupidly made an impromptu detour over here to see Kitty after my interviews.'

'Still not run out of conversation, then, you two?' Rob teased, directing the comment at Kitty, but his voice sounded strained. 'Who were you interviewing?' he asked, his stiff body language belying the easy-going chat.

'Min and Olive.'

He raised an eyebrow. 'Fun day.' He shifted position, shoving a hand into his trouser pocket. 'How was Min? I haven't seen her for ages.'

'Yes. Very well. It all went well,' she fudged. Now wasn't the right time to confront him with the truths she'd learnt today.

'Have you eaten, Rob?' Kitty asked. 'There's some stew left.'

Rob held up a hand. 'Thanks, I'm fine. I had lunch out today.'

'Well, can you stay for a drink?' Kitty asked hopefully. 'We can give Joe the post-mortem.'

'I'm not sure I like the sound of that,' Joe protested, making Kitty giggle and slap his arm affectionately.

'Verbier, you wally!'

'To be honest, I really ought to head back,' Rob said, thumbing towards the door.

'Not even one drink? Please?' Kitty pleaded. 'It would be so fun.'

Rob hesitated, his eyes on Laura's red toenails. 'Well . . . just one. But it'll have to be quick. It's still snowing and you don't want *me* stranded here overnight too,' he said, giving a forced laugh.

'Let's move into the other room,' Joe suggested convivially, picking up the bottle and leading the way, leaving their second helpings untouched on the table.

They went through to a room Laura hadn't been in before. It was tiny but more formal – well, not covered in dog hairs anyway. There was only just enough room for two two-seater sofas and an under-the-window bookcase. The walls were painted port-wine red, with a green carpet and a black fire-place that, unlike the blacksmith's furnace in the kitchen, had a low, simmering flame.

Laura crossed the room to the far sofa. Etiquette demanded that she sit next to Rob – there was nowhere else to go – and she fussed as she sat down, taking care to wrap her legs round themselves like wisteria vines so that she took up as little space as possible.

'So it sounds like I missed a cracking weekend,' Joe said to Rob, handing him his glass.

'You were sorely missed, mate.'

'You'd have loved the Secret Santas,' Kitty giggled, patting Joe's knee. 'There were some really rude ones. Poor David's face when he saw that glow-in-the-dark thingy! Of course, Alex made sure he ended up with it, didn't he, Laura?'

'Uh, yes, I think so,' Laura replied vaguely.

'Kitty said Alex was up to his usual tricks,' Joe muttered.

'Of course,' Rob nodded, and Laura felt her cheeks burn. Was Joe referring to what had happened on the skidoo trip?

'Have you spoken to anyone from the trip since getting home?' Rob asked, turning to Laura.

'Uh, just Kitty. And Cat Skyped me yesterday, obviously,' Laura replied, managing to keep her eyes dead ahead.

'Not Orlando? Or Alex?' There was an intimation in his voice.

Laura deliberately let the question pass. As far as she was concerned, she'd already answered. She stared into her glass, bemoaning the pyjama situation. It was hardly the most dignified appearance since their last, eventful meeting. She bet he didn't want to kiss her now.

'So all the interviews are finished, then?' Kitty asked, throwing her legs over Joe's lap.

Laura nodded. 'Yup. All done, and the charms are almost completed. I'll be out of everyone's way before you know it.'

'I hope that's not code for you disappearing on us,' Kitty said quickly. 'You will keep in touch, won't you? I'd love to make a day trip over to see you. I love the seaside.'

'Don't worry, Kit. Laura's not going anywhere as fast as *she'd* like,' Rob said with authority.

Laura looked across at him.

'You haven't interviewed me yet,' he shrugged.

'Yes I have. I interviewed you on the plane.'

A moment passed. 'Briefly. It hardly counted as an interview.'

'Maybe, but you told me a lot on the glacier too, and I did have a weekend to watch you together. That's more telling than words.' She took a swig of wine. 'You asked me to encapsulate the essence of her relationships, not signify particular memories, and I believe I understand absolutely the essence of your relationship with her.'

'You do?'

'I do,' Laura nodded.

'Mind-sharing?' he asked, giving a small, forced laugh.

'She's the fixed point of your world. She's the sun you rise to every day and the moon who guides you. You're the luckiest man on the planet, Rob – you married your own dream.' Her voice had risen an octave and her smile was rictus tight.

Rob stared at her. 'That's what you see?'

'Wow, Laura,' Kitty breathed. 'You're like a poet or something.'

'I will be if I can find a way of translating all that into a single charm,' she smiled, draining her glass, unable to bear Rob's continued scrutiny. She didn't think she could keep up the act for much longer. Sitting here on this sofa with him was too close, too soon. She looked across at Kitty. 'Well, I'm afraid I'm shattered. I've been working non-stop since we got back and I'm so tired I could sleep on a spike.'

'But it's not even nine,' Rob said incredulously, checking the mantel clock.

'Like I said, crazy hours,' Laura replied tightly, rising. 'And I've imposed on you guys enough for one day. You must want some time to yourselves before the ankle-biters are up again. Thanks for dinner, Kitty. It was delicious.'

She crossed the room, feeling conspicuous and ridiculous in the pyjamas.

'Actually, I'll just, uh . . . have a quick word with Laura outside,' she heard Rob say as she got to the door. 'About payment for the necklace.'

Laura spun on her heel to find him standing up, ready to follow. 'There's absolutely no need, Rob. Don't you remember? You've already paid in full. We're all square.'

He looked back at her, stunned. 'But—'

'Trust me. Our account is settled. Just enjoy your drink with your friends,' she said casually, leaving him no option but to sit down again. 'You owe me nothing.'

# Chapter Thirty-Five

The light woke her. Laura sat up blearily. Even without opening the curtains she could tell the snow had fallen hard.

She kicked the blankets off and the floorboards creaked beneath her weight as she went to the window to peer out into the world. There was probably a foot and a half of snow now. It was so deep that everything outside had lost its edges, blending shapes so that bird baths blurred with garden chairs, cars into garden walls. She remembered her old enemy Sugar and wondered how she was coping with the snow, in spite of her adaptability.

A shiver ferreted up her spine from the old, cold glass and she moved away to lean against the ancient radiator. It was only warm in the top-right corner, so she perched there whilst her brain slowly booted up and reminded her of the ruin that was her life now. Jack, Fee. It was Thursday. This would be the third whole day since she'd left home, the longest the three of them had ever gone without contact. She kept catching herself worrying about Fee – knowing she of all people couldn't cope with silence – before remembering in the next instant how Fee didn't need her concern. Fee had proved more than capable of looking out for herself and getting what she wanted.

Laura breathed slowly, painfully. She still hadn't cried

properly yet and was beginning to wonder whether she ever would. Maybe she just couldn't any more; maybe her body couldn't absorb any more hurt.

She washed at the sink and got dressed in yesterday's clothes. She had no idea how she was going to get home today. She'd have to fit Monster wheels on Dolly to get her over this snow.

She could hear Kitty talking as she came down the stairs.

'Well, I haven't had an email or anything to say that school *isn't* going to open, so I guess I'm going to have to try to make my way in,' Kitty sighed, setting down the tea and a platter of sausages, bacon and baked beans. Scrambled eggs were in a separate bowl. She looked up at the sight of Laura in the doorway. 'Good timing! Come and sit . . . Of course, the children will want me to pull them in on their sledges.'

'Well, you're not to, Kits,' Joe said firmly from his high-backed chair. He didn't actively acknowledge Laura's presence, but he didn't scowl at her either, which had to be taken as a positive step up in his books. 'They're too heavy now for you to be dragging them behind you like that. You'll do your back in again. I'd take them myself if I didn't have to clear the roads.'

Kitty looked over at Laura. 'The council's asked him to clear the local roads. It couldn't have come at a better time, could it, Joe? A little more cash before Christmas.'

Joe gave a terse, scarcely perceptible nod. Laura already knew enough of the man to know he would abhor any kind of comment about money in front of strangers. 'Don't change the subject, Kit. You are not to pull them.'

'Yes, you're right,' his wife replied, busying herself with cutting her sausage into tiny pieces.

'Kit!' Joe warned, frowning at her. 'I mean it.'

Kit sighed and stopped what she was doing. 'Okay. I promise,' she said, making eye contact with him. Laura quickly looked away, feeling strangely intrusive, pouring herself some tea from the pot.

Joe helped himself to another rasher of bacon.

'Well, obviously I can help you,' Laura said after a minute listening to everyone munching whilst she held her mug between two hands.

'You've not got suitable clothing for walking around in these conditions,' Kitty argued.

'What are you talking about, woman? You've got loads of things she can borrow,' Joe muttered. 'She may as well make herself useful.' He looked at Laura. 'The roads are closed and there are no trains. You'll have to stay here tonight as well.'

It was the most graceless offer of hospitality Laura had ever heard.

'Thank you,' she said quietly.

Kitty peered over at Laura as she spread her home-made marmalade on toast. 'Sleep well?'

'Like the proverbial, thanks.'

'Huh, that's because you don't have the literals,' Joe mumbled.

Kitty's phone beeped beside her and she picked it up. 'Oh. There it is. Confirmation that school's shut.'

A collective roar from the children made Laura jump. Kitty shook her head, smiling, as they all started dancing around the kitchen, jubilant. She raised an eyebrow at Laura. 'How are your snowman-making skills?'

'Rusty.'

'Well, tuck in,' she said, pushing the sausages towards Laura. 'You thought skiing with Rob was hard core?' She shook her head and gave a small snort of disdain. 'He's nothing compared to what my lot will expect from you in the snow.'

Laura sniffed loudly as Samuel wriggled on her lap. Lucie put her arm around her and squeezed tight.

'Laura?' Kitty frowned, peering her head round the door of the snug and finding her feral children sitting in a heap around Laura. They were supposed to be having 'quiet time' after lunch, but it appeared Laura was the one most in need of time-out.

'Mufasa just died,' Laura hiccupped, pointing towards the TV. It was the third film she'd watched in a row and she was almost cross-eyed with grief.

'Ah yes . . . *The Lion King*. One of my top-five films of all time,' Kitty said earnestly, watching her closely. Laura had started weeping the second the opening credits had come up and basically hadn't stopped.

'Mine too. After *Nemo* and *Toy Story*,' Laura sniffed again.

'I think *Toy Story* 2's better,' Finn piped up from under her arm. 'We'll watch that next.'

Kitty smiled at him. 'Well, do you think I could borrow Aunty Laura for a bit first?'

Laura nodded and got up. Instantly, five sets of arms wrapped around her. 'No!' the children cried.

'I'll have her back before Scar does you-know-what,' Kitty winked.

They fell back on to the little green sofa reluctantly.

'What's up?' Laura asked weakly, her nose red, as they tiptoed out of the snug.

'Is everything all right, Laura?' Kitty asked, placing an enquiring hand on her arm.

'Absolutely,' she sniffed. 'Why d'you ask?'

'Only the fact that you've been crying for two hours solid.'

Laura swallowed. 'Disney,' she said, thumbing back towards the door. 'Killing me. I don't know how the kids do it. They are so *hard*. How can they not sob when Mufasa is betrayed by his own son like that? *His own son*, I ask you?'

'Uh-huh.' Kitty watched as a fresh veil of tears fell. 'Well, listen, I was going to ask whether you wouldn't mind doing me a favour. But if you're too upset, I —'

'No, no, no. Anything. What can I do?' Laura asked, wiping her nose with a piece of kitchen roll that Samuel had given her – only to discover the little devil had used it himself. 'Ugh!'

'I'm just finishing the costumes for the nativity tonight, but I'm out of ribbon for Martha's headdress. Joe's going into town to get some more salt, but frankly he wouldn't know a petersham from Peter Jones. I don't suppose . . . ?'

'Of course.'

'Great! I've got a small sample you can match. I need three point two metres.'

'Sure.'

'Oh, you are a love. Joe's just getting the tractor. Take my ski jacket from the porch. I'll just go get that sample for you.'

Laura nodded, sniffing again as she slipped on Kitty's jacket and wellies by the door.

'Here you go.' Kitty handed over a small strip of cinnamon-coloured grosgrain ribbon. 'See you back here shortly. I should have pretty much finished by then and we can have a cuppa.'

'Lovely.'

Laura marched into the snow. It had been well compacted down thanks to their strenuous activity in the morning – a snowman competition: yes, why stop at one when the children can have one each? – followed by a particularly vigorous and evil snowball fight that saw the children target Laura with a well-planned ambush campaign, resulting in handfuls of snow being shoved down her back. And when she'd fallen, laughing, in the snow, the children had followed suit, swinging their arms and legs out to make snow angels.

Joe's blue tractor rumbled around from the barns at the back and he threw open the door for her without cutting the engine and the cab wobbled perilously on its hyper-suspension. Laura clambered up, looking around for a seat belt, and found with alarm that there wasn't one. The snow-plough Joe had used earlier when he'd been clearing the roads was still fitted, and Laura watched, mesmerized, as they pulled away and the fresh falls parted before them like a holy sea.

'You're quiet,' Joe muttered after several minutes of silence.

'Am I?' she replied, staring out of the panoramic wind-screen.

'Yes, given that every time I pass, you and Kitty are always chatting away like you've known each other for years.'

'Well, I'm sure Kitty's like that with everyone. She's so friendly and warm.'

Joe shot her a sideways look. 'You'd be surprised.'

Laura looked across at him. This was almost passing as a conversation. 'Are you saying Kitty's *shy*?'

'I'm saying she's not as robust as she comes across. She gives too much and she gets easily hurt. That's what I'm saying.'

Laura frowned as the tractor swept down the lanes. The comment felt targeted. '*I* would never hurt her, if that's what you mean.'

'No?' Joe looked dead ahead. 'That's what her other friends

said too, till their lives took off and they dumped her like a sack of potatoes because she wasn't rich and thin and glamorous enough to fit into their shiny new circles.'

'Do you mean Cat?'

'Who else?' he snorted.

'She's just . . . abandoned her?'

Joe looked straight at her. 'Nail on the head.'

'And that's why you've hated me on sight. It was nothing to do with Pocket's diet at all. You feel I'm perpetuating the glossy myths around her, when all she's done is hurt your wife.'

Joe was silent for a minute. 'It breaks my heart to see her talking up that woman like they're still so close. Reminiscing about their glory days when, in reality, Cat hasn't bothered with her for years.'

'But they got on so well in Verbier.'

'Yes. Because Mrs High and Mighty had an audience.'

'I really don't think Cat's like that,' Laura said quietly. 'She went out of her way to be friendly to me when she really could have just ignored me altogether, and there's no agenda there – she doesn't have any idea that I'm doing the necklace for her.'

'Then there's another reason she's currying favour with you. Cat Blake doesn't do anything for anybody unless there's something in it for her. Kitty outlived her usefulness years ago.'

Laura fell quiet. There was no point in arguing the toss. He'd known Cat since childhood. Who was she to tell him he was wrong? He didn't need her to lecture him that friends very often do just grow apart. She watched him discreetly as he stopped at a junction and pulled out on to the main road. His chin was thrust forward defiantly, proudly. She might not like what he was saying about Cat, but she liked what he was doing for his wife. And for the first time, Laura began to understand what it was that Kitty saw in him.

Laura leaned against the wall, her clasped hands resting against her mouth – partly to stop her from laughing, partly because the scene in front of her ranked as one of the most adorable she'd seen in her life. On the darkened stage, the children of Ottersbrook Primary School were singing 'Little Donkey' in joyous tunelessness and Kitty's chaotic home-made costumes. The shepherds had tea towels fixed down on their heads, jam jar-style, the donkey was boasting a Rasta mane Bob Marley would have been proud to call his own, and poor Mary and baby Jesus were being completely upstaged by the stars – the pretty little girls in reception who were twinkling gloriously in white tutus and LED fairy lights. Laura had so far successfully managed to identify Lucie, Kitty's second, who was the inn-keeper's wife, Tom, who was a king, and Samuel, who was a rather blotchy-faced sheep. The fact that he was holding on to his companion duckling for grim death suggested he had thrown a major tantrum backstage and refused to go on without it.

Kitty and Joe had managed to bag seats in the third row, but Laura – despite Kitty's entreaties that she sit with them – had insisted on not taking a place intended for proud parents and was perfectly happy leaning against the back wall instead. She could see equally as well from there, she'd said.

It was just as amusing for her to watch the families as the children anyway. Before her lay a sea of inclined heads – some greying, some balding, many blonded – the shoulders beneath them hunched with anxious anticipation until lines had been safely delivered. The dark space running up to the stage was lit up like a circuit board as hundreds of red blinking lights recorded the play for posterity and absent grandparents. Five, eight, ten years earlier, these very people would have been holding up white lighters at festivals and concerts, but this performance – better than anything they'd ever seen at the $O_2$ – marked their new life stage as clearly as stretch marks and baggy eyes.

She let her eyes swing over the audience like a beam of light, watching their profiles as women leaned in to whisper to their husbands during the carols, or their hands fluttered to their mouths nervously as their children spoke their lines. This was what it was to be a mother, she saw – pride and fear intermingled with something fierce and tender all at once. Something complicated, something universal, but uniquely theirs all the same. Had she been wrong to walk away from it so lightly? Had Jack? If she had been pregnant, would he really have left her?

Laura searched out Kitty again, and she noticed Joe lip-synching as Tom delivered his lines. She watched for a couple of minutes, enchanted. The man was secretly soft!

And then she saw him – Rob – sitting two rows back, slightly further to the left so that he was almost directly in front of her. It was his curls, so identifiable even from behind, that she noticed first. To his right was Cat, hair gleaming as though the lights were trained on her. Even from behind they made a beautiful couple. Laura looked back at Rob again, feeling her heart galloping like a thoroughbred. All day last night's veiled conversation had lingered in the back of her mind like a shadow on her heart. What had he wanted to say to her in the hall? She had lain awake for hours afterwards, wondering, wincing as she heard the front door close twenty minutes later.

She watched him tilt his head to listen to something Cat was whispering in his ear, and he appeared to frown and shake his head in reply. Suddenly she lost them as the weighted hem of the curtain landed on the stage with a *thwump!* and they were swallowed up by the upsurge of cheering parents who took to their feet.

Laura craned to see them in the crowd, but it was impossible to keep tabs on anyone as mothers cried, grandparents roundly congratulated, children ran into outstretched arms, and fathers swapped cordial handshakes for their 'good to see you' once-a-term meetings. Over the crowd, she could hear Kitty, boisterous in her happiness, as she tried to simultaneously congratulate the music teacher and round up her brood. All around her, people jostled and laughed and chattered, children darted past her knees, and her toes were run over several times by mothers with sleeping babies in prams.

'Aunty Laura, Aunty Laura,' a little voice called up, and she felt a strong tug on the hem of her jumper. She looked down to find Martha squinting up at her. 'I can't find Mummy.'

'What? Oh, but she's just down by the stage,' Laura replied distractedly, her eyes falling upon Kitty, who was conducting an impromptu nit-check on Tom.

'People keep treading on my toes,' Martha whined.

'Well then, just stay here with me. Let's just . . . let all these people get through first, shall we?' she said, taking Martha by the hand and gesturing towards the bottleneck of people shuffling through the narrow doors, only to find, just twenty feet away, the Blakes.

Rob's eyes met hers a split second before Cat's.

'Laura!' Cat gasped, waving a manicured hand across the sea of heads. 'What are you *doing* here?'

'Snowed in!' Laura called.

Cat cupped her hand to her ear. 'Sorry?'

'I'm snowed in!' Laura shouted. But it was useless. They were being swept away by the nativity tide.

'Meet us outside!' Cat called as she disappeared from sight.

Laura nodded, squeezing Martha's hand excitedly. She let the crowds rush past, and Laura looked back for Kitty and Joe, just catching sight of them as they disappeared through the emergency exit beside the stage.

'Oh, come on, Martha. Let's go this way.'

'I always knew Tom would make a great king,' Kitty was saying proudly, clutching the poor mortified boy by his shoulders, as Laura and Martha met up with them in the car park. It was all but deserted — no one was stopping to chat in the freezing night temperatures. Fluffy snowflakes were fluttering down, illuminated in the pools of light thrown out by the lamp posts.

'He'll make a better farmer,' Joe snorted.

'And as for Lucie – I mean, the way she delivered her lines. I never had that kind of composure when I was her age.' Kitty had her hand smacked over her heart in utter amazement.

'She was great!' Laura beamed, stopping next to her. 'And I loved Sam holding his duckling too. So sweet.'

'Huh! That's what you call it,' Joe muttered.

Kitty rolled her eyes. 'Ignore him, old Misery Boots,' she mouthed.

But Laura just gave him a knowing smile. His secret was out with her. She hadn't forgotten his quiet pride beaming out in the dark hall.

'You really ought to have sat with us, though,' Kitty

tutted. 'There was honestly no need for you to stand at the back.'

'No, it was packed in there. I was fine. I had a great view.'

'You could have sat with us, Laura,' Cat smiled, looking richer than the Three Kings in a honey-coloured sheepskin coat. 'There was plenty of room next to us proud godparents.'

Laura shrugged, wishing she hadn't borrowed Kitty's coat – a Millets fleece-lined parka that was better suited to fell-walking in Cumbrian rain than Christmas plays in the Home Counties.

'So how come you're here?' Cat asked her again. 'Are you staying with these guys?'

'Yes. I got snowed in. Apparently I was the only person in the country *not* to know that it was going to snow this week and decided that driving cross-country to London and Surrey was an absolutely cracking idea.'

'What were you doing in London and Surrey?' Cat asked.

Laura stalled. It was a reasonable enough question, but Laura couldn't answer it – not without giving away Rob's secret present. She saw Rob shift his weight nervously.

'Oh . . . you know . . . visiting friends,' she nodded.

Cat looked between Laura and Kitty, and Laura saw the flash of hurt that she hadn't been included in the grand tour. 'You must have seen Laura last night when you went to get the cakes?' Cat asked Rob. 'Why didn't you tell me?'

He gave a careless shrug. 'Laura went to bed early. I didn't think to mention it. What was there to say?'

'I would have liked to know! I could have come over today for some girly chat and some of Kitty's world-famous cake.'

Kitty puffed up with pride. 'Well, if you want to come over tom—'

'How long are you staying for?' Cat asked Laura.

'Hopefully I'll get back tomorrow. I need to start getting everything ready for the launch party.'

Cat's face fell. 'You're going so soon?'

'I've imposed far too much as it is. I'm eating these guys out of house and home, using up all the hot water . . .'

'Nonsense!' Kitty admonished. 'We love having you to stay.'

'Well, if it's a bother for Kitty, I've got a fabulous idea,' Cat gasped suddenly.

'But it's not a b—' Kitty tried.

Cat's hands gripped Laura's forearm excitedly. 'There's a big charity auction tomorrow night at the Mandarin Oriental. And you'll never guess who's chairing it.'

Laura shook her head. She was quite sure she wouldn't.

'Bertie What's-his-name.'

'Penryn, Cat,' Rob muttered. 'Christ, why can you never remember his name?'

Cat swatted his arm lightly. He wasn't the one in her sights. 'What do you say? Come with! It'll be the perfect opportunity to introduce you, and then we can work on him to come to the party next week.'

'Oh, Cat, it's so kind of you, but I couldn't possibly. I'd be a gate-crasher and, I mean, I don't have anything to wear –'

'So? We'll go shopping! And I'll take you for lunch at my favourite place.'

'But it's far too late notice. Surely there are seating plans organized, and I probably can't afford a ticket anyhow.'

'Oh, don't worry about all that! Rob's company's taken a

table. We can have whoever we want.' She pointed her finger at Laura, Kitchener-style. 'And I want you!'

She burst out laughing, and Laura giggled nervously, starstruck and stunned. 'I'm not sure.'

'Rob, tell her.'

But Rob did nothing at all other than shake his head and stare at his feet. The last thing he was going to say to Laura was that he wanted her too!

'Tch. Ignore him. He's just worried about his Amex bill. Oh, please say you'll come.'

'But how are we supposed to get into London from here? There are no trains running. The auction might even be cancelled, mightn't it?'

'We're not relying on public transport, Laura. Heaven forbid. They can scarcely do the job on a summer's day. We're hitching a lift in a friend's chopper. They're shooting in Lincs, but sweetly said they'd drop us off at Battersea heliport on the way past.' She tipped her head pleadingly. 'What were the chances of me bumping into you like this? It's a sign. I know it is. You're meant to be there.'

Laura looked from Rob to Joe to Kitty. It was hard to say who looked more thunderous. She had no such conviction that she was supposed to be anywhere other than her studio in Suffolk in the middle of a creek.

'In fact, let's make it easier still,' Cat said, clearly on a roll. 'Come back with us now. That way, you're out of the Bakers' hair and we're all ready to go straight off in the morning.'

Laura looked over at Kitty, who was holding a child on each hip. Martha was leaning against her legs and sucking her thumb. The poor woman could scarcely remain upright.

'I suppose it *would* make things easier for you guys if I skedaddle off,' Laura said.

Kitty opened her mouth to say something but then appeared to think better of it, and closed it again.

'You're right. You go,' Joe said coldly, wrapping an arm tightly around Kitty's shoulders. 'It'll mean we can turn the heating off in that room tonight.'

'Great!' Cat beamed. 'So it's all sorted, then. We'll take Laura off your hands and give you guys a break.' She leant over and kissed Kitty roundly on each cheek before ruffling the children's hair. 'And you kids were superstars tonight. Well done, you!'

Laura hung back awkwardly – Joe's body language was warning her not to hug his wife. 'Thanks so much for everything, Kitty,' she nodded lamely. 'I've loved staying with you. And you really were all brilliant tonight, you lot. You really were . . . superstars.' Five pairs of blue eyes blinked back at her warily.

'Come on, Laura, the car's over here,' Cat said, looping an arm through hers and leading her away.

'Oh, Kitty! Your coat,' Laura said, suddenly stopping and turning back as she remembered she was wearing the parka.

'Keep it. You'll need something to wear in these temperatures,' Kitty said quietly.

'Don't worry about that. I've got loads of coats Laura can borrow,' Cat interjected.

Kitty took the coat from Laura without a word as Cat led her towards the gleaming black Range Rover, chatting away excitedly. The doors closed with an expensively muffled *dock* sound and she looked out through the tinted windows at the big, bustling family standing unusually still and quietly in front of the little village hall.

A helicopter, huh?

# Chapter Thirty-Six

Rob was the one who retired early that night. He didn't say a word on the journey back – only taking his eyes off the road to throw furious looks at Cat every time she absently stroked his leg – and he didn't give her 'the tour' of the house this time, either. It was down to Cat to show her to her room – one of five 'spares' – before cracking open a bottle of champagne for them both, even though it was gone ten when they got in. By the time Laura fell into bed – and she did quite literally fall, the room was spinning so fast – it was well past two.

'Morning,' Cat said cheerily as Laura staggered into the kitchen the next morning in yesterday's clothes. Cat was sitting at a long white granite breakfast bar swirled with chocolate, wearing a black skinny jumper and even skinnier poppy-red jeans. Her skin glowed, her hair shone – and Laura felt even more deathly. How did she do it? How could she look so sparkly on four hours' sleep and several litres of champagne?

'Here, try this,' she smiled, taking in Laura's wan pallor. 'My secret weapon. It'll give you some zing.' She pushed a tall orangey-pink juice towards Laura. 'It's full of antioxidants and vitamins. Goodness in a glass. Here, sit down.' She pulled out a stool.

Laura sat down and sipped it suspiciously, not convinced that imbibing anything within the next ten hours was a good idea, but it was delicious. A cook in a grey uniform came over to her. 'What would you like me to prepare for you, madam?'

'Oh, nothing for me, thanks,' Laura said, shaking her head.

'Laura, this is Anchee, our cook. Fix her a Benedict royale, please,' Cat instructed, before looking back at Laura. 'You're going to need some carbs or you'll pay for it later in the chopper.'

'What time's it coming?'

'About ten-ish.'

'Is it just us going?'

'Rob's coming too. He's working in the study at the moment. There was no way the roads would be clear enough to get him into the office from here.'

Laura sipped some more of the power-juice and looked out through the arched windows at the beautiful garden. It was as if the snow itself had been topiaried, with conical trees and sharp hedges rendered in white.

'When do you buy your Christmas tree?' Laura asked, looking around curiously. There had been nothing festive in the cavernous hall or in any of the rooms she'd snuck a glance into as she'd passed. It seemed sad to think of the beautiful tree standing fully dressed and moulting quietly in the chalet in Verbier, its lights turned off and no one at home.

'I prefer not to get the decorations out until Christmas Eve. What with the two events being so close, I've always delayed the onset of Christmas until after my birthday. That was how my parents tried to make it special for me. I can't tell you the number of times I had a birthday party and people would turn up with my Christmas present instead.'

'Oh no, I can imagine,' Laura said, just as Rob came into the kitchen carrying an empty cup. 'It must have been so disappointing. One of the things we always loved about having a May birthday was that it staggered the year into almost equal halves between the present bounties. Also, we got to have our birthdays in the garden.'

'*We?*' Rob asked, the word more like a stab than a query, as he rinsed out the cup, his back to her. 'Is that the royal "we"?'

'Don't be a pig, Rob,' Cat snapped protectively. Rob shot a cold look at the two of them as he walked straight back out again.

'Please tell me your man's as grumpy as mine in the morning,' Cat muttered, her mood noticeably flatter.

The plea floored Laura as she thought of the daily ritual that had kicked off her days until this week: Jack waking her with tea and toast and a host of light kisses. His face came to her in a composite of separate parts – his surf-bum hair, patchy stubble, those clear blue eyes that opened on to a gentle soul – and she felt a flash of dizziness from the strain of keeping up the pretence. It felt like a feat of endurance not to have told anyone that she was drifting, anchorless, without him now. Answerable to no one. Belonging to no one.

Anchee set down in front of her a perfectly poached egg and smoked salmon covered in hollandaise sauce.

'Oh my goodness, that looks amazing.'

'Great. You tuck in. I'm just going to finish packing,' Cat said, rubbing her shoulder. 'Honestly, I've got three dresses I just can't choose between, and knowing me, I'll end up taking the lot . . .'

Laura tried not to moan with pleasure as she ate her breakfast alone, and she could feel her body beginning to rally with every bite. Switching her phone on for the first time in four days – and finding her message box predictably full of calls from Fee, which she deleted without listening to – she called one of her suppliers to place an order for twelve extra sheets of gold and three bags of links. Now that the interviews for Cat's necklace were complete, her mind had begun to scroll over what she needed for the launch party next week. She had a good stock of ready-to-go charms to display, but they needed fixing to chains, and she'd had a couple of ideas too: she'd woken up the night before last with the brainwave of fixing some charms to a giant nappy pin for a bridal 'something old, something new, something borrowed, something blue' theme. It would attach nicely to the inside of the gown for the big day and could easily be transferred to a chain for posterity. And what about kilt pins? Each clan had not only its own tartan, but a crest and motto too. There was scope for translation on to charms there too . . .

The ideas flowed quickly as she ate. When her phone rang, she answered without hesitation.

'Hello?'

'. . . Laura?' Fee's voice came down the line. Except that it wasn't Fee's voice, just a pale imitation, tremulous and hollow, lacking the falsetto laughter or gullible wonder.

The fork dropped out of Laura's hand and fell on to the plate with a clatter.

'Laura, please, wait! I am sorry! I know what I did was wrong. Please . . .' Fee gabbled desperately, knowing only too well that her friend was this very moment struggling to disconnect her. 'I was trying to help.'

Laura gasped in outrage at Fee's sanctimony. 'Since when

has betraying your best friend's confidence ever been considered helpful?' she hissed.

'I was wrong to tell him – I know that now. It wasn't my place,' Fee said pleadingly.

'Tch, *you think*?' Laura asked sarcastically. 'And how about sleeping with him? I suppose you've since figured out that that wasn't your place either.'

'You don't understand—'

'Oh, I understand perfectly! Everything is very clear to me now. I made a huge mistake thinking you could be my family. I'm better off alone. I don't need *you*. I don't need any—'

Her finger found 'disconnect' and pressed it. The phone fell from her hand to the floor and she dropped her head in her arms, holding her breath, knowing that even just to exhale would be enough to open the floodgates. She held on . . .

'Laura?'

She looked up with a start. Cat was holding out her phone, concern written all over her beautiful face.

'Who was that?'

Laura met her eyes and Cat's face fell as she saw the overwhelming expression of heartbreak reflected back at her. 'Oh, sweetie,' she whispered, opening her arms out wide.

Laura walked into them and let the sobs come at last.


'So we'll meet you in there, then?' Cat asked Rob, rifling in her bag on the pavement as Laura ducked into the taxi ahead of her and slid along the back seat.

Rob nodded. 'I'll change at the office. If you've got Laura to walk in with, there's no point in me travelling all the way over to Kensington only to have to go back to Knightsbridge again.'

'I promise we won't be *too* naughty,' she pouted.

Rob gave a knowing sigh. 'Yeah, yeah. I'll believe it when I see the Top Shop label.' He threw a quick glance over at Laura as he stepped into his car, but luckily her expression was impossible to read behind the sunglasses Cat had given her to hide her puffy eyes.

'To South Molton Street, please, driver,' Cat said as she got in and sat beside Laura. 'First we shop,' she smiled, patting her knee. 'Then we talk.'

Laura took a deep breath, trying to keep it together. She'd been bang on about the floodgates. To paraphrase Paxman, she'd started, so she'd finish, and she felt as barely held together as the Hoover Dam with Sellotape.

'Have you decided what you're wearing yet?' she asked Cat, giving it her best shot at being 'okay'.

Cat swivelled round to face her excitedly. 'Well, I've got it down to two. The front-runner's a Marchesa gown I bought in Rome last month. Silk chiffon in that baby, baby pink that's just so good for us blondes,' she purred, running her hands down her arms. 'With waterfall ruffles and a black velvet bow at the waist.'

'It sounds amazing.' Laura nodded, utterly hypnotized by just the sound of it. It could have been pudding.

'Mmm,' Cat said, wrinkling her nose. 'But is it just a bit . . . blah?'

'Well, what's the other one like?' Laura asked, sniffing inelegantly.

'Now that's the interesting one. It's a bit out there for a do like this. Everyone will be in full-length, but this is short – I mean micro-short – but it swings out, like a baby-doll style, so it's not tacky or anything.'

Laura nodded. She knew that if there was one thing Cat didn't do, it was tacky. 'What colour?'

'Grey, but kind of fringed on a jacquard.'

Laura blinked, lost, and Cat laughed at her beleaguered expression. 'It's a satin that looks like it's got distressed feathers on, as though the threads have pulled. It makes you want to tickle your hands against it.'

'I think I'd have to see it to . . . understand it.'

Cat nodded. 'I'll take it in to Browns with us. See how it looks compared with your dress. It might look odd for me to wear short if you're in long.'

'I think I'll probably go short,' Laura said quickly, surmising that a short dress must surely cost less than long, given the discrepancy in the amount of fabric used.

'What about your hair?'

'What about it?' Laura asked back. Her hair needed a *decision*? She'd planned just to wash it.

'Up or down?'

Laura swallowed. 'What do you think?'

Cat tipped her head in consideration. 'I'd say down.'

'So then I'll go with down.' Laura sighed with relief, sinking back into the seat. It definitely sounded the easier option.

'Oh God, and shoes!'

Laura shot forward again. 'Shoes?' She'd been planning on wearing some. What was the calamity?

'I so badly want to wear my new Valentino shoots, but they'd really only go with the Marchesa.'

Laura hesitated. 'What's a shoot?'

'A shoe-boot,' Cat explained, looking bemused that this wasn't the common parlance she'd assumed. 'They're divine. Black with a sheer gauze over the top of the foot and tying in just the diddiest drawstring below the ankle.' She sighed.

'He's got such an eye for the details. If that drawstring was just an inch higher and above the ankle?' She pouted and shook her head. 'Uh-uh. Entirely different proposition altogether. We can't all be Bolivian supermodels with legs up to here, can we?' she giggled.

Laura shook her head, even though Cat was the closest flesh and blood approximation of a supermodel that *she'd* ever seen.

The taxi pulled up outside a run of boutiques painted in a distinctive clotted-cream colour. Cat paid, not bothering to get either a receipt or change, as Laura hauled herself out of the other door.

'Ready?' Cat asked, looping her arm through Laura's and walking with authority and purpose towards the nearest door.

'You lead the way,' Laura smiled, taking a deep breath. 'I'll follow.'

# Chapter Thirty-Seven

*Now* she understood why smart restaurants had doormen. Laura smiled gratefully as Scott's door was held open for her and she walked through sideways, like a crab, to squeeze her bags through. Cat was already kissing the maître d', her bags abandoned in the middle of the floor in the absolute confidence that someone would pick them up and store them safely for her.

'May I take your bags for you, madam?' a waitress asked.

Laura handed them over with the same strangled expression Jack reserved for Fee and a tomato-based sauce; their contents equated to almost two mortgage payments in value and it was a nerve-racking experience letting them out of her sight.

'Over here, Laura,' Cat called softly, settling herself at a table by the window. It was one o'clock and the restaurant was already at capacity.

'Just as well you booked,' Laura said, looking around at the mushroom-coloured walls, tobacco-leather chairs and plush, deep red flower arrangements on the tables.

'Oh, I didn't book,' Cat shrugged, just as Laura caught wind of the jealous looks being thrown at them by the people sitting along the bar in the centre of the room. A magnificent display of *fruits de mer* was arranged behind them all on a platter – two-tiered for extra opulence.

Laura looked down hungrily at the menu. Carbs. She needed more carbs. And some fat. But no alcohol. She felt a raging thirst and was desperate for a pitcher of water.

'I've already ordered for us,' Cat said, patting her menu. 'I come here all the time and honestly, trust me, the Dover sole is just heaven.'

Did it come with chips, though? Laura wondered as the waiter came over with a bottle of Dom. More?

'Could we, uh, also have some water, please? Laura asked. Tap would be fine.'

The waiter smiled and went off to find a tap, clearly not sure whether they had one.

Cat raised her glass and waited for Laura to follow suit. 'To new friends,' she winked, clinking their glasses together delicately.

Laura sipped.

Cat put her glass down slowly and began brushing imaginary wrinkles out of the beautifully ironed tablecloth. 'So . . . are you going to tell me? Or shall I guess my way to the truth?'

Laura realized she was holding her breath again.

Cat laid a warm hand over Laura's, watching the way Laura's bottom lip wobbled. 'Okay . . . well then, I'm guessing that this is about your boyfriend?' she said kindly.

Laura swallowed.

'And your friend?'

Laura blinked.

'Getting together?'

Laura sniffed.

'And you discovered it recently?'

'Monday night,' Laura whispered.

'Monday? *This* Monday?'

Laura nodded.

Cat's eyes scanned hers. 'So what – you just left?'

Laura nodded.

'Is that why you went to Kitty's?'

'No, that was genuine stupidity on my part. I really didn't know it was going to snow. I never would have gone over if I'd known I'd have to stay. It's not like they're not busy enough with five small children and a farm to run.'

'Mmmm, tell me about it. I hardly ever get to see Kitty now.'

Laura looked at her. 'You don't?'

Cat shook her head. 'She's had five children in seven years. If she's not breastfeeding, she's trying to get them to sleep or doing the school run or going to toddler classes or NCT or . . . I don't know what.' She gave a hopeless shrug. 'It's almost impossible to just see *her* any more. She comes with an entourage these days. That was why it was so nice seeing her in Verbier.'

'Oh, I didn't realize.' Clearly, neither did Joe. He'd been too quick to judge. Laura admired him for protecting his wife, but he'd failed to see how it might feel from Cat's perspective. She'd lost her friend to her children. Ultimately, who had really dumped who?

'It's life, I guess.' Cat arched an eyebrow. 'And I try to look on the bright side. It also creates room for new friends.'

'Yes,' Laura laughed. 'I guess so.'

They were quiet for a moment, reflective again.

'Do you think you can forgive them?' Cat asked.

Laura shook her head. 'They were all I had in the world. I never knew my father, and my mother died when I was six.'

'Oh, Laura,' Cat gasped, upset. 'How long were you and your boyfriend together?'

'Four years.'

'Did you ever discuss marriage?'

'He did. At least he did to begin with.'

'To *begin* with? Hey, most guys don't go into a relationship looking to get married, Laura. It's usually the endgame when they're all out of get-out clauses,' she quipped, taking a large sip of her champagne.

'Jack's different. He wanted to take care of me.'

Cat stared at her. 'He sounds sweet. Didn't you want to marry him?'

'No.' Her answer was swift and decisive, taking Cat by surprise. 'There were such good reasons why we should, but it just never felt right enough.'

Cat paused, thinking. 'By which you mean, you didn't love him the way he loved you.'

'I don't know. Maybe.'

'Do you think he knew?'

Laura looked up at her through her lashes. 'Yes.'

'So then maybe that's why he . . . I mean, I'm not making excuses for him, Laura,' Cat said quickly, seeing Laura's expression change. 'But don't you think maybe it might have been . . . crushing for him, knowing that he loved you more than you loved him?'

'Yes.' Laura's voice was a whisper. She knew it with absolute certainty. 'I knew he'd run out of patience with the situation one day. I almost felt like I was waiting for it. I know it sounds weird, but I think the thing that's almost surprised me the most is how much it *hasn't* surprised me – him and Fee, I mean. It never crossed my mind before I found out, and yet now, when I think of them together, it makes perfect sense. They'd be great – I can totally see it.'

'Damn, you're nice. Remind me to have an affair with your husband when you marry.'

Laura shot her a pained smile and felt another sharp start of guilt at her actions and feelings for Rob. 'I'm not saying I forgive; just that I . . . kind of understand.'

'Were the two of them friends before this?'

'Totally. We just had our little gang of three. We were so intertwined, I thought nothing could ever break us. I mean, Fee's always got disastrous boyfriends on the go, but they never last very long. No one could ever really break into our group. We were too bonded for outsiders. But then she started seeing this guy, Paul, a few weeks ago. She was really keen on him, but I kept trying to talk her out of it. I think maybe I sensed she could get serious about him and it made me feel threatened. I didn't want to lose her.'

'So instead, she hooked up with Jack last weekend and you lost them both? Great friend she is.' Cat gave a heavy sigh. 'I don't know what to advise, Laura. I mean, I've got sympathy with Jack, up to a point. If the relationship wasn't going to go the distance, then I suppose you knew this day was coming. But sneaking around with Fee behind your back? That's hardly the way to break it off with you.' A thought came to her. 'Unless he deliberately *wanted* to hurt you. Could he have been trying to make you feel the way you make him feel?'

'No, Jack's not like that. He's not got a vindictive bone in his body.'

'Well, he's no saint either, Laura,' Cat said, squeezing her hand. 'Don't make him out to be blameless. There was no excuse for what he did. It's not your fault.'

Laura looked over at her. 'But I'm not faultless, am I? I kissed Alex,' she said quietly.

'No. Alex kissed you. There's a difference. You have nothing to feel guilty about.'

Laura looked away as Rob flashed up before her eyes again. She had plenty to feel guilty about it, even though Cat was right – it was nothing to do with Alex.

'Was it Fee you were talking to this morning?' Cat asked.

'Yes.'

'And what does she have to say for herself?'

'Not much. She was wrong; I've misunderstood – everything I would imagine passes as usual in this type of scenario.'

'She'll say whatever it is she thinks you want to hear.'

Laura nodded. 'I know.' The tears threatened her composure again, and she hurriedly took a large glug of her drink.

The waiter came over to refill their glasses. Clearly he hadn't yet found the tap.

'Is there any chance it's been going on longer than you think?' Cat asked when he'd gone again.

'The affair? No. Definitely not.'

'How can you be so sure?'

Laura paused. 'I'm fairly certain it only happened when I broke Jack's trust.'

Cat fell still. 'Broke his trust?'

'One of the reasons I agreed to go to Verbier was because I thought I was pregnant. I confided in Fee about it, but I didn't tell Jack.' She sighed heavily. 'So Fee did.'

Cat gasped. 'The bitch!'

Laura winced to hear Fee called that, but wasn't it true? She'd chosen Jack over Laura. She'd made her choice, found a way to lever a crack between them.

'I just wanted some time, you know? I wasn't trying to

deceive him; I just didn't know how I felt about it. We hadn't been trying, and to be honest the topic had never even come up. We'd always just plodded along quite happily, just the two of us. When I realized I was late, I panicked. It meant everything would change and my instincts were telling me it was wrong. But maybe Fee was right,' she sighed. 'Maybe I should have told him the second I suspected.'

'Oh no, Laura, I totally disagree. How could you have a baby if you had doubts about the relationship? I would have done exactly the same as you.'

Laura smiled gratefully for the support, even though she knew it couldn't possibly be true. A baby was the one thing the Blakes' money couldn't buy them, and neither one of them would need 'time to think'. They knew what she was beginning to realize too late – a baby was a blessing. Being up close and personal with the Bakers had shown her that much.

The waiter came over with their steaming Dover sole. Neither of them said a word as he set it down before them. Cat fiddled with the cutlery on either side of her plate.

'It's weird, isn't it?' Cat said finally when the waiter had gone. 'I feel I can trust you. I knew it from the moment we met. I don't get that with many people. I usually feel like most people want something from me.'

Laura felt herself swell at the compliment. She felt it too. 'I don't suppose this has ever happened to you, has it? No one's ever broken your heart?'

'Oh yes they have,' Cat replied, spearing a minted pea.

'Really? Let me guess – Alex?'

Cat laughed, a tinkling sound. 'No. No, bless him, although I know I broke his a long time ago. I think he's forgiven me, though.'

'Who was it, then? Was he wildly handsome and romantic?'

'Yes, yes and no. He was wild and handsome, but not romantic. In fact he was cruel. He took pleasure in watching me humiliate myself for him. He thought I was such a princess when we first met – he actually told me that. He liked seeing me broken.'

'Broken?' Laura stopped cutting. 'He sounds sadistic.'

Cat stared into her plate. 'Maybe he was. He just liked the game and having that kind of power over me. He threw just enough scraps to keep me hanging around him in vain hope. All my passion for him went completely unrequited. We only consummated the relationship once; I was so desperate for him, I actually begged him for it. But when we did it, it was like he was . . . bored.' Her voice had become tiny.

She inhaled suddenly, coming to. She looked up at Laura, taking in her dismayed expression. 'But what are you gonna do? I personally think all the most interesting people have had their hearts trampled upon by someone at some time or another. It makes you tough; it forces you to find ways to survive and adapt and go on. Don't you agree?'

'I do,' Laura replied quietly, resuming nibbling her sole. She'd never felt less hungry. 'Thank God you found Rob.'

'Yes, absolutely,' Cat agreed heartily, squeezing a half-lemon in its gauze. 'Thank God I did.'

# Chapter Thirty-Eight

Laura smiled at the woman looking back at her. She was poised, groomed and rich. Her hair shone like spun gold, her make-up, thanks to the expert hand that had applied it, was immaculate, and the dress she was wearing – baby-pink Marchesa with waterfall ruffles – hit all the right notes: formal but still funky, expensive but young. She barely recognized herself.

The knock at the door made her turn and Cat came in, quivering delicately in a long strapless grey feather dress. 'Oh. My. God.' Cat grinned at the sight of her. 'Jack who?'

Somewhere inside, Laura winced at the mention of his name, but her smile didn't slip. That bottle of Dom at lunch had kept her on a mellow ride all afternoon.

'Are you absolutely sure about me wearing your dress?' Laura asked. 'It's so expensive. What if I knock wine down it or something?'

'It looks sensational on you. Far better than it looks on me.' She came and stood behind Laura, staring at their mutual reflections in the mirror. They were like Gemini. Apart from their eyes, they really didn't look dissimilar. Cat was prettier, blonder, skinnier and taller, obviously, but they were the same 'type'.

'I still don't know how you've managed to make my eyes

look like this,' Laura said, peering closer in the mirror. 'Whenever I've tried it before, I've ended up looking more like a victim of crime.'

'Years of practice,' Cat smiled, changing position to see the dress from another angle. She popped a hip, model-style.

Laura picked up her clutch bag, wondering whether she should stand like that when they were at the party. Cat grabbed her palest grey fur shrug, Laura the shahtoosh Cat had loaned her, and they caught the lift together, striding across the hotel lobby looking like it was Oscars Night in Bel Air.

The car Rob had ordered for them was waiting outside and they slid in with perfect synchronicity, the pavement in front of their boutique hotel miraculously clear of snow and ice as though it had been heated with hairdryers. Laura looked out of the window as they drove past the ornate black and gold gates of Kensington Palace and alongside the gardens into Hyde Park. Christmas was in the air as definitively as cinnamon and cedar; tracks left from bikes, walkers and animals criss-crossed the snowy lawns like dot-to-dot drawings, and pools of light punctuated the dark paths as office workers, Christmas shoppers and residents all hurried homewards. Laura looked across at Cat, excited that they – by contrast – were on their way out. When she thought of the evening she ought to be having – home alone in the studio listening to the tide rushing past and rifling through her trinket boxes; when she thought of the night she'd just had – sitting in Ottersbrook village hall watching the primary school's nativity concert. . . And last weekend in Verbier. Where would she be next week? What was her baseline now? Not Suffolk, of that she was certain.

'What's the name of the charity this is in aid of?'

Laura asked, shuffling around so that she was facing Cat side-on.

'Who knows? We go to so many. But this is one of the biggies. It makes bucketloads. Honestly, what some of the lots go for . . . even my eyes water!'

Just the minibar prices had brought tears to Laura's eyes. 'Will there be lots of celebrities?'

Cat laughed, amused. 'No doubt. So brace yourself – there'll probably be lots of pappers outside. Don't worry. They'll leave us alone as soon as they see we're not famous.'

Laura nodded happily, feeling strangely invincible knowing she had Cat as her ally.

Traffic was light along the park and they were cruising into Knightsbridge within minutes. Laura looked on, dazzled, at Harrods' year-round lights, which seemed so especially fitting at this time of year, and the opulent Christmas windows that had passers-by, even now, congregating in front of them. They passed Burberry, flying its distinctive checked flags and plastered with enormous black and white billboards of sulky, beautiful, young Brit things who could rival anything in Times Square. Laura was glad the traffic lights turned red before they could pass Harvey Nichols, and she and Cat scrutinized the displays hungrily: psychedelic snowflakes, ice caves, frozen stalactites and swooping snowy owls were the backdrops for insouciant mannequins draped in beaded dresses and felted wool coats.

'I love that skirt,' Cat gasped, pointing indistinctly to one in a row of eight windows.

'Mmm, me too.'

The lights changed and twenty seconds later they were pulling up outside the hotel. As predicted, banks of photographers were huddled, shivering, on the pavement, waiting to get their money shots before they could go home and thaw out. Laura and Cat got past without much bother, just one or two 'complimentary' flashes for the effort they'd clearly put in.

Champagne was in their hands the moment they walked through the door – when was it *not*, in Cat's world? – and Laura clocked Jemima Goldsmith and Boris Johnson within moments.

'Come on, we'll start over here,' Cat said, nudging her gently with her elbow. Laura tagged along happily, smiling back as famous and frozen faces looked at her, the oblique question in all their eyes: have we met? Simply being in the room meant you were in the club.

Laura took in the room discreetly as they walked towards a table at the back where the lots were displayed. Cat had been right: long was de rigueur, and there was an astonishing number of variations on how men wore black tie these days. The ceiling was a vaulted golden rotunda, and deep, thick, red velvet ribbons had been swagged from corner to corner of the room so that it felt gift-wrapped. The magnificent tree – as wide as it was tall – was decked in hundreds of smaller velvet ribbons, and microscopic vanilla fairy lights made the room prickle with starlight.

Cat stopped by the table. 'Fancy that?' she asked, holding up a thick cream card. *Lot 21: Private tennis lesson with Rafael Nadal*.

'I think Rafa would be the only person capable of getting me to a decent baseline return.' Laura giggled. 'I usually play like I'd do a better job with my arms in plaster.'

Cat laughed, moving along. 'How about this?'
*Lot 14: Dance class with Lady Gaga.*

'I'd be terrified,' Laura hissed, eyes wide.

'I know! What the hell would you *wear*?' Cat gasped.

'Ooh . . . that looks fun,' Laura said, noticing Lot 12: *One week at Donna Karan's villa in Turks & Caicos.*

'Been there . . . Not to Donna Karan's place, obviously. But let's face it – nowhere's slumming it out there,' Cat remarked.

'Are you going to bid on anything tonight?' Laura asked curiously.

Cat looked around to check nobody was listening. Nobody was, although plenty of people were staring. 'Well, I have to play my cards very carefully at things like these. Rob will refuse to put his hand up even for extra water if he thinks I'm expecting anything. *But . . .*' She took Laura by the hand and walked further along the table. 'Between you and me, I'm rather hoping he'll go for this. It is my birthday after all.'

Laura looked at Lot 18: *Styling session with Rachel Zoe.* 'Who's she?'

'Laura!' Cat laughed. 'She's only Hollywood's uber-stylist. She does everyone.'

'But you don't need to be styled. You always look great.'

'I look passable,' Cat said with raised eyebrows. 'We both know there's a lot more I could be doing.' She saw a waiter approaching and drained her glass quickly, nodding for Laura to do the same. 'What would you bid for?' she asked as their glasses were refilled.

'Ummmm . . .' Laura walked slowly down the table, reading the cards: *Share a table at Annabel's with Kylie. Drive the Amalfi coast with Jenson Button in a '63 Alfa Spider. A weekend charter on P Diddy's yacht in St Tropez.*

Laura stopped at Lot 19, and Cat read it over her shoulder: '*Paragliding in Scafell.* Seriously?' she laughed, squeezing her arm affectionately. 'You're an absolute riot!'

'Cat.'

The distinctive voice made them both turn, and Cat's laughter died in her throat. A man with shaggy black hair, a beard and Arctic-blue eyes was standing in front of them.

'Ben,' Cat replied in an unfamiliar voice, prompting Laura to look over at her.

'How are you?' His Highland accent was tumbling and melodic; Laura knew instantly who he was.

A heavy, black silence settled between the three of them like a thundercloud.

'You must meet Laura,' Cat said suddenly, bringing Laura round so that she could 'present' her.

'Hello,' Laura said, smiling dutifully. 'Laura Cunningham.'

'Ben Jackson,' he said, shaking her hand gently. 'It's a pleasure.'

Cat looked around the room as though searching for an emergency exit, making no effort to engage.

'Are you, uh . . . are you bidding tonight?' Laura asked, reaching for conversation.

'Possibly. But I'll be honest, I'm more interested in knowing how much my lot will go for. I'm up for grabs tonight.'

'Oh.' Laura didn't miss the way his eyes darted fractionally towards Cat. 'You're the artist.'

His eyes came back to her with her use of the determiner. 'That's right. Have you seen my work?'

'Not . . . not in person, no. But I've heard about you. Lots.'

He watched her, his eyes keen and sharp on her face. 'Well, come over here. I'll give you a private view.'

Laura glanced at Cat – eyes wide with excitement – as he led them towards an easel shrouded with a black cloth in the far corner of the room beyond the serving station. He lifted one corner of the cloth and stepped back to allow Laura and Cat alone a fleeting glimpse of the canvas beneath. It was a landscape in oils, so thickly daubed that in some areas the paint had clotted like cream into knobs you could hang a hat on. Its moorland vista was wild and open, the palette a smoky green, charcoal and black with just a vein of acid yellow streaking through it. It was like looking through a window into another world – fresher, blowier, wilder than the cultivated scents intermingling in this room. Rather like him. He looked incongruous, so wild and ungroomed in his dinner jacket, which was boxier than the waisted styles most of the men were wearing and appeared more likely to have belonged to his father – or at least his father's generation.

'It's stunning,' Laura breathed, looking up at him. He smiled back, quietly satisfied. 'Can you see it, Cat?' Laura asked, stepping away so that she could take a closer look.

But Cat merely gave a slight tip of the chin. 'It's lovely,' she smiled, drumming a finger on her glass.

*Lovely?* It was like saying the Sistine Chapel was pretty. But Ben appeared not to be offended.

'Our beautiful friend thinks I have sold out, I fear.'

Cat shook her head lightly. 'Not at all, Ben. We all have to make a living.'

'Well, some of us do,' Ben replied, smiling, and Laura saw Cat straighten herself stiffly. 'That was below the belt, I apologize.' He looked at Laura. 'It is to Cat that I owe my illustrious career.'

'Yes, I know,' Laura replied loyally.

'You do?' Cat frowned.

Laura faltered. 'Orlando told me.'

'Oh.'

'We were talking about your great eye and everything you've done at the Cube,' Laura shrugged. 'And your job came up, at Min Hetherington's gallery in Holland Park.'

Cat didn't react to the mention of Min's name.

'Are you still there, Cat?' Ben asked her, with a certain amount of incredulity. 'I'd have thought you'd have moved on to Mayfair by now.'

'It suits me working for Min. She's happy to let me do only three afternoons a week. I know how to handle her, and it's good for the motorways. '

Laura winced at the lie, but was this just pride talking? After all, Cat had enjoyed enormous success with Ben's exhibition. Laura could well see how she might not want him to know she'd been sacked.

'Ah yes, *Surrey*,' Ben teased with sparkling eyes. 'And how are the Home Counties? Still so neat and tidy? Green and pleasant?'

Cat shot Laura an unimpressed look. 'Ben prefers to live in mossy caves and under gorse bushes.'

'Not strictly true – any more,' he grinned, but Cat looked far from amused. In fact she looked positively icy. Min had said she hadn't represented Ben after the Exposure exhibition, and now she could see why. The atmosphere between Ben and Cat was glacial; how the devil had she persuaded him to exhibit in the first place?

'There you are! I've been looking everywhere for you,' Rob said, finding the three of them tucked away in the corner. He looked at Ben. 'Hi. Rob Blake.'

'Ben Jackson,' Ben replied, shaking his hand.

Rob paused a second. 'Are you *the* Ben?' Rob looked at Cat for clarification. 'At Min's?'

'That's right,' she nodded.

'You must be Cat's husband. Sorry not to have met you that night,' Ben replied.

397

'I was in New York, if I remember rightly. The private view was a great success, by all accounts.'

Ben nodded. 'Thanks to Cat. Your wife's a remarkable woman, so much more than just a pretty face.'

'I'm always trying to tell her that, but . . .' Rob shifted his weight. 'She still spends three hundred pounds on face cream!'

Everyone, bar Cat, laughed.

'Well, if you'll excuse me, I just stopped by to say hello. I'm supposed to be schmoozing my newest patrons. They've just commissioned four giant murals for the lobby of their new HQ in Farringdon.' Ben widened his eyes just enough to show his real feelings about the project. 'The commercial reality of artistic life.'

Rob watched Ben disappear into the sea of smartly tailored backs before he turned to face them. His eyes fell upon Laura for the first time and she breathed in nervously as he clocked her in his wife's £1,000 dress.

'I thought you bought that dress to wear here? You bought it specially,' he said to Cat.

But Cat seemed lost. Laura watched as she stared at the floor, unblinking.

'Uh, to be honest, she was helping me out,' Laura interjected. 'Nothing suited me in the shop, and the things that did I couldn't afford. Cat said I could borrow this instead.'

That wasn't quite how it had happened. Laura had set her heart on the grey dress herself – it matched her eyes – and she did have just enough to splurge on it if she lived on baked beans for a month. But she'd seen the fleeting wistful expression on Cat's face in the mirror as she'd tried it on, and it had been the least she could do to let her have it after everything Cat had done for her.

'So you're telling me Cat bought a new dress so that you didn't have to? Well, that's certainly what I'd call redistribution of wealth.'

'Don't be horrid, Rob!' Cat said coldly. 'You know full well that most of the women in this room are in couture gowns worth ten times the cost of this.'

A tense silence settled, as Rob looked away from the two of them and Cat downed her glass. Laura turned her head away, embarrassed. It wasn't the first time she'd been caught between them.

'Maybe you should slow down a little,' he said pointedly.

Cat shot him a hateful look. 'I'm going to the ladies', Laura. I'll be back in a minute.'

Laura made as if to go with her – she had rapidly become accustomed to doing everything with Cat in the past twenty-four hours – but Cat had already turned and disappeared. Falling back, Laura kept her eyes on the crowd, pretending to celebrity-spot as a waiter appeared from nowhere and refilled both their glasses.

It was the first time they'd been alone together since their kiss in the lift.

'Having a good time?' Rob asked her.

'Can you point out Bertie Penryn to me?' she asked briskly. 'I need to make myself known to him tonight.'

Laura noticed how his mouth flattened at the comment. 'Fine. I'll introduce you after dinner.'

'No, there's no need. I'll introduce myself. I'm perfectly capable.'

The way his eyebrow lifted fractionally showed he wasn't so sure she was.

'What?' she demanded.

'Nothing. If that's what you want.' He pushed a hand

casually into his trouser pocket, making no effort to hide his scepticism.

'I don't need your help,' she reiterated.

'No? You're sure? Because it's just that I'm seeing you in this room on my wife's ticket, wearing my wife's dress, with your hair and make-up exactly the same as hers . . .' His intimation was clear.

'Cat has invited me here tonight to make a valuable new business contact. And that's precisely what I intend to do.'

They were quiet for a minute, staring at the people laughing and talking all around them. Laura watched the way the jewels on the women's necks, wrists and ears sparkled beneath the lights, how the men expressed one-upmanship with back slaps and power handshakes.

'Did you get my email?' he asked in a quieter voice, looking straight ahead.

Laura sniffed in affirmation, and he turned to face her.

'I was wrong to do what I did.'

She turned the other cheek to him, not wanting to have this conversation, to meet his eyes. 'I know.'

Her answer wasn't what he'd been expecting and they fell quiet again.

'Should we talk about it?' he asked after a moment.

She gave a humourless laugh. 'No.'

He stepped into her line of vision, apparently irritated by her response. 'Have you even thought about it?'

Laura felt her heart pound wildly, suddenly, within her ribs. Nought to sixty in an instant. 'No.'

'*No?*'

She looked away, worried he would see the lie. 'I've had other stuff going on.'

His eyes narrowed as he remembered the way Cat had

shepherded her into the helicopter, loaned her the sunglasses. 'You mean whatever you and Cat were talking about this morning?'

She said nothing.

'You seemed upset.'

'I'm fine.'

'Is it Jack?'

'It's none of your business.'

'But it is Cat's?'

'She's a friend.'

'And I'm not?'

'What do you think?' she said sharply. 'From the moment we've met, you have – in chronological order – tried to bully me to get your way, been rude, abrupt and aggressive, *jumped on me*, and for the past twenty four hours you've been blanking me. I wouldn't say we're close, no.'

He watched her quietly as she studied Keira Knightley wafting past in Chanel.

'I was angry at you for the way you treated Kitty yesterday.'

'And how did I treat Kitty?' she retorted.

'You abandoned her the second Cat clicked her fingers.'

'That is not true. Cat offered me the opportunity of my career coming here tonight. Bertie Penryn could transform my business. Kitty totally understands that.'

His expression showed he disagreed, but he didn't bother to argue further. Laura turned back to studying Keira. Kitty did understand, didn't she?

'As for the rest of it – well, you frustrate the hell out of me,' he went on. 'I thought you were – I don't know, a kindred spirit or something on Combin. I thought you felt the same escape, exhilaration, freedom . . . But now I think you probably just liked riding in a helicopter.'

'That is not true!'

'I know!' he said, pouncing on her indignation. 'I saw it in your eyes then, and I can see it now. I get flashes of this wild spirit with you, and then just as quickly you revert to creeping around like—'

'I don't creep!' she hissed.

But he was unrepentant. 'You creep around like you're apologizing for the very space you take up in a room. You put less food on your plate than anybody else. When we sat on the sofa at Kitty's, you tucked yourself into a tiny ball because God forbid we should actually *touch*!' His eyes burned into hers. 'It's like you feel guilty for breathing. You want to be invisible.'

Laura stared at him defiantly. 'I don't care what you think.'

'You're hiding something.'

'No.' She shook her head.

'Yes! But my mistake was thinking that it made you interesting. I got it into my head that there was something about you that was different from everyone else. You intrigued me. I thought you were only *trying* to be ordinary. I thought it was all an act. But maybe I was wrong. I was obviously trying to see something that isn't there.' He was goading her, daring her to prove him wrong – she could see it in his eyes. But she wouldn't play this game.

'Th-that's right. You were.' She stared back at him, refusing to back down, aware that her breath was coming fast and shallow.

'Why is it that every time I try to apologize, we end up arguing more?' he asked, taking in her upset.

'You're the one with an agenda. I just want to be left alone to do my job. You asked me to interview Cat's friends and family, and I've done that.'

'Except that you've done *more* than that, haven't you?' he pressed. 'They've become your friends too – Kitty, Orlando, Cat. Even Alex – you've kissed her first love too. It's like you want to *be* her.' He leaned in fractionally towards her. 'But what are you going to do next week when the necklace is finished, Laura? Are you going to just disappear back to Suffolk and leave them behind you? Go back to Jack?'

She stared at him, devastated. He had unwittingly stumbled across her Achilles heel.

He stepped closer again. 'Or are you going to stay in our spare room? Live with me and Cat? Is that how it's going to be? I commission a necklace from you and end up with a lodger in return?' His words were hard and angry.

'She's become a friend. What's so wrong with that? I can keep out of your way if that's what you want.'

'How would you know what I want?'

Laura stared back at him, determined not to cry. 'I don't know why you're attacking me like this. I didn't ask for any of this to happen – I didn't ask you to walk into my studio. I didn't ask you to take me to Verbier. I didn't ask you to kiss me—'

'I didn't ask to kiss you either, but it still fucking happened.' He inhaled sharply, his hands on his hips, and he wheeled away from her, grabbing a brandy from the tray of a passing waiter. He downed it in one, wiping his mouth with the back of his hand. 'You have to go, Laura. As soon as the necklace is handed in, you have to cut ties with everyone. Not just Cat, but Kitty and the others too.'

'But *why*?' she asked, aghast. 'What does it matter to you who I'm friends with?'

'I don't want you around us.'

His words cut her to ribbons but she could see the same

high emotion in her face reflected in his. 'You don't want me around Cat? Or around you?'

'Laura? It is you!'

Laura looked to her left. A tall man with short cropped hair and a shaving rash was peering at her.

'*Timothy?*'

'My God, it's been so long!'

He swept her up in an exuberant hug.

'How are you? Wowzers, you look sensational! And who's this lucky chap?' Timothy asked, reaching out a friendly hand. 'Don't tell me you're married now?'

'God, no!' Laura replied quickly, prompting a look from Rob. 'This is Rob Blake, a clie—' She had been about to introduce him as a client when Cat reappeared, fresher and more glowing than ever.

'I'm afraid he's my husband, poor soul,' Cat smiled, proffering a hand. 'Although I'm quite sure he'd have asked Laura instead if he'd met her first. I am the world's worst wife: can't cook, won't iron, never been inside a Waitrose.'

'Well, th-that's what staff's for . . .' Timothy mumbled, dazzled by her radiance.

'What do you do – Timothy, was it?' Her eyes were bright and interested; she was clearly restored to her vital self.

'Yes. Yes. Timothy Gresham,' he said eagerly. 'My company has donated one of the lots for tonight.'

'Oh, which one?' Cat asked excitedly. 'There are so many excellent things up for grabs. Such a worthy cause.'

'Paragliding off Scafell in the Lake District.'

There was a short pause.

'Oh,' Cat said, looking at Laura and giggling. 'That's the one you were going to bid for, wasn't it, Laura?'

'No, no, no, I wasn't actually going to bid,' she replied

hurriedly, placing an apologetic hand on Timothy's arm. 'I think the bids in this room are going to be somewhat out of my league, you understand.'

'Yes, but it was your favourite,' Cat insisted.

'Well, pipe dreams and all that.'

'Laura, you know that *you* don't need to bid tonight to take to the air.' Timothy smiled down at her. 'You've done more than enough hours to just turn up at ours.'

'You paraglide too, then, Laura? Why am I not surprised?' Rob asked, with sarcasm posing as interest.

'Tell me, how's Caroline? Is she here?' Laura asked quickly. 'I'd love to see her.'

'Uh, yes, yes – she's over there somewhere.'

'Would you mind? I'd love to catch up with her.' Laura grabbed his arm as she smiled at Cat. 'I'll come and find you in a bit. Must just say hello.'

'Yes, of course,' Cat nodded, thoroughly bemused by the sudden exit. 'You go mingle. We'll see you later at the table.'

Laura let Timothy lead her into the heart of the crowd, away from Rob's cold words and watchful eyes. Her friendship with Cat wouldn't survive if he was opposed to it. He wanted her gone and – she remembered Sam's words, slurry and indistinct, in the bedroom in Verbier – what Rob Blake wanted, Rob Blake got.

Laura rested a rosy cheek in her hand as she leant against the table, watching the goings-on as the chairman of Sotheby's expertly wooed the crowd into shelling out small fortunes with every £25,000 increment. The bidding had been furious and ostentatious for over an hour now, and the atmosphere in the room was giddy with excitement and testosterone.

The woman on her right, Simone Cappell, Rob's COO,

was knocking back Cîroc vodka shots, having already lost out twice in the bids: once for the week in Donna Karan's villa, which went for almost as much as a trip to the moon, and again for backstage passes for a Black Eyed Peas concert at $O_2$. The man to her left, Garth Kesswick, Rob's CEO, was far more interested in trying to find out why, at the grand old age of thirty-two, she still hadn't been 'snapped up'.

'To be honest, I'm not convinced that I'll ever marry,' Laura said provocatively, knowing just how combustible this comment would be. As a waitress moved between them, removing the dinner plates, she took another sip of wine – one of hundreds this evening – feeling increasingly defiant and angry. Who the hell did Rob think he was? Ordering her to drop her friendship? Laura didn't answer to him, and from what she'd seen, neither did Cat.

'What? A pretty thing like you?' Garth flirted, clearly under the impression that he was much more of a catch than his ruddy cheeks and subtly highlighted hair would suggest. 'You might find you don't have much say about it. Some lucky chap will just march you off to the nearest registry office and, hey presto – trouble and strife, you're a wife. If I wasn't already shackled, I'd do the job myself.'

'I don't think so,' Laura said archly, which only seemed to excite Garth further.

Rob, who was seated opposite her, and who was entertaining Garth's wife, Camilla, so much that her mascara was running, glanced over at them.

The auctioneer broke up their conversation for the fifteenth time.

'And now for Lot fifteen, ladies and gentlemen: an original oil by a man who has already, in his short but illustrious career, been hailed as one of Britain's greatest living artists

– Ben Jackson. Measuring two point six metres by two point three, and entitled *Wind IV*, it is the final oil in a celebrated series that achieved record sales in Manhattan last month. I have with me here a starting bid of a hundred and fifty thousand pounds. Who'll give me one seven five?'

Laura settled back in her chair and rested her eyes on Ben Jackson, three tables away. He was leaning forward with his elbows on the table, his chin down modestly, listening to something the man next to him was whispering in his ear. He was as striking as his paintings to look at, and Laura wondered how much of the untamed wildness of his work was inspired not only by nature, but his own character. Many of the women in the room were far more interested in scrutinizing him than the painting on the easel as the biddings rapidly topped the half-million mark, but Cat wasn't one of them. Her eyes caught Laura's.

'Loo?' she mouthed.

'Now?' Laura mouthed back. Etiquette demanded the room was quiet and still to allow the easy observation of bids placed. Getting up now would be like leaving Wimbledon in the middle of a final.

But Cat scraped her chair back and rose like a goddess. Laura followed suit, aware of the eyes swivelling as they passed. They walked together, conspicuously, through the seated room, and the auctioneer broke off from the escalating bids to call them back.

'Ladies, please – was it something I said?' he cried jocularly, prompting a rumble of titters.

Cat turned as if she was on wheels and smiled. 'On the contrary, we'll return when the real bidding begins.'

A chorus of laughter rippled through the crowd.

'Surely Ben Jackson is enough to tempt you to stay?' the

auctioneer asked, delighted by this unexpected repartee with the beautiful stranger.

'He's sweet, but sadly not . . .' Cat replied loftily.

Sweet? Ben Jackson? He was as sweet as a wildcat.

Even in a room full of celebrities and the super-rich, Cat commanded attention. Laura stood next to her, mute and stricken with panic that the auctioneer was going to turn his attentions to her next.

'I already have him hanging in our drawing room, you see. I'm after someone new.'

'Ooooh!' rumbled the audience, absorbing the veiled insult in her words. Ben Jackson was motionless in his seat.

'Mrs . . . ?'

'Blake. Cat Blake.'

'Mrs Blake. And your sister?'

Cat squeezed her arm tightly. 'Laura.'

Laura looked at her in surprise. Cat hadn't corrected him? She felt her heart quicken. So Cat saw it too, then, their similarity? Maybe that was why they'd been so drawn to each other – maybe that was why she'd helped with her hair and shared her clothes. In a way she'd lost her sister too; after all, Olive had made it very plain their relationship was beyond repair.

'Mrs Laura . . . ?'

'Oh no. Laura's not married,' Cat purred, eliciting a roar of anonymous wolf whistles and cheers that made Laura blush furiously. 'She's deliciously single.'

'Not for long, apparently,' the auctioneer joked. 'Well, you set a high bar, Mrs Blake, if Ben Jackson can't whet your appetite. I'm not sure whether your husband is one of the luckiest or bravest men in this room. Where is the great man?'

Garth stood up instantly and pointed eagerly at his boss. 'Here!'

Rob, leaning one cheek against a fist and looking thunderous, gave a reluctant nod as the room erupted into laughter and cheers.

'Mr Blake, so good to make your acquaintance. I have a feeling we're going to be getting to know each other better tonight.'

The crowd roared with laughter, and Rob could only roll his eyes as Cat – playing to the crowd – blew a kiss and sashayed out of the room, pulling Laura after her.

'How are you able to do that?' Laura asked as they strode down to the loos. 'I'd have *died* if he'd spoken to me in front of the entire room. I mean, all those celebrities . . .'

'Follow me,' Cat smiled, opening the door to the marbled bathrooms.

She disappeared into a cubicle, and Laura went to go into another, but Cat called her back. 'In here.'

Laura threw a look at the toilet attendant, who was wiping down the immaculate basins, and tiptoed over to where Cat was standing. 'What is it?'

Cat closed the door behind her and locked it. She opened her bag. 'This is the secret,' she smiled, pulling out a tiny plastic bag and compact.

'Cat, I . . .' Laura stared at her, agape, as she carefully sliced some white lines on the mirror. 'Look, thanks but it's not really my thing.'

Cat looked up at her with knowing eyes. 'Have you ever done it before?'

Laura shook her head. 'No, but—'

'So then how do you know you won't like it?' She pressed a soft hand against Laura's bare arm. 'It's just a little fun,

Laura, and it'll give you some confidence. You've had a shitty week and this will just give you a lift. Tonight's supposed to be fun!'

Laura looked away nervously.

'Laura, it would be easier to count the number of people in that room who *aren't* on this. You trust me, don't you? Would I ever steer you wrong?'

Laura looked at Cat, so like her that they could be sisters – wasn't that what the auctioneer had assumed? And Cat had encouraged him to think it; she felt the same way as Laura.

She nodded.

Cat winked. 'So, okay then. Let's live a little.'

# Chapter Thirty-Nine

'Ladies!' the auctioneer hailed as they returned. 'We've been eagerly anticipating your return. We're just about to commence the bids for Lot eighteen: the styling session with Ms Zoe? I can see by your dazzling dresses tonight that her name will not be foreign to you?'

'On the contrary,' Laura laughed boldly, putting a little sway in her hips as she wove her way seductively through the chairs. 'It's Cat's birthday in a few days, and her husband is under strict orders to win this bid tonight. Or *else*.'

The room erupted into excited laughter, with lots of sympathetic back-slaps on Rob's shoulders, as Cat grabbed Laura's arm and they walked arm in arm towards their table.

'That should drive the price up another twenty thousand before it even begins,' Cat whispered.

'I thought it might,' Laura giggled back

'Well, I'm so delighted to hear it,' the auctioneer called at the front. 'The prospect of the "or else" alone should ensure somebody in this room wants to outbid him.' This comment in particular was met by a crescendo of male cheers, so that it sounded more like a rugby club than a Knightsbridge hotel.

Laura slid down into her chair happily, defiantly meeting Rob's eye. She knew exactly what she had done.

'Well, shall we start the bids at thirty thousand?' the

auctioneer asked, staring pointedly at Rob. 'A small price to pay, I think you'll agree, for keeping such a beautiful wife so well dressed.'

The room held its breath as they waited for his nod – and when it came, they almost lifted the roof. The numbers escalated quickly and Rob's colour with it. Every man in the room was throwing his hat into the room, knowing that Rob's honour would demand that he outbid them again and again and again.

Garth leaned in close to Laura. 'I hope your game with the boss's wife isn't going to wipe out the bonus pot,' he murmured, so close that his breath tickled her neck.

'Why? What would it mean?' Laura replied coquettishly. 'No new Bentley? Purchase of your private island on hold?'

'I would have to hold you personally responsible for my impoverished state.' His eyes met hers, the innuendo clear.

'We'd better hope he doesn't spend all of your money, then,' Laura whispered, her face close to his.

'One hundred and thirty thousand. Do I have any advance on that?' the auctioneer pleaded.

But the room had fallen quiet. It was a good game, but nobody wanted to get caught out at these numbers should Rob call a bluff. There were other lots they actually wanted to win – notably the drive with Jenson Button, the lesson with Rafa . . .

'Going once . . . going twice . . . gone to the valiant Mr Blake!' he proclaimed grandly. 'May his wife always be so beautifully dressed!'

Everyone was on their feet stamping and clapping, Rob nodding gamely as everyone cheered his good humour. Laura leant across the table and high-fived Cat, who was lapping up the attention.

'That was a priceless PR exercise for Blake & Somner's profile,' Simone said to Laura, taking her seat again and returning to her vodka shots. 'It'll be interesting to see the calls we get on Monday as a result of this. These guys love a bit of balls-out bravado.'

'And next up, ladies and gentlemen, we have one of my favourite lots of the night: a day's paragliding in Scafell in the Lake District. May I implore any of you who have never tried this magnificent activity to consider it now. There is no more beautiful way to survey the English landscape than this – and yes, I do mean the view beats the one from your Lear.'

A ripple of laughter.

'As I'm sure many of you are virgins – at *this* – let us begin the bidding at five thousand pounds. Do I have five?'

A hand went up at the back of the room.

'Thank you, sir. Who'll show me seven? I have seven . . .' He looked back at the original bidder. 'Ten, sir?'

The original bidder shook his head.

'Ten, anyone? Come, come, don't tell me you're all intimidated by Mr Blake's largesse? Nine, then. It's for a worthy cause, ladies and gentlemen . . .'

Laura's hand shot up.

'A new bidder! Thank you, Miss Laura . . . ?'

'Cunningham,' Laura smiled.

Another cheer went up.

'Laura! What the hell are you doing?' Rob hissed across the table at her. 'You can't—' He stopped himself short of announcing to the table that she couldn't afford it.

'Miss Cunningham is our new highest bidder. Is anybody going to go to ten and deny the lady what she wants?'

The auctioneer and Rob looked around the room. It appeared nobody was.

Rob looked back at her in concern. He raised his hand.

'Mr Blake! Oh dear! Betting against your own guest.' The auctioneer looked at Laura in glee. 'Will you go to eleven?'

'I will,' she nodded.

Rob's face paled. 'Laura . . .'

Everyone in the room looked at him expectantly. 'Twelve?' He gave a brief nod.

'Thirteen, Miss Cunningham?'

'Yes.'

'Mr Blake?' the auctioneer asked expectantly.

'Fifteen,' Rob replied, boring his eyes into Laura's profile, though she wouldn't meet his gaze.

'Twenty,' Laura replied, quick as a flash.

The room gasped. Laura could feel Rob's anger shooting across the table at her like electric bolts, but she didn't care. He didn't call the shots in her life, no matter what he may think. He didn't get to choose her friends, nor how she spent her money.

There was a long silence. Even the auctioneer, who was no doubt reading the body language between the two of them – Laura's body turned away, her chin up; Rob's anxious expression – didn't intrude. They were running this show for the moment.

'Thirty,' he muttered.

'Forty.' She didn't hesitate. She was going to win.

'Fifty.'

Laura looked over at him. 'One hundred.'

A collective gasp whipped everyone's breath away. No one stirred. You *really* had to like paragliding to go to these figures.

'Mr Blake? Can you beat the bid?' the auctioneer asked breathlessly. As the most inauspicious lot of the night, it should have gone for ten max.

Laura stared back at Rob, feeling the adrenalin pump through her, enjoying the rush. She knew perfectly well that he *could*.

Rob saw the fight still in her eyes and shook his head. 'No. I'm done,' he said quietly.

Laura felt herself exhale.

'So then, at one hundred thousand pounds, one day's paragliding in Scafell going once . . . going twice . . . gone to Miss Cunningham!'

The audience was on its feet before the gavel made contact with the block, and Laura felt Cat throw her arms around her neck, screaming with delight as Garth clapped with undisguised lust.

'Laura! You were incredible,' Cat trilled. 'I've never been so excited.' Garth's head snapped round at that.

'Oh my God,' Laura cried, putting her fingers to her temples. 'What have I done? I must be mad.'

'You must be loaded,' Simone quipped, rubbing her shoulder.

'Well, it's for charity,' Laura shrugged. 'What else am I going to spend my money on?'

'Laura Cunningham,' Cat grinned, plonking herself down on Laura's lap and kissing her on the cheek. 'You just get better and better.'

Garth shifted position in his chair to get a clearer view. 'Much like this night.'

Throughout the rest of the auction, Laura succeeded in keeping her eyes well away from Rob's. Simone and Garth were her new best friends, and people kept stopping by to congratulate her as they passed the table on the way to the bar. The atmosphere was highly charged now, money having been splashed about with abandon, everyone turned on by the displays of power.

The band started up and the dance floor was flooded in an instant.

'Laura, you are mine,' Garth said, reaching down for her hand.

'I don't think I am, actually,' Laura laughed, draining her drink and letting him pull her along anyway. She felt too light-headed and carefree to resist further, and he immediately spun her into a twirl. The hem of her dress fanned out around her ankles, her hair a golden waterfall that lifted off her shoulders with the movement. She didn't consider herself an accomplished dancer, but Garth was reasonably good for someone who'd drunk the best part of a jeroboam of wine, and managed to catch her hand as he flung her out.

'You're not bad,' she said as he pulled her into him for a second.

'No, I'm not,' he grinned, spinning her back out again.

'You're making me look good!' she laughed as he quick-stepped her around before dipping her so low that her hair brushed the floor. He brought her back up so that they were face-to-face.

'Oh no. I think it's very definitely the other way round.'

'Do you mind?' a curt voice asked.

Garth stopped dancing, surprised to see Rob standing there. 'Camilla's not looking too happy. Thought I'd better warn you.'

Garth pulled a face. 'Oh. Yeah. Thanks,' he sighed, casting a rueful look at Laura.

Laura watched him go and went to walk off the floor herself, but Rob caught her by the wrist and spun her back into him.

'Not so fast. The song's not over yet,' he said, placing one hand on her back, one leg between hers, and leading her around the floor quickly.

'Maybe. But I don't want to dance with you,' she replied, trying to pull away, but he was too strong.

'You and I are going to talk,' he said.

'I don't like talking to you. It always ends up with you insulting me,' she said, turning her face away from his.

'What the hell were you doing back there?' he asked, his voice a growl in her ear that made the hairs on her neck stand to attention. 'Couldn't you see I was trying to help you! You know perfectly well you can't afford that bid.'

'Do I?'

He laughed, unamused. 'Come off it. You got carried away. You were showing off, enjoying your moment in the sun with Cat.'

She pulled back. 'You're just mad because I stitched you up like a kipper,' she jeered. 'You had to spend a hundred and thirty thousand pounds for Cat just to save face.'

He was quiet for a second. They both knew it was the truth. 'And I expect you think I'll cover the cost of your shopping trip too.'

Laura shook her head. 'Nope.'

'You've got a bloody nerve. Of course you do.'

'Why do you assume I'm poor, Rob?'

The question surprised him.

'Because I'm *just* a jeweller, is that it?'

He swallowed, watching her as she swayed beneath him.

'You already know that I had a career before this one. I told you I worked in corporate finance. My bonuses were exceptionally generous, thanks very much. Maybe not in your league, but I have my own money saved away. I don't need *you* to come in and rescue me.'

'Who do you need, then?'

'No one. And that's just the way I like it.'

'I don't believe you.'

'Suit yourself,' she shrugged.

He frowned at her, baffled by her belligerence and the marked change in her behaviour. 'How much have you had to drink?'

'Not enough, actually. Good point!' she smiled, turning to make a beeline for the bar.

But he caught her again and spun her back into him so that she slammed against his chest. He looked into her eyes.

'What've you taken?'

'Nothing, guv'nor. All the money's still in the till. Promise.'

He flinched at her sarcasm. 'You're high,' he sneered, shaking her lightly by the arms.

'So what if I am? You're not my keeper.'

'No, I'm not.'

'No. You're not.'

He dropped his arms away from her. 'I was wrong about you in every way. You're utterly ordinary.'

'You've already said that tonight. Think up some new material,' she replied, turning to leave.

'Miss Cunningham?' asked a grey-haired man walking towards her. 'Bertie Penryn. I'm the co-chair for tonight's event. I wanted to come over and thank you personally for your contribution to the evening's success. Your bid made quite an impact.' He stopped and looked across at Rob, who was standing motionless and ashen beside her. 'Hello, Rob. Good to see you again.'

Rob nodded as they shook hands. 'Bertie. It's been a great evening.'

'You were very generous, indulging your wife for our benefit again this year.'

Rob nodded. 'Well . . . she's worth it, and it is such a great cause.'

'We do appreciate it.'

Rob paused for a second. 'Actually, I was going to come and find you this evening anyway. Laura here's got a jewellery company that's got Cat enthralled. She's hosting a launch party for Laura next Friday evening, and wondered whether you might be able to make it. I think her ultimate ambition is to exhibit at the tents in Fashion Week. Have I got that right, Laura?'

Laura glared at him. He'd done this deliberately. He knew perfectly well she'd wanted to network herself and not rely on his 'help'. She looked back at Bertie. 'Yes. But I completely understand you must have a very full diary, especially at this time of year . . .'

'I'd be delighted to pop by. Take my card and leave the details with my assistant. I'll make sure I'm there.' He handed Laura a business card. 'One good turns deserves another. Tonight's cause is very dear to my heart. I'll do whatever I can to help you in return.'

'What is tonight's chosen charity?' Laura asked, inspecting the card. 'My ticket here tonight was very last-minute. I'm afraid I'm not up to speed on who we're supporting.'

'It's a charity I set up in memory of my beloved wife, Barbara. She died from burns sustained in the Covent Garden bombing five years ago. We've raised almost twelve million pounds so far and have built a new plastics wings at the Marsden, and all funds raised tonight will go towards equipment and training specialist nurses. In my opinion, your money couldn't have been better spent. There are many people out there who will be immensely grateful for your generosity.' He smiled. 'But look at me, keeping you from having a good time. I must let you get back to your dancing. I just wanted to say thank you. I'll see you again on Friday.'

Rob took a step towards her. 'Laura? What's the matter? You've gone—'

She fell to the ground like a stone.

# Chapter Forty

Except for the smoke, there was only silence, and it was hard to determine which was the heavier. Certainly it was the smoke she noticed first as she lay on her back. Black and billowing, it descended like an avalanche towards her, falling from the sky with a red rain that stung her eyes and forced them shut, so that she did not see the precise moment that the smoke struck, only felt it. It was dense and sticky like fibreglass, gumming up her airways with glue and suffocating her with shocking speed. Automatically she hacked and coughed, her body contracting violently as it tried to squeeze the noxious gas back out, but then in the very next instant, undoing itself again as her lungs, screaming for air, forced a gasp that brought the black march even further into her airways.

She twisted away, pressing her weight forwards on to her hands to bring her face lower to the ground. The smoke seemed to rebound away from there, scudding back up to the dark sky again, and she lay with her cheek to the ground, grabbing dirtied oxygen pockets in staccato breaths.

The temptation to stay there – breathing, only breathing – was overwhelming, but something else was beginning to impinge upon her mind, demanding her attention. A dazzling light show was refracting right in front of her eyes, and she saw that she was lying on a carpet of millions of glittering crystals. She went to sweep a hand over them, to gather up the riches like a pirate, but *her own hand sparkled and she stopped it in mid-air. There was nothing familiar about it. The love line that folded so deeply beneath her knuckles and the bisected life line around the base of her thumb were completely obscured. Instead, reddening gems pitted the flesh like a jewelled glove. It was strangely beautiful. Mesmerizing. Reality had been skewed. Nothing was as it should be – snow was black, rain was red, diamonds blanketed the ground – and she knew she was dreaming. She forced herself to rouse her inert body, which so longed to stay still and sleeping.*

*She sat up, and as she did, she felt the weight of silence push down on her like another form of gravity. For all its initial rolling malevolence, the smoke was spinning into airy evanescence and leaving only an acrid tincture as its calling card; but the silence that remained was pulsing and rounded, pregnant with an unborn life force that demanded to be let out. For a moment more, as she took in the distorted dreamscape that surrounded her, the walls of silence held. Then, as her eyes fell upon the burning van, she heard the beat of her own heart and the vacuum was released. Suddenly life – what was left of it – sprung into sound and the screaming started.*

*Wherever she looked, her eyes fell upon twisted metal, broken limbs, blown-out windows and charred flesh. A lamp post was bent double, hanging down like a wilted tulip; a row of scooters was blasted a hundred yards further down the road like skittles; cars lay on their sides, wheels still spinning; a dog's lead was attached to warped metal railings, hanging limply to nothing at all.*

*It wasn't the screams that clamoured at her ear, although she was aware of the shouts for help, hysterical tears, of names being called. It was the low, meek groans, the scarcely audible whispers, the pleas that hovered fractionally above the ground. They were the sounds that barely escaped the silence that contained them, the* ones with not enough life force in them, the sounds that would return to silence sooner than the rest. They were the ones she heard loudest in the din.

Behind her, she saw a boy. This morning, shaving in his boxers, nursing a hangover, his girlfriend still sleeping, he probably would have said he was a man. He was wearing a bike helmet, so she couldn't see his hair, but she could see his eyes – they were pinned on her – and he was just a boy. Nineteen, maybe twenty. Too young for this. His right arm had gone and the red fountain that had gushed out of him and over her was slowing to a trickle; the shaking was beginning to subside. He lay in silence, staring at her, and she crawled over the glass towards him, her eyes never leaving his. Unwinding the scarf at her neck, she slid one end beneath his neck and tied it tightly against the open joint of his shoulder. The silence around him was getting louder, and she cupped his face. A single tear slid down his cheek.

'Dan.'

It wasn't even a whisper. Just a small expulsion of air, easy to lip-read, his meaning clear.

'Dan,' she echoed, giving him confirmation. Shifting her weight off her knees, she turned her body and stretched out her legs so that she could rest his head on them, but the weight of him caused a sharp, sudden pain in her thigh and she cried out. She recognized the terror in his eyes as she looked back down at him, and she tried to smile, to reassure him as she undid the clasp of his helmet beneath his chin and gently eased it off so that his brown hair, unexpectedly long, flopped out. There was a pressure groove across his forehead from where the helmet had rubbed, and she smoothed it away gently as a hum started to sound out from somewhere deep inside her. The ground began to feel warm as she hummed and stroked him, lying here in the glass, in the glow of the blazing van. His skin was cool to her touch, in spite of the *heat behind her, and looked dove-grey in the blue lights that suddenly whirled up.*

*'They're here, Dan,' she whispered, gripping his chilled hand more tightly. 'They've come for us.' She twisted to see a fleet of ambulances pull up, green-uniformed paramedics spilling out into the desolation. They didn't stop to cast pitying glances or catch their breaths. They just ran headlong into the noise. One, catching sight of her red hair and the blood-soaked tourniquet round Dan's torso, ran over.*

*'His name's Dan,' she said as he knelt over them, two fingers pressed to Dan's neck.*

*The man put his hand on her arm instead. 'He's gone, love,' the man said. 'I'm sorry.'*

*She blinked at him, her eyes blank.*

*'He's died.'*

*'No. You're here.'*

*'We were too late. I'm sorry.'*

*Sorry? She looked back down at Dan. His eyes were opaque and distant, unblinking, but the tear was still sliding down his cheek.*

*'I have to help those I can do something for. I'm sorry,' the paramedic said, picking up his bag again and standing up. 'You'd better get yourself seen to at the station over there. Some of those cuts are deep. You're going to need stitches.' And he ran back into the noise.*

*She hadn't heard. Her eyes were on Dan's, waiting for another tear to form. But it didn't. The first, only, final tear just slid to the edge of his cheekbone, where it hung for a few seconds, elongating out of recognition, before smashing with silent violence on to the crystals below.*

*Carefully, she closed his eyes with her fingertips, taking care not to graze his face with the glass embedded in her hands. His body may have been blown apart, but his face had escaped untouched; a small mercy for his mother when she came to kiss him goodbye. And she would make sure that she did get to kiss him goodbye, that he wouldn't go unaccounted for in the body count. His name was Dan and she alone here knew it. She would stay here with him till the fire went out and the screaming stopped and someone came to get them both. 'I won't leave you, Dan,' she said, stroking his hair. 'I won't leave you.'*

*The lights whirled and the fire roared, and she watched in silence as people staggered and crawled and were carried into the pristine white safety of the waiting ambulances. She made no attempt to move, even though she could feel her skin beginning to blister in the radiant heat. A river of blood had made its way along the ground and was creeping around her, keeping her warm, because dusk had fallen now and the first evening chill was mixing with the smoke. And she found that the longer she sat in the glass with Dan, the safer she felt. It was as if she was watching from behind a plate of glass.*

*'Are you okay?' The voice sounded far away, but a man put his hands on her shoulders lightly as his eyes scanned her body. She looked down at herself with vague curiosity and saw that all that remained of her clothes were ribbons of sooted fabric flapping like bunting in the fiery breeze. Beneath those scraps, her entire body glimmered and gleamed, tiny red rivulets racing each other between the sparkling glass shards that peppered her skin. She went to pull them out, but the man stopped her, his fine hands suddenly on hers.*

*'No!' he protested, and she thought how very blue his eyes appeared against his charred skin. 'Some of these are pretty . . . pretty big.' He swallowed, his eyes snagging on a large jagged slice that was embedded in her thigh. 'Let's get you over to the ambulances. Can you walk?' His arms were under hers, trying to get her to stand up, but she shook her head.*

'Dan.'

He seemed puzzled. 'I'm not Dan.'

'No.'

He followed her gaze down to the dead boy in her lap, a look of dismay rippling over his face as he clocked his missing arm.

'This is Dan?' He looked back at her, his eyes narrowed in scrutiny. 'He's dead.'

She shook her head and looked at Dan's face. There was no trace of the tear now. Its track had completely dried up, taking evidence of his sorrow at dying too soon, on a beautiful winter's afternoon, with it. 'I promised.'

'Promised what? Look, you need help. You're bleeding heavily.' He tightened his grip around her arm, tried to pull her up, but she wrested herself out of his grip and fell back on to the glass. The ground instantly felt wetter and warmer than it had a minute previously, as though she'd landed in a puddle.

'No.' Her voice was weak but firm.

The man dropped his head in his hands for a moment, then stood up. He started calling out, waving his arms in the air. 'Over here! I need help here! Please!'

A paramedic came running over, a different one from before, throwing out questions as he jumped over the already dead. 'What have you got?'

'Her leg's bleeding badly, but I can't get her to leave this dead guy here.' He dropped his voice a fraction. 'I think she's in shock.'

'Show me someone who isn't.' The paramedic knelt down next to her and began studying her leg.

'I'm Patrick. What's your name?' he asked as he unceremoniously moved Dan's head to the side to get a better look at her leg wound.

'His name's Dan,' she said, tightening her grip around his head protectively. The paramedic noticed the possession in her gesture, *the way she'd blindsided his question, the flatness in her voice. He grabbed his radio and issued some hurried instructions into it. Then he opened his bag and grabbed a strap and tied it tightly round her thigh. The pain made her cry, but she kept her grip around Dan. She wasn't stupid. She knew what he was going to try to do.*

*The paramedic looked straight at her, just as three more ambulance men rushed up with a couple of stretchers. 'We need to get you to a hospital right away. I think you've got a nicked artery.' He touched her arm, anticipating her response. 'But Dan can come with us, okay?'*

*So he understood. She nodded weakly and let her grip on him loosen, just for a moment, but that was all it took to find herself suddenly rising through the air and then laid flat and strapped down.*

*'What's her name?' the paramedic asked the blue eyed man as she was ferried through the air. 'Look in her bag there.' She kept her eyes on Dan. No tricks.*

*'Does it say anything?' the paramedic asked, placing a mask over her face. His voice was the last thing she heard before the darkness rushed in. 'Lily. Lily Cunningham.'*

*And then the silence won.*

'Lily!'

Laura awoke with her usual sudden terror, heart pounding, her muscles clenched rock-hard as reality asserted itself slowly. She threw the covers off her, trying to cool down. It was hot in the room, and even lying down she could feel her heart racing. She brought her hands to her head. She'd never felt so bad. She opened her eyes and bright light instantly clamoured at her. She squeezed them shut again, but white light streaked behind her eyelids – there was no escape.

She tried again, opening first one eye, then another as her sight adjusted. The room was actually pretty dim, with just a strobe of pale December light whimpering through a slit in the curtains. Rolling on to her elbows, she pushed herself up into a half-sitting position, moaning.

The first thing she took in, other than that she was back in the hotel room, was her dress lying crumpled on the floor. Cat's dress. A thousand-pound dress that should be hanging up on a padded hanger in acid-free tissue paper in a dehumidified vault. Not lying on the floor. She went to get out of bed to retrieve it, but her head wouldn't let her, and she allowed her arms to slide along the sheets so that she fell face first on to the mattress.

'Owwwwww,' she whimpered softly, wrapping her hands behind her head and beginning to cry.

'Please don't,' a voice said quietly from across the room. She whipped her head up – a bad move – to find Rob slumped in a chair behind her by the far window. He shook his head at her. 'It's been a bad enough night. Please don't cry.' He looked shattered. His skin was grey, with black circles beneath his eyes and those healthy first signs of a beard that she'd admired so much in Verbier. If she looked anywhere near as bad as he did . . .

She swallowed back the tears, trying to remember the sequence of events. Rob had caught her, only just, as she fainted. She remembered coming to in the lobby as the fresh air hit her face and a taxi was hailed. She recalled the lift in this hotel and Rob struggling to find her room key in her bag. 'How did I end up . . . ?' She looked down at herself to find she was in just her underwear.

Rob raised a weary eyebrow. As if it mattered about him seeing her in her underwear. For a brief moment she recalled

Alex's lascivious look that first night in Verbier when he'd 'accidentally' burst in on her. The difference between the two men's reactions almost made her laugh. Almost. Except she couldn't laugh. Her body had forgotten how.

'I'm sorry,' she whispered, sitting up further. 'You needn't have stayed with me.'

'It was your first time, of course I did.'

'How do you know it was my first time?' she asked. But he just raised another weary eyebrow.

'Where's Cat? Shouldn't you be with her?'

'It's not *her* first time. Besides, she's not back yet.'

'Not back?' Laura echoed in alarm. 'But where is she?'

An unrecognizable expression – almost like a spasm – crossed his features before he shook his head. 'With friends. They'll look after her.'

Laura's face fell again and she dropped her head, trying to hide the tears. What had she done?

'Do you remember much?' he asked her, getting up from his chair and picking the dress up from the carpet.

Laura watched him, feeling more wretched with every act of kindness.

'I remember forcing you to buy the styling session for Cat,' she murmured.

'What else?'

'I remember . . . spending a fortune on paragliding.' She groaned.

He stared down at her. 'I can cover it, Laura,' he said after a moment.

She looked up at him sharply. 'No! It's my mess. I'll sort it.'

'You were out of your head.'

'I'll still sort it.'

'Do you have that kind of money? Were you lying about that?'

She shook her head. She still couldn't bring herself to touch the inheritance money, but she could sell the investment trust she'd built up working at Goldman. 'No. It was the truth.'

He paused, then nodded, relieved. 'What else do you remember?'

She inhaled slowly. 'I remember dancing.'

'With?'

'With Garth.' The moment she said it, she regretted it. Why was she trying to hurt him, even now? As if Garth featured anywhere in her memories. He turned away from her and walked to the window to draw the curtains tighter together so that the blindingly sharp sliver of light was blocked out. 'And you. I remember dancing with you,' she whispered to his back.

He fell still, his back to her, his head bowed. 'What then?'

'I remember talking to Bertie Penryn. He's going to come to Cat's party.'

'And?' He turned, his hands jammed in his trouser pockets, his dinner shirt rumpled and untucked. She saw his jacket and tie slung over the desk.

Laura was quiet for a long moment. 'And he told me about the charity we were fund-raising for.' Her voice was tiny.

Rob came and sat on the foot of the bed, and she instinctively tried to shuffle back a bit to create more distance between them. But moving wasn't going to be her strong point today.

'You went sheet-white when he mentioned the Covent Garden bombing,' he said in a low voice, the tips of his fingers lightly spreading over the tips of hers. 'Is that what it's all about?'

Laura looked at their hands, connected by the merest of touches, and nodded.

'You were there?'

'Yes.'

'You survived.'

'But many didn't,' she murmured.

'Like Lily. She's the "we"?'

The sadness in his eyes made sobs rise up in her like air bubbles. She struggled to swallow them down. 'Yes.'

They sat in silence for a long time, Laura trying not to wince as her body struggled with gravity, Rob's finger just skimming lightly over hers, back and forth, in a meditation.

'Do you hate me? For what I did to you last night?' she asked after a while.

He gave a small smile, his eyes meeting hers for the merest of moments. 'I wish. It would make everything a lot . . . easier.' He looked away again.

'Why do we get so angry with each other?' she whispered.

'It . . .' He swallowed hard. 'It signifies that we have a problem.'

'What?'

'That we're under each other's skin.'

'No.' She shook her head feebly.

'I'm not saying I like it, Laura,' he said slowly. 'I'm married.'

'And she's my friend.'

His eyes met hers. Her message was clear. She would put Cat before him.

'It's just one of those things. We can wait it out. It'll pass,' she said quietly. They fell still.

He withdrew his hand and stood up. 'Yes, you're probably right.' He crossed the room and picked up his jacket. 'I'd better see if she's back. I'll order some room service for you. Have plenty of fruit and juice, but keep off anything dry, and whatever you do, don't go anywhere near caffeine.'

'I'll never go anywhere near any of it again,' she sobbed, resting her forehead in the bridge of her hand.

He stopped at the door and looked back at her. 'Try and rest. I'll come back and check on you in a bit.'

Laura listened to the sound of his door open and close in the room beyond the wall. She slid back down under the sheets, tucking herself into a foetal position around a pillow and letting the tears fall, untrammelled, down her face. She couldn't believe what she'd done in the course of one night. She scarcely recognized herself. Who was she now? Not the shy, quiet jeweller coasting along in a flatline life with a boyfriend she couldn't love. Not the aunty figure who could eat her bodyweight in cake and mime all the words to 'Little Donkey'. Certainly not the party girl snorting coke in the loos and blowing the cost of a flat on an adrenalin kick.

She wasn't any of those women. Because, without Lily, she simply wasn't anyone at all.

She awoke three hours later to find a glass of freshly squeezed juice sitting on the table beside the bed. Rob? She stayed lying down, staring at the curtains and smelling the acrid scent of the damp, sweaty sheets. She knew she had to get up sometime; however much she didn't want to move, she had to get home.

Pushing herself up, she drank the juice in one go, feeling the cold liquid soothe her raw throat and cool her head. She found she could move more easily now and she swung her legs, one at a time, out of the bed. Yesterday's clothes had been folded and placed on the chest of drawers. Gingerly, she stepped into them, splashed her face with water and brushed her teeth before taking a sheet of paper from the complimentary pack and writing with a shaky hand:

*Didn't want to disturb you. Have gone home to prepare for the party. Back Friday.*
*Love Laura xxx*

She stared at it for a moment. Would it appear rude not to thank them for last night? Or ridiculous if she did? After all, it had hardly been the evening they'd all anticipated.

Grabbing her bag and the dress, which would need to be dry-cleaned, she let herself out of her room, sliding the note beneath the Blakes' door. She rode the lift with her eyes closed and took a moment to react when the doors opened. With her back pressed against the wall, she stared out miserably into the small lobby, straight through the doors on to the streets beyond. A low-slung sports car had pulled up. A flash of grey chiffon that was trapped in the door flapped like a wing in the snowy breeze.

Laura focused immediately and started crossing the hall to greet her, for it was clearly Cat in the car. Laura saw the door open and watched those long legs slide out with a grace that was far beyond Laura's reach this morning.

Laura stopped dead in her tracks as Cat swung the car door shut with an exuberant panache – something in the movement was flirtatious, victorious – and Laura quickly darted behind a pillar. She felt her heart hammering in her ribs as Cat strode through the lobby, radiant in last night's clothes, with stale make-up and mussed hair. Her body was clearly not crashing; it was soaring. She angled her head very slightly in Laura's direction as she passed, but Laura took a further step back, out of sight.

Laura looked back through the doors at the car pulling away from the kerb. It was a matt-black Porsche. She couldn't see who was driving, but she clocked the first few characters on the number plate: B5H.

She leaned against the pillar as she heard the lift take Cat back upstairs, back to Rob, waiting alone in their room for her. She wondered what Cat was going to tell him – what lie? Because it was abundantly clear from where she was standing that the man in the car was no mere friend.

# Chapter Forty-One

The studio was freezing – literally. Small icicles were forming on the insides of the windows, and Laura had to put on a pair of gloves to set the fire. She boiled the kettle four times too, just to get the steam to heat up the air temperature. The snow was newer and thicker on the ground here in Suffolk, though thankfully her train journey home had been unproblematic and the roads had been gritted so the taxi had had no problems getting her to the yard.

Laura wandered over to the east window, a mug of hot chocolate in her hands to warm her up. The flame in the stove was still green and cool, but the sounds of it flickering brought a little life into the room, at least. The locksmith had done his job and it was clear neither Fee nor Jack had been able to enter in her absence.

Her breath quickened at the thought of them, just a mile away from here. She tried to imagine them cuddled up on the grey sofa, watching the *X Factor* final and ploughing their way through a cheap bottle of red. She wondered whether Fee would have succeeded where she'd failed and persuaded Jack to let them have their Saturday-night take-away on their laps after all. She tried to envisage Fee lying in his arms in *her* bed, with *her* clothes still hanging in the wardrobe, *her* book still sitting unread on the table. Fee stepping into another woman's life, picking up the pieces just like . . . just like *she* had done four years earlier.

It had been five days since Jack had turned his back on her, five days since she'd left their cottage and drifted between four different homes – here, Kitty's, Cat and Rob's, the hotel in Kensington . . . She would have to go back to the cottage tomorrow and pack some fresh clothes. There was no washing machine in the studio and she couldn't keep buying new socks and knickers every few days. She also needed some more milk and proper food. Dinner tonight would have to be the emergency tin of chicken soup she'd managed not to eat in almost three years – it was going to be a long way from the kobe beef she'd enjoyed last night.

Last night – another land. She closed her eyes and a slideshow of images flashed behind her eyelids like cine film, jerky and silent. She remembered the look in Rob's eyes across the table as he'd tried to stop her – save her – during the bids; the way his body had felt, pressed against hers, as they'd danced; the exhaustion in his face after he'd sat up all night to make sure she was okay; the sadness in his voice this morning as they'd retreated from each other . . .

Had it been for nothing? Were the two of them battling with doing the right thing when the marriage was all but dead anyway? She'd been up close and personal with them for over a week, and for all Rob's insistent declarations of passionate love, there was also a constant dissatisfaction between the two of them that hummed like a high-volt cable, as though there was *too much* power. But then weren't people most desperate – most alive – in their death throes? Didn't a drowning man fight for survival with an intensity that was never required in normal life?

Or was it all the other way round? Was she the desperate

one – looking for reasons that could justify her feelings for Rob? What if Cat really had been with friends? Perhaps she had simply mistaken her chemically induced euphoria as love? Cat had, after all, been as high as her, and look what she'd done – blown a small fortune on a bid, just to prove a point.

Laura stared out into the night, watching the distant lights of a tanker ship blinking on the horizon. It had begun to sleet again, and the occasional snowflake fluttered past the windowpanes, startling her slightly each time. She was jittery and confused – still crashing – and her head was pounding – hardly ideal, given that she had to work for the next two days solid if she was going to pull together the stock for the party as well as finish Cat's necklace.

Of the three charms that remained – Rob's, Olive's and Min's – she knew what she was doing for only one of them. She turned away from the night and unlocked the safe – hidden behind a cardboard box beneath the bench – pulling out stackable trays of charms she had built up in the past four years and setting them along the counter. Some had been fashioned purely to develop her technical ability; others were ideas she hadn't been able to resist, like the silver squirrel holding a real acorn, inspired by a 1950s children's print. One tray was of antiques, bought as happy-go-lucky aides-memoires on her travels before she'd decided to make this her career.

Another tray was filled with the earliest charms she had made. She couldn't take them to London with her – they weren't anywhere close to being good enough quality to sell; she'd just been cutting her teeth when she'd made them, but she had a strong sentimental attachment to them. Her eyes tripped over them like a child's over sweet jars:

the old-fashioned phone box, a Venetian mask where one of the eyes was misshapen; a jack-in-the box that didn't open properly; an enamelled emerald-green four-leafed clover; a slightly lopsided wedding cake; a lockable treasure chest; an Easter egg; a dice on which she'd repeated the 'four' dots twice; a rocking horse that looked more like a rocking donkey . . .

There were hundreds of charms in total, stockpiled as references, waiting to tell a stranger's story. But what would tell Olive's? She looked at them each in turn, her eyes falling upon every single one. She could remember almost word for word the torturous interview and ran over some obvious images – Truffle the pony, a bit, a horseshoe, a grooming brush? Or their last holiday in Cornwall – the crab, the shell, a bucket and spade? But they seemed too shiny, too idyllic, to honestly represent that fatally fractured relationship, and she well remembered Rob's smile as he'd insisted on warts. He wanted the truth spelled out – *Don't edit to be kind* – and she couldn't pretend the sisters were close. The reality was that their relationship was defined by the loss of Daniel, but how did you put an image to something that wasn't there?

She sat down on the sofa, positioned the digital recorder beside her and switched it on. Min's uncharismatic voice filled the room.

*'I couldn't go on justifying her salary when she was basically a glorified tea-girl.'*

Laura stopped the machine as she remembered another small detail that had been lost in the broad strokes of last night's events – Cat had told Ben Jackson she was still working at Min's gallery. She had fluidly and easily lied. At the time, Laura had put it down to pride. It was one thing saving face in front of an estranged acquaintance, but her own husband? They certainly didn't need the money. Laura bit her lip. She knew Cat – for some other reason – must be lying about it to Rob too. It was the only explanation for why he didn't know his wife had been sacked; if he did, he surely never would have included Min on the project. They weren't friends, colleagues or even in touch. She switched it on again.

*'I do often see her around and about, but she never comes in.'*

She clicked it off again. Laura felt her head begin to swim with too much and too little information all at once. She knew Cat was lying about her job, but she didn't know why; she knew Cat was still travelling into Holland Park every week, but she didn't know why. And she knew it meant Cat had been lying to her husband for two years. *Two years!* But she didn't know why.

Old Grey woke her early the next morning with his droning wing beat outside the east window. She'd worked till late, but her body was still on hyperdrive, her mind racing with what had to be done. Her eyes focused slowly and she remembered that there was nothing to be done now. On the necklace anyway. It was finished.

Laura reached out from the sofa and picked it up off the table, the attached charms tinkling delicately like wind chimes. She held it up, feeling a rush of pride at what she had created. Even without the emotional resonance behind it, the bracelet was an object of stunning beauty. Any woman – the glamorous Cat Blake included – would wear this with pride.

Her fingers brushed the individual charms lightly. She had done it again – a life remembered, another one recorded for posterity. It wasn't a perfect life by any means, though many people held it to be: its incumbent was beautiful but flawed, spoilt and selfish but also kind and unquestionably generous; a woman who couldn't be pinned down to just one interpretation. She was a polished jewel honed from inauspicious beginnings, and as multifaceted as a diamond: a wife, a sister, a first love, a friend – not necessarily excelling in any of those capacities, but then who ever said she had to? She was loved by the people on this necklace, anyway. Laura didn't have the answers to all her questions about Cat, but then did anyone ever know someone else in complete fullness? Did anyone even have the right to complete ownership of another person's history, secrets and dreams?

No. She had fulfilled her brief. Hand on heart, with the information she did have, every charm was honest and true – even Min's. She had listened to the interview over and over until, as the last traces of the drug disappeared and her mind became more balanced again, she had realized that Rob had wanted her to represent not a personal relationship but a professional achievement – the Exposure exhibition.

Laura looked at the charm she had given *him*: a tiny compass with red arrowed hands. She had known from their conversation on the plane that this would be his charm, simply from the way he'd talked about his beautiful wife. Cat was, in the words of Auden, his north, his south, his east, his west. His everything.

Her hand fell to her chest, the charms pressed against her skin like little knuckles, as she fought back the tears that sprang at her eyes. All the people she'd once been everything to were gone for ever. She was nothing to anyone.

Laura dressed quickly, defiantly converting desolation into action. It wasn't yet eight, but Jack and Arthur would be out for their walk before breakfast and the cottage would be empty. (Well, if Fee wasn't sleeping in, that was. She still slept like a teenager.) She wanted to get this over and done with, without confrontation or angry scenes. Jack and Fee – if they were even bothering to check for her – would see that Dolly wasn't parked in her usual spot in the yard and would assume she was still away. Where did they think she had gone to? she wondered. They both knew there was no family to take her in, nor friends. Or at least, not friends *they* had met. Would Fee guess? She had been jealous enough of Kitty.

The towpath was slippery – semi-thawed snow had iced over the mud during the night – and Laura trod carefully beside the brown and swirling water. She had scarcely been here in the past week, but she still instinctively knew the tide times. She would have just under two hours to get back here before the water level rose too high to cross.

In town, it was quiet. Sunday. The shops wouldn't be opening for a while, and down side alleys the bins bulged with black sacks, waiting for the council refuse collections on Monday. Laura stopped outside Dorothy Perkins – the shaggy 'rock princess' jacket she'd been considering for Fee was in the window. It would have looked so good on her too.

She continued walking, shivering without a hat or gloves to put on, and she made a mental note to remember to pack those too. She pulled out her phone and called for a taxi to collect her from the cottage in half an hour. There would be too much to carry all the way to the studio, but at least if she was dropped at the top of the footpath, she could manage the rest.

She stopped as she turned into Pudding Street. The thatched roofs looked so pretty in the snow – like snowflakes caught on eyelashes – and the whitewashed walls looked greenish by comparison. She could see all her neighbours' Christmas-tree lights sparkling in the matching bay windows that were repeated in every house, and her own red door gleamed back at her, naked. There was still no wreath above the knocker.

Laura looked up at the bedroom window. The curtains were open and neatly pulled back, a faint light from the landing beyond just visible. She couldn't see any movement inside. She waited ten minutes, feeling self-conscious to be loitering outside her own house, before walking up to the door and pressing her ear to it. There was nothing to be heard. She crouched down and peered through the letterbox. There was nothing to be seen either – just her Joules mac hanging on the peg above her red wellies besides Jack's mustard duffle coat and Timberlands. Arthur's lead – which hung from its own hook – was gone. They were out.

Quickly, she let herself in, shutting the door behind her as quietly as she could in case Fee should be up there still sleeping after all. She crept silently up the stairs, her heart pounding from fear of what she'd find, but the bed was empty; no one was in.

She sagged against the door frame, looking in at her own bedroom. Already she'd lost her sense of ownership over it. It was like looking around a house that was for sale, feeling slightly voyeuristic, peering into the intimacy of other people's lives. The patchwork quilt she'd loved so much at the market – Jack had bought it for her even though it was overpriced and clearly not antique, in spite of what the stall-holder had said – was neatly pulled to the top and smoothed in typical Jack fashion, and the lace cushions were arranged on their points, just the way she liked them to be. The square box on the mantelpiece was untouched – she could tell by the faint dust lines; there was water in only one glass on Jack's side of the bed, and his favourite grey Nordic jumper had been draped carefully over the bottom bedstead.

Laura turned and walked into the bathroom. She looked around for make-up, cheap perfume, neon bangles or glittery nail polish – anything that told her Fee was here – but all she could smell was Jack's deodorant. She wasn't fooled. Fee wouldn't move in before Laura had moved out.

Unless . . . unless they were staying at Fee's. They knew she would have to come back sooner or later to collect her things. How much easier it would be for everyone if they continued their affair away from home until it was clear Laura wasn't coming back.

Well, she'd make it easy for them. Marching back to the bedroom, she heaved down her large suitcase on wheels. She pulled out her underwear drawer and tipped it upside down angrily, so that bras, knickers, socks and tights fell out in a jumbled mass. Then she took her two other pairs of jeans, a funnel-necked fleece, all her T-shirts and pyjamas, the snazziest party dress she owned – beige lace, Reiss in the sale – and her high heels (all red), and jammed them into the suitcase. She walked over to the dressing table and had just begun to rifle through her make-up and jewellery box when she heard the front door slam.

She froze. Downstairs she could hear the muffled 'pop' of Arthur's padded feet on the stone floor as he trotted over to his water bowl, the tinkle of the brassware as Jack replaced the lead on the hook. There was no sound of his footsteps, though, and she imagined him standing at the foot of the stairs, sensing her presence.

Then she heard him turn into the kitchen, the sound of water hissing through the pipes as he opened the taps and filled the kettle. Laura looked around the room as though scanning for exits, but she knew perfectly well there was nowhere to go. The back door led straight off the kitchen. The only way out was the way she'd come in.

She sank on to the bed, her face in her hands. How could it be she was hiding from Jack? Him of all people. He'd always been her safety net. That had been the point – he was safe! He would never hurt her or leave her or let her down. They were connected in ways no one else could ever understand. No one except Fee. Her tears fell quickly, but they were silent at least.

Laura listened for sounds of him moving around downstairs, but everything was quiet. She thought of Arthur curling up in his bed, happy to sleep after his run. But what were they doing back so soon? Sunday was always Arthur's treat day when she and Jack took him on an extra-long walk up to the lighthouse.

In her pocket, a text buzzed on her mobile – the taxi was outside. She had to be quick. The bollards meant the driver wouldn't be able to get down this street, and anything more than a minute of waiting and he'd get out and ring the bell.

Zipping her bag as quietly as she could, Laura heaved the suitcase off the bed and carried it to the top of the stairs. It was so big her hands didn't meet round it, but her adrenalin was pumping and she felt at that moment that she could have carried a car. Carefully, knowing exactly where the creaks were, she zigzagged her way down the staircase. One misstep would tell Jack she was here.

At the bottom she stopped, hoping Arthur was already zonked out in his bed. If he detected her scent . . . She was desperate to see him and ruffle his ears, but not right now. He would lead Jack straight to her. The doorway to the kitchen was on her right and she held her breath, listening. She could hear Jack breathing – he was close, just a couple of feet away. In her mind's eye she could see him perched on the arm of the small teal sofa opposite the tiny fireplace reading the Sports section. She almost thought she could smell him – that sweet, familiar smell that had soothed her like balm in those first terrifying days . . .

Slowly and silently, she reached her arm out and put her hand on the handle. The latch retreated into its shell and she pulled open the door without a sound. The world – still sleepy – gently poked its head in and she could hear the sound of the taxi's engine rumbling further down the street. She lifted the suitcase over the threshold in both arms and stepped out on to the pavement. And the only sound she heard before the door clicked shut was a single escaped sob.

# Chapter Forty-Two

'So.'

'So.'

'How are you feeling?' Cat asked tentatively as Laura buckled her seat belt.

'So-so,' Laura shrugged, folding her hands in her lap. 'You?'

'Okay, I guess.' Cat looked down sheepishly. She was looking radiant in her sheepskin coat, a butterscotch knitted dress and suede boots. 'Look, Laura, before we go any further, I want to apologize to you. I never should have dragged you into it with me. It was wrong. Rob's completely hauled me over the coals about it.'

'Really, it's fine. I'm a big girl. I can make my own decisions. You didn't make me do anything I didn't want to. You were right – I'd had a tough week. It gave me a chance to escape myself for a while,' she managed, diplomatically.

'Yes, but it all got a bit out of hand, didn't it? I mean, a hundred thousand on paragliding? You wouldn't have done *that* on champagne alone. I'd be happy to swap my styling session with you.'

Laura smiled, knowing that although the offer might be sincere, she'd be anything but happy about it. 'I really appreciate the offer, Cat, but I'll have a ball; I love paragliding. And it's an incredible cause. I . . . I honestly can't think of a better charity to give my money to.' That much was true at least.

Cat blinked at her with some considerable amazement, probably as much because of the revelation about Laura's secret wealth, which she assumed Rob had mentioned to her, as at her generosity of spirit. 'Well, you're incredibly sweet,' Cat replied, pulling the car into the traffic heading up Kensington High Street.

'Let's not say any more about it,' Laura said determinedly, relieved the formalities were over. 'It is, after all, *your birthday*!'

'I know!' Cat squealed excitedly, tossing her head from side to side like a thoroughbred as the lights turned red and a mob of pedestrians crossed in front of them, eyeing Cat's latest-model Evoque and her equally rich golden mane with unconcealed envy. She was wearing her Prada shades to protect her from 'snow glare', even though the pavements had been swept clear and all that remained was sludgy, grubby banks of compacted snow along the kerbs and gutters.

'Happy birthday!' Laura clapped, leaning over to kiss her on the cheek just as the lights changed and Cat moved the car back into gear. Embarrassed, Laura sat back hastily in her seat.

'So what did Rob get you?' she asked quickly. 'Apart from the small matter of the Rachel Zoe styling session, obviously.'

Cat shrugged. 'He hasn't given it to me yet. He says it's a surprise. I'll get it at the party tonight.'

'You must be so excited.'

'I am! He always puts so much thought into it, but I'm getting the impression he's gone the extra mile this year.'

Laura smiled to herself. The necklace was wrapped up in her suitcase, ready to hand over to him. She felt a burst of butterflies in her stomach, feeling ridiculously nervous at the prospect of Cat finally receiving her work as a birthday gift. Would she find it sufficiently beautiful? Would she think it was enough?

Cat swung a left at the lights to go up Kensington Church Street, getting stuck behind a taxi that was picking up a fare.

'How was it back home, anyway? Did you see either of them?' Cat asked, overtaking a bus.

'No. I just hid away in my studio and worked all week.'

'They must have come looking for you, though? It's the first place I'd look.'

'My car's still at Kitty's, so they'll see it's not in my parking space and think I'm away. I haven't had time to go and collect it – I've been so busy making stuff for the party.'

'What about all your clothes? You said you'd have to go home to get them,' Cat asked, taking a swift left and then turning left again into a tiny dead-end street flanked on either side by five white stuccoed houses, a leafy garden square no bigger than a sandpit but filled with a magnificent magnolia sitting in between them all. She reverse-parked, pulled out a resident's parking permit from her bag and stuck it on the windscreen.

'I popped in when I knew Jack would be out walking Arthur.'

Cat cut the engine and turned to look at her. 'That must have been weird, going back.'

'It was.'

'Any sign of the Wicked Witch?'

Laura winced. 'She's . . . she's not really li—'

'Uh-uh-uh. Remember what we said? Don't make excuses for them!' Cat warned, patting her hand.

They jumped out, and Laura heaved her suitcase awkwardly from the boot. It seemed to weigh a ton now – especially given that she had also packed in thousands of pounds worth of jewellery from the studio too – and she wondered how she'd managed to steal it away so deftly from the house.

Thank God Cat had offered to pick her up from the station. They only had about three hours till the first guests arrived and there was so much to do – it would take an hour alone just to arrange all the different charms. Cat had been adamant, when she'd tried bringing it up the other day, that all the party arrangements were 'in hand', but Laura was determined to contribute and had packed a few bottles of Piper-Heidsieck champagne that she had found on offer in Sainsbury's, plus several large bags of Kettle Chips and some olives from the deli.

Cat opened the door on to a narrow communal hallway with Prussian-blue walls and a parquet walnut floor.

'Leave that there, Laura. One of the guys can take it up for you,' Cat said, indicating her suitcase as she started up the staircase.

Guys?

They climbed two flights to the top floor. The door was already open, and a stream of people were bustling about from one room to another.

'Cat!' a thin woman in charcoal-grey cried, kissing Cat on both cheeks as they stepped into the flat. It wasn't huge, but the rooms still had a grandness to them, and light flooded through from the tall windows. The pear-green hall was galleried with tens of watercolours, charcoals and pencil sketches all the way up the walls. Laura thought she saw a Hockney, but couldn't be sure.

Smoky panelled *verre églomisé* mirrors lined the far wall in the drawing room, reflecting another galleried wall opposite, and a duck-egg silk sofa glistened against a delicate vanilla antique Persian rug that seemed to emit a glow like moonlight.

But it wasn't really the sumptuous decor that grabbed attention today – it was the staggering amount of greenery in the room. It was like walking on to a film set. Low-lying crystal rose bowls were stuffed with profuse white peonies that looked like heaps of giant snowballs, and a team of florists were arranging enormous woody sprays of mistletoe – the stems sprayed with white glitter – to sit like splayed frosted hands. Laura counted three potted bay trees, whose narrow trunks were bound with wide red velvet ribbons and finished with extravagant bows at the tops, like bow ties. But the centrepiece had to be a magnificent white-flowering miniature blossom-tree, no higher than six feet but beautifully shaped, with a venerably twisted canopy that looked like a gymnast's ribbon caught mid-flight.

Laura's mouth dropped open. Frankly, it would have been rude if it hadn't.

'Oh, it came in time after all!' Cat cried, stroking the blossom-tree admiringly.

'You do *not* want to know the numbers I had to call to get this through customs in time,' the grey-clad woman laughed.

'It's imported?' Laura asked in disbelief.

The woman looked over at her as though noticing her for the first time. 'Thankfully the Japanese are so efficient, it meant we could absorb the two days it spent sitting at Heathrow. But next time, Cat, darling – a little more warning? I've not slept since last week!'

Cat chuckled. 'Laura, this is Tana, my party organizer. She arranges everything for me.' She looked across at Tana. 'Do you remember my thirtieth in Marrakesh?' Cat dropped her bag on the sofa and ran her hands through her hair, her eyes on her vague reflection in the dappled mirror.

'As if I could *forget*,' Tana laughed, rolling her eyes. 'If I never see another camel . . .'

Give Surrey a wide berth, then, Laura thought to herself. 'Pleased to meet you, Tana. It all looks amazing.'

'It's Laura's designs that we're launching tonight,' Cat said, twisting her hair into a chignon. 'What do you think? Up or down?'

'Up,' Laura and Tana chimed together.

Tana turned and smiled at her, and Laura recognized the same territorialism in her that she'd encountered in Sam and Min.

'So, things seem to be running smoothly,' Cat smiled.

'Of course! The balloons have arrived. It was a bit of a rush, but . . .' She leant down and pulled out a balloon, hastily and rather inelegantly inflating it on the helium pump. Laura looked on as a pale grey balloon fattened, revealing an intertwined LC monogram printed in white on the side. 'You were right *again*. The monogram works much better than the logo.'

What logo? Laura wondered.

'Don't they look pretty?' Cat smiled, looking over at her.

'They do,' Laura agreed, nodding enthusiastically.

Cat let her hair fall from her hands and it billowed like a silk parachute around her shoulders. 'So, I've spent a lot of time wondering how we can make the charms look interesting en masse, because, I mean, obviously they're so teeny-tiny they could easily get lost in a room like this – there's just so much else to look at. So I thought what we'd do is . . .' She walked over to the balcony and opened the doors. A man was out there, chiselling away at a block of ice. 'Andrei here is working his magic.'

Laura stepped on to the balcony after her, amazed by the sheer beauty of the work-in-progress before her. The reindeer was almost finished and it appeared to be pulling a beautifully carved sleigh.

'We're going to use this red velvet ribbon here as reins, and we'll thread some charms on to it like jingle bells!'

Laura gasped at the idea. She loved it!

'But that's not all,' Cat said, grinning at her excitement. 'Now that we're here, Andrei's going to make a solid-ice sack to sit inside the sleigh, with the charms suspended on invisible wire and frozen inside it.'

Laura's jaw dropped again. 'It'll be so beautiful,' she whispered, completely overwhelmed by the time, money and trouble Cat was going to for her. 'Is there time, though? There's only—'

'Plenty. Andrei's got a blast freezer that'll give him the ice block he needs in ninety minutes. After that he's chiselling and sculpting. He can't work further ahead than this anyway, as it'll melt before anyone gets here.'

'Oh. Okay,' she nodded dumbly.

'We'll get the charms to you in five minutes, Andrei,' Cat assured him, leading Laura back into the warmth of the flat again. The fire had been lit – being central London, it was only a gas one and the flame was still blue, but it did the job. 'Then we're going to thread the charms for the blossom and bay trees on to very low-wattage LED lights, and wind them in and out of the leaves. It should make them glitter in the light.'

Charms twinkling in trees? 'How do you even think of these things?' Laura asked her in wonder.

'I remembered this book I read as a little girl: *'I had a little nut tree; nothing would it bear, but a silver nutmeg and a golden pear. The King of Spain's daughter came to visit me, and all—'*

'For the sake of my little nut tree!' Laura laughed, joining in. 'Oh my God! I'd totally forgotten that! It's brilliant!'

'Isn't it? I was always so fascinated by the idea of this tree with the treasure fruit . . .' She arched an eyebrow. 'I don't suppose you've actually got a silver nutmeg or a golden pear?'

Laura considered for a moment and then clapped her hands together. 'I do! I actually do! I've always got a silver nut in the collection – it's a popular motif for luck. And I've got a prototype golden pear that I made . . . I made one each for twins. They're a matching pair? Get it?'

'Dreadful!' Cat laughed, nudging her arm. 'And so we'll have the remaining charms dangling on the mistletoe fingers and then the complete pieces – a necklace, a couple of bracelets – sitting on little scarlet pillows under these,' she continued, pointing to several enormous Victorian bell jars sitting on some of the surfaces.

'My gob has been well and truly smacked,' Laura muttered as she saw a courier come in and hand over several mint-green Ladurée bags. In the kitchen beyond, she noticed black-clad catering staff preparing canapés and cocktails, and watched as the rainbow-coloured macaroons were immediately arranged on porcelain-lace plates. 'How can I ever thank you? I had no idea you were going to all this trouble.'

'Cat either goes to this trouble or none at all,' Tana remarked.

The intimation was that Laura was special to her, and she felt herself swell with pride.

Cat checked her watch. 'Oh God, is that the time? I'm

running late. Listen, I've got to pop out to get my hair done, but let me show you the room where you can get ready.'

She led Laura through to a cream bedroom dominated by a mahogany sleigh bed. A striking oil of a woman reclining nude on a bed hung on the wall behind it, but there was nothing on the surfaces – no photographs, no books, no dust, no life. Cat hadn't told her who was so generously loaning out her flat, but she must live out of town.

'There's a private bathroom just through here,' Cat said from a doorway at the far end. 'No one will disturb you.'

'That's great, thanks,' Laura nodded.

'Okay,' Cat shrugged. 'So then, I'll leave you to choose the charms for Andrei so he can get on with the sack. I should be back in just over two hours.'

Laura followed her out to the sitting room, watching as Cat grabbed her coat, kissed Tana on both cheeks and dashed back out again. She saw that one of the 'guys' had carried her suitcase up the two flights of stairs for her and it was sitting on its end in the hall. She went to retrieve it, almost colliding with one of the party planners who was officiously and blindly carrying a festoon of grey balloons from the study into the sitting room, having to squeeze them through the doorway in batches. The bag caught on the skirting board as she moved, leaving a vivid black drag mark along the pristine paintwork, and she heard a quiet tut behind her.

'See to that, will you, please?' She watched Tana direct an underling and then turn away to move back into the drawing room to carry on overseeing preparations. Laura felt her smile slip. She had a sudden sense that Tana wasn't going to be quite so chummy with Cat gone, and she banged her way down the hall, feeling awkward and alone in this flat full of strangers.

# Chapter Forty-Three

Laura sat on the edge of the bed drying her hair, her towel pinned tightly under her arms just in case anyone, in all their enthusiasm, should burst the locks and come in. It was certainly a risk. Outside her door, she could hear the commotion of florists, party planners, the ice sculptor and caterers all doing their separate things.

She needed to get ready quickly and join them. She had over two hundred pieces to sort through and help thread on to ribbons and lights, and she was beginning to shake so much from nerves, she wasn't sure she'd be able to pick them up.

She rifled through the suitcase left open on the bed, looking for her hairdryer. It took several frustrated attempts before she realized she'd never packed it – Jack had come home before she'd had a chance.

Feeling the first seeds of panic take root – society party with air-dried hair? Really? – she hurriedly threw open the wardrobe doors and looked inside. There was bound to be one here, especially if this was just a bolt-hole. A solitary black suit swung from a hanger, a narrow silk tie draped casually round the neck. Curious, Laura checked the label on the back – Ermenegildo Zegna. Pricey.

She shut the doors and tried the bedside cabinet. Nothing

on that side of the bed. She crossed to the other and checked that too. Found it!

Quickly she finished off drying and styling her hair, pleased with the way it fell, rather than hung, around her face for once. Her trouser suit – a blood-red velvet tux with skinny cropped trousers – flattered her, making her look particularly long-legged; Cat had picked it out for her last week, possibly as compensation for whisking the grey feather minidress from under her nose.

She peered at herself in the mirror. She looked lean and uncharacteristically cosmopolitan and reprimanded herself for never having had the vision (or occasion) to wear trousers as a 'cocktail' option before. She felt urban and young. This was her second dressy event in a week so she'd better get used to the vagaries of party dressing – this was simply how life was with the Blakes. Cat had told her to wear the suit without anything underneath, but Laura wasn't that brave and had bought a mannish ivory silk shirt. Her red ankle boots could have been considered overkill, but the poppy versus the crimson tones clashed rather nicely, she thought.

She applied her make-up with new speed – Cat had passed on a few tips last Friday – and quickly zipped her clothes and accoutrements into the suitcase, smoothing the bed covers and replumping the pillows. There! As if she'd never been here.

She walked across the room, and as she wrapped the lead round the base of the hairdryer and replaced it in the drawer, her eye fell on a tiny white corner that was clearly the edge of a Polaroid photo. Ordinarily she wouldn't have looked. Ordinarily. But she clocked who it was instantly.

Laura bent down and peered into the drawer, finding a stack of photos pushed to the back. It must have been dislodged and fallen forwards as she'd opened it. She flicked through them, knowing she should feel guiltier than she did for prying like this. But *she* had nothing to feel guilty about. Not compared with this. She looked at tens of images of Cat sleeping, Cat laughing – and they'd all been taken in this bed. The photographer wasn't revealed in any of them.

Or was he? Laura peered closer at one that showed Cat leaning back on her elbows, her eyes straight to camera. To her right, on the table, was a bottle of champagne and a three-quarters-drunk glass, and beside that a gold signet ring.

Laura knew full well that Rob didn't wear one. But she plainly remembered who did.

'So where's your boat kept?' Laura asked, writing everything down furiously as Michael Bublé crooned in the background and the fire flickered. Mistletoe garlands had been draped over the fireplace and great bunches of balloons that could lift the house, *Up*-style, bobbed in the frantic air currents – frantic from the amount of hand-waving, hair-tossing and air-kissing going on. The flat had been mobbed for the past hour and a quarter, and she was getting cramp in her hand and a sore throat. She kept looking around, but there was no sign of Cat.

'Falmouth Harbour, Antigua,' the brunette replied with a mid-Atlantic twang.

'And you'd be able to get a photo of it to me?'

'Sure. I want you to get it absolutely spot on.'

'Okay. Well, with that one on top, that would take you up to five charms.'

The brunette clapped her hands together. 'I'm so excited! I've always wanted one since I was a little girl, but all the ones I've seen are just either really heavy and old-fashioned, or these meaningless fashion ones.' She picked up a bracelet threaded with three charms. 'Yours are so light and pretty, and they look so modern. I think it's genius threading them on the velvet too.' She said it with a sense of wonder, as though Laura had unlocked the genome code with her designs.

'Thanks,' Laura replied modestly. The idea for the leather or velvet 'ribbon bracelets' had come as she'd been setting up, and worked well for a more casual edge.

'What does this pigeon mean?' another brunette asked, holding up a charm.

'It's a dove. Commonly it represents love, but in some instances peace. I had a client who lost her husband after a long illness, and she found it comforting to think of him at peace at last. But this interpretation was also private – no one else looking at it knew what it meant unless she wanted to tell them.'

'Oh, I like the sound of that! Secrets hidden in plain sight?' the woman said, nudging her companion knowingly.

'I thought Cat was supposed to be here,' a woman in a pink blazer asked, her glass in her hand, as she surveyed the tables without touching anything.

'She will be. She was at the hairdresser's. She must have got held up.'

'Oh, I'm sure,' the woman murmured with a distinct undercurrent of sarcasm. ''Cause it just gets so busy in there at this time of year.'

'It's the day before Christmas Eve,' Laura said pointedly. 'Of course it does.'

'There are roadworks in Queen's Gate,' the woman who'd been looking at the dove remarked. 'Traffic's backing up all the way past Gloucester Road.'

Laura shot the rude woman a look, as if to say, 'See?'

Above the sea of hennaed heads, Laura suddenly caught sight of Bertie Penryn looking distinguished in black tie again as he made slow progress over to her. Not for the first time in the past hour she sent up a prayer of thanks to the assistants the party planners had hired to work as sales crew so that she could 'mingle'. She gave the assistant next to her the chart she had hastily drawn up that showed what each charm symbolized, and a price list.

'Mr Penryn, I can't believe you made it!' Laura said, shaking his hand as he came and stood in front of her.

'Bertie, please,' he said, almost panting from the effort. 'And I'm afraid I don't have as much time as I'd like,' he smiled, pulling slightly on his barathea jacket to make his point.

'I understand. I'm so grateful you b-bothered at all.'

He noticed her nerves. 'On the contrary, I'm intrigued. You've got this crowd in a frenzy. Tell me what's so different about what you do?'

She stepped aside so that he could look at it all. 'I call it interpretive jewellery. For my bespoke work, I interview my clients for the stories or memories they want to remember, and come up with a motif unique to them. But there's also an off-the-pillow line for more generalized charms – so beans and shamrocks for luck, that kind of thing.'

Bertie peered closer at the gold nightingale necklace protected under a bell jar.

'That's a nightingale to denote a "songbird", my client's nickname for his wife. It's their golden wedding anniversary and it was through her singing that they met.' Laura swallowed as she remembered Fee's wide eyes and breathy anticipation as Laura had recounted the story to her.

'I like it,' Bertie remarked, his eyes scanning quickly over the tables. 'You've got a very distinct look, Laura. You can see that the same hand worked on all the charms on each piece. It gives them a coherence that many charm bracelets lack.'

'Thank you. I want them to be beautiful in their own right, as well as emotionally significant. But they have to feel fresh and modern too if women like these are going to wear them. '

She watched as he picked up a gold hair slide – one of her newest designs – with a red enamelled heart swinging from it on a chain. 'Well, this has a much younger feel to it.'

'Yes. I thought with Valentine's Day coming up, it would make a good gift for boyfriends to give. And it's nine-carat gold, so a lower price point too.'

'For the off-the-pillow range?' Bertie smiled. 'I like that name.'

'I'm thinking about expanding the slide to include other motifs too, like a diamond star or two crossed arrows.'

Bertie frowned. 'Crossed arrows? What do they connote?'

'It's a Native Indian symbol for friendship.'

Bertie nodded as he examined a hammered-gold cuff with a circular cutout and, inside that, a charm of a baby bear lying on its back, legs in the air. 'Droll.'

'Off-the-pillow again. The bear stands for strength, and of course the cuff itself is almost like a piece of armour, so I liked the juxtaposition of making the bear more playful and cute. Katie Hillier's done so well with her bunnies . . . Ultimately, it has to appeal to a girl shopping on the King's Road, not a warrior princess.'

Bertie chuckled, watching with interest as the women clamoured at the tables and peeked into the trees.

'I really like it, Laura. You have not just a great idea but the skill with which to back it up. You're very, very good. Have you met Marsha Keble at Liberty yet?'

Laura shook her head, her heart leaping at the mention of the L word.

'I'll arrange a meeting. I know she'd be very interested in you, although she might press you for exclusivity.'

'Is that a bad thing?'

'You might think so when you're mobbed by the buyers at Fashion Week.'

Laura gasped, her hands flying to her mouth. 'You mean . . .'

'I most certainly do. If I don't snap you up, it'll only be a matter of time before the CFDA is calling you.' He laughed at Laura's confused expression. 'The BFC's American cousins. Don't worry, you'll learn. I'll get my secretary to send you all the paperwork. In the meantime, you've got six weeks till show time to get these new ideas for off-the-pillow made up. Think you can do it?'

'Absolutely!' Laura cried, her cheeks pinking up before him.

She walked him to the door. 'I can't tell you what this means to me,' she said.

'Oh, I imagine I can guess,' he nodded. 'You've timed it very well. The accessories market has been dominated by bags and then shoes for the best part of this decade, but jewellery's moment in the sun is coming – that's how the fashion pendulum works. I hope you realize you're going to be rushed off your feet.'

'I can take it,' Laura replied firmly.

'I get the feeling you can, yes.' He smiled. 'Have you booked your paraglide yet?'

'Not yet. It's a bit chilly up there at this time of year.'

'Yes, quite. You've done it before, then, I take it?'

'Many times.'

A grey monogrammed balloon poked its way round the door. 'Well, we'll speak soon. I'll get Laura Cunningham Designs on the tents list as soon as the office reopens after Christmas,' he said.

Laura heard a car door slam in the street below and looked out of the hall window. It was the matt-black sports car again, the same one – B5H 5TK. She darted to the window, looking down to try to see who was in it, but the reflection on the windows made it impossible.

'Someone you know?' Bertie asked.

'Uh . . . yes, yes,' she said in a strained voice. 'It's Cat. She's here at last.'

Bertie's right eyebrow twitched ever so slightly. 'Well, I'll push off before I get caught in more conversation. My driver's outside. *A bientôt*, Laura. Merry Christmas!'

'Yes, thanks, Bertie. And to you. See you soon.' As soon as he was out of sight, she turned back to the window. Cat was leaning through the car window, talking animatedly to the driver, still wearing the clothes she'd left in earlier, her hair untouched.

Laura listened as she heard Cat's heels clicking on the parquet floor, and then the sound of gentle running up the stairs. If Cat found her here, she would know Laura had seen her and firmly, unequivocally knew what was going on.

Turning, she dashed back into the flat, weaving her way through the crowd of women all laughing and drinking and chatting, and positioned herself behind the blossom-tree. She interrupted a conversation between two women who were arguing over the meaning of a butterfly charm.

'Butterflies always represent change and transformation,' one of them was saying. 'It's really nothing new to see that represented in this charm,' and she put the charm down with an element of disdain.

'You're absolutely right, but in Chinese culture, they also represent long life,' Laura said, forcing a smile.

'Most butterflies live for a few days,' the woman contradicted.

'The Mandarin word for "butterfly" is "*hu-tieh*". "*Tieh*" means "seventy years", which is why it has that association. I used a butterfly like this for a single-charm necklace I was commissioned to make for a woman celebrating her hundredth birthday by her great-grandchildren.'

'Oh.' The woman was silenced.

Laura heard the small gasps that immediately preceded Cat's entrance, and she kept her eyes down, pretending to care about what these women – who thought they knew it and had seen it all – were saying.

'Now this goddess figure is a particular favourite of mine, and one of the most versatile charms,' Laura murmured, just as Cat swept straight over to her.

'They love you!' Cat whispered in her ear, hugging Laura to her tightly. 'I knew they would. They've all got such monstrous egos, they can't think of anything better than jewellery that's all about them,' she giggled.

Laura pulled back and looked at her. How could she pretend everything was hunky-dory when she'd clearly just been with another man? *Him* again. 'You didn't get your hair done,' she said pointedly.

'Tch, yes, I know,' Cat sighed. 'Roadworks in Queen's Gate. We were sitting in traffic for three-quarters of an hour before we decided to turn back. Everywhere's gridlocked. Do I look a fright?'

Laura stared at her, crushed by how easily Cat lied to her face.

'Listen, I'll just go get changed and then you can tell me what's been going on. It looks like it's been a blast. I'm so cross I've practically missed it.'

Laura nodded, grateful for the brief reprieve. 'How could Cat have seen *him* again on her birthday of all days? She watched as Cat wove her way through the crowd, kissing, smiling and squeezing hands with earnest declarations of getting together after Christmas.

The crowd was beginning to thin out quickly. It was coming up to half past seven and everyone seemingly had eight o'clock appointments. Laura quickly scanned the notepads the busking sales assistants had written in – there were further orders and her eyes bulged at the sight of the total someone had quickly calculated for her.

She sank on to the arm of a sofa and bit her lip. What Cat had done for her in the course of one night was beyond anything Fee could have hoped to achieve in five years. She might even get to be stocked in Liberty, for heaven's sake! Could she really turn round and accuse Cat of cheating on Rob? What business was it of hers, anyway? Their marriage was their business.

'Why so sad, pretty lady?'

Laura looked up with a start.

'Alex!' she cried, jumping up. 'I didn't know you were coming!'

'We're all travelling to Cat's birthday together. I must say, I thought from the number of drivers sitting along the street this party had been a triumph, but then I see you over here looking forlorn in the corner and I'm not so sure. What's up?'

Laura looked around them. 'Where's Isabella?'

'I— Turin with her family. Why?'

She paused for a moment, looking at him with vehement scorn. Everything made perfect sense. The photos. The two-year lie.

'This is your flat.' It was more of an accusation than a statement.

'Yes,' he nodded, shrugging limply. 'So?'

'So it's five minutes from Min Hetherington's gallery . . .'

'Yes. So?' he repeated.

'So you and I both know she hasn't worked there for two years.' She watched the pupils in his double-ringed eyes contract. 'She's using it as a cover for her affair with you. She meets you here every week, doesn't she?'

She licked her lips and watched him, but he was impassive, clearly calculating his defence strategy.

'I was a decoy, wasn't I?' she continued, determined to provoke him. 'You made a big show of coming on to me in Verbier so that Rob wouldn't suspect you were actually sleeping with Cat.'

His sigh was all the confirmation she needed.

'Are you going to tell him?' he asked after a moment.

She looked down, conflicted. The affair made a mockery of the necklace and the all-encompassing love it represented, but Cat was her touchstone in this new life she had been thrown into without Jack and Fee.

But what about Rob? She couldn't pretend he was just her client; she couldn't pretend he meant nothing to her. He was in her head the whole time, no matter how hard she tried to banish him. To see him humiliated like this, and he didn't even know about it? How could she just stand by?

She was in an impossible situation. To defend him would be to betray Cat. And to protect Cat would be to betray him. 'I don't know. I don't know what I'm going to do,' she replied, forlornly.

'How did you find out?'

'I found the photos of her in the bedside table.' She saw the cloud darken his face. 'And before you say it, I wasn't snooping! I was looking for a damned hairdryer! It was hardly discreet to keep them in there.'

He looked away, angry that the secret had been so carelessly given away, all because of this party. 'They're old photos, taken years ago,' he said. 'You know that Cat and I were lovers for years. Of course I've got photos of her.'

'Don't try and bluff your way out of this, Alex. She's wearing her wedding ring in the pictures,' Laura disputed, bluffing herself. She hadn't noticed one way or the other whether or not Cat was wearing her ring, but she knew – absolutely knew – that it was Alex with whom Cat was having an affair. All the half-truths and part-revealed secrets had fallen into place. 'Plus I saw her getting out of your car outside the hotel on Saturday morning, and again just now. What did you do? Agree to wait ten minutes before coming up?'

Alex took a step back. 'What car?'

'Why? How many have you got?' she asked sarcastically.

He bent down so that his face was level with hers. 'When did she get out of my car?' he pressed more urgently, his eyes pinned on something behind her.

But he was too late.

'Oh good, you're here already. Are you set to go?' Rob asked over her shoulder.

466

Laura got up off the sofa arm at the sound of his voice and whirled round to face him, her wide eyes darting nervously between him and Alex.

'Everything all right?' Rob asked, his gaze taking in Laura's high flush and nervy behaviour.

'Fine.' It was good to look at him again. She hadn't seen him since the morning after in her hotel room and she felt her pulse quicken. His gaze lingered on her, but he made no move to touch her or stand closer. They had both drawn their lines in the sand.

'Where's Cat?' he asked after a moment, remembering Alex.

'Getting changed.'

'Well, do you want to give me the necklace now, then, before she comes out?'

'Uh . . .' Laura's gaze drifted towards Alex. 'No, if it's okay, I'd rather give it to you when we get there. I just need to, uh, decide on some things first.' She saw Alex shift his weight apprehensively. 'There's something I'm still deciding on.'

'But surely it's finished, Laura,' Rob said intently. 'We're presenting it to her as soon as we get there.'

'Yes, yes, it is – it's all done. I just need to be sure I've . . . I've got it exactly the way I want it. Sometimes I, uh . . . make some last-minute tweaks.' She couldn't look at him.

Rob stuffed his hands into his pockets and stared at her through narrowed eyes. She gulped under the scrutiny, and not just because he looked so damned good in his black velvet jacket and ivory shirt. Alex was doing the same – the two of them were trying to read her mind.

'Alex, would you excuse us for a moment?' Rob said suddenly. 'Laura and I need to talk.'

'Sure,' Alex shrugged, his eyes texting to Laura a desperate plea to keep quiet.

Rob took Laura by the elbow and steered her down the hall, past the stragglers, past the room where Cat was even now applying the finishing touches to her birthday look. He shut and locked the bathroom door behind them. Oh God. Rob Blake in a confined space. This was a bad idea.

'You know,' he said, turning to face her.

'What? What do I know?'

'You've found out about the affair. That's why you're dithering about handing over the necklace.'

'You *know*?' Laura cried in disbelief. This wasn't what she'd been expecting him to say.

'Of course I know.' He gave his words a moment to settle. 'It's what all this is about.'

'But . . .' She was floored by the revelation.

'I know perfectly well that Cat and Min aren't close. Including Min in this necklace is an anomaly that will stand out to Cat immediately, and will show her that I know about the affair.' He inhaled sharply. 'I – and that I forgive her.'

'You're going to just forget about it?'

'I never said *that*. But it's in the past. The affair was never about *him* anyway – he's just a symptom of her problems. Cat's damaged, Laura – you know that now. She's spent her whole life feeling like her birth had to compensate for Daniel's death. She had to be her parents' saviour, even though it meant destroying her relationship with her sister in the process, and for what? They divorced anyway. She failed. Wherever she looks at her family, she failed. She thinks she let them down, and now she thinks she's let me down. But I won't give up on her, Laura –' his voice dropped '– not even for you.'

What? Laura felt the shock ricochet through her at his unexpected words. 'I . . . would never ask you to,' she faltered.

A beat pulsed. 'I know.'

His eyes held hers and the world stopped spinning – just for a second, but enough to make her feel weightless and giddy, as if she was floating from one world into another. What couldn't – wouldn't – be said crashed off the walls, buffeting them both with a physical force that almost knocked her off her feet.

He turned away, shaking his head slowly. 'But it's . . . it's pointless to . . .' His voice trailed away. It was pointless to even finish the sentence. They let silence fill the air. Rob paced back to the window.

'I can't just turn my back on her. She's my wife. Another man broke her heart and she's been through hell because of it. I've had to stand back, pretending I didn't know, but I can't do it any more. The guilt's destroying her. She wouldn't let me near her for months after the affair ended; she even went to see a therapist, supposedly to talk through her child-hood, but it isn't going away, not really. She pretends to care about clothes and parties, dabbles a bit in design projects, but you saw for yourself on Friday what she does to get through. She's sinking – she can't do it alone. It's time for her to know that I know and that we'll get through it together.'

'But why don't you just confront her, then? Why bother with this necklace at all? Why did you have to drag m-me into it?' Laura cried. *Couldn't he see what he'd done to her?* Her life had imploded as a result of this necklace . . . as a result of him . . .

He walked up to her in three strides, placing his hands on her trembling arms. 'I'm so sorry, Laura,' he said in a low, urgent voice. 'Getting involved with you was the very last thing I thought would happen. I never imagined I could feel for anyone else what I feel for Cat. Falling for you was *not* part of the plan.'

Laura felt herself reel from his words as he immediately stepped back away from her, back to a distance they were both safe with.

'But if she's going to believe that I forgive her,' he continued, 'then she first has to believe that I understand her too, and this necklace is my best chance of proving that to her. I have to try, Laura.'

Laura watched him, letting her heart break in silence. He mustn't hear it. His love for Cat was unconditional, untouchable, as it should be. There was nothing more to be said.

'It's in my bag. I'll go and get it for you,' she said with effort, unable to meet his eyes, too scared they'd betray her.

She unlocked the door and walked towards the sitting room. Only Cat and Alex were in there now, chatting nonchalantly by the windows and surrounded by the party planners tidying away around them. Laura saw that all her charms had been neatly packed into the boxes as someone checked off the inventory she'd made. She watched the charade as Cat, dressed in a strapless gold crêpe minidress, chatted amiably to Alex in low tones, his gaze soft and smitten on her face.

'Oh, there you are!' Cat said, hearing Laura's footsteps. 'And what exactly were you doing locked away in a room with my husband?' she teased, standing up.

'Rob was talking me through a tax-break set-up for the business, now that it's gone to the next level,' Laura replied, thinking on her feet, as Rob followed down the hall after her.

'Well, if we're all ready . . .' Alex said, jumping up nervously, his eyes diverted from Rob's as he motioned towards the door.

Rob caught Laura's eye and gave the barest of headshakes. She would have to give him the necklace at the party.

'Okay, so let's go,' Rob said with a tight smile, making a beeline for Cat and bending down to kiss her. 'It's no good having a birthday party with no birthday girl.'

'I can't wait to find out what you've got up your sleeve this year,' Cat smiled. 'I didn't think anything could beat last year's surprise party in the Serpentine Gallery.'

'We'll be right with you. I'll just help Laura with this bag,' Alex called after them as they descended the stairs.

'What happened? What did he want?' he demanded, anxiety crawling over him like ants as soon as they were out of sight.

Laura shot him a look of withering disdain. 'He knows all about you and Cat. He has done since the beginning. But he's not going to give her up, Alex. He doesn't see you as a threat. He refuses to roll over and let his marriage die.'

Her words settled like blows. No threat?

She reached down and snapped shut the lid on a tower of stackable boxes. 'It's over, Alex. Tonight he's going to let Cat know that he knows. That's what the necklace is all about.'

'No, I don't believe you.' Alex stared at her. 'I know Rob. He scarcely tolerates me as it is. He'd knock ten bells out of me if he knew I was sleeping with his wife and he *certainly* wouldn't invite me to go skiing in Verbier.'

'Actually, he would. Every charm on the necklace tells Cat's story, right up to the very last one that points the finger at your affair. He knows that Cat's a product of her past, and he's using the necklace to show her that he not only knows about you both, but he forgives her too. He's going to show her that her relationship with you only began as a direct result of her broken childhood.'

Alex laughed softly. 'When we were seventeen, maybe. But *this* affair with me began as a direct result of the miscarriage.'

'Miscarriage?' The shock was like a slap. 'But Rob's never once mentioned they were pregnant. Why wouldn't h—?'

His expression stopped her.

'Oh God. *They* weren't . . .' she whispered.

Alex shook his head and Laura instinctively held her breath as the full ramifications of his words sank in: their affair started up only after the miscarriage? So then the baby hadn't been his either.

'Whose baby was it?' she demanded.

'She never told me his name, and I never asked. I didn't want to know who the bastard was – he'd succeeded where Rob and I failed. But he propelled her back into my arms, so what did I care? I was just happy to get her back.' He sighed heavily at the memory. 'God, she was a mess. I'd never seen her like that. She just turned up on my doorstep in Milan one day and seduced me in my own damned porch – straight back to our old ways. Because when the chips are down, it's *always* me she comes back to.'

He looked back at Laura. 'What? Why are you looking at me like that? Cat knows I know the score. She knows I'll never ask more from her than she's prepared to give. Don't you get it? Rob can't help her, Laura! He suffocates her. Do you have any idea what it's like for her living with a man who adores her so completely, and who she just doesn't feel anything for in return?'

Laura stared at him, mute. She knew *exactly* how that felt.

Poor, sweet Jack had been alone in their relationship too; she had never been able to match his devotion. Was this what had drawn her and Cat together?

'Their entire life is an act, Laura. Look, don't get me wrong. Cat doesn't want to hurt him. She loves him as much as she can, but it's just not in the way he wants. He knows the marriage is on its knees. Her husband is not the man she loves – but neither am I.'

Laura looked at him and saw all the devastation in his eyes she would have expected to find in Rob's. For all his two-faced treachery to Rob, Alex's love for Cat was true. She had known it in Verbier.

'Then who is? I saw her with my own eyes. When she got out of that car, she practically floated across the floor.'

He winced at her words. 'I don't know. But *I* don't have a car in this country.'

'So then it's *his* car,' she murmured. 'She's cheating on both of you. She's seeing *him* again.'

# Chapter Forty-Four

Even in the dark, a camel with territorial issues has a distinctive sound all its own, and Sugar scored a bullseye on the passenger-side window as they passed, indicating that they had arrived. At only just gone half past eight, they were pretty much on time; traffic had been forgivingly light, which they had all – for their own reasons – been grateful for. Laura could feel a definite edge in the atmosphere between the four of them, as though there were invisible blades hanging from the ceiling that only showed themselves in the glint of the lights of passing cars. Occasionally, Rob had stretched his hand over from the steering wheel on to Cat's lap, squeezing her thigh – a gesture not missed by either Laura or Alex in the back seat – as Cat turned the music up higher and higher, ready to party, and drowning out the possibility of easy conversation.

Laura had taken the opportunity to think and reassess, ignoring the weighty stares Alex kept throwing her in the dark as newly revealed facts tumbled around in her head. Rob's motives for commissioning the bracelet had been more double-sided than she'd ever realized. Its message was as much about forgiveness as about love, but Rob didn't know as much as he thought he did. How prescient he'd been on the plane when he'd said she'd end up knowing more about his wife than he did.

Laura almost groaned with relief when she set eyes upon Kitty's crooked cottage again. The lights inside glowed orange and welcoming, and after chandeliers and marble, it felt so good to scale back down to an ordinary home – particularly this one, with its round-the-clock cakes, animal residents and feral children.

Cat clearly didn't agree and she shot Rob a shocked look as they parked. *'Seriously?'* she whispered.

'What? Don't be like that,' he murmured back. 'Kit wanted to do this for you. She pleaded with me. You know she's been asking for years. It gets embarrassing having to keep coming up with excuses for you, Cat. Why can't you just let her, for once?'

'It's my birthday, Rob,' Cat hissed. 'You said it would be somewhere special.'

The front door was on the latch, and Nat King Cole was crooning not too loudly on the record player in case he should wake the kids. Pocket, who deigned to come to the door to greet them for once, was wearing tinsel round her neck and a forlorn expression since her sofa had been requisitioned for the party and had a tower of coats thrown over it. The small Christmas tree in the hall had taken a significant turn for the worse since Laura's last visit a week ago, and now looked like it had been shaved, the gingerbread decorations openly half eaten.

Joe looked up from pouring some drinks as they trooped in, smiling broadly at Rob, marginally less at Cat and Alex, and not at all at Laura.

'Well, that's what I call timing!' he said, placing glasses in everyone's hands. 'Cat, happy birthday,' he said, kissing her properly on one cheek (he didn't approve of continental-style double kisses). The fire behind them was leaping so high, Laura wouldn't have been surprised if you could see the flames peeking out of the top of the chimney, and she took a step away. She was quite warm enough in her velvet tux.

'Thanks, Joe. Where's Kit?' Cat asked, carefully lifting her foot over Pocket's water bowl, which had somehow been pushed into the middle of the kitchen floor. Joe – looking surprisingly distinguished in a loden blazer and cranberry-pink cords rather than his usual boiler suit and mud – removed it without comment.

'Still upstairs, having a wardrobe freak-out. Nothing fits apparently.' He shook his head. 'But then she says that every time and she always ends up looking lovely.'

'I'll g—' Laura began.

'Let me go sort her out,' Cat smiled, patting Joe's hand. 'I've got her birthday present in the car.'

Laura closed her eyes in dismay, remembering too late that it was Kitty's birthday in four days – Kitty had told her they'd always shared their parties as children – and realizing she had nothing to give. Yet again, she was impinging upon their hospitality and turning up empty-handed. She wondered whether the bottles of Piper still in her bag would suffice.

Cat disappeared, the light wattage in the room appearing to dim with her departure.

'It looks like you've got everything nicely under control here,' Rob said, making small talk as Laura and the three men lapsed into an awkward silence. She instinctively knew that her presence was inhibiting them from diving straight into talking about the Premiership and poor pheasant numbers.

'Yep. Kitty's been cooking for England these past few days – there's been no stopping her. It's like therapy or something. She's got herself in a right state about tonight.' His eyes – flint-hard and cold – met Laura's for the briefest of moments. 'The others are in the drawing room waiting for you – let's go through and talk in there.'

They filed through the tiny hall into the drawing room, Laura quickly ducking into the boot room to deposit the bags. When she'd stayed here as a guest, the drawing room had been out of bounds, with the heating turned off and the door very firmly shut ('to keep the ducks out,' Kitty had sighed). Tonight, it had come to life and twinkled like a tree decoration. Long and low-beamed, with an antique pink and brown marble fireplace in the middle, home-made stockings were hanging from nails banged into the walls ready for tomorrow night. There were thick, squashy sofas in faded strawberry velvet, pale green curtains and table covers trimmed with heavy braided bullion, and a deeply pocketed square ottoman sat squatly amidst all the sofas. Although the scheme was undeniably 'tired' and Eighties, it still managed to evoke a faded grandeur.

There were a few – not many, but nice – antiques dotted about too, and an abundance of candles cast a gloriously flickering and flattering light. Laura particularly liked the unfashionable cut-crystal bowls that had been filled with glistening pomegranate seeds so that they looked like pirates' treasure, and the door and window frames were draped with thick home-made (so therefore slightly uneven) swags of eucalyptus and holly berries that hung extravagantly to the floor like fur scarves. And in the middle of the room, just to the right of where they were congregated, a huge swirl of mistletoe hung from the central beam like a piñata, swinging so low that Rob, Alex and Joe had to dodge to avoid it.

Laura took one look at the Christmas tree in the corner and instantly forgave the pale imitation in the hall – Christmas wasn't anywhere near as patchy in the Baker household as she might have been led to believe. Thick, bushy and the blackest of greens, Laura guessed it had been hacked from the nearby woodland; the fresh pine scent fragranced the room more beautifully than any Jo Malone home spray. Beneath the lower fronds, dozens of parcels wrapped in snowman paper (obviously a jumbo roll) were peeking through. At the back, Laura could see a shape that was clearly a bicycle, but wrapped nonetheless from handlebars to wheels, with an enormous yellow rosette on top. From the size of it, she guessed it was for Tom.

Laura took in the other guests as she stood at the doorway – David, Sam and Orlando were standing by the ancient fireplace – and realized it was Verbier Mark II.

'Finally!' Sam exhorted with customary charm and grace as she caught sight of them.

'Sorry, we got a little caught up,' Rob said, soothing her with a kiss. 'The girls had a party in London first.'

'The girls . . . ?' Sam echoed.

'Cat and Laura. It was a launch do for Laura's business.'

'Oh! And what was I? NFI?' Sam asked tetchily.

'Cat knew she'd be seeing you here. Besides, it was just a business thing, wasn't it, Laura?' Rob said diplomatically as he looked across at her, giving no indication of the intimate and emotionally charged conversation they had shared just an hour earlier. 'By the way, did Penryn show?'

'Yes, he did,' Laura nodded, scarcely able to meet his eyes. He had a right to know what was going on in his own marriage, but did it have to be her who told him? 'It's all going ahead for the Fashion Week tents. And he's going to introduce me to the buyer at Liberty.'

'What an achievement – congratulations!' David said, leaning down to kiss her. 'And I trust your family emergency was sorted? We did so miss you, even just for those last few hours.'

Laura blushed to remember her flight from Verbier and she kept her eyes well away from Rob's. 'Thank you, yes. A false alarm.'

'*Bella!*' Orlando roared, bounding over. 'You look divine! Such a fashion plate – who knew, uh? You look just like one of my ladies.'

'I look nothing like your ladies, Orlando,' Laura smiled. 'I would stick out like a robber with a swag bag next to them.'

'Mmm – before maybe. But now . . . I love it, this suit. It reminds me of someone else . . .' he said meaningfully, and Laura realized he was referring to his and Cat's escapade in Milan. 'I think I can guess who took you shopping.' Orlando pulled the jacket forward a little and caught a glimpse of the floppy silk shirt beneath. 'Although it would have been even sexier with nothing underneath it,' he grinned.

'Funnily enough, I like to be fully dressed when I go out,' Laura chided, prompting an amused chuckle from David.

'Enough of this chit-chat – where's Cat?' Sam interrupted. 'I want to get on with the main event and see this damned necklace once and for all. I want to see how Laura's represented *me*.' Her tone suggested there was an 'or else' element to the statement. 'You have got it with you, I hope? We wouldn't want any awkward best man moments.'

'Yes. It's here.'

'Cat's upstairs with Kitty. I'm sure they won't be lo— Oh!'

Rob said, his eyes focusing on something behind Sam, prompting her to turn.

An astonished silence fell as Kitty entered, although no one could be a hundred per cent certain it *was* Kitty. Her hair was as straight as a rod, her eyes were blackened, and she was wearing a dark plum lipstick on her bow-shaped mouth. There was no sign of her freckles – had they been lasered off? – and she was squeezed into a silver cocktail dress that was very clearly several sizes too small.

Everyone watched in degrees of wonder and horror as her bosom wobbled magnificently, scarcely contained by the cutaway neckline and balconette bra Cat had put her in. It had to be said, though, that her ankles looked magnificent.

'How sexy is your wife?' Cat demanded of Joe as Kitty skittered in, almost having to walk diagonally, the skirt was so tight.

'What have you done to her?' Joe asked, aghast, as Kitty took a drink gratefully from David and necked it.

'My birthday present,' Cat sighed happily. 'Cost a bomb, but when you've been friends for as long as we have . . .'

Laura looked over at Kitty's panic-stricken face. She was barely recognizable under all the make-up. 'Hi, Kitty,' she smiled.

Kitty nodded. 'Laura.' But she made no move to enfold Laura in her arms the way she usually did – partly, no doubt, because she was terrified to even breathe in that dress. But Laura instinctively understood now the new settings of their tentative friendship. Joe's look in the kitchen had been the first indication that Rob had been right – by skipping across the car park with Cat that night, she had hurt her new friend. She'd done exactly what Joe had predicted she would and chosen the bright, shiny girl instead.

And wasn't she just! Laura looked at Cat standing next to her, glistening like a new penny in the firelight in her pale gold dress, her champagne-blonde hair smoothed back into a low, self-tying ponytail that was now draped over one glossy shoulder. She looked gilded, as if she'd been sprinkled with fairy dust, and even knowing what she now knew, Laura could still feel herself falling for the illusion of perfection all over again.

But it was all a shimmering mirage, she knew that now. The closer Laura got to Cat, the more she saw that her life was a house of cards on the brink of collapse, with secrets whistling past like eddies of wind. Behind the dazzling image, Cat was flawed, broken and fragile, and guilty of actions that only a past as dark as hers could begin to explain.

Laura's attention slid over to Alex. How could he do it – stand here in front of Rob and pretend he wasn't stabbing a friend in the back every time he smiled? Except that he wasn't looking so cocksure right now. His eyes were on the floor, he had one hand in his pocket, and she knew he wasn't listening to the spirited conversation – he was back in his Kensington flat, learning from Laura that the only lover who'd ever captured Cat's heart was back in the game. He looked depressed and defeated, she thought, and Laura wondered whether he was tiring finally of playing third fiddle in Cat's life, of remaining a secret.

Not that ending the affair was going to be his call. Rob may only know half the story, but he knew the half that mattered. Cat didn't love Alex; he wasn't the threat. By Alex's own admission, their affair – for Cat at least – was a consequence of comfort and habit, not passion. Alex was but a mere footnote in the sweeping passions of Cat's love life and everything was going to change tonight with the presentation of the necklace. When Rob showed Cat that he knew about the other affair – the one that had really threatened their marriage – they would be able to wipe the slate clean of all her old mistakes and start facing everything together. And if Rob could forgive, how could Cat not try to move forward too?

Kitty sidled off – quite literally – to get some canapés from the kitchen. Laura wanted to go after her but Sam demanded to know where she'd bought her suit, and Laura sensed her stock had risen since she had become closer to Cat.

'So what are you doing for Christmas?' Sam asked, peering over the rim of her glass. She was wearing a black dress with a cutaway 'racing' shoulderline, and an organza rose swirled at her throat.

'Nothing extraordinary. Just spending it at home.'

'In Sussex.'

'Suffolk.'

'Are you near the sea where you live?'

'Yes, very. I can see it from my bedroom window. I love it. Have you ever been?'

'No reason to,' she shrugged. 'I grew up in Cheshire, boarded in Berkshire, straight into London. I suppose unless you know someone there, or there's a specific reason, why would you go?'

'I suppose.'

There was a small silence, but Laura didn't begin to try to fill it for once. She had to talk to either Rob or Cat – but which? Should she warn Rob about the full extent of his wife's lies, or try to convince Cat to do the right thing by Rob?

'So what's your boyfriend getting you for Christmas?' Sam asked.

Laura inhaled. Dammit – of all the questions. 'Actually, he won't be getting me anything. We broke up.'

'Oh shit,' Sam replied in a quiet, tactful voice. 'That's out of the blue, isn't it?'

'Yes. But I guess that's how it goes. Something's fine until it's not.'

'Is that why you scarpered, then?'

Laura tossed her hair to check Rob wasn't listening. His eyes were on the fire, but something about the angle of his head made her think his concentration was on her conversation and not his. Unsurprisingly. He was probably checking she wasn't about to drop him in it with his wife's best friend. She looked back at Sam. 'Yes, that's right.'

'Bugger. I'm really sorry for you. How long were you together for again?'

'Four years.'

'Ouch! And you're not getting any younger.'

Laura couldn't help but smile. Sam was abrupt, but there was no malice that Laura could detect in the comment. 'Yes. I'd better start getting serious about finding a husband,' she joked.

'Well, you'll have no worries – you've been Catted. Actually, I bet she's got some eligible fellas lined up.' Laura's irony had been lost on her and Sam's sincerity was almost sweet. 'Hey, Cat!' Sam called across. 'Know any nice single guys for Laura?'

All conversation ceased and Laura sighed in despair.

'Oh! I know, poor Laura,' Cat smiled sympathetically, coming over and clutching Laura's arm just as Kitty came back in with a tray of mini beef Wellingtons. 'I mean, how could anybody cheat on *her*? She can do so much better.' She turned directly to Laura. 'We'll find you someone.'

Kitty thrust out the tray, and a series of manicured hands

dived forwards. Laura saw the hurt on Kitty's face that she was the last to learn about something as major in Laura's life as this.

'Honestly, I was joking,' Laura protested, embarrassed that this line of conversation had hijacked the party. 'I'm really not looking.'

'Yeah, but you're what – thirty-five?' Sam protested.

'Thirty-two.'

'Exactly. Time's not on your side.'

Cat looked over at Rob. 'What about Valentine Garson? Isn't he divorced now?'

There was a slight pause. 'Yes, on account of his incessant wanderings.'

'Hmmm.' Cat wrinkled her nose. 'Well, you've had quite enough of that for one lifetime. Oooh, Mike Kemp?'

'Just married his third wife.'

'Ah, shame,' Cat tutted.

'No, not really. He's fonder of his hookers than the various Mrs Kemps.'

'Ugh! How about Marcus Higson?'

'Too short.'

'Henning Thingamabob?'

'Weak handshake.'

'Oscar Shipton?'

'Tends to spit when he talks.'

'Dan Ashley?' Cat asked with narrowed eyes. 'He's gorgeous.'

'And yet to discover personal space. Practically stands on your toes when talking to you.'

'Stop, please!' Laura laughed, desperately trying to make light of the situation. 'Really, I'm not interested.'

'It's just as well, Laura! According to Rob, there's no one

out there good enough for you.' Cat looked back at her husband. '*I've* never had that with Dan.'

'That's because you always sit on his lap when you talk to him, darling.'

Sam chuckled, delighted by this unexpected foray into character assassination, especially from someone as measured and diplomatic as Rob. 'Well, if I was single, I can tell you who I'd be going after,' she said, winking at David. 'Don't worry, darling – I'm not wishing you dead quite yet.'

'Who?' Orlando asked with an intonation that suggested he might join the race.

'That artist chap, Ben Jackson. He's lush.'

Her use of the word 'lush' drew Laura up short. It was such a Feeism. She felt a stab of pain again at their separation; it had been more than ten days now, and as the days were ticking by, she was beginning to miss her old friend more, not less.

'Why would you go after *him*?' Cat asked with disdain. 'He's hairy and looks like he hasn't washed for years, and he's unspeakably arrogant. He was a nightmare to work with.'

'Yes, but he's got that twinkle, hasn't he? We saw him at a charity thing in New York a few weekends ago, and if I was any less principled than I mercifully am, I'd have been in there. He was hitting on me big-style. He's one naughty boy.'

'Really?' Cat asked.

'He was mobbed when we saw him last week too, but I don't see it either,' Laura shrugged.

'Trust me, that boy can conjure more passion with a single brushstroke than Nadal playing a Wimbledon final in his undies.'

There was a small silence as the image rebounded in

everyone's heads. Orlando looked particularly happy, but Laura felt distracted. Something was niggling in her mind like a tickle. What was it?

Kitty gave a light clap of her hands. 'Well, Olive's called to say she's been held up at work but will be here shortly.'

'Like hell she will,' Cat muttered. 'It's just her usual game-playing, trying to show me how important her job is. Why's she coming tonight anyway? I didn't ask her. It's my birthday. It's supposed to be a celebration.'

'*I* asked her to be here. I thought it was important,' Rob said, stroking her arm soothingly.

'Did you have to promise to make a donation to one of her charities in return?' Cat asked, a cruel sneer twisting her beautiful mouth.

Rob hesitated. His wife's mood and behaviour were plummeting fast. 'It'll be okay, darling.'

But Cat just moved away.

'Well, shall we give a few of the other pressies now, while we wait?' Kitty asked hurriedly, diverting attention from the tension.

A murmur of assent rose up and everybody moved towards a small heap of presents piled on to one of the sofas. Cat wasn't looking especially excited about the prospect. In fact, she was looking far from it. Laura dashed to get hers, which was still in her bag in the boot room. Something was still niggling annoyingly in the back of her mind.

She returned carrying a soft silver-wrapped parcel significantly bigger than any of the others and put it down amongst the rest of the presents, where it sat looking like the foil-wrapped Christmas turkey. She was embarrassed by its lack of finesse. All the others were neat rectangular packages gloved in smart matt bags.

Cat sat down and started on the pile. Sam and David's present was a leather-buckled Ralph Lauren photo frame with a black-and-white photo of Cat in it, taken in Verbier. Orlando had bought her some Crème de la Mer products. Alex (and supposedly Isabella) gave her a light pink cashmere travel blanket, and Kitty and Joe presented her with a hamper of Kitty's jams and chutneys, fruit cake and half of one of their pigs presented as sausages, chops, ribs and belly.

Laura shifted nervously as Cat opened the unwieldy parcel. Her response to the other gifts had been muted, to say the least, and Laura was beginning to harbour serious doubts that she'd chosen wisely.

Cat pulled out the black shaggy 'rock princess' jacket as if it was a dead dog.

'Oh! I've never had anything from Dorothy Perkins before. How . . . exciting.'

'I thought it would look nice with your black jeans and those new ankle boots,' Laura mumbled, wishing the ground would swallow her up.

'. . . Yes . . . Great idea. Thanks.'

The jacket fell to the chair, lifeless and unloved, and she knew it would have been better appreciated if there'd been a Roberto Cavalli label inside instead.

Everybody looked embarrassed and the party atmosphere fizzled out like a damp firework.

'Cat?' Rob asked, taking a step towards her again.

'Oh, don't fuss, Rob! I'm just hot next to the fire. I'm going to run some water over my wrists.'

She left the room.

'Is anyone else too hot?' Kitty asked solicitously. 'I could open the windows.'

But they all protested they were absolutely fine, falling

into small groups again and picking up the conversations they'd been having before Laura's search for a husband had come to dominate.

Kitty noticed a crisp on the floor and automatically bent down to retrieve it. The way she stopped – as if frozen – halfway down, was as telling as the unmistakable sound of too much flesh escaping too little fabric. There was a collective tilt of heads as everyone struggled to identify what they'd heard before giving up and turning back to their partners.

But Laura knew what had happened and she immediately took a step in front of Kitty, blocking her off from the rest of the party.

'Kitty,' she said quickly, taking her by the elbow and rotating her out of view. 'I know you're busy, but do you remember saying you'd give me the recipe for that plum cake? I'd love to get it off you now if I could, before dinner.'

'Okay,' Kitty replied, the mortification and gratitude both easy to read in her eyes.

Kitty turned, with Laura hot on her heels to shield her from behind, Kitty's turquoise knickers clearly visible as they walked. But it was easier for Kitty to move now, and they were out of the room within moments. Kitty hid her face in her hands the second they were out of sight.

'Oh, Kitty, please don't cry!' Laura beseeched her as her shoulders began to heave. 'I swear no one noticed. Really. Kitty?'

Kitty dropped her hands away to reveal the tears that were streaming down her cheeks. 'I can't believe that just happened,' she laughed, leaning against the wall. 'Isn't that just my bloody luck? I can't even begin to think what Joe will say later. I know he heard it – I saw his face.' The laughs came faster again and she doubled over, leaping away slightly as her exposed bottom touched the cold plaster. 'Bloody awful dress anyway.'

She turned and showed off her peek-a-boo knickers and laughed even harder, and Laura joined in as she saw, properly, how enormous the split was, running for six or more inches down the back seam.

'Do you think we can sew me back in?' she cried, hiccupping madly and making them laugh even harder again.

'I don't think so, Kit, not without an industrial sewing machine,' Laura managed through her own tears.

'Oh noooo! What am I going to tell Cat? She'll be livid. She said it cost a bomb,' Kitty sniffed as her giggles subsided finally. 'I can't just walk back in wearing something completely different.'

'We can, uh . . . we can say you had to change because you got some gravy on it and you're soaking it out before it stains. Then just get it repaired. She'll never know.'

Kitty's shoulders sagged. 'But what shall I wear instead?'

Laura thought for a moment. 'What about that waisted Fifties dress that was hanging up in my room when I stayed over? The teal one. I bet you look lovely in it.'

'But isn't it a bit . . . old-fashioned? I mean, look at you and Sam and Cat . . .'

'Kitty, it suits *you*. That style flatters your shape. You'll look a thousand times better in something you're comfortable wearing. And I bet Joe loves you in it, doesn't he?'

'It is his favourite. It was his mother's, actually.'

Of course it was! In this house, if it wasn't inherited . . . Laura smiled, her head tipped to the side. 'Now I have to see you in it.'

'Okay,' Kitty replied, relieved at the thought of putting on something that actually fitted and would accommodate tasks such as breathing. 'And do you think, while I'm up there, the make-up . . . ?' She wrinkled her nose.

Laura wrinkled hers back. 'Yeah, I would. It's a bit . . . harsh. Bring your freckles back.'

Kitty took Laura's hand and squeezed it. 'Thanks for saving me in there. I'd never have heard the end of it if Sam had caught wind of what happened.'

'I've got your back. That's what friends are for.'

Kitty hugged her suddenly. 'Yes. It is.' And she covered her bottom with her hands and ran knock-kneed up the stairs, giggling again.

# Chapter Forty-Five

Laura turned to go back to the others, feeling her heart lift inside her like a bucket being pulled up a well, when she caught sight of Cat leaning against the bathroom door, staring.

From the look on her face, it was clear she had heard every word.

Laura gulped. 'Kitty's dress split when she bent over,' she said quietly.

Cat gave a small disgusted snort and disappeared back into the bathroom again. Laura hesitated before following after her. She was shocked to find Cat leaning with her face against the mirror, her hands either side of her head as though she was trying to push through the glass to the other side.

'Cat? What's wrong?'

Cat simply shook her head, rolling her forehead from side to side across the cold glass, her eyes closed, a thick make-up brush held in one hand like a cigarette.

'Are you feeling okay? Do you want me to get Rob?'

But that merely prompted a dismissive laugh. Cat remained pressed to the mirror as though she was trying to cool down, and as the minutes passed, Laura began to wonder whether she was dozing or had forgotten she wasn't alone. In the eerie stillness, her eyes fell to the brush in Cat's hand and finally her brain made the connection she had been reaching for, and she felt the shock burn through her like a blazing comet.

'Cat, after the auction on Friday . . . where did you end up staying?'

The question seemed to bring Cat round and she inhaled sharply, pushing herself away and staring appraisingly at her own reflection as though she was deciding which lip gloss to wear.

'Nowhere special,' she murmured. 'I was flying by the time I heard Rob had taken you back; I went back with some friends who were carrying on the party at their place. It was easier to crash at theirs.'

'Oh right.' Laura watched as Cat closed one eye and dabbed a charcoal-grey powder on her lids. 'So then in the morning . . . ?'

'I caught a cab back. I think I probably only just missed you.' She caught sight of Laura's expression in the mirror and pulled back. 'What? *What?*'

Laura hesitated. 'You didn't miss me. I saw you. I saw you getting out of his car.'

Cat's hand dropped, sprinkling grey powder on to the white porcelain. 'Whose car?' There was a coolness in her tone.

'Ben's.' The number on the car she'd seen was personalized, not random, and proudly boasted its owner: B5H 5TK, aka brushstroke. Sam's comment just now – '*That boy can conjure more passion with a single brushstroke*' – had triggered the association. He was the man Rob had been referring to, when he'd told Laura he knew about the affair. Alex had been right. They *had* been talking at cross-purposes – not simply because he knew nothing about Alex, but because he had no idea whatsoever that things with Ben had been rekindled. He thought the affair was a dusty and cold relic of the past, his wife haunted by the weight of harbouring her guilty secret. But as Laura stood before her, Ben's name drifting like a feather to the ground between them, she knew it wasn't memories that haunted Cat, but panting anticipation and yearning for a passion that was alive and pulsing and threatened at any moment to break her heart all over again. Rob thought the future of his marriage lay in forgiving the past. But would he feel the same when he discovered it was living with them in the present?

Without a word, Cat opened her make-up bag and began dusting her face lightly with bronzer, pulling that particular 'blank' look that women the world over pull when applying make-up.

'Well, why didn't I see you?' she asked after a moment.

'I was behind a pillar.'

A ghost of a smile washed over Cat's face at the ridiculous image. 'You were *hiding* from me?'

'I was shocked to see you with another man like that. I panicked.'

Cat stared at her for a long moment. 'Laura, I'm afraid your overactive imagination has run away with you. It's not what you think. Ben's a friend.'

'He's anything but that,' Laura repudiated. 'I saw the way you were when he came over on Friday night. You couldn't look at him, you couldn't speak – you were completely thrown. It's why you insisted on upstaging him by walking out in the middle of his lot. It's why you ridiculed him in front of the entire room. It's why you had to get high. He's the one you told me about at Scott's. I assumed you were referring to someone from university or further back in your past, before you met Rob, but he's the one who broke your heart, isn't he?'

Cat fell silent, and Laura could see the quiver of self-control rippling down her skin. 'Well, let's not be bourgeois about it, Laura – people have affairs all the time. A lot of marriages only stay together *because* of them. It doesn't have to mean anything.'

'It doesn't have to, no,' Laura agreed. 'Your affair with Alex, for example, is classic rebound. Even he knows it.' She saw the utter surprise cross Cat's features. 'But it's not like that with Ben. It means everything to you.'

A long moment stretched out and Laura wondered what the next round of denials would bring. But they didn't come. Instead Cat crumpled, literally folded in on herself as hoarse, angry sobs racked her frame. She tried to shield her face with a hand, but the convulsions were too strong and she rested herself against the mirror on two locked arms, the hot tears falling smoky and black, straight from her mascaraed lashes, to mix with the charcoal powder scattered in the basin.

'I'm not judging you, Cat,' Laura said, moving over to her and resting an arm gently on her shoulders. 'I'm your friend. Talk to me. Let me help.'

'How? How can you help? How can *you* help *me*? You don't know what it's like to love someone you can't have.' The words were like individual stabs and the irony made Laura want to laugh out loud – or scream. 'Anyway, there's nothing to do about it. You heard what Sam said out there – he was chasing her tail too the other week. He doesn't care about me. He just enjoyed the fight.' She gave a small hiccup. 'It excited him, me treating him like that in front of everyone. He thought it meant I'd be more of a challenge . . . but I was a big disappointment on that score.'

Laura flinched. 'He doesn't deserve you. You're worth more than that.'

'It doesn't work like that, though, does it? We don't get to choose who we love. Your ex-boyfriend knows that only too well,' she added bitterly, her mood as volatile as the wind.

Laura refused to rise to the provocation. 'Rob loves you so much. He could make you far happier than Ben if you'd let him. He loves you unconditionally.'

Cat stared at her. 'Why would you say that?'

'Because it's true.'

Cat turned to face her, her expression intent. 'Have you told him?'

'No.'

'But you're going to.'

'I don't have to.' Laura took a deep breath. 'He already knows.' She watched as Cat – in spite of the fresh bronzer – paled before her.

'*What?*'

'He knows you had an affair with Ben and he forgives you.'

Laura watched for the relief to seep through Cat's bones as she learnt that she was so truly and wholly loved. But it never came.

'And what am I supposed to make of that?' Cat asked finally, contempt dripping from her words. 'What kind of man tolerates being married to a woman who loves someone else? How can he want to stay married to me when every breath without Ben is like a fire that scorches my lungs? I don't even know how to get through the days without him. My body hurts unless *he's* touching it. Has Rob got no self-respect?'

Laura felt a sudden flash of anger burst through her at Cat's response. 'I don't know, Cat. I guess he sees the affair as surmountable. But then he doesn't know about the baby. Maybe *that* would change things.'

The mention of the baby made Cat crumple like balled-up paper, and she sagged forwards, clutching the basin again. Laura instantly regretted her outburst.

'Cat, I—'

'I'll bet you were stunned when Jack turned round and said he didn't want you to have his baby,' Cat whispered coldly. 'Just like I was when Ben said it to me. He was glad I lost it. Did you know *that*? He knew the baby would mean I had a piece of him, even if he didn't come back to me. He knew it would have made everything bearable.' Tears flooded her haunted eyes.

Laura recoiled in shock. 'Are . . . are you saying you would have let Rob think the baby was his?'

'Why not? He wants a baby. Tons of babies. It was the ultimate win-win situation,' she replied blankly. 'Don't assume you know me because we went shopping, Laura. I won't bring a baby into the world for the wrong reasons, like my parents did. For me more than anyone, a baby has to come from love or nothing at all.'

Laura looked back at her sympathetically. Cat wouldn't realize how very much Laura did know and understand about her until she received the necklace. 'If you're saying you won't give Rob a child, you have to tell him. You owe him that much.'

Cat straightened up. 'But I am going to give him a child. We've been trying for a while now. I've moved on. Ben is in the past.'

Laura stared at her in disbelief. Cat was such an elegant

liar – no wonder Rob had been fooled. Laura leant in closer, her hand accidentally knocking the make-up bag off the edge of the sink as she did so. 'No he's not. I saw you getting out of his car today.' She crouched down to replace the contents.

'It's just a fling. I'm not stupid, Laura. I don't harbour any expectations that it'll ever be more than that.'

'I don't believe you. I know you're still in love with Ben. I saw what you were like with him.'

Cat shifted her weight, arms folded across her chest as she watched Laura scoop numerous bronzers and highlighters into the bag. 'What is this? What are you trying to do here?'

Laura looked up. 'I'm just trying to help. You have to be honest with Rob about everything if the two of you are going to move forward.'

'No. You're trying to split us up. You know Rob would leave me if he knew about the baby. You know he'll leave me if he finds out I'm seeing Ben again. You want me to press the self-destruct button on my own marriage so that you can have him for yourself.'

'What? No!' Laura stood up quickly.

'You really must think I'm blind. I've seen you *bonding* – going on your dawn skiing trips together, holding him just that bit too tight on the skidoo, dancing just that bit too close at the auction, getting him to take you back, alone, to the hotel.'

'Nothing happened.'

'Maybe not yet. But you want it to, don't you?'

'No!'

'Don't lie, Laura. You're not very good at it. This becoming blush gives you away every time,' she murmured, running a finger along Laura's cheek. 'I can almost see why it's worked such a treat on him. He's properly rattled by you – always trying to work you out and know what you've said, as though he thinks I believe that we're all "just friends". Bless him, I think he really does believe it himself.'

'My loyalty is to you.'

A beat passed between them. 'Well then, if that's true, you'll make sure Rob never finds out any of this.' Cat stared back at her reflection, smoothing her ponytail as if it was a pet.

Laura felt her heart thumping wildly. This was it – the moment when she had to choose. 'Does anybody else know? Sam? Orlando?'

'It's just you and me.' Cat's eyes met hers in unison.

You and me. She was part of a unit again. Not alone after all. Laura looked down despairingly, her eyes falling on a small purple packet by Cat's foot. She automatically picked it up to return it to the make-up bag when she noticed the short row of white pills still sitting in the foil. Aghast, she looked back at Cat. 'You're trying for a baby, are you?' she asked sarcastically.

'Give me that!' Cat tried to snatch the pills out of her hand, but Laura was too fast and pulled her arm away.

'You've got no intention of giving Rob a baby. Unless . . .' She looked at the packet closer – none of the pills had been taken since Friday, the day of the auction. The night she'd reignited the affair with Ben. Laura started to laugh, a dry, brittle, joyless sound more like a cough. 'You just stood here and told me you don't harbour any expectations that this will be anything more than a fling. But you're doing it all over again. You're trying to get pregnant with *Ben*'s baby.'

'Don't try to take the moral high ground with me,' Cat hissed, grabbing the pills suddenly and pushing them into her bra. 'You couldn't have Jack's baby, and I can't have Rob's.'

'If you won't tell him, I will. He deserves to know.'

Cat's hand dropped to her side, her eyes icy. 'Funny. Isn't

that *just* what Fee said when she told Jack you were pregnant? You told me yourself it was your body, your call. You've been in my shoes, Laura, and you took exactly the same stance. We're the same, you and me.'

Laura stared at the beautiful face, so similar to hers they'd been mistaken for sisters. But the woman staring back at her was a stranger. 'No we're not,' she murmured. 'We're nothing alike. I was going to tell Jack about the pregnancy. I only needed time. I could never do what you're doing.'

Cat was on her in an instant, slamming Laura against the wall, her face so close their noses almost touched. 'Understand this,' Cat hissed. 'If you say one word out there, I *will* come back fighting. I'll leave them all in no doubt about your creeping intentions towards my husband. And who do you think they'll believe?' A small, cruel smile played upon her lips 'Who do you think they'll choose?'

Laura didn't respond. She couldn't. She felt numb. She had walked into this room wanting to help a friend in need, and was walking out pitched as an enemy. She watched as Cat calmly zipped up the make-up bag, checking herself in the mirror one final time before stalking out. Laura slumped against the wall, deeply shocked.

She vaguely heard the doorbell ring and then Olive's clipped voice in the hall.

Everybody was here now and Rob would be coming to find her any moment to ask for the necklace. It was the moment he'd been waiting for, the moment he got his wife back. Cat was his golden girl, and now, thanks to Laura, had had her entire life cast in gold to prove it. But it was all a sham. Far from representing Rob's love and forgiveness, the necklace was going to confirm Cat's lies.

And there was nothing Laura could do about it.

# Chapter Forty-Six

Laura shuffled into the boot room. Her suitcase was behind the door, bulging. Carefully she tipped it over and unzipped it, lifting out the champagne suede box that was next to the stackable trays inside. She peered in at the necklace, so beautiful and so untrue – just like the woman it was intended for. Of the seven charms, only five could be deemed to be accurate: Rob's, Olive's, Kitty's, Sam's and Orlando's. But Alex's and Min's? They were connected by the same lie, a vein of poison that tainted everything.

She heard the conversation level rise and a small round of applause come from the drawing room, and realized Kitty had reappeared as herself again. They were all just waiting for her now – or, more specifically, the necklace. The reason for entering Cat's life was upon her, and within the hour, all reason for staying in it would have gone. As much as she loved Kitty (and even Joe, for she saw what lay behind his gruffness now); as much as Orlando made her laugh and even Sam made her smile; and as much as Rob found in her the passion and vitality she tried so hard to suppress, they all belonged to Cat, and always would. Deciding between her and Cat wouldn't even be a choice.

She glimpsed a glint in the crease of her folded jeans and pulled out a stray charm that had escaped one of the trays.

She rolled it in her palm. It was one of her favourites – enigmatic, with multiple meanings . . . She gasped and quickly rummaged in her tools.

Suddenly, she knew exactly what she had to do.

Rob met her at the door as she walked back in, and she wordlessly handed the box to him. Everyone fell silent as they saw it in his hands. Cat's eyes flickered to hers as she saw her gift, understanding instantly what she was getting and exactly why Laura had come into her life; and Laura saw in that instant the disappointment register in Cat, that deep down she had always known she would find. It wasn't enough for her, but the difference was that now Laura knew nothing ever would be. What Cat really wanted, money couldn't buy and Rob couldn't give her.

'Cat,' Rob began, a tentative smile on his face, his hand over the top of the box, even though its contents couldn't possibly be a surprise. 'You're a hard woman to buy for. Every year I drive myself to the edge of insanity trying to find the one thing that will show you exactly what you mean to me, and every year I never quite make it. But this year, I *know* I've pulled it off.' He tapped the box. 'A month ago, I asked Laura to create a charm for every one of us here – with the exception of one absent friend – that encapsulated what each person meant to you. She's worked incredibly hard interviewing us all to get the stories and memories that we've each made with you, and although I haven't seen it myself yet – secretive much?' he joked at Laura, '– inside here there's a visual landscape of your entire life. A shorthand, if you like, of everything that matters to you. It includes the highs as well as the lows because I've always believed it's not fortune that shapes us but adversity – and I do love your shape!' he grinned, prompting wolf whistles from Orlando and David.

'Seriously, though, I specifically asked Laura not to airbrush what she learnt about you and your relationships, not because I want to hold a light up to your faults—'

'What faults?' Orlando interjected loyally.

Rob grinned. '. . . But because there's *nothing* I could hear about you that could ever change the way I feel.' His expression became more serious. 'I don't love you because you're perfect; I love you because you're not. I know many people look at you and see you in a certain way – they think you've got it all – but the people in this room know you've been through hard times like anyone else: your crazy childhood, your parents' divorce . . . You know what it is to have your heart broken.' His voice cracked and he paused as Cat's eyes locked with his. Laura caught the current of recognition that flashed between them – they both knew what he was really saying. 'But nothing can diminish you. You're complicated and exciting and I wouldn't have you any other way. So I want you to wear this knowing that it's made with full awareness of who you are in your entirety, and given with the entirety of my love. Happy birthday, darling.'

A single tear slid down Cat's curved cheek. 'Oh, Rob,' she whispered, placing a hand on his chest and looking up at him. 'I don't deserve you.'

'Never say that,' he murmured, bending down to kiss her lightly on the lips. Laura stared into the fire as everyone clapped and cheered, apart from Sam, who was shaking her head and saying to David, 'What's wrong with Cartier?'

Carefully, Cat opened the box, a gasp of genuine surprise escaping her as the firelight caught the precious metal and it twinkled before her. 'Oh my God, it's beautiful!' she whispered in amazement, automatically catching Laura's eye and forgetting the ferocious threats she had made not ten minutes earlier.

After a moment's polite restraint, everyone else leaned in and peered at it too, gasping and cooing as if it was a baby bird in a nest.

'Oh, Laura!' Kitty cried. 'It's absolutely gorgeous. How on earth did you *do* that?'

'Fuck me,' Sam muttered, looking up at David. 'Scrap what I just said. I want one of those.'

'Thanks, mate,' David said, rolling his eyes as Rob patted him on the arm consolingly.

Rob looked over at her, respect mingling with something else – sadness? – in his eyes, and she realized he was saying goodbye. The solitary moments they had shared – glimpses of another path – were in their rear-view mirror now. He was moving forward with his wife.

Cat's finger lightly pushed over the charms and they jingled prettily.

'Can you guess which one's mine?' Rob asked in Cat's ear, as much in the dark as she was.

'What am I?' Sam demanded, frowning.

'Well, I'd have to say bossy, noisy—' Alex began, earning himself a wallop in the stomach.

Cat shook her head. 'I'm trying to guess.'

'Would you like Laura to tell you?' Rob asked, and Laura took a deep breath in readiness.

But Cat, seeing the anticipation of a month's work explained, shook her head. 'No. I'll work it out. It is my life after all.'

Rob looked across at Laura, as stunned as she was. 'Sorry,' he mouthed.

'It's fine.' She was all done. It was over, then. Cat had specifically warned her not to say one *word*. There was nothing else she could do. She couldn't jeopardize Rob's hopes of making a new start with his wife. 'But if I'm not needed, then I'm afraid I have to get going.'

Six heads whipped round. *'What?'*

Kitty rushed forwards. 'But you can't! What about dinner? And we've . . . we've got some catching up to do.'

'And we will, I promise. But not tonight. I've got to get home. I've got a long journey ahead and I won't be home till after midnight. Tomorrow's Christmas Eve and I've got so much to do. But before I go, this is for you, Kit, for your birthday. You don't have to open it now if you don't want to. It can wait.'

Kitty's mouth dropped in surprise as Laura pressed a narrow suede box into her hands. 'Are you kidding? I *have* to open it now. I'll die of curiosity if I don't.' She flipped open the lid to reveal a necklace with a single charm – a golden boot with a tiny mouse peering over the top.

'Shall I explain it to you?' Laura asked.

'I already know it. *There was an old lady who lived in a shoe; she had so many children she didn't know what to do,'* Kitty giggled.

'That's right, and it's meant with fondness and affection. I'm not saying you're old, either! But you're an amazing cook and mother, and you could make a home in a car or a tent or a shoe. I love the noise and chaos in your house, with all your children and animals, and it's shown me that a quiet life isn't an ordered life, it's an empty one. I only realized when we arrived here this evening that you remind me of my own mum. You make me feel safe, like she did, and you've shown me that home's what matters – something

I've spent a long time trying to pretend wasn't really true.' She took a deep breath. 'You are one of the few people in this world I feel truly at home with.'

Kitty had her arms wrapped around Laura's neck before she'd got the last word out, big tears wetting her neck. 'Oh, Laura!'

'I'm sorry I messed up before,' Laura whispered into her hair. 'It won't happen again.'

Kitty blinked back at her and Laura knew she was forgiven. Cat might keep the others, but Laura was going to put up a fight for Kitty. 'I'll ring after Christmas, okay?'

Kitty nodded as Orlando rushed over for his hug and Alex, Sam and David lined up behind.

'I think *I'm* probably going to be giving *you* a call after Christmas,' David said wryly. 'You can imagine the headache I'll get if I don't.'

'Damn right,' Sam quipped. 'You think Cat's life's colourful? You ain't heard nothing yet!'

Laura laughed. 'Well, I'll look forward to hearing it!'

Alex paused in front of her with a degree of trepidation when Cat suddenly broke in. 'Oh, tell me, then! I know you're all dying to hear.'

Everyone looked back at her. In the shock of Laura's imminent departure, she'd been momentarily forgotten.

'I mean, I guess until I get the interpretation behind the necklace, it's just another piece of jewellery, right?' Cat held the necklace out in her hand.

Slowly Laura walked back and took it from her. Her bluff had worked. What was the saying? Curiosity killed the Cat?

Straightening her fingers into a corona, Laura draped the necklace over her own hand, feeling everyone's interest peak. She looked for the first charm and then took a deep breath.

'Well, this is for Olive,' she said, picking out a charm of a pea pod split open to reveal three peas; the two at either end were golden, but the one in the middle was a small, cultured pearl. 'The pod represents the fact that you came from the same womb, or pod, and are sisters. There's a pea for each of you, obviously, but this pea here,' she said, pointing to the pearl, 'represents Daniel and the fact that he came not only between your births, but his death has come between your lives too. The impact of what happened the day he died has been devastating for you both – even though you were only a baby yourself, Olive, and Cat wasn't even born. Your parents failed you when they put all the blame on you, Olive, and when they put all the hope in you, Cat. I chose a pearl for Daniel because they historically represent forgiveness, and although you couldn't see this yourselves as children, I hope that you can see it now and perhaps try to work towards forgiving each other. Sisters are . . . They're such important people. You should treasure each other.'

An uncomfortable silence followed as everyone avoided Cat's and Olive's eyes. Cat had strapped her arms across her body as if she was wearing a straitjacket, although the blanched skin of her arms beneath her fingertips betrayed her high emotion. Olive must have seen it too, for she suddenly crossed the room and wrapped her arms around her sister, kissing her hard on the cheek.

'I'm sorry I blamed you for stealing away Mum and Dad's love. It wasn't your fault. They should have had enough for us both.' Olive's voice was low and dignified.

'I-I-I'm sorry too,' Cat stammered quietly. 'I wasn't good enough to—'

'You're good enough for me,' Olive rebutted. 'I just had to have someone I could pass the blame on to, that's all.'

'What else are little sisters for?' Cat managed.

Rob looked at Laura in amazement and winked at her. It was such a casual gesture but it almost floored her, and she looked away quickly. She could see the hope rising in him like a full moon and she couldn't bear to see it. The necklace might go some way in helping reconcile Cat and Olive and heal past hurts, but it couldn't change what Cat had done or was still doing.

Laura found the charm of the flower fairy and rested it in her palm; she could almost hear everyone hold their breath as they waited to discover the identity of the next charm.

'This one is for Kitty. Fairies represent eternal youth, and that's where your relationship is rooted. Kitty's your oldest and dearest friend, who just loves you so much. You're not as close as you once were, but you should be,' she said, defiantly looking up at Cat. 'You shouldn't drift away from her because your lives are different now. You are each other's childhood and you can't leave that behind you. Kitty was the only reason you have any happy memories of your childhood at all, so keep her with you.' Laura paused. 'Plus she can cook – frankly, you could learn a lot!'

Everyone burst out laughing; everyone except Cat, and Kitty, who was weeping quietly into Joe's lapel as the farmer smoothed his wife's shaking shoulder. He caught Laura's eye and nodded at her approvingly.

'Too much sherry,' he snapped as Sam cast one of her quizzical looks.

Laura smiled hesitantly and looked straight back down. She moved the necklace round on her hand so that they could see a helter-skelter slide, complete with a staircase disappearing up the inside. 'This helter-skelter is for your friendship with Sam. It represents all the wildness and wind-in-your-hair freedom of your university years.'

'Yeah!' Sam beamed. 'I reckon that's spot on. The wind in our hair . . .'

'I was thinking, originally, about a stirrup. You could pretend it was from Gucci and it means "taming the wild", but I'm not sure anyone's ever going to tame you two when you're together.'

Rob and David high-fived each other at that.

'Orlando, this one's yours,' Laura smiled, looking up at him. He was beaming down at her, arms crossed proudly. 'A wishing well, because you and Cat made each other's dreams come true. And look, if you see here, the little handle turns,' she murmured, giving a demonstration and hearing a small admiring gasp come from him.

She took a deep breath. 'Alex, I'm sure you'll be happy to hear I've given you a horse—'

'Wa-hey!' he cheered, but his joy was hollow; she could see the apprehension in his eyes.

'It's not actually as transparent a symbol as you might think,' Laura warned him. 'In the Bible, for instance, horses are a symbol of intelligence and diviners of danger. They also represent strength and power. And of course there's the most famous horse of all – the Trojan horse, which hid enemies in plain sight, bringing traitors into the midst.' She gave a long pause, watching the Adam's apple bob up and down in his throat, before she finally smiled. 'But you were Cat's first love, the man who introduced her to passion, and it seemed fitting to represent that vital chapter in Cat's life with the virility of the horse.'

He nodded, relieved. 'Great. I might get one myself and wear it round my neck.'

'Go for it,' Laura replied coolly, wiping the smile off his face.

She turned her attention back to Cat.

'Your boss, Min, isn't here tonight, but this charm of the apple is hers. I had to think long and hard about this charm because your relationship with her is so much . . . "looser" than it is with everyone else on this project. In fact, I soon discovered you scarcely have any personal relationship with her at all. Rob only really asked for her to be included because of what she represented to you –' she watched as the corners of Cat's mouth drooped '– which is, of course, your great love of art. Because it was while working for Min at the gallery that you achieved one of the greatest highs of your life – securing Ben Jackson.'

Cat set to stone before her eyes, her breath shallow, her blinking significantly slowed. Was Laura really going to do it? Laura saw Rob tense too.

'I would have liked the charm to represent Ben directly, but his exhibition was called "Exposure", and I'm afraid I still can't work out how to cast the wind in gold.' Laura smiled. 'So I decided to use art itself to represent him, hence the apple. It's one of the most enduring symbols throughout the history of art – from early religious iconography, where it represented the Fall of Adam and Original Sin, through to its use as a symbolic prop in Renaissance art, as a still-life form in the seventeenth-century Dutch movement, and through to modern art, where it's been celebrated by artists like Cézanne and Braque . . . But what really confirmed for me that the apple was the right charm was the Greek myth about the Judgement of Paris. Do you know it? It's very famous.'

Cat slowly shook her head. 'Why don't you tell me?'

'It was a contest between the three most beautiful goddesses – Hera, Athena and Aphrodite – for the prize of a golden apple that was inscribed with the word "*Kallisti*", which means "the most beautiful one". Paris of Troy was chosen to select the winner. Hera, the goddess of marriage, tempted him with land and power. Athena, the goddess of war, tempted him with military skill and wisdom. And Aphrodite, the goddess of love, tempted him with Helen of Sparta, the most beautiful woman in the world, as his wife. Of course Paris fell in love with Helen and Aphrodite won, but when Paris abducted Helen to be his wife, it triggered the ten-year-long siege of Troy, which only ended when the Greeks sent in the Trojan horse. All that because of a golden apple.' She shrugged.

Rob snapped his eyes up to Laura's as her words settled.

Cat looked over her shoulder at Rob. 'Darling, you're the classics scholar. Are you keeping up with this?'

Rob was silent for a long moment. '. . . Laura's drawing the causal link between the golden apple and the Trojan horse.'

'Yes, I got that – but what's it got to do with me?' Cat asked.

'Most people would call you a modern-day Helen. Men fight over you too,' he replied, his jaw tightening like a screw.

Cat met Laura's eyes triumphantly before reaching a hand to his cheek. 'Would you, baby?'

Rob, standing stiffly, didn't reply as she reached up and kissed him with an open mouth.

'There's just one charm left,' Laura said quickly, resting a plumed bird in her palm. 'Your charm was really very simple, Rob: the cuckoo.'

'The cuckoo has many meanings,' Rob said quietly.

'Yes, it does,' Laura agreed.

'I know one!' Sam called out. 'They lay their eggs in other birds' nests so that another bird raises their young.'

'That's right, they do,' Laura murmured, her eyes steady on Rob's. 'In fact the word "cuckold" is derived from "cuckoo".' Cat's hair swished as she looked up at Laura sharply. 'But in this instance, I've referenced it as one of the birds of Hera, the goddess of marriage.'

'Her again? You've mentioned her already,' Cat said archly.

'Yes. Because everything interlinks, Cat.' Laura's unruffled tone stopped Cat in her tracks, and she looked back down at the bird charm suspiciously as though it was calling out secrets.

'I couldn't think of a better motif from someone who prizes marriage so highly and would do anything to protect it. I know you realize how lucky you are.' Laura held out the necklace for Cat to take. 'Happy birthday, Cat.'

Cat lifted her ponytail so that Rob could fasten the necklace. Laura had shortened the chain so that it sat at the very base of her neck, the middle charm resting in the hollow of her throat. It looked magnificent next to her dress, her skin, her hair.

'Wow! So then this is my life – a pea pod, a fairy, a helter-skelter, a wishing well, a horse, an apple and a cuckoo.' She looked at Laura with a respect that belied the fractured friendship. 'I was right about you. You're the bomb.'

Laura nodded. Yes, she was.

She looked around the group for the last time – though

Rob wouldn't meet her eyes – and quickly said her good-byes. She knew that, bar Kitty, she wouldn't see them again. Her infatuation with the Blakes was over.

'Alex, can I see you for a sec?' she heard Rob ask as she walked out of the door.

Outside, it took three starts before Dolly jumped into life, shaking on her wheels as she shook off her snowy slumber. Laura was just throwing her into reverse when she looked up to find Rob and Alex talking in the garden. By the time she'd shifted into first, Alex was sprawled in the copper-beech hedge, and Rob was massaging his fist. Laura knew she ought to laugh – Alex deserved everything Rob could land on him – but for some reason, she found she could only cry.

# Chapter Forty-Seven

Laura put the match to the coals and watched as they started to smoke, gentle plumes spinning up to the clouds. She checked her watch again – forty minutes had passed since she had pressed 'send' – and looked in both directions along the beach. It was deserted. Everyone was still in bed, of course, only the most excited children already up and unwrapping presents, but Laura hadn't been able to wait for an acceptable hour to call. She'd been up half the night, fretting over and plotting this.

Urchin looked beautiful. The fairy lights she had threaded along the apex gently nudged away the early morning mist, and the plastic wreath on the door looked passable from a distance. She'd been so busy yesterday getting the final painting done, she'd only made it to Homebase last night with eleven minutes till closing time, so she hadn't exactly had time to browse – but the balding Christmas tree made a festive statement, at least. She'd wound a red-lettered 'Happy Sixtieth' banner that she'd mistaken for 'Happy Christmas' round it in lieu of tinsel, and tea lights twinkled in every window, giving it an ever so slightly Dickensian feel. *Ever* so slightly.

Jack was only forty feet away when the mist revealed him, a multi-striped scarf wound four times round his neck, obscuring half his face. But it was only his eyes she needed to see.

He stopped, stunned, as he saw the beach hut glow in front of him, and Laura standing on the veranda, waiting.

Haltingly, he stumbled over the dry sand to her. 'Laur!' he said, stopping a foot away and marvelling at the sight of her. 'Where have you *been*?'

'A world away,' she blinked, thinking how lovely it was to rest her eyes upon him again, her old friend. He had grown a beard during her thirteen-day absence and was visibly thinner, neither of which had been intentional, she knew. He looked so good. So real.

Jack saw the love in her eyes and embraced her, his arms the home that had given her shelter all these years.

'Where's Fee?' she asked after a moment.

He shook his head. 'I don't know.'

'Did she get the message?'

He looked down at her. 'Laur, I haven't seen or spoken to Fee since that weekend.'

'You . . . ?' She looked down towards the retreating water. So then Fee had been telling the truth. She hadn't stolen Jack; her only crime had been to choose Jack's right to know over Laura's right to decide – and that had been no crime at all, she knew now.

Arthur bounded up, his beloved discombobulated purple ball in his mouth. He whined ecstatically at the sight of her, shaking the surf out of his coat before falling on to his back for a tummy rub from his mistress. Laura laughed, raking him lightly with her fingers. 'Oh, I've missed you drenching me, you smelly mutt.'

Jack looked up at the beach hut, the only one inhabited

in the Christmas dawn. 'Whose is this?' he asked, one slim hand stroking the planed veranda rail admiringly.

'Mine,' she murmured, kneeling in the sand, watching him. 'I've been doing it up as a project. It was practically falling down when I bought it.'

'But when . . . ? I mean, how did you—'

He saw the shivering ghost at the same moment she did, as pale and wispy as the mist, hair wet and plastered to that tiny heart-shaped face, bare legs like straws in polka-dot wellies and a denim mini.

Laura had to suppress the urge to scream with joy at the pathetic sight. 'Will you *ever* dress for the weather?' she demanded with laughing eyes, striding towards her and enveloping her in a bear hug.

She felt Fee's tiny shoulders shake beneath her, and she let her tears fall too, as another layer of warmth came to protect them and Jack encircled them both. They'd all lost more than each other through this; their separation had let the world in and there was no going back for any of them.

'Come and have a bacon sandwich to warm you up,' Laura said finally as Fee sniffed like a schoolboy, making Jack laugh.

They trudged up the sand on to the veranda where the picnic barbecue tray was smouldering nicely. She threw on a couple of rashers and they sizzled noisily, breaking the anxious silence. Laura watched Jack standing in the doorway, taking in the tiles, the freshly painted ceiling, the rolled-up futon . . . Fee was sitting on an upturned fire bucket, wearing Jack's duffle coat, at Laura's insistence, and the arms dangled down to her knees. She kept blowing into her cupped hands to distract from the fact that she wasn't talking.

'Here you go,' Laura said, handing her a bap and a cup of tea in a blue-striped enamel mug. 'Happy Christmas.'

Fee smiled, bringing her hand to her mouth, before dropping it dejectedly, and Laura knew she couldn't eat. Not yet.

'Fee, I'm sorry,' Laura said, dropping down beside her and squeezing her knee. 'I know I put you in an impossible position.'

'No! You trusted me. You needed to think and I totally betrayed you.'

'You were looking out for Jack. You did the right thing,' Laura said, so calmly that it took a moment for Fee to register her words.

'Huh?'

'You were right to tell him. *I* should have as soon as I thought I was pregnant. It was never just my decision.' She looked up at Jack. 'And you were right, too, calling time on us. You made the decision you knew I couldn't. You knew I could never leave you.'

Jack sighed and slid down against the wall. 'I just couldn't bear to see you so unhappy any more. You were so like her, it was easy for me. I truly believed I could make you love me through sheer force of will. It was stupid of me to think that just because Lily loved me, you would.'

'It wasn't stupid, Jack. We all wanted it to happen like that; it made us feel like we could keep her with us somehow. But she's . . .' Her voice faded instantly and she had to gulp down the air to bring it back. 'She's gone and she's not coming back. I look in the mirror and I see her face looking back at me and I want so badly for it to *be* her looking back. But it never is. It's just me, and I can't stand it.' She rested her cheek on her knuckle, her face turned away as tears skinned down her face in sheets. 'I thought that if I could just stop being me and be like her instead, it would make the loss easier to bear. But I only look like her. I'm not as funny or sweet or kind. I'm not patient; I'm not tolerant or encouraging or brave or—'

'How can you say that?' Fee demanded furiously. 'After what you did for Dan, how could you ever doubt your kindness or bravery? My brother died with your arms around him! The last thing he ever knew was your kindness,' she cried.

A sob escaped her. 'But it meant—'

Fee dropped to her knees beside her, her bap rolling, forgotten, on to the floor and straight into Arthur's mouth. 'Lily died alone? Yes, I know. And I'm so sorry . . . I'm so sorry for you that you didn't get to say goodbye. But you were a victim too, Laura. It wasn't your fault you didn't know she was there. You were in shock. Your injuries kept you in hospital for weeks.' She grew still. Older. 'And it wasn't your fault that you missed the funeral. The doctors were right not to let you out.'

Laura's face crumpled and she wept into her hands.

'But you know you've got to say goodbye to her one day,' Fee said quietly, her voice low like a prayer.

'My head knows I have to, but I just *can't*.' Laura shook her head vociferously.

'There's an old Jewish proverb I heard once: "If I am her, who will be me?"' Fee shrugged as Laura looked at her in amazement. 'You have to let her go and just be you again. I don't think I've ever really met *you*.'

'You wouldn't like me,' Laura sniffed.

'Huh, you wish!'

Laura looked at her, so defiant in her loyalty. 'I still remember your face being the first thing I saw when I came round in hospital.'

'Poor you!' Fee said, trying to joke.

'You wouldn't leave me.'

'You didn't leave Dan,' Fee said, her fragile smile sliding off her face like a gently melting candle. 'We're connected for ever, Laur. I'm the baby sister you never wanted and I'll *never* not be your friend. But you only followed me here because you couldn't bear to go back to everything that had made you happy. And, Jack,' she said, turning to look at him, 'you followed Laura here because you were chasing the face of the girl who made you happy. We've all been clinging on to each other as though it will bring Lily and Dan back, but it won't. It may have helped us in the beginning, but now it's only hurting us and we all have to move on, even if . . . even if that means moving apart.'

Silence fell like a shadow upon them and Laura felt her sense of separation solidify. She had sensed it in Verbier, but now, hearing it from her scatty, wise friend, she knew it was true, and it felt like absolution.

She looked at Fee and Jack – her family – standing at opposite ends of the veranda, their eyes down, cloaked in feelings that they didn't dare to acknowledge, much less explore. She knew that it had to come from her. She had to give them her blessing before they even knew they wanted it.

Laura managed a laugh, her eyes falling on Arthur pulling on a piece of rind. 'Well, so much for breakfast.'

'It's only just gone six; there's plenty of time,' Jack said. 'I don't think I've ever been up so early on Christmas Day before. Not even when I was seven and asked for my first Scalextric.'

'What can I say? I felt like a chat,' she smiled, shrugging lightly. 'I knew I couldn't go without fixing things between us.'

'Go? Go where?' Jack asked.

'I'm flying to Peru tomorrow with Shelterbox. I'm going over as part of the response team to help the victims of the mudslide.'

'Peru? You mean like Paddington Bear Peru?' Fee asked.

Laura couldn't help but smile. Darling Fee. 'Exactly.'

'But for how long?'

'For as long as they need me. A few weeks to begin with, maybe longer later on in the year.'

'But what about the business?' Fee asked, her eyes getting bigger and more anxious by the moment.

'Well, I rather hoped you'd take care of that for me while I'm away. I've managed to get in to London Fashion Week, so I'm going to need you on the case to sort out all the admin.'

'Fashion Week? Since *when?*'

Laura sighed. How was she ever going to explain what had gone on between her, Cat and Rob? 'It's a long story. I'll tell you over the turkey.'

'When I said . . . when I said we all had to move on, I didn't mean like right away,' Fee objected tremulously.

'But you were bang on, as usual, Fee. It's for the best, and I know you two will make each other happy. I'm sorry I was so selfish. I closed my eyes to the obvious for so long because I was scared of being completely alone. I thought – if you've got each other, who's got me?'

Both Jack and Fee jumped as if they'd been burned.

'We're not together, Laur,' Jack protested.

'I know. But you *should* be. You're perfect for each other. Think about it – you both love brown sauce on your salmon and drinking milk with tea in it. You're both addicted to *X Factor* and *Most Haunted*, and neither one of you seems to understand why acrylic is objectionable. Plus with Jack being such a neat freak and you such a slob, Fee, there's a definite upside for you. And I imagine, Jack, that Fee's probably the only female in the whole of East Anglia who's over ten but has hips narrower than yours.' She smiled at them both. 'And last but not least, you laugh like two hyperventilating hyenas together, and you're best friends who are so much happier together than apart.'

Fee, who was blushing furiously, carried on staring at the floor. Jack looked at Laura for a moment – a look of understanding passing between them – before he looked across at Fee. Laura could see from the change in his facial muscle tone that she'd been right.

'I'd have to agree with you, Laur,' he said quietly, prompting Fee to look up in amazement.

An electric flash zipped between them, but neither one moved.

'Please . . .' Laura nodded, knowing what was going to happen. She held her breath as Jack got up to kiss Fee lightly but tenderly, the kind of kiss that precedes hungry passion and is the first of thousands. It was so different to the parched kisses Laura had shared with him, where each one was a cork that kept their mutual grief stoppered.

They both looked over at her apprehensively.

'Yes, well, maybe it's slightly weird, but I'll get used to it,' Laura laughed, scratching her ear, embarrassed. 'By the way, I've got some pressies for you both,' she said, leading them into the hut. She handed Fee an enormous soft silver parcel that looked like the foil-wrapped Christmas turkey.

'Oh, Laur!' Fee gasped delightedly as she pulled out the 'rock princess' jacket. Laura had grabbed it off the chair on the way out from Kitty's – no way was it staying with Cat, who was clearly going to give it to her cleaner. And besides, it had been Fee she'd wanted to buy it for all along. It had been *made* for her.

'And for you, Jack.' She handed over an envelope.

He pulled out a key from inside, puzzled. It wasn't the cottage key.

'Urchin is yours. I bought her for you. I figured it was one dream I could make come true for you.'

Jack's face was a gift. 'It's the most perfect present anyone has ever given me,' he said, hugging her to him like a big brother.

'Yuh, well – you may not say that when you hear the catch.'

'The catch?'

'Okay, the condition.'

'The condition?' he echoed nervously.

'It applies to you both '

Now it was Fee's turn to look nervous.

Laura walked to the pegs on the far wall and held up two of the three wetsuits. 'You've got to put on these.'

'*Now?*'

'I told you not to thank me too soon.'

Jack looked out at the mineral green-grey sea. 'Please don't be saying what I think you're saying.'

Laura wrinkled her nose. 'I did say you might not like the real me,' she said, pulling her jumper over her head and indicating that they should follow suit. 'The first thing you need to know is that I'm competitive. Really damned take-your-eyebrows-off competitive.' She pulled off her boots and socks. 'The next is that I absolutely *hate X Factor* and apple turnovers.' She unzipped her jeans and started pulling on the wetsuit. 'And finally, I'm mad. Completely certifiably insane and have never yet turned down a bet or a dare.' She swished her hair out of the way and pulled up the back zip by the tape.

'And that's what this is?' Fee wobbled as she and Jack climbed into theirs. 'A dare?'

Laura stopped and thought for a moment. 'No!' she pooh-poohed. 'A Christmas-morning swim? This is just our new tradition.'

And with her arms outstretched, Arthur, Jack and Fee at her side, she ran laughing and screaming towards the perishing-cold water.

# Epilogue

## Three months later

Laura could hear nothing, not the blare of the tannoys and horns two thousand metres below, nor the distant scream of a golden eagle circling above the next peak. But she could see everything. Up here she could see Italy in one direction, France in another, and above her – so close she felt she could touch it – heaven.

She dropped her backpack on to the snow and rested for a moment, bending forward with her hands on her thighs, her breath coming fast and strong. It had taken an hour to walk up this mountain with her kit on her back, and getting back down again wasn't going to be any less exhausting. Fifty metres away, she could see the tip of the red triangular gates that told her she'd made it, but that wasn't her destination. Not yet.

Opening the bag, she pulled out the small Elizabethan walnut box that had sat for nearly five years over her bedroom fireplace. She ran her fingers over the silver oval plaque. *Lily*.

'So . . .' she murmured. 'This is where we say our goodbye, at last . . .' Her voice faltered and she put a hand to her mouth to stop her lips from trembling. 'I thought you'd like it here. It's about the only place I could think of that was as pure and beautiful as you.' She swallowed hard. 'Also I think this counts as "sweeping the sky", don't you? Mum told us to do that, do you remember? "Brush the floor and sweep the sky." So that's what this is . . .' She bit her lip. 'I'm terrified, if I'm honest. I don't mean about how I'm going to get down this mountain again, although I am pretty scared of that too. I mean of going on without you. You were always my mirror – one of those flattering ones that made me feel better about myself. I've managed to put it off for quite a few years now, but . . . I just never wanted this day to come.'

She inhaled sharply, sniffing back the tears.

'I hope you're looking after Mum, by the way. Tell her I miss her every day, like I do you, and tell her I'm going to make her proud again. I'm going to live like she wanted us to, only now I'm going to do it for you too.' She crossed her fingers and held them up to the sky. 'So wish me luck. And w-wish me love.'

A sob escaped her, in spite of her best efforts, and the world that was plated out in front of her blurred out of sight. She closed her eyes and the sun found her like a spotlight, drenching her with a gentle warmth that seemed to sink right through to her bones. Her fingers slid back the lid of the box and a thermal current swooped down, lifting Lily high into the sky where she could fly with the eagles. Within a moment, she was gone.

Laura watched through freezing tears, wanting to follow, wanting to bring her back. But she knew she'd spent too long chasing ghosts. Finally, picking up her backpack, she walked the last fifty metres to the red gate, nodding as the steward relayed her vest number to the finishing post. She clicked on her skis, fastened her helmet, adjusted the strap of her goggles and looked down the vertiginous drop.

'This is for you, Lily,' she whispered. And balling all her fear into love, she pushed off, determined to set the snow on fire.

Laura could hear nothing above the blare of the tannoys and horns, and the screams of the crowd circling as she swept through the finish gate. Hers wasn't the fastest time; hers wasn't the cleanest line – far from it: she'd wanted to get down in one piece after almost wiping out on one cliff jump – but as one of the five wild cards in the event, not to mention a woman, she was the underdog they were cheering for. Verbier erupted as she screamed to a stop, spraying the spectators with snow, and an overexcited presenter in an orange unitard and jester's hat raced over to her.

'Laura Cunningham, from Great Britain, your first freeride on the tour! How did that *feel*?' he shouted, waving a mic dementedly in her face.

Laura pulled off her goggles, laughing and half crying as she looked back up the intimidating mountain she'd just jumped off. 'Exhilarating! Absolutely unbelievable. I can't . . . I can't believe I did it!'

A cheer erupted as she wiped away the tears of joy.

'Two falls and a safe line kept you off the podium today. Can we expect to see you in Chamonix on the tour next year?'

'God, no! That was enough for me. It took all my skill and courage to get down there. These guys competing here are incredible – a whole other level.'

'No! You can't be serious?'

'Oh, I am . . . Once is enough, and "enough is as good as a feast", as my mother always used to say. I'll remember this for ever.'

'What made you do it?'

Laura bit her lip and gave a small smile. 'It was kind of a dare.'

'You jumped off the legendary Bec des Rosses for a *dare*?' the presenter repeated for the benefit of the crowd, whipping them into a frenzy. If there was one thing this extreme-sports crowd loved, it was extreme behaviour. 'Well, Laura, I hope you change your mind before the next stop on the WFT, because we want to see you again!'

Laura laughed, waving her poles deliriously, and the crowd cheered as she skied over to the competitors' area. She had promised Jack and Fee she'd ring as soon as she was down. One of the French guys slapped her on the shoulder as she collapsed on to the bench to unbuckle her boots. 'Great ride!'

'I cannot believe you did that,' a voice said behind her as she took off her helmet and dropped her head in her hands. 'You weren't supposed to actually do it . . .'

Laura froze.

'If I'd known you were this reckless, I'd have given you a Laura Ashley voucher instead,' Rob said, throwing one leg over the bench and straddling it beside her.

She looked up, the sight of him making her heart beat even faster than the Alpine drop. Really *nobody* should be that handsome. 'What are you doing here?'

'Isn't it obvious? I'm watching you.'

'How did you know I was h— Oh.' She gave an embarrassed smile. Of course he wasn't out here because of *her*. They were staying at the chalet.

But he lifted her chin with his finger, turning her to face him. 'Jack and Fee told me.' His eyes danced over her skin, making her shiver.

'You went to my house?' she croaked.

'They were very welcoming. And helpful. They explained a lot. Clearly *you* weren't going to – at least not about your own life. Mine, on the other hand . . .' He gave a rueful laugh.

'I'm so sorry, Rob.'

He looked down momentarily. 'Don't be. You simply helped make a decision that had previously seemed impossible actually very easy indeed. I knew that everything was built on lies; I just hadn't appreciated the full extent.'

Laura could see the toll the past few months had taken on him. His eyes looked tired and reddened, and he was pale, although he hadn't shaved, which she always thought was an improvement. 'The affair with Alex starting up after Ben, for example.'

Laura swallowed. 'Did you understand about *your* charm?' she asked cautiously. What if he'd missed her inference?

'You mean a cuckoo's egg in my nest? Yes, I got it, although not immediately. It was only later, when we were going to bed and the pills fell out of her dress, that I realized what she was doing,' he nodded. 'But why didn't you tell me directly?'

'I didn't know if you wanted to hear it. You had so much hope. If you could accept the affair, maybe you could accept that . . .' She shrugged. 'And besides, Cat threatened to tell everyone we were . . . you know.'

'Sleeping together?' Just hearing the words come from his lips made her blush, and his eyes held hers so that all she could do was nod. His hand found hers and he smiled. 'How can you be trembling, sitting here with me, when you've just bombed down that mountain?'

'This is much more scary,' she mumbled.

'For you, maybe. You didn't have to stand by and watch you jump cliffs on a one-one gradient. Have you got any idea what you did to me?'

'Taught you not to set me dares?'

'Can't you be trusted, then?' She saw the excitement flicker in his eyes.

'I've never turned one down yet.'

He stared at her, his eyes searching hers. 'And now I know why. It was your mother who told you never to shy away from trying new experiences.' He leaned back to reach into his trouser pocket and pulled out a silver charm bracelet, tarnished with age. He saw the emotion rise in her face as she saw it out here.

'Fee gave it to me to bring to you – she said the matching bracelets were your mother's final gifts to you and Lily. She said that after Lily died, you wouldn't wear yours.'

'I couldn't . . . I couldn't bear being reminded of what I wasn't.' She shook her head quickly. 'It made my life too big. It was what Mum wanted for us – she was such a free spirit. But after I lost Lily too, I couldn't bear to feel so much any more. My heart couldn't take it.'

He raised a hand and gently stroked her cheek. She let herself tilt into him.

'Fee showed me the letter. She's talked me through it,' he murmured, examining the bracelet. He held up a charm of a silver book. 'I know, for example, that this represents Roald Dahl. Your mother wanted you to read all his books. She said his was the only imagination that could actually match a child's capacity to create and dream.'

Laura blinked at him.

'This spanner was to tell you to learn how to change a wheel, the rolling pin for you to learn how to make a basic shortcrust pastry – both essential life skills. She wanted you to be capable and independent.' He moved the bracelet round on his palm. Laura's eyes watched every charm as closely as a mother guarding her young. 'This halo – she wanted you to see the aurora borealis. She said it was the closest you'd ever get to seeing heaven from earth.' He looked at her. 'Have you?'

She shook her head.

'Then I'll take you. We'll see it together.' He looked back at the charm, deliberately ignoring her surprise. 'This rabbit signified that you should have pets – your mother thought it was a way for children to express love, especially those children who'd experienced loss.'

'She was right,' Laura murmured.

'This flag was to encourage you to learn a language, so that you could make your way in the world. The Aga was for you to make a home . . . and this matchstick denotes the story of the little match girl and the freedom to live – or die – on your terms.'

He turned the bracelet round again as he continued his tour of the bracelet – *her* life.

'The balloon and the starfish she had a saying for: "Brush the floor and sweep the sky." I'm guessing that's what the balloon safari and gap-year diving project were all about?'

'Mum wanted us to go to the very tops and bottoms of the world. She thought we'd feel most alive at the extremes of human experience. Lily and I did one of them every year.'

'Like paragliding?'

Laura nodded.

Rob stared at her. 'You mother sounds an amazing woman.'

'She was,' Laura said, nodding, her eyes instantly filling with tears again – she had put her emotions on the line too many times today – when suddenly she felt Rob's kisses falling like rain on her eyelids, her temples, her jaw, her nose, her mouth . . . He pulled away, but only enough to look at her as though checking she was real. His hands stroked her cheeks, and she felt his love colour her up, making her heart swell and her soul relax.

'Found you,' he whispered, looking at her with keen intensity. 'To anyone else, this bracelet is a hieroglyph, but it tells me everything I wanted to know about you. Thanks to your mother, I've got the guidebook on Laura Cunningham.' He shook the bracelet lightly so that it jingled in his hand. 'There's just one thing missing.'

Laura looked up at him. 'What?'

He pulled something from his other pocket and placed it flat in his palm. It was a tiny red enamelled shoe. Carefully he attached it to a link on the bracelet. 'I asked Fee about the red shoe thing – she told me it's what you were doing together the day Lily died.'

Laura was silent for a moment. 'She was going to a party. She wanted a pair so badly to go with her dress. I've never been able to look at a pair since without thinking of her. It was the last time we ever laughed together.'

He smoothed her hair, cupping her cheek with his hand. 'So, then – this is to signify remembrance.' This time, as the tears fell, he slid her along the bench into him, kissing her hair and enclosing his arms around her until she could look at him again.

He fastened the bracelet on her wrist – a mother's hopes and dreams cast in silver to be un-erasable, and her daughters' for ever. 'Laura Cunningham,' Rob murmured. 'Beloved daughter, devoted sister . . . nymphomaniac girlfriend,' he grinned.

'You wish!' she laughed as he caught her in his arms, kissing her again and again and again.

'Oh really?' His copper eyes bored into hers, devilry dancing in them. 'Is that a bet?'

# Acknowledgements

My gorgeous husband, Anders. I say it every time, but it seems to become truer with every book, I couldn't do what I do without his support. Calm, tolerant, wise, he's a rubbish editor – far too kind to me – but it's always his opinion I seek. May he never leave me for one of my characters.

My three beautiful children, who put up with me saying, 'I'm on deadline!' every time they want me to play football in the garden and haven't yet put me up for adoption – in spite of the threats. All the love in the prologue is inspired by them.

My mum for being my touchstone in everything and ringing me every morning, cup of tea in hand and ear ready.

Sally, Mhairi and Muirne for inspiring the last scene in the last chapter; Rebecca O'Connor for giving me a camel to work with – yep, he's alive and well and living in Sussex; Camilla Fenning for her red shoe wisdom; Tamson Martin for her beautiful cat like eyes; Carole Bennett for canine inspiration; Aunty Flora for keeping sales buoyant in Scotland; and any friend who hasn't dumped me while I've gone to ground on this book.

And most of all, my editor, Jenny Geras, and agent, Amanda Preston, for keeping the wheels on with this one!